Real Dragons Don't Cry

For,

Noya & Naama & Omri &

Eyal & Hadas.

With love

BY THE SAME AUTHOR

Close Your Eyes and Open Your Mind: A Practical Guide to Spiritual Meditation

Real Dragons Don't Cry

Dada Nabhaniilananda

InnerWorld Publications
San Germán, Puerto Rico
www.innerworldpublications.com

This is a work of fiction. Names, characters, places, and incidents either are the product of the author's imagination or are used fictitiously.

Copyright © 2015 by Dada Nabhaniilananda

All rights reserved under International and Pan-American Copyright Conventions. Published in the United States by InnerWorld Publications, PO Box 1613, San Germán, Puerto Rico, 00683.

Library of Congress Control Number: 2015909003

Cover design and illustrations © Iana Zaalishvili

No part of this book may be reproduced or transmitted in any form or by any means, electronic or mechanical, including photocopying, recording, or by any information storage or retrieval system, without permission in writing from the publisher, except for the inclusion of brief quotations in a review.

ISBN: 9781881717409

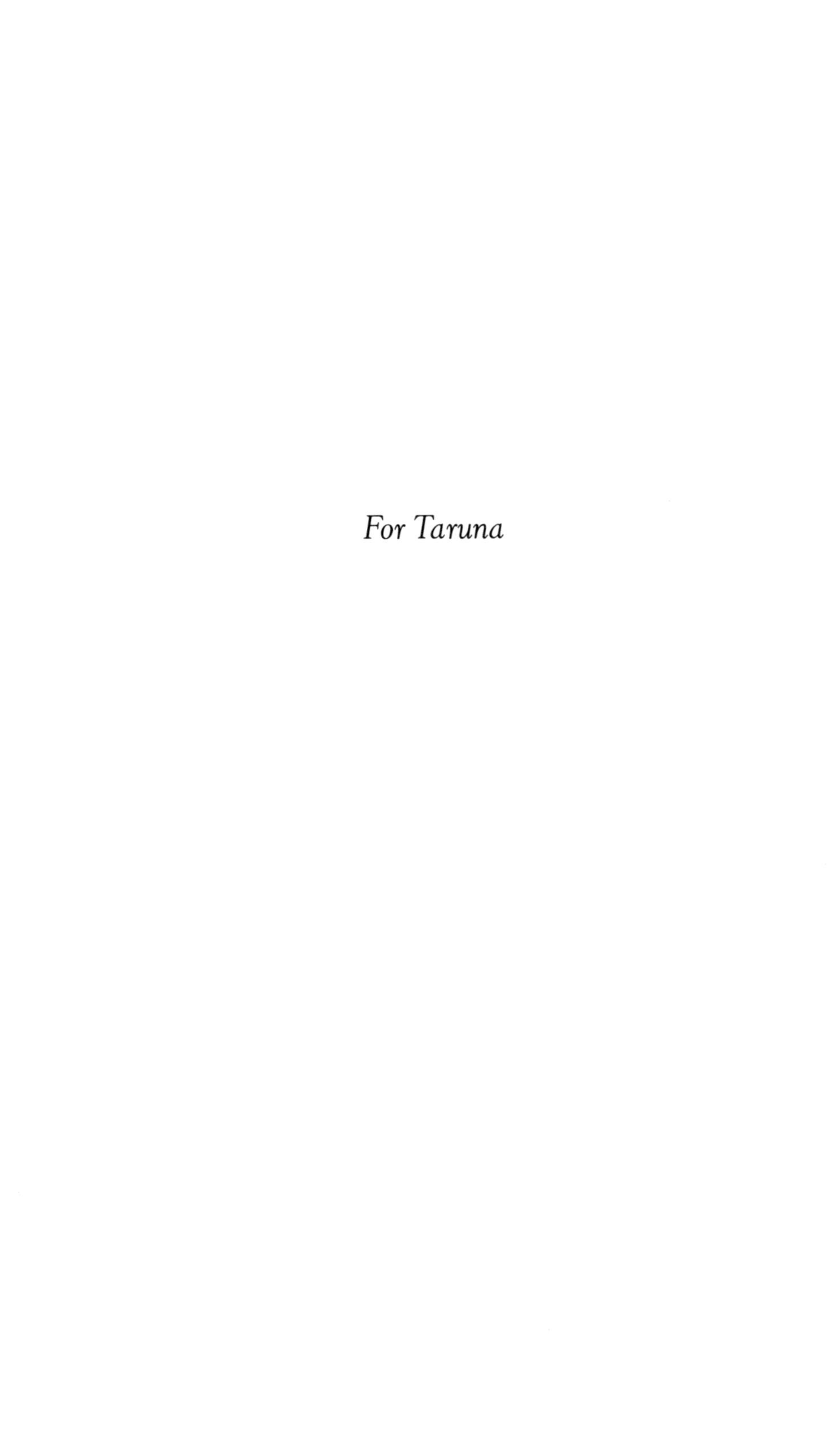

For Taruna

Contents

Space Nurse Miranda

Location: Dr Dogalogue's Spaceship, en route from Zondgraz to Earth.

"Would you have had the courage to challenge the master as Lucifer did?" said Dr. Dogalogue.

"Sure, I would!" said Miranda. "I'm not scared of anything. But what happened then? Did Lucifer really leave the school? Did you really go back to the training center for hundreds of years? How long do Zondgrazians live, anyway? You must be really ancient!"

"Hold on," the doctor laughed. "Too many questions at once. By Zondgrazian standards, at 2011 of your earth years I'm still a young adult. Our master is more than twelve thousand years old."

Miranda's eyes opened wide.

"And yes, I did go back to the training center, but Lucifer left the school altogether. But that is all part of a very long story, far too long to tell you before you go to bed tonight. But, since you're not scared of anything, how about I begin by telling you about the time I challenged a dragon?"

"A dragon? Great! Tell me everything. I'm not sleepy at all." Miranda curled up on the couch, her eyes all eager.

Dr. Dogalogue adopted his best storytelling pose, draped languidly over the arm of his comfy couch, one tentacle dangling in an imaginary stream, gazing dreamily at the ceiling with five of his eyestalks. The other three watched the earth child.

"The first time I went to your planet, about seven hundred years ago, I was obliged to go out and fight a dragon." He hesitated. "Are you quite sure a dragon story isn't too scary right before bed?"

"But dragons aren't scary at all; they're all furry and cuddly and purry."

"I suspect, my child, that you are thinking of what is known as a pussy cat."

"Oh, no," Miranda gasped. "Everybody knows they're *awful and scaly and greedy and unreasonably aggressive."*

"Do you mean to tell me that when you asked me for a pet dragon, 'just a small one,' and I told you what terrible pets they make, you were talking about the furry purry variety of dragon that normal people call a pussy cat?"

"Of course, silly. I want one of those pretty stripy ones—a small one, about ten feet long."

Dr. Dogalogue was fast regretting getting into this conversation. It was time to take command of the storytelling. He sat her up straight on the couch and began.

"Now pay attention. This story is about a dragon. Watch my lips—a dragon, which in common English parlance means terribly awful and scaly, enormously vast, possessing seemingly innumerable large, sharp teeth that it incessantly gnashes, an apparently inexhaustible appetite, egg-laying, carnivorous in the extreme, loud-mouthed, and fire-breathing. A monster beautiful and hideous at once, so fearsome as to strike terror into the hearts of the most stalwart of heroes. In short, the most unreasonably aggressive piece of work you're ever likely to set eyes on, even in your darkest dreams."

"How could you see it, if the dream was so dark?"

Dr. Dogalogue breathed out a small tongue of flame and Miranda jumped in fright. "Just a little trick I learned from a dragon I befriended," he said with a chuckle. "It helps stop little girls from interrupting."

As I was saying, in spring of the year 1357, according to your earth calendar, I had the misfortune to enter into the field of combat with a terrible monster such as I have just described. Since I was impersonating a knight errant, I was wearing a human suit and armor on top of that, so it was all a bit cumbersome.

My search brought me to a medieval town in southern England. The villagers were complaining of a dragon that had taken up residence in a nearby cave. It was apparently supplementing its regular diet of oxen and bears with village maidens. The people were all in a panic because the dragon was about to eat a princess whom they had courageously allowed to volunteer as tribute to appease the monster so that it would not eat them.

Appealing to my sense of honor, the townsfolk asked me to fight the dragon and rescue the princess. Since I was supposed to be a knight, and also because I didn't much like the idea of the dragon eating the brave princess, I accepted the challenge. But I had a secret motive. I needed to talk to the dragon. My master back on Planet Zondgraz had told me that to have any chance of success in my mission, I needed to consult a dragon, and this seemed like too good a chance to pass up.

So early that fateful morning I mounted my charger with the aid of a couple of serfs. I thanked them with some coins and urged my steed forward into the chill dawn, eager to rescue the hopefully still-intact princess. A short way up ahead, a barely visible figure loomed out of the mist. As I approached, the swirling fog cleared to reveal a drab crone crouched atop a mossy stone wall, chewing on a dead crow.

"Fare well, oh oddly optimistic knight," she croaked, fixing me with her one beady eye. "I don't suppose we'll be seeing one another again so I'd like to congratulate you for so willingly throwing away your life in the name of honor. By the way, the dragon really made a mess of the last knight he ate. Perhaps you could ask him in advance to clean up after himself this time." She cackled horribly.

Zond! I thought. That wasn't the kind of motivational lecture I was looking for. I tried to ignore her, but her words had planted a seed of dread in my heart that grew with every step as my horse carried me toward the dragon's lair.

"Thanks a million, you old bat," I muttered, but when I looked back I froze, for there was naught but stones and moss on the crumbling wall. Was she a phantom come to haunt me or was it the voice of my own foreboding? But no, she had sounded quite real, as real as the tread of my horse bearing me to my doom. I spied a vulture crouching on the road ahead. It looked up as I approached, croaked once, and flapped away, the remains of a small animal dangling from its beak, dripping blood.

"I don't like this story, Dr. Dogalogue," Miranda whimpered, clutching his tentacle. "It's way too scary." She looked at the doctor in

sudden suspicion. "And where did the vulture come from? There aren't any vultures in England."

"How should I know? Perhaps it was on holiday. Anyway, what happened to my brave space nurse who isn't afraid of anything? Why are you worried? Obviously the dragon didn't eat me or I wouldn't be here talking to you."

"I guess so." She wriggled closer, trying to look brave. "All right, you can go on."

Suddenly the sun came out in a dazzle of rainbows, and a dozen bouncing bunny rabbits popped out of the spring grass and started practicing the piano. The shining morning erupted in a chorus of fairies and pixies and talking beavers, and a wobbly gnome with a red hat and brass buttons on his waistcoat marched up and offered me some tea and cake and a special bottle of guaranteed dragon repellent, costing only sixpence.

"Stop it, Doctor!" Miranda snapped. "What do you think I am, a three-year-old? Be serious and tell the story properly. And leave out the vultures."

"OK, OK. But are you quite sure about the vulture ban? This was a very friendly vulture with a charming Irish accent and a master's degree in particle physics."

"Doctor!"

"All right, got it. No vultures. Now where was I?"

A Fork in the Road

Once I'd passed beyond the village, I left the main road and took a lesser path leading up into the hills, just wide enough for one rider. The trees closed in above me and I only glimpsed the sky from time to time through the foliage. A patch of new spring growth caught in a stray sunbeam shimmered like green plastic. I halted for a moment and stopped to inspect the leaves on the nearest trees. Remember, this was my first time on an alien planet. Every new variety of tree and shrub was a curiosity, each fern or bush a revelation. I could hear the plants whispering in wet, breezy voices, wondering at my intrusion into their quiet world, never imagining I could understand their thoughts. Bathed in the bliss of the now, I rode on slowly through the forest, allowing my sphere of consciousness to expand and encompass the world around me, absorbing sounds, smells, and color through my sixth sense. Insects buzzed within this enhanced awareness, a magical inner world of flowing energy and shimmering life force. It all glowed and shifted subtly so that everything, from the forest floor to the tops of the tallest trees, seemed a part of me.

I cast my mind back to my arrival on earth a few days earlier. The master had sent two of us on this mission, myself and my commander, Dr. Eikelbohm, a shape shifter and a great fighter, capable of throwing lightning bolts and destroying enemies with ease. I thought back to our last conversation.

"We'll divide forces," Eikelbohm had declared. "The first thing we have to do is locate Atlantis. Only the dragons and the old wizard know its whereabouts. Your job is to track down a dragon and slap it around a bit or whatever it takes to persuade it to cough up its secrets.

Meanwhile, I will find the magician, overcome any resistance, and try to get the location out of him. I'll meet you in six days' time. There we can assess our situation. The good news is, I've arranged transportation for you. Check out this amazing talking horse."

I looked at the sleepy-looking animal, unsure which end was the front or how to make it go.

"What about you? How are you going to get around?"

"I'll take the spaceship."

"But the master said not to use it once we landed. We have to keep a low profile."

"I'll fly at night. In any case, if someone sees it they'll just think it's a weather balloon or swamp gas or an elaborate hoax."

"I don't think these people have weather balloons."

"Well, they're not so dumb that they don't know what a hoax is, and they've got swamp gas. Everyone has swamp gas."

"So let me get this straight. I ride this unreliable-looking hairy thing with four legs and fight a huge fire-breathing monster that can fly, while you get to ride in a modern spaceship, and your main job is to beat up an old man."

"Got it in one."

I didn't want to complain, so I said nothing. I knew my place. But in truth I wasn't very comfortable with this arrangement.

Anyway, it was time to get moving. I had a mission to fulfill. A princess awaited my rescue and a dragon was about to be deprived of its breakfast. I nudged my horse, Amble, trying to get him to walk a bit faster, but he ignored me, and true to his name, continued at a leisurely pace. The last of the early morning mist dissolved and I began to warm up inside my armor.

We rounded a bend and came upon a rocky outcrop dividing the road. Leading away to my left was a well-worn track. A sign carved into the rock read: *The Path of the Wimp. This way, shameless cowards, for a route free of dragons and other anti-social elements.*

The right-hand path was so overgrown it would have hardly caught my notice were it not for a freshly painted wooden board that read *Dragon's Lair: The Path to Certain Death*, featuring an alarmingly realistic painting of a dragon eating a knight. I found the picture quite disturbing. I don't generally go in for senseless violence. In fact, I'm not really the hero type at all. I've been known to break out in a sweat when my vegetables are too sharp.

I looked first at one path, then the other, uncertain which to take. Back on Zondgraz, when I'd put my name down for foreign assignments, I'd envisaged sunny beaches and exotic food. But the food wasn't supposed to be me!

I considered the problem logically. Obviously, as a brave and loyal disciple of my master, I should take the right-hand path. That is what knights errant on book tours always claimed they did. But they were clearly lying. The Path of Certain Death didn't look as though a horse had passed that way in a long while, whereas the Path of the Wimp was suspiciously well-worn. Anyway, the knight being eaten in the picture wasn't going to be doing a lot of book tours.

I found the whole image so discouraging that my initial zeal for the mission shrank to a disquieting sense of obligation. I wondered if anyone would mind if I were to go back to the village and explain that my horse had a sore hoof. Perhaps I should try to find a smaller, less nasty-looking dragon to talk to. Why, with any luck I might find one that was sick, or had a wooden leg, or one that had just eaten a huge meal and couldn't move at all. But what about the princess? How could I leave her to be eaten by the dragon? Suddenly I had an inspiration. What if she was an ill-tempered girl? I might be sparing a perfectly decent prince an unhappy marriage. I'm sure the prince would thank me. He might even reward me. But then I remembered that she had offered herself to the dragon to save the village. Darn it!

Lest you get the impression that my reluctance to play the hero was due to cowardice, allow me to explain. My difficulty in making up my mind was primarily a result of Zondgrazian physiology. Every time we think "but then on the other hand," another mental tentacle appears. Rather than the two points of view of a biped, I have fifteen. We Zondgrazians have a lot of trouble making decisions. You can't possibly imagine what it is like shopping for shoes with a Zondgrazian female. Selecting a single set of shoes can take several earth years, during which time their male consorts frequently strangle themselves.

Sure enough, a fresh doubt came to my mind. (Only eleven to go.) What if the dragon didn't speak English? I needed more information lest I do something rash. Telling myself to be more practical and less romantic, I tried to turn Amble around so we could go back to the village and do a bit more research, but the horse, who had discovered a patch of lush grass, was quite unconcerned with my dilemma.

"Having a little trouble making up your mind, young man?" a high-pitched voice croaked from behind me.

Zond! An enemy!

I wanted to turn around to identify the speaker but I was locked inside my armor, unable to move my head more than a few inches in either direction. I tried to turn the entire horse, simultaneously drawing my sword, a standard maneuver no doubt for an experienced knight, but my unrehearsed version quickly turned into a major clown show. The horse, rudely interrupted in the midst of its third breakfast, turned its head with a puzzled expression, the ends of several grass shoots sticking out the sides of its mouth.

My heavy sword was equally uncooperative. At first it refused to slide free at all. Then on a sudden impulse it changed its mind and leapt out of the scabbard, throwing me completely off balance so that I was leaning dangerously to my left, waving my arms. The stupid animal chose this moment to take a wild guess at what I wanted it to do and turned abruptly in the opposite direction. I pitched forward and would no doubt have looked as elegant as a high diver in his finest hour, except that my legs became caught in a tangle of stirrups and straps and ropes and pulleys sufficient to rig an ocean-going galleon. I ended up swinging upside down from the saddle, my helmet inches from the dirt.

Meanwhile, my sword had embarked on a mission of its own. The moment I released the weapon from its scabbard, it began showing off. It leapt from my hand in a graceful arc, casually assassinating a few million oxygen molecules as it sliced through the air and stabbed into the bare earth with a satisfying thunk. In this way I managed to dismount and disarm myself in one smooth motion.

Perhaps you doubt the truth of my tale. Perhaps you are thinking, in a somewhat mocking tone, how hard can it be to turn a horse? Before making any assumptions regarding my equestrian prowess, I ask that you imagine yourself doing the same: First donning fifty pounds of ill-fitting armor that allows you roughly the same range of movement as a straitjacket. Then asking a friendly passerby to lower you by winch into the saddle of a horse whose Intelligence Quotient is on par with that of a slice of cheese. Add a sword possessed of the enthusiasm and good judgment of Don Quixote and remember that your natural form is that of a fifteen-tentacled Zondgrazian cephalopod, and that since you have inhabited this clumsily forged human body for only two days, your position might reasonably be compared to that of a newborn child attempting to pilot a large piece of earth-moving equipment.

As I swung there contemplating the leaves and sky above my feet, I heard another peel of laughter. There on a jutting rock I spotted an old crone rocking back and forth with such mirth I feared she might topple off her perch altogether. Great. Another old hag offering inspiration.

"You look like you could do with a hand down there," she cackled, starting to climb down from her throne.

"No, no thank you," I replied, casually crossing my arms behind my head as I dangled upside down. "Very kind, I'm sure, but I'm fine, very comfortable in fact. Why, I could happily remain like this all day. This posture is very good for the spine. Don't they teach you how to do this in hag training? It's called Upside Down Horse Rigging Brain Inversion Therapy, or yoga for short. I'm rehearsing for my *Yoga on Horseback* demonstration at the local castle next week. The Duke was kind enough to invite me to display my skill before the court."

My horse looked around at me in astonishment but was at least loyal enough not to contradict my extravagant lie.

I struggled for a moment to free my legs, but with the weight of the armor, enhanced by earth's somewhat rigorous gravitational field, it was impossible to reach the straps to untangle them. Finally I surrendered my pride and asked the old crone, "As a matter of fact, this is a tad awkward. One of these modern-type saddles, you see—not at all what I'm used to. If you could be so kind as to untangle the stirrup straps, I'll have it all under control."

With her amused assistance and some obstruction from the horse, I was able to free myself and stand upright.

"Well, that was impressive," said the hag, standing back and taking my measure. "Are you planning a similar performance for the dragon? Actually that's not a bad idea. There's a good chance it will die laughing."

"'Chance does not seem to be favoring me much these days," I said. I sat glumly on a tree stump and removed my boots. They were pinching my feet. I felt quite peckish, so I reached into my saddlebag and removed a muesli bar and a drink. Hey, there was the perfect gift for my witch friend: a carob-coated newt. I'd been wondering what to do with it. I certainly was not intending to eat it myself.

I offered her the delicacy, "Would you care for a carob-coated newt, madam?"

To my surprise she demurred.

"But aren't you a witch? Witches are always bleating on about how they love newts."

She was staring at my boots, or rather my feet. She looked confused for a second. "Oh, you mean newt! I thought you said boot. A carob-coated boot—that didn't sound very appetizing, ha ha."

But I detected a hollow note in her laugh. There was something fishy about this witch.

"'Newts, eh?" she babbled on. "Why, I could eat an army of newts without batting an eyelid. And bats, now that I mention it. Bring on the newts, that's what I always say. Ha ha, but what kind of real witch would eat a carob-coated boot?"

Still she showed no sign of actually eating the newt.

"Well, that makes me all the more glad I could offer you this one." I was now almost certain that this woman was an imposter. Perhaps she was an innocent village maiden who had murdered the real witch.

All this talk of newts naturally brought to mind the age-old philosophical question: how much money would someone have to pay me to eat a dried newt? I had pondered this puzzle for weeks during my Zen training. I had never been able to come up with an exact figure, but I had concluded that it would have to be an awful lot.

The hideous sight of the witch gingerly nibbling the carob coating off the newt brought me back to the moment. In that instant I conceived of a cunning plan to determine if this was a real witch or not.

"So what's it like being a witch then?' I asked, trying to sound casual.

"'It's a living. Barely. You know, the usual routine: brewing love potions, cursing people, figuring out new excuses to avoid being burned at the stake, and of course the odd newt-nibbling competition. Keeps me out of mischief."

But does it? I thought. "Ah yes, newt-nibbling competitions. Evidently one of your specialties. I heard it will soon be an Olympic event." The newt in her claw was now free of carob coating, but still entirely uneaten.

"I've been doing a bit of study, and I dare say I know a fair bit about witches." I shifted my position, apparently to stay in the shade, but my true intent was to be within easy reach of my sword. "I wonder if you'd be so kind as to tell me a bit more about yourself. After all, being so old and decrepit you must have been in the business a long time. Are you a famous witch?"

"Indeed I am. Have you not heard of Megan the Child Munching Evil Maniac of Mongolia?"

"You're her?" I cried, taking a step back. I had no idea who Megan was, but her name gave me reason for caution.

"The same," said Megan with a smile that lost its charm as it exposed a leering row of snaggy teeth and rotting gums. They really knew how to make scary witches on this planet. Her face was so hideous and warty, and her hair so green and lichen-thatched, that I didn't see how anything short of decapitation could solve her problems in the looks department.

My opponent—for now I viewed her as such—shifted uneasily. She grinned and clutched her twisted walnut staff with her gnarled hands. I eyed the staff warily. This must be her arcane weapon. A magical device for casting ruinous spells. Pitted against such a formidable foe, I played for time.

"I'm so sorry, I'm forgetting my manners," I said, raising my chin in defiance. "I have not introduced myself. I am Sir Dogalogue. Current occupation dragon slayer, princess rescuer, and evil witch decapitator."

Sweat collected on my brow. I tensed my body, readying myself to spring. Now that had I issued my valiant challenge there was no knowing what terrible powers this creature might unleash on me. But the witch burst out laughing.

"Forgive me, Sir Dogalogue, I couldn't help myself. You are the worst rider in Britain, you handle your sword like a croquet mallet, and you demonstrate all the courage of a jellyfish stranded in the hot sun. A dragon slayer? I think not. Where are you from anyway, the moon?"

"Interesting guess but wide of the mark," I said coldly. So wounded was I by her unkind mirth that my pride got the better of me and I declared, "I am from the planet Zondgraz in the Arcturus System and on my planet we do not munch children!"

Oh dear. I hadn't meant to reveal my alien origins to this untrustworthy creature. It would not do at all to have her rush off to her ignorant peasant friends and tell them I was from another planet. I mean, if they burn witches here, Zond knows what they would do to a cephalopod from the Arcturus System!

"Why," I said, facing away from the witch lest my face reveal my disquiet while trying to dance a little jig in my heavy armor in order to appear nonchalant, "that must have sounded as though I were saying I was from another planet. How amusing you must find my little joke. After all, only a crazy person would claim that, and I have a certificate of sanity from the Zondgrazian College of Intergalactic Psychology."

I sensed that I was not handling this well, but in my panic I blundered on. "And I happen to have an IQ of 1079, which is more than most entire earthling families between them, even Catholic ones." Oh, Zond. Did I say 'earthling families?'

"Ha, ha, silly me! Of course I meant human families, as opposed to monkey families or perhaps lemur families." I paused for breath, unsure of what I'd actually said, hoping that she was as confused as I. I dared not look at the witch lest she see the agony in my eyes. Cringing inwardly and picturing her raising her fell staff with which to end my life, I abandoned myself to the will of Zond and grabbed my sword, crying, "Avant thee, mistress of doom; your child munching days are over!"

As I cried out my challenge, sword upraised, I spun to face my enemy and froze.

The witch was gone. In her place stood a fair maiden. "Greetings, Sir Dogalogue of Zondgraz," she said. "Welcome to earth. I am Princess Iris of the Kingdom of Navarre. I am the one you have come to rescue."

Picnic with a Princess

The princess curtsied gracefully and proffered her hand for me to kiss.

"Well, I must say, this is a stroke of luck," I said when I'd recovered from my shock. "I'm so glad to discover that not only are you not a dangerous witch, but that I don't have to fight the dragon to rescue you. But what leads a princess to disguise herself as a hideous hag lurking atop a rock in the forest? Is this normal behavior for earth princesses?"

Princess Iris laughed, a pleasant sound quite unlike the grating cackle of her witch persona. "Not at all, Sir Dogalogue. Right willingly will I tell thee my tale, but first I deem it wise to remove ourselves from this public highway. I have no wish to be discovered attired thus, for I dare not risk any word of my whereabouts getting back to the village. Let us ride a little ways down the Path to Certain Death. None will be so rash as to follow us there."

I hesitated. "But that's the way to the dragon's lair. Are you sure it's safe?"

The princess laughed again. "Don't worry, brave knight. We'll just go a short way down the path. We won't go anywhere near the dragon."

With this assurance, I allowed the princess to lead me to a spot where we could relax without fear of interruption. We made ourselves comfortable on the grass in front of a small cave that was evidently her temporary abode. She spread a checkered cloth and laid out fresh victuals. After a short prayer of thanks to Zond, I set to eating. Dealing with witches is hungry work and my human body craved frequent sustenance—a lamentably inefficient mechanism compared to my latest model Zondgrazian body.

After eating my fill, I paused to look about and savor the freshness of the spring morning. A few surviving dewdrops, nestled in the grass, shone like tiny stars that changed color, shifting through the spectrum when I moved. The listening ground quietly soaked up the morning warmth and the hoary oaks and looming elms seemed as delighted as I to be in the company of a real princess rather than a hideous old witch. I was enjoying my first earth picnic. This dragon-hunting caper didn't seem so bad after all.

Suddenly a terrible sound echoed through the woods, like unto a hundred metal rodents striving for supremacy in a tin bath. I jerked upright, accidentally flicking a pat of butter in an arc through the air that landed on Amber's nose. The horse shied and started for the woods, but Iris leapt up, caught his reins, and threatened to cut off his pension if he ran away, so he stood shivering and sweating, rolling his eyes and licking the butter with his long tongue.

"What in the world was that?" I said shakily. "It didn't sound all that far away."

"That would be the dragon," said Iris, as though making an observation about the weather. "Nothing to worry about. He's just singing. It means he's happy. He makes a noise like that around this time every morning. He is practicing for the Euro-Roaring Dragon-Song Contest."

"People actually *like* to hear that kind of noise?" These earthlings had even worse taste in music than I'd suspected.

"Generally they're afraid not to like it. And if you think that's bad, you should hear the other contestants. Entire ecosystems have been known to uproot themselves and migrate to the northern tundra just to avoid them."

"Well, now I'm even more impressed by your volunteering to be the dragon's sacrifice for the year. The villagers think you are terribly noble and brave!"

"It's not really like that," said Iris. "The dragon is not as bad as people say. He's fat and lazy and really quite small for a monster. Not much more than an overgrown lizard."

"A lizard? The creature on the sign didn't look much like a lizard!"

"That's just propaganda. A wild exaggeration. I painted it myself."

"What on earth for?"

"That's a long story. First, pray tell, have you had enough to eat?"

"Yes, thank you. My bodily appetite is quite satisfied, unlike my curiosity."

The princess sat up like a schoolmistress and began her tale. "Very well, I will tell you my story. I live in Northern Iberia with my parents. Everyone thinks being a princess is all glamour and excitement and throwing scarves to handsome knights at tournaments but what they don't know is that it has a major downside. I'm supposed to marry whichever noble or king my parents need to make an alliance with. We're not talking intelligent, handsome young princes here. My most likely suitors include an ancient madman who thinks his mother is a goat, a ruthless tyrant whose breath could slay an ox at twenty paces, and a simpleminded fourteen-year-old who is about as masculine as I am, if you take my meaning. I'd rather die than marry any one of them. I managed to delay matters by arranging for my brother and me to spend a season with my English uncle. He's the local duke around here. He's got a castle and everything. Offering myself as a sacrifice to the dragon was my golden opportunity. Now everyone thinks I'm a heroine, and better still, they think I'm dead! No one will come looking for me, trying to marry me off to an ogre. I'm free!" She couldn't resist performing a little pirouette on the grass.

"But what about the dragon? How come it didn't eat you?"

"I've always been good with animals. And my brother is a genius at negotiations. He gave me a few tips. Even so, the dragon was tricky to manage. But I'd done my research. I discovered that this dragon is bored with fighting knights. He wants to lead a more contemplative life, practicing his music and working on his memoirs. His problem is, he needs to maintain his reputation as the fiercest dragon in the known universe. So I offered him a win-win solution. He doesn't eat me on condition that I help with his public relations. My job is to boost his reputation through the local media, gossip circles, and witches covens, so that everyone will be so scared they will leave him in peace."

It was my turn to be impressed.

"No fair, it's my turn," chirped a blue finch from a nearby branch.

"Get in line," growled the hawthorn bush the bird was perched on. 'I've been standing here for twenty years waiting for my turn and you just flew up and pushed in."

"My turn, my turn," came a chorus of trees, birds, bushes, and beetles. It really can be a pain sometimes, being able to understand the speech of so many living things. I tried to ignore them.

"So that's why you painted the scary sign at the crossroads and hung about in the witch suit to discourage any overeager knights from confronting the dragon. Ingenious."

"I think Princess Iris is wonderful!" said Miranda, her eyes aglow. "I want to be a brave, beautiful princess like her when I grow up."

"You're going to get bigger?" said Dr. Dogalogue in surprise.

"Of course, silly," laughed Miranda. "Don't you know anything? I'm going to be tall and graceful and I'll be an expert shot with a laser pistol."

Dr. Dogalogue looked worried. "Wouldn't you rather stay this size?"

He liked Miranda as she was. He wasn't sure how he would feel about a pistol-wielding larger version.

"It's not like I have a choice," said Miranda. "Humans grow to a certain size. It's nature."

"Hmm." Dogalogue looked pensive. "Well, that's something to think about. Anyway, you really must sleep now. We'll continue the story tomorrow, OK?"

Zond, Dogalogue thought. Looking after an earth child is way more complicated than taking care of a pet tortoise.

"One thing I don't understand," said Miranda. "How could Princess Iris change from looking like a witch to being a princess, so quickly?

"She had a really cool one-piece witch costume, specially designed by a talented local artist. They were quite the rage amongst village maidens. They all disguised themselves as witches so that they could run off with knights and wandering troubadours. It seems there was quite an epidemic of elopements at the time. It must have been the spring air."

"Well, that is romantic. I could use a witch costume like that. Do you think they have them in my size?"

"I don't know. Perhaps you'll find one under your pillow," he said.

"OK, OK, I'm going to bed. But tomorrow you have to tell me about earth all day, OK? If you promise, I'll go to sleep without torturing you for even a second longer."

"OK, it's a deal. Goodnight my little two-legged monster."

"Goodnight, Dr. Dogalogue." She hugged him and retired contentedly to her egg. The doctor watched her until the capsule door slid shut, his eyestalks pulled together in a thoughtful frown.

The next morning he continued the story, as promised.

"Princess, I need to know. How come you were so ready to believe that I was from another planet?"

"By the time you told me, it was already pretty obvious you weren't from anywhere around here. Your story didn't fit. Clearly you weren't a real knight, and you spoke English with an octopus accent! Even without all that, I knew something very weird was going on the moment I saw your feet."

"Why, what's wrong with my feet?" I said, looking down.

"Are you serious? Don't you know they're the wrong way around? Look. Your big toes are on the outside. They're supposed to be on the inside like mine, see?" She slipped a small foot out of her shoe. Sure enough, her big toes were on the inside and the little toes on the outside, the opposite of mine.

This was quite a blow. I'd paid good money for that human suit. "You're absolutely sure they're supposed to be like yours?" I asked. "Maybe some people have feet like mine, like being left-handed." If what she said was true, I was going to file a complaint with those dratted human-suit manufacturers.

"I have never been more sure of anything in my life. Look, if you really want to keep your alien origins a secret you're going to have to be much more careful. You have to keep your boots on for a start. And try to be less, er..., less *weird*. And for heaven's sake, be careful what you say. You went and told me you're from another planet. What if I'd been a real witch? You can't go around trusting everyone like that. Earth is a dangerous place."

"Right," I said. "Got it. Don't say anything unusual, wear my boots, and trust no one." I drew my cape before my face, trying to look dangerous, and hunched my shoulders, glancing around mysteriously beneath my hooded brow.

The princess burst out laughing. "You're so funny! You should have posed as a court jester, not a knight. Then people would expect you to be strange. Look, if you want to keep out of trouble, just try to be slightly normal when we're around other people. If you let me do the talking we should be all right. Now I want to hear about you and your mission here on earth. I love quests and adventures!" She lay face down on the grass, resting her chin on her elbows. Her eager eyes watched me like a child. It dawned on me that for all her cleverness and confidence, she was still very young.

I hesitated. How much should I tell her? She'd just told me to trust no one but something about her felt right, so I decided to tell her the whole story. I needed allies, and right then, on a world where everything was new and strange, I really wanted a friend.

"As you already know, I'm from the planet Zondgraz. I'm a student at the Sadvipra School for Saints, Messiahs, and World Saviors. My spiritual master sent me here to find the lost seed of the microvita tree. He wants it as a gift for his mother, who is an avid gardener. There is only one such tree and it was lost in the ruin of Atlantis."

"Atlantis?" Iris gasped and sat up. "My ancestors were from Atlantis! According to family tradition we're descended from the last Atlantean kings. There's a prophecy that says that our family will help to restore Atlantis's lost glory." She stared at me in wonder. "And the prophecy refers to a visitor from another world who is supposed to fall off his horse."

That piqued my curiosity. "What else does the prophecy say?" I asked.

She was still staring at me in disbelief. "I don't remember all of it. It is written in some dusty old books in our library. But I definitely recall the part about falling off a horse."

"What remarkable attention to detail."

"What do you mean?"

"That prophecy was undoubtedly written by one of our Zondgrazian agents hundreds of years ago and planted in your culture to help prepare the way for my coming. We write prophecies informing everyone that our future agent is a savior or a prophet or the new messiah. Have you ever noticed how most of the prophecies sound so similar, especially the ones anticipating the advent of world saviors? It's a standard formula: a virgin birth, the father was the sun god, some special star appears in the sky and the world savior appears—"

"And falls off his horse?"

"Sometimes, yes. We write from a template. We're supposed to improvise a bit and add some variety, but some agents get lazy and stick with the standard form, so a lot of prophecies come out kind of cookie cutter. But this author evidently put some thought into his work. That's clever, the part about the horse."

"But how could he know that would happen? It's miraculous!"

"It's actually quite simple. He knew I'd be in a human suit and that I'd be an inexperienced rider. It was safe to predict that I'd fall off a horse, your main mode of transport. It looks like magic, but it's just logic. We learn all about it in prophecy-writing class."

Iris thought for a moment, trying to take this all in. "So, according to scripture," she said, "you're a savior, but in reality that's just a story someone made up thousands of years ago that somehow has come true." She paused. "Well, anyway, I think it's very special that you came seeking Atlantis, and you met me, and my ancestors are from Atlantis. That's miracle enough for me."

"Indeed, it is remarkable. So do you know how to find Atlantis? That's what I came to find out from the dragon. I'd far rather ask you than ask a dragon."

"I don't think anyone knows how to find Atlantis. It's lost in the mists of time, it was so long ago. Some people believe it was off the coast of Iberia, but no one is sure exactly where. But all the stories agree that it sank into the ocean ages ago."

"That figures. Only the dragons are old enough to remember."

"So what's so important about this tree that you had to come all this way to get it?"

"As I said, my master's mother is an avid gardener." Suddenly I realized how lame I must sound. How could I explain that our master often made seemingly pointless requests and set impossible tasks to test his disciples?

But the princess seemed to take it in stride. "I've always wanted to go on an adventure. Can I come with you?"

"I don't know. I wouldn't want to be responsible for taking you into any kind of danger."

"Danger? I just faced down a dragon and everyone thinks I'm in its stomach. And if you're worried about being responsible, I'll convince my brother to come. He will take care of me. You'll like him. He's almost as weird as you. Plus, you don't know our world. You'll need my help." A dreamy look came into her eyes and she ended as though to herself, "and somehow I feel it is my destiny."

"Well, I could use some assistance," I said, after a moment's thought. "And it does seem appropriate, you being an Atlantean princess and all."

"Wonderful! That's settled then. So what do we do first? You said you have to interrogate this dragon. It's not going to be easy. Dragons are secretive and slow to trust humans. When you consider that we've been trying to kill them for thousands of years, it's understandable. But maybe if you befriend him, we can convince him to help us."

"But aren't you already friends with him?" I said. "Why don't you talk to him?"

Iris looked away. "Well, he's not exactly my friend. He's more like my employer. I'm supposed to keep people away from him, not bring him visitors. He's not an easy animal to understand. He's reluctant to discuss anything about his personal life. If you want him to tell you the lost secrets of Atlantis you're going to have to win him over."

"Then how are we going to approach him? Oh, I have an idea." I rummaged in my satchel and pulled out a medieval health bar. "How about bribing him with this? What do you think?"

Iris gave the muesli bar a dubious look. "I don't think bribing someone who has the purchasing power of a dozen kings is going to work. I'm afraid you're going to have to challenge him in combat."

"WHAT! Are you crazy! You have a peculiar idea of how to make friends. How is it going to help my mission if I get eaten?"

"Dragons respect courage. If you are brave enough to fight him, he will definitely respect you. And I'm certain he won't eat you. At least, I'm fairly certain."

"I'm afraid I don't find that very reassuring!"

"He's really quite a coward. He's scared of the dark, and his teeth aren't sharp at all. They're mostly just grinding molars."

"I have no intention of being ground up by a dragon's molars!"

"Don't get excited. He's been in a good mood lately. In fact, he rarely eats people. Especially on Tuesdays."

"Your dragon doesn't eat people on Tuesdays? What is he, a religious dragon?"

"I don't think so, but he loves nature, and in spring he's been known to become quite gay and dance about like a little child."

"He sounds really peculiar. How come you know so much about this dancing dragon if he's not your friend?"

"A hermit told me about him."

"Did he eat this hermit, by any chance?"

"Too skinny, not enough flesh. Honestly, he's not that bad. He hasn't eaten anyone in more than a week. He seems to be on some kind of health kick. You know, plenty of trees and shrubs and thorn bushes. And lots of liquids—he drinks a fresh lake every morning."

"What if he's in a bad mood after eating all those thorn bushes? I would be."

"Look, I'm sure it'll be OK. He's always chirpy after his singing practice. In fact, now would be the perfect time to catch him."

"Now? You want me to fight the dragon now? What about tomorrow? Or next week? I need to think this over." I backed away, nervous as a sardine fleeing a hungry dolphin. Zond, I thought. This was turning into a nightmare. Some of my friends thought I was a wimp, but this wasn't fair. The real problem was my imagination. I could scare myself half to death just by thinking. Plus, I had a perfectly natural aversion to being eaten alive by huge, fire-breathing monsters. What could be more reasonable than that?

Up until now everything had been looking up. The witch had turned out to be a princess. She knew the dragon personally, and it didn't eat her. Even the vulture was only on holiday. But now I was stuck with that ghastly Path of Certain Death after all. I had to talk to that dragon. I took a deep breath, realizing that I couldn't turn back now.

"You're absolutely sure that a personal introduction won't help?"

"I'm certain. He'll think you're a coward hiding behind a girl's skirts, and he really hates cowards. Your best strategy is to face him boldly."

I sighed and turned to my horse. "OK, Amble. It looks like we're going on a little adventure."

"Hang on a minute." Amble backed away from us, shaking his mane. "What happened to the 'we're not going all the way to the dragon, just a short distance down the path' idea? I thought that was a good plan. What's the need of getting all carried away and noble? Was anyone planning on asking my opinion? I know I'm only a horse, but I do believe that I have an interest here. Dragons eat horses too, you know."

Iris cried out in delight. "What new marvel is this! A talking horse! I stand amazed, Sir Knight. I deem that on your world you must be a powerful magician."

The horse snorted. "It's not him that's doing the talking. It's me. You should be praising *me*. Yet another instance of unfair discrimination against horses. Which only serves to illustrate my point: no one has even bothered to inquire whether or not I'm interested in embarking on this suicide mission."

"Now look here, Amble," I said. "I need you to get with the program. We have a mission to fulfill, enemies to avoid, identities to conceal, Barnard's stars to subdue. Oh no, that's a different mission. Anyway, I have to do this and I can't do it without you. Who ever heard of a knight fighting a dragon on foot? I'll look foolish. Come along and be a good fellow. Where's your sense of destiny and adventure?"

"Where it belongs: in a story book for fillies and foals. I'm not big on destiny, and I crave adventure about as much as I desire to be turned into a talking amphibian by a French sorcerer with a penchant for frog's leg soup. I believe in common sense, which is to say, horse sense."

Hard to argue with that. But in the end we managed to strike a deal.

"Look," he said. "I want double wages for this caper or you can walk. And I'm only going if I can wear a sign saying I'm a noncombatant, like medical personnel or journalists have."

"Consider it done," said Iris. "I just happen to have a noncombatant sign right here." She hung the sign around Amble's neck as the horse and I stared in bewilderment. Where in the world did she get that sign? This princess was passing strange. But resourceful.

Iris patted Amble on the neck. "Amble, you're a wonderful, brave horse. I'll never forget you. Now take good care of my friend Sir Dogalogue and I'll give you the juiciest carrot you ever saw."

"Gee, really? That's a great offer. Maybe I'll get to eat it in heaven. I might even get lucky and contract the plague. A nice drawn-out agonizing death looks quite attractive right now. Lord knows, I'd prefer it to being chewed up by dragon molars."

"He's just being negative," Iris said to me. "Don't listen to his silly talk. Now, all you have to do is follow the path beside the stream. It leads straight through the forest to the dragon's cave. You might even meet him on the way. After singing, he sometimes takes a little stroll around the hill. You know, watching butterflies and picking daisies and such."

"'And devouring herds of innocent cattle and sheep," muttered the horse.

The princess ignored him. "Farewell, brave Sir Dogalogue. I wish you success in your mission. And remember, don't go asking the dragon questions about Atlantis until you are sure he trusts you. He's very sensitive about anything to do with his past. Good luck and long live Zondgraz!"

"I'll do my best," I said glumly. It was not the life expectancy of Zondgraz that concerned me right then. "I really hope this creature is as harmless as you say."

Iris embraced Amble, kissing him on the nose.

"Hey, whoa!" said Amble, snorting in embarrassment and stepping back. "Just because you're a princess doesn't mean you can go kissing whomever you please. I'm a not a frog, you know. I'm a married horse!"

But I thought he looked rather pleased.

Iris laughed and waved her embroidered handkerchief as we rode down the path and out of sight. The birds were twittering and little yellow and white butterflies flittered among the flowers, seeking those most laden with nectar, as though nothing were more important in the world.

Buttercup Dreaming

Miranda frowned.

"There's one thing I don't understand, Dr. Dogalogue."

"What's that, child?"

"Well, I don't wish to be rude or anything but how come you were the one they picked to go on the mission? I mean you're really nice and really smart, but you're not exactly the superhero type."

Dr. Dogalogue looked abashed.

"I was not their first choice."

"Why? What happened?"

"The recruiter from the Planetary Adventure Club came to our campus and called a meeting for anyone interested in getting out of crucifixion practice. I remember the meeting like it was yesterday. Everyone was there. Only total nerds with a martyr complex actually liked crucifixion practice. The problem was, they wanted someone from the second-century group. That included me, Lucifer, who refused to go on the grounds that earth was 'infested with meaningless creatures,' and Lumbago, the top contender—strong, intelligent, skilled in combat, easy to get along with, good at thinking on his feet—in short, a born leader. It was a done deal. Lumbago would get the gig and I'd spend six hours a week hanging from a cross until I got used to it and began to sing. Until one fine morning when Lumbago got his fourteenth tentacle caught in the kitchen blender. I still remember the gloom in the selection room when everyone discovered that I was the only candidate.

"The head mission planner looked around the room. 'Is there really no one else?' he asked.

"My philosophy professor, Dr. Non-Existent, looked apologetic. 'I'm afraid not. The other students already have their mission assignments. These three are the only ones still available.'

"'The dregs, eh? I guess that's the penalty for applying late.'

"The mission planner sighed and turned to me. 'So, minion. I would ask you why you think you're up to the task, but there's no point. We have no other choice.'

"I was trying to feel brave, but actually I was more than a little intimidated. 'I haven't been briefed with the details, sire. But I'm eager for adventure and always love to serve our great cause of bringing awareness to the universe.'

"The mission planner looked skeptical. 'OK, here's the deal. You have to accompany the mission commander, Dr. Eikelbohm, thirty-seven light years to the planet Earth, third out from Sol; find the last remaining microvita tree seed that was lost in the ruin of the island of Atlantis ten thousand years ago; and bring it back here so that our master can plant it in his mother's kitchen garden as a special surprise for her birthday. To retrieve the seed you will first need to interrogate a dangerous man-eating dragon and/or a homicidal, megalomaniacal necromancer. Then you will have to fight off the guardians of the seed, which may or may not include a giant sea monster. At no time may you utilize our advanced technology in the form of weapons, navigational instruments, or transportation devices.'

"The mission planner fell silent, waiting for my response. I hesitated, then stammered, 'Sir, that sounds kind of hard.'

"Anyhow, I got the job."

The path to the dragon's cave turned south, following the stream that ran down the spine of the valley. Silver birch trees gathered near its banks, lured by the sweet water that tinkled and whispered as if it would never run out of gossip. Meanwhile a drama was playing itself out at the level of my horse's hoofs.

"Here, watch where you're walking," yelled a buttercup as Amble almost stepped on her. The horse did not hear, so the flower turned to her neighbor to complain. But her friend lay squashed with a hoof mark imprinted on her back.

"Oof!" gasped the injured flower. "That was a fat one! That knight should put his horse on a diet. I won't be able to stand up straight for a week. And with my luck, he'll probably trample me again on the way back."

"I doubt they'll be back, Carnice," said the first flower. "It looks like they're off to fight the dragon, which usually means that the horse is bringing the dragon breakfast in bed."

"Serves them right, clumsy brutes. I hope it eats the horse as well," said the aggrieved Carnice. Buttercups can be vindictive when roused.

"Hey, I've an idea. Why don't we start taking wagers on the outcome of the fight? We could start our own betting shop."

"No one is going to bet on the knight. How would we make any money?"

"We could spread rumors that the knight is a magician. Or we could take wagers on how long the knight would last. You know, even odds for the knight lasting sixty seconds, that sort of thing."

"Hmmm. That could work. Winifred, I believe your plan has possibilities."

But as everyone knows, buttercups are dreamers. They seldom act on their own fanciful notions. If it were not for the sharp ears of a passing mouse, Winifred's idea would have died where it was born.

Dragon vs. Cephalopod Round One

Amble and I rode on down the valley. Dust motes caught in sunbeams floated in the air like snow, calling to us in tiny golden voices. Small birds flitted and darted, catching insects stirred up by our passing, chirping out high-pitched cries of thanks. I tried to stay positive and trust that the princess knew what she was talking about.

"Has it occurred to you that this so-called princess might really be a witch after all?" Amble said, interrupting my reverie. "This whole thing might just be an elaborate ploy. Witches are always pretending to be princesses. She might just be a particularly cunning witch pretending to be a princess who is pretending to be a witch. And even if she's not a witch, you've got to wonder about her state of mind. I mean what kind of girl paints gory pictures of dragons eating knights? Either way, I wonder about her reliability."

I wondered how Iris would feel about being psychoanalyzed by a horse. But the animal's words made too much sense to be entirely discounted. Maybe she *was* a witch after all! A chill crept over me as I considered that possibility. What if she was in league with the dragon, luring victims toward its lair with her pretty wiles and other deadly clichés. Maybe she got to eat the scraps once the dragon was satisfied. Horror! Perhaps her claims about the dragon being afraid of the dark and not eating people on Tuesdays and dancing about like a little child were just a ruse to allay my fears and persuade me to walk into their trap.

The forest sounds took on a new and horrible significance. We had entered the dragon's domain and every rock, tree, and fallen leaf carried an echo of the wicked reptile's malevolent spirit. The very earth groaned in memory of the worm's passing. Since I'd been on earth, I had shared the thoughts of the living creatures wherever I'd gone, but here my mind was clouded by a fog of dread. The memory of unnamed horrors pervaded the air. A raven cawed and I started in fear at a white stone that stared at me with hollow eyes like a skull.

Amble was trembling. "Well, what's the verdict, boss? I'm not sure how long I can keep up this brave front. I'm not a hardened battle stallion, you know."

"I never would have guessed," I said, but my weak sarcasm cheered neither of us. "Look, Amble, I've got to tell it to you straight. I know this seems like a bad idea, but I feel bound to go on. You can leave now if you want. I might as well walk to my doom as ride."

Amble snorted. "I never thought I'd hear myself say this, but I, too, feel bound. We horses are loyal creatures, you know. I wouldn't want to let the species down. Let us put ourselves in God's hands and pray for the protection of Mary, the mother of horses."

"You're a Catholic? I've always thought of horses as atheists, or perhaps nature worshipers."

"What? And risk ending up in horse hell? No, thank you. My money is on the Jesus story and the Holy Bible. With one important correction."

"Which is?"

"According to the current human version of the Bible, the Lord Jesus rode into Jerusalem on a donkey. What an insult to our Savior! Jesus rode into Jerusalem mounted on a fine horse, whom I believe to be none other than my ancestor Bartholomew the Substantial. It's all due to a mix-up in the translation from Aramaic into Greek. The ancient Aramaic word they translated as 'donkey' actually has three meanings. It can mean either 'undignified-looking load-bearing quadruped,' 'noble creature suitable for carrying divine beings into large cities,' or 'deep-sea fish notable for its fondness for word games.'"

Amble snorted in disgust. "Obviously the first interpretation is fictional. No self-respecting world savior would consider riding on a donkey! There is at best a remote possibility that the third interpretation is correct, despite the claims of a hugely unpopular sect that believes that Christ rode into Jerusalem mounted upon a literate fish. The most logical translation is clearly the second, which implies that Jesus loved horses above all other creatures, including humans. Furthermore, there is evidence to suggest that Mother Mary herself was part horse."

I was about to respond with incredulity but I was startled by a dark shape moving through the bracken on the far side of the stream. "What was that?" I hissed. Amble froze, his skin twitching, afraid to go forward or back, scanning the undergrowth with fear-stricken eyes. But there was no sign of movement so I shook the reins and urged my nervous steed onward, each step taking us further into the heart of the dragon's realm. I wondered how many brave souls had perished on this road, how many scattered bones and broken swords lay buried beneath the damp earth, relics of forgotten fights and desperate last stands.

Tendrils of noisome mist seeped from the ground as I rode, coiling like serpents around the boles of the dark trees that loomed over us, creaking and watching, whispering fell messages in half-heard voices. High in the branches a wind arose, stirring leaves that rustled and sighed, obscuring the stealthy tread of prowling beasts and the slavering of hungry lips.

The path led downward curving deep into the forest. Rows of pines stared down coldly, casting long shadows over the path, filling the air with their sharp scent. Driven by fear down the darkening avenue, I drew breath and summoned the last dregs of my valor. A raven watched from a high branch as I rode reluctantly toward my doom, pressing forward through a thickening cloud of dread.

I've never fully understood what sustained my spirit in that hour. Was it some unsuspected reservoir of courage, awakened by my simple faith that the master would not have sent me on a needless mission? Was it pride that made me unwilling to admit defeat? Or was it simply the certain knowledge that I had no idea how to turn my horse around? Whatever my motive, continue I did, and my determination served for two, for loyal Amble carried me every step of the way.

And so we emerged at last from the bitter gloom of the trees into a clearing beneath a grassy hill covered with white flowers. I drew rein. The air was filled with the sound of wind among the leaves, the rustling of small, furry creatures, the carefree twittering of small birds. I felt calm despite my fear, and strong despite my youth. My self-doubt left me, for in that moment I knew that whether I lived or died, I had the courage to face a live dragon.

The monster lay crouched beneath the flower-clad hill. Coiled about a grassy knoll, the huge spiked serpent, turquoise scales shining in the sun, watched me with intelligent eyes. Then he roared. That awful sound was too much for poor Amble. His courage broke and he reared wildly, dumping me on the ground and running for home.

I lay on my back on the grass, dazed and disoriented, wondering why all the forest creatures were fleeing, wondering what was causing that earth-shaking sound, wondering why all the birds had become silent, wondering if I would ever taste pizza again. Mentally I began to formulate my letter of knighthood resignation.

"GET UP AND FIGHT LIKE A MAN, PUNY MORTAL, OR I WILL TEAR THEE LIMB FROM LIMB AND DEVOUR THEE WHERE THOU LIEST," a dreadful voice blared, all in capitals.

I sprang to my feet, reluctantly recollecting where I was and what I was supposed to be doing there. I whipped out my sword and pointed it at the huge creature that loomed in front of me, a terrifying apparition that bore no resemblance to the princess's description of a small, ancient, toothless, overgrown lizard. In fact, it was the spitting image of the ferocious monster in the painting, only much, much bigger! I drew little comfort from the thought that if I were to strike it from close range, I couldn't miss—there was so much of it! But instead, I thought it prudent to begin with a few formal threats.

"Foul spawn of hell!" I stammered. "Get thee back to the shadows whence thou came or I will smite thee such a grievous blow with my vorpal blade that thou shalt long remember it, and even if thou slayest me, the anguish of the wound I deliver shall bring thee torment for all thy evil days."

A rather impressive little speech, I thought, considering the stressful circumstances under which it was delivered. I'd tried to be realistic and allow for the possibility of my defeat, while conveying the clear impression that though I might be small, I was fierce and determined to die bravely. In truth, I wasn't interested in dying at all, bravely or otherwise, and I've never been considered fierce.

The dragon ambled forward like a shuffling hill and the horror of it smote my heart. I quickly decided that I had no clear evidence of its evil deeds and therefore was not really justified to smite it with my vorpal blade thus unprovoked, and that if I did, it would be perfectly within its rights to charge me with aggravated assault.

"Would you like me to read you your rights?" said the dragon in a tone of amusement. 'Now, if you'll just stop waving that silly vorpal blade about, perhaps we can have a little talk."

At this point I was hiding behind an oak tree. Please do not be too hasty and attribute this to cowardice. It is an amazing thing that just at that moment I suddenly became fascinated with the patterns on the bark of the aforementioned tree and became inspired to begin a research paper on the subject, which was bound to keep me very busy and make me unavailable for any appointments for the foreseeable future, particularly for barbaric engagements involving swords and crude violence, which I opposed on principle. Surprised by the dragon's gently mocking tone, however, I instructed my newly appointed research assistant, a nearby toadstool, to make an exception and schedule a meeting. I poked my head out from behind the tree.

"Why don't you begin by telling me why I should not sue you for calling me a nasty name and hit you with a trespassing charge for riding on my land?"

I considered being flabbergasted, but I settled for being merely astonished.

"You've got cheek, threatening to bring petty charges against me!" I retorted, adopting a spirited tone, not in order to scare the monster (dragons are not easily frightened), but because I remembered what the princess had told me, that dragons appreciate boldness.

"How many innocent maidens have you devoured? How many innocent cattle have you stolen? How many innocent local by-laws have you violated parking your vast bulk in inappropriate places? Try removing the boil from your own cheek before you comment on the innocent pimple on another's."

I paused, becoming somewhat confused in my excitement. Arguing with dragons is heady stuff.

"What a distasteful analogy. Is it biblical?" The dragon sounded pained.

I was touched by the monster's sensitivity. It seemed like the princess was right, after all—Amble's fears were just paranoia. Which is not so surprising when you consider that he thought that Jesus's mother was part horse.

"'Forgive me, I see I have offended you with the uncouth figures of speech I have picked up from these wretched English peasants. I am a foreigner and unacquainted with the proper manner of address for prodigious and valiant fire-breathing monsters." I thought a little flattery might appease the creature.

"You show signs of being a civilized human, an unusual combination. I once heard about a dragon who came across a civilized human but it was all rather unfortunate. Sadly, the dragon ate him before he realized he was civilized. Anyway, no point in crying over eaten people. On to brighter subjects. Allow me to offer you a vat of tea in my cave. We can talk matters over there like gentle reptiles."

6

The Badger's Betting Shop

Mina the mouse hurried off to tell her friend, Brains the badger, about Winifred's idea. When it heard the mouse's report, Brains's entrepreneurial spirit roused itself from slumber. Ah, how he loved the thrill of danger, the exhilaration of risk-taking. Thinking of the risk, the badger decided to avoid discussing this with his mother.

"Just going out to help some old beavers cross the pond, mum. Hope that's OK," called Brains.

"Fine, dear." She muttered to herself, "He's such a good boy!"

Brains, as the newly elected Mayor of Not Enough Hugs Valley, didn't like having to ask for his mother's permission every time he went out, but he didn't have the courage not to. As soon as he was out the door, he called a secret meeting with his business partner, Maurice the mole.

Word of the coming fight and the newly opened Brains's Betting Shop spread quickly among the forest creatures. Soon they had all laid extravagant wagers on the contest and were hastening toward the dragon's lair to watch the fight. Naturally most money was on the dragon, but as per the buttercup's creative suggestion there was a complicated range of betting options, taking into account whether or not the man ran away and what kind of sauce the dragon used when eating him.

The severely squashed condition of Carnice the buttercup boosted the martial reputation of the horse, and Winifred's report of its enormous girth and the great ferocity of the knight gave the forest creatures pause to wonder: perhaps the challengers had a chance after all. This added fuel to the lively speculation and betting was running hot.

Lance the lemur leered at Brains. "How can we be sure that you'll pay out when I win," he snarled.

"*If* you win," said Brains, standing his ground. These lemurs were no joke, but he couldn't afford to show fear. Actually, it didn't matter because they could smell fear, and he reeked of it.

"Don't worry. The money is deposited in escrow with Slime the snake."

Which was true, but it wouldn't cover their losses if the knight proved to be a complete chicken and didn't fight at all.

The lemur grunted. "OK, but if you try to rip us off, you're toast."

His husky brothers gathered round, flexing their lemur biceps and laughing in derision at Brains and Maurice. Lance drew his claws across his throat, in case Brains didn't know what toast was.

But he did, and he definitely didn't want to be it.

At first the animals hid, peering between the grass blades at the battle from their observation post on the hilltop. But as their curiosity and their concern about the funds they'd staked on the outcome got the better of their fear they emerged one by one, creeping out into the open for a better view of the fight. Brains was counting the bets and trying to calculate the odds. He looked worried. "What's the square root of minus three and a half?" he whispered.

"Unreal number. Can't do it," said Maurice the mole absently. "Must be a mistake."

"This accounting is really complicated," said Brains, glancing nervously at the lemurs. "I need Slime the snake to help me. He's the only one around here who doesn't have to count on his fingers. We'd better get it right or we'll have the internal revenue service on our backs. Not to mention that ruthless lemur mob."

He turned to Mina the mouse. "Mina, go fetch the snake."

"*Me*?" said Mina. 'You want *me* to fetch the snake? Are you sure that's a good idea? Snakes eat mice, you know."

"It's OK," said Fenugreek the fox from his nearby perch on a flat rock. "She's sleeping off her last victim. She won't be hungry yet."

Mina gathered her courage and flitted between the tall grass stalks towards the snake's burrow.

"Excuse me, Madam Slime," she squeaked timidly at the entrance. A snore came from within. Mina crept into the hole and found the snake dozing with a suspicious-looking lump in her abdomen.

"Mrs. Snake. Madam," squeaked Mina. "The other animals want your help with some advanced math. Mayor Brains said it's important."

"I'm not going anywhere," growled Slime. "I'm digesting. If they want advanced math, tell them to come here."

Mina ran to fetch the other animals. Soon they were assembled in the gloom of the snake's den, standing respectfully in a row.

"What's that suspicious-looking lump?" whispered the mole.

"'Oh, it's nothing," Slime said, trying to hide the bulge behind a bowl of Christmas decorations. "It's an apple. You know, from the Garden of Eden."

"Wow," said Maurice. "You ate a mythological apple. Are you that famous snake they mention in the Bible?"

"I'm not an apple," said the lump. "Maurice, it's me, your cousin Joslyn. This lying snake swallowed me whole. I'm not from the Garden of Eden. I live just down the hill in my molehill. At least I used to."

"Oh," said the snake, looking guilty. "I thought you were an apple."

Maurice put his paws on his hips. "How could you mistake a mole for an apple! You ate my cousin! Well? What do you intend to do about it?"

"Excuse me," said the lump. "I'm getting a bit bored down here. Could someone please send down a magazine?"

The snake looked ashamed. "I didn't know she was your cousin. But you heard her, she's OK. I can regurgitate her, if you like. But perhaps you would like me to solve this math problem first."

"OK," said Maurice, "but you'd better regurgitate her right after that. In the meantime, swallow this magazine." He passed Slime a copy of *Molehill Monthly*, and the snake obliged by scarfing it down.

"That tasted terrible," said the snake.

"Serves you right. It'll teach you to be more careful in future."

Miranda interrupted Dr. Dogalogue's narration. "But how could the mole read the magazine in the snake's stomach? It would be too dark to see."

"It didn't matter," said Dr. Dogalogue. "Don't you know moles are blind? And anyway, they can't read."

"Oh, I didn't know that."

"Can I go on now?"

"Yes, Doctor."

Brains approached the snake. "Look, we've collected all these bets on the outcome of the fight between the dragon and the latest suicidal knight errant. But we're confused by the figures. There are some complicated betting odds. Could you have a look at it for us, please?"

He spread out a large sheet of paper on the dirt. The snake studied it thoughtfully.

"OK, let me see now. Aha. Look at this. Here's your first problem. You can't divide a hieroglyphic by an antigen. What on earth are you trying to do? Here, give me that." The snake took the paper in her jaws and savaged it, growling and shaking her head like a dog. The numbers were now complete chaos. She spread the mangled paper out proudly before them. "Now it makes sense. See that row of Paleoliths? Now they all add up. And I don't think you'll be getting any grief from the integers any more. They've been demoted to prehistoric numbers."

Brains stared at the paper, bewildered. "I'll take your word for it. It all looks prehistoric to me. So what does it mean?"

"Four," said Slime. "You each get four pieces of walnut if the dragon eats the knight with Italian sauce, as seems likely."

"Hey, you guys," called the raven from the entrance. "The fight's starting. C'mon."

They rushed outside. Even Slime crawled along after them. She was not going to miss the excitement, digesting or not.

Brains and Maurice lagged behind. "There is going to be trouble if we can't sort out these bets," said Brains in a low voice. "Did you get the tickets for South America?"

"Quiet, everyone!" hissed Fenugreek. "There's a human coming."

The animals hid in the grass and a moment later Iris appeared. She climbed down the hill toward the dragon and hid behind a tree so she could watch the fight unobserved.

Once she was gone, the animals gathered together again.

"What's she doing here?" said Carl the magpie. "She looked like a princess. Do you think she wants to place a bet, too?"

"How should I know?" said Brains. "If she's a princess, she's probably dessert. Forget about her. What's happening with the fight?"

Maurice crept down the hill to get a closer look.

"Very disappointing so far," said Wallace, an adolescent weasel. "Look at that. They're just yakking. It's not a proper fight at all. Who ever heard of a dragon talking so much? And that stupid human is pointing his sword at the ground. What kind of warrior is he?"

"Hey!" he called out. "Moron! Keep the point up!"

But his small voice was too slight to carry down the hill.

The magpie had bet heavily in favor of a brief but vigorous struggle ending in a Chinese sweet-and-sour dish. "This smells fishy," he cawed. "Hey, Brains. What's going on? They seem to know one another. Looks to me like someone fixed this fight. You didn't tell us they were friends. I want my money back!"

Lance the lemur barred his teeth. "Yeah, this looks mighty suspicious to me, too. What's going on, Brains? You'd better not be cheating us, if you know what's good for you."

"Go on, you idiot knight," Brains muttered to himself. "Strike when he's not expecting it." He prayed that it was a ploy on the knight's part to get close enough to the dragon to get in at least one blow with his vorpal blade. He knew it wouldn't alter the final outcome of the struggle, but if the moron would just provoke the dragon a bit, the struggle would be over in a few seconds and Brains would make a fortune.

Maurice came panting back up the hill. "You'll never believe the conversation I overheard down there," he announced to the little group of animals. "That knight is as crazy as a bandicoot, and the dragon is a total wimp! They just argued a bit and now they've made friends, for Cernunnos's sake!"

"No way!" the group cried in unison.

There was a chorus of objections: "That's impossible; your ears are full of dirt; you must have misheard; how could a monster like that be friendly? This is unheard of."

"Don't ask me. How would I know? But I know what I heard. And now they are going off to have a vat of tea together in the dragon's cave."

"I once saw a documentary that explains that dragons are descended from birds, not reptiles," piped Mina.

"That's ridiculous," said Fenugreek. "How could a great fat dragon like that be descended from a bird?"

"It's not only ridiculous," said Maurice. "It's incorrect. Mouse, you are a nincompoop and belong in the wrong end of a flowerpot. The theory you refer to concerns dinosaurs, not dragons, and it's the other way round—birds are descended from dinosaurs. By Cernunnos, you're stupid."

"Oh," said the tiny mouse. She seemed to shrink even smaller and withdrew from the circle to search for her pet nut.

And so the animals debated whether or not it was really possible that the monster they'd feared so much could make friends with a human.

"We need to confirm this," said Brains. "Perhaps the dragon is tricking the stupid man. Maybe he just wants to lull him off guard and lure him into his cave where he'll eat him."

"But why would the dragon go to all that trouble?" objected the weasel. 'Why doesn't he just step on him?"

"Shut up," said Slime. He turned to the group. "We have to send a spy into the cave to find out what happens. Who wants to volunteer?"

"I'd love to, of course," said Paul, the unidentifiable rodent, "but I have an urgent appointment with my Egyptologist."

"And I'm expecting to be transported back to the Pleistocene Era at any moment," said Bertha, the beaver. "I couldn't possible go. Though of course I would love to help if I could. I only regret that I have but one set of intestines to sacrifice for my country."

"I'm really interested in going," said Paula, the pet persimmon. "There is just one small problem. I am an article of fruit and do not qualify for the job."

Brains nodded sagely. "Noble sentiments, my friends. I quite understand." He looked around at the crowd of excuse-oligists. He spied Mina and glanced at Slime.

"You look like you want to volunteer, Mina," said the snake. They all turned to the mouse.

Mina looked up. "I do?" She hadn't been paying attention. She'd been too busy trying to bite a hole in the shell of her hazelnut.

"Yes, you do, and that means that your inner self surely wants you to do it," said Cynthia the psychic lizard.

"Really? I never thought of that."

"Well, you'd better start thinking of it quick," said the fox. "You don't want to go to hell. do you?"

"No." Mina glanced about, unsure what to do.

"Then it's clear," said Brains. "You'll sneak into the dragon's cave and then report back to us. And while you're about it, see if you can pick up a slice of pizza. Henceforth, you will be known as Supermouse. OK?"

"Supermouse? Wow! OK, I'll do it." Mina ran off through the grass in the direction of the cave, her whiskers twitching.

Fact Checking for Aliens

Miranda was quiet during breakfast the next morning, absentmindedly sculpting her Greek super-thick yogurt into the shape of a badger. She had a lot to think about. One thing in Dr. Dogalogue's story about his first visit to Earth didn't seem to make sense. How come the dragon didn't eat Dr. Dogalogue? Dragons eat everybody!

And then there was St. Lucifer. There were only the three of them on the spaceship, but she'd hardly seen Dr. Dogalogue's mysterious friend. Of course, it wasn't as though she wanted to see him. He gave her the creeps, stalking about on his long legs like a big insect. The only time he moved quickly was when he went into the kitchen to get some food and scuttled back to his lair like a horrid cockroach. He never said anything or even looked at her. Sometimes she spotted him lurking in the corner, listening to the doctor telling her his story. He really got on her nerves.

Great! she thought. I finally get to travel to my home planet, and I'm stuck on a spaceship for a week in the company of a giant insect! The worst part was, she felt uncomfortable asking Dr. Dogalogue about Lucifer because he was his best friend. Why would the ultra-nice Dr. Dogalogue have such a weird friend?

Anyway, the first thing was to get the doctor's story straightened out. She didn't want to arrive on her home planet without having the full picture. She wanted to understand more about this dragon. After all, when she arrived on Earth herself, she might run into one.

"Dr. Dogalogue, how come Joe didn't eat you? I thought dragons were greedy and aggressive and eat people. Joe seems so friendly and kind and he's really funny. I know he's a bit of a tease and seemed to enjoy frightening you, but he never intended to hurt you, did he?"

"No," said Dr. Dogalogue. "He never meant me any harm, and he became a good friend. But if you want to know how he came to be so different from other dragons, I have to tell you about The Amazing Sweep."

Enter The Sweep

One fine morning, further up the very valley where Dragon Joe lived, a mouse sniffed at the entrance of a cave as the sun began to burn through the mist.

"Smells like human," she whispered to her companion, a large badger.

"That can only mean one thing," replied the badger gravely. "This must be a holy man, come to contemplate the meaning of existence in the quiet of our valley. What a blessing! Mina, run and fetch Maurice the mole and bring refreshments so that we may greet our new resident and pay our respects."

"Yes, Brains, sir," said Mina, who skittered off to do his bidding, for Brains was the mayor of Not-Enough-Hugs Valley and far more important than a mouse.

Inside the cave, The Amazing Sweep, T. A. Sweep for short, prince of Navarre, awoke to hear a robin teaching her young to sing in tune. He lay still, eyes closed, listening to the robin's song, to the twittering and chirping of the finches, blue-tits, and jays, and the soft buzz of insects welcoming the morn like a tiny orchestra. He was in no hurry to get up. He didn't have much to do today, a fact of which he was very glad.

Finally The Sweep opened his eyes, sighed with pleasure, rose and stretched. The first sunbeam was just touching the back wall of the cave. Looking out from the entrance, he could see a stream below, weaving between the birches like a thread of silver. Across the water the valley floor ended in a rocky slope, rising swiftly towards the cliffs. He thought he could see another cave upstream in the distance and he wondered if anyone lived there. A broad flat rock lay before the cave mouth, the sunlight creeping slowly across it like spilled honey. The Sweep sat on a log, soaking up the warmth and, right on schedule, did nothing. It felt so pleasant that he did it some more.

What a relief to be away from the city, he thought. Here a man could think in peace. No merchants shouting, no hags gossiping, no carts clattering on the paving stones as dogs yelped and dodged the horses' hooves. It sure beat having to be a prince all day. He'd never been comfortable with all the bowing and scraping and he'd long tired of managing the kingdom's business and navigating court intrigues. Yearning for a simpler life, he'd left it all behind and become a hermit.

The prince hermit rose and re-entered his cave. The sandy floor made it feel cheery in the daylight. It was clean and spacious, the more so since it had come unfurnished, which was perfect for a hermit. He'd gotten it cheap from the previous occupant, another hermit who had been eager to get out of the lease, claiming he'd been offered a new job as a court jester. The Sweep doubted the truth of this. The fellow was glum and husky, more like a ruffian than a jester.

The Sweep considered the demographics of his new neighborhood. According to the last census, he was far from alone, although he was the only human resident. A wide variety of creatures shared the valley with him: voles, moles, badgers, rabbits, mice, crows, owls, muskrats, foxes, lizards, robins, finches, hawks, snakes—a veritable menagerie of varmints and critters. Satisfied with his new quarters, he went out in the sun again to study his new book, *Hermit Living for Dummies*.

Page one of the illuminated manuscript displayed a gaunt figure so bony and hairy he seemed hardly human. The caption read: "*Austerity Bob—Top Hermit for the year of 1356. Voted most miserable man in the world, three years running. Generally regarded as the very embodiment of the sacred hermit principle of unnecessary, self-inflicted suffering.*"

Inspiring stuff to be sure, but The Sweep found it daunting. Ordinarily as confident as a giraffe in a neck-length competition, he was experiencing an uncharacteristic bout of self-doubt. Though he was an expert in many fields, the one thing he did not know how to do was nothing. And doing nothing is, of course, a hermit's primary occupation.

Amongst The Sweep's many skills was that of falling asleep while reading chapter four of any boring philosophy book. Sure enough, just as he was about to learn why hermits are so bad at predicting the future, he dozed off. Meanwhile the sun edged higher. The chorus of birds subsided to a gentle twitter and the insects buzzed on happily in accompaniment.

The Sweep awoke to the touch of whiskers on his face accompanied by a gruff snuffling sound. He opened his eyes carefully and found himself staring into the grey-and-white-striped face of Brains the badger. Next to the badger, a field mouse stood on her hind legs, carrying a tray of drinks. A black mole peered at his book where he'd dropped it, open to page four.

"Welcome to Not-Enough-Hugs Valley, noble hermit," squeaked the mouse, offering The Sweep a glass of fresh apple juice with a slice of lemon and a tiny umbrella sticking out of it.

The Sweep sat up straight in surprise, like unto a wise king who has just been informed that his castle is made of milk.

"Welcome once more to our valley, sir," said Brains, who paused, waiting for The Sweep to respond. When the silence became uncomfortable he continued. "This sunshine is provided for you through the sponsorship of the Not-Enough-Hugs Valley Committee."

Finally The Sweep shook his head and said, as if to himself, "This is passing strange. How come you animals can speak like humans? I am astonished, and it is not easy to astonish a Sweep."

"Ah," said Brains, grinning modestly. "That is because we are no ordinary animals. We are blessed by the goddess."

"Did you notice that I can talk too?" said Mina, "even though I have only a very small brain."

The mole ceased poring over the book and joined the conversation. "Maurice the mole at your service, sir hermit. Allow me to suggest a more plausible explanation for our remarkable powers of speech than this piece of superstitious folklore proffered by my badger friend. It is my understanding that there exists in the vicinity of this valley a mysterious power that enhances the intelligence of all the creatures born and raised here. Mole scientists have observed that this effect increases as the generations pass."

"Incredible," breathed The Sweep.

Mina piped up. "I heard that the source of this wonderful magic is an ancient giant cheese buried deep under the earth, right beneath us, so potent that none might smell it and live."

Maurice laughed. "Yes, well, some people will believe even the most fanciful of tales. We moles, however, prefer the rational approach."

"Well, I'm right glad that I have chanced to settle in such a blessed place," said The Sweep.

"Indeed," said Brains. "And I see that you have elected to rent Jake's cave."

"That's right, Jake was his name," said The Sweep. "He said he'd decided to become a court jester."

"Hmm. I fear he sought to deceive you. He was known around here as Jake the Hit-monk," said Brains. "Not the kind of hermit you want to get on the wrong side of. We're glad to be rid of him."

"He's mean," said Mina. "He once threatened to dip me in batter and make me into a mouse fritter."

"Total barbarian," agreed the badger.

"Listen, Sir Hermit," began the mole.

"Please, call me Sweep," said The Sweep.

"As you wish. Sir Sweep, I have a little friendly advice for you. Nothing official, completely off the record. Everything should be fine with you living at this end of the valley, unless, by some incredibly unlikely stroke of bad luck, it should turn out that there is a monstrous dragon living nearby who happens to be known throughout the land as Joe, the most Fearsome Dragon in the Universe, and is very large and omnivorous, with teeth the size of fence posts."

"Ah," said The Sweep, unwilling to bounce, having nearly exhausting his bouncing quota for the day, but nevertheless concerned. "Would those be English fence posts or French fence posts?"

"Do you mock my warning?" said the mole. "I must advise you that in this valley mocking a mole is a punishable offense."

"No, no, not at all. I meant no insult! I just happen to be a bit of a fence post expert. I was in charge of procurement for our kingdom, and French fence posts are known to be lean and thin due to the extreme weakness of French cows, whereas English fence posts, out of necessity, are more stalwart, built to withstand the onslaughts of powerful English cows, known for their savagery."

"Ah," said the mole. "I see. Well, I think you're probably looking at the English fence post."

"That is a worry," said The Sweep. "And just how unlikely might this proposed stroke of bad luck be?"

"Oh, not very unlikely at all, so far as these things go, taking into consideration that this is known to be a dragon-infested area and that just last week two dragons were sighted by the previous tenant of your cave. Whoops. I wasn't supposed to have said that."

"Why not? What's going on?" demanded The Sweep.

"Look, you can't tell anyone I told you this, but you seem like a decent fellow and I feel obliged to warn you. In case you're wondering why you got such a great deal on this nice cave, your friend Jake the Hit-monk was desperate to get out of the lease because a dragon who used to live here and had been away on a sabbatical for two hundred years recently moved back into his cave further down the valley. It wasn't mentioned in the lease papers because it is a recent development, so Jake managed to fob the problem off on you."

"But why didn't he just leave?"

"Violation of contract. The cave troll who owns the place would have had his head. Would have hunted him down to the ends of the earth, knew where his family lived and all that. Your predecessor had a choice between being eaten by the dragon or being hit over the head with a mace by the cave troll. Until you came along, that is."

"Oh, dear," said The Sweep. "I thought I was getting a cheap holiday resort."

"Well, it is cheap," said Maurice.

"But what am I to do?"

"So far as I can see, you only have one chance," said the mole, looking thoughtful.

"What's that?" said The Sweep eagerly.

"I've been developing this idea. It hasn't been fully tested, mind you. In fact, this is the first opportunity to try it."

"So what is it? What's your idea?"

"Are you sure you want to hear it? It may not work. In fact, some people think it's not a good idea. I don't want you to blame me if it doesn't work. Of course if it doesn't work, the dragon will eat you, so that shouldn't be a problem."

"Just tell me!"

"OK, keep calm. Don't panic. It never helps to panic. My plan goes like this: to persuade the dragon not to eat you, you have to convince it to become a vegetarian."

The Sweep stared at Maurice. "That's it? That's your plan? To convince a man-eating, fire-breathing monster to give up meat?"

"Well, you are made of meat, aren't you? And anyhow, there's more to my plan, just listen. This is a European dragon. Right now the whole of Europe is Catholic, except for the occasional escaped druid. So it goes without saying that most dragons are Catholics."

"Dragons are Catholics? Are you mad?"

"Possibly, yes. But my theory is logical. Dragons are sentient beings. They're not dumb, like most animals. They can speak and think. Like me." The mole looked confused for a moment.

"Yeah—and breathe fire and eat people."

"Well, yes, but that doesn't stop them from being Catholics."

"OK, suppose this dragon is Catholic. What am I supposed to do? Start reading to it from the Bible?"

"That's one option. The important thing is to make it feel guilty."

"How about if I just leave town instead?"

"The cave troll is lying in wait in case you try, remember? He doesn't want his cave left vacant. He will lose value on his investment. He may even lose possession. It has to remain occupied; it can be taken over by squatters and he'll never get them out because of the tenancy protection act."

"Who's going to squat there with a dragon for a neighbor?"

"All sorts of riff-raff: bats, rats, dormice, voles, lizards. The property's value would plummet!"

"And the property value won't drop if the occupant is eaten by a local monster?"

"Ah yes, I see what you mean. Well, what can I say? Trolls are not deep thinkers. Anyway, that's the word on the ground. I really do think you should consider my suggestion and talk to the dragon about his diet. I believe it's your only way out."

While The Sweep was becoming acquainted with his new home, Joe, the Most Fearsome Dragon in the Universe, was not idle. It was time for breakfast and he was feeling a little peckish. Rousing himself from his bed of treasure, the beast shook off any stray jewels or gold coins that had attached themselves to his person and crept forth from his cave. Once outside, he paused and cast about for any whiff of fresh meat. He paused for a moment to gnash his teeth. An astute observer would have noted that they did indeed bear a remarkable resemblance to the common English fence post.

Suddenly the dragon raised his head and sniffed the air. A fresh scent—human! His favorite! Grinning, he eagerly set off down the trail.

Of Reptiles and Sweeps

The Sweep spent an otherwise peaceful afternoon trying not to think about his dragon neighbor. He took a stroll up the valley and returned to reread the first four pages of his book. When the shadows grew longer he ventured down to the stream to replenish his drinking water so that he could get back before dark.

As he walked up the hill with his jug full of water, The Sweep was deep in thought. He was not certain whether the mole had completely lost his marbles or not, but just in case, he kept a sharp eye out for dragons, wondering if Maurice could possibly be right about dragons being Catholics.

By the time he neared his cave, his spirits had risen somewhat. The dragon didn't seem to be around, and anyway, he had come up with an improved version of the mole's crazy idea.

Rounding the last corner on the path to his cave, The Sweep stopped and bounced without spilling a single drop of water. Sweeps generally prefer to bounce only on Thursdays but today he had a special reason to be surprised: he had almost walked into a huge ferocious-looking dragon. It was even huger and more ferocious-looking than he'd expected, and it was looking at him.

Seeing The Sweep for the first time, Joe, the Most Fearsome Dragon in the Universe, almost bounced too, but he didn't. Being a lot heavier, dragons don't bounce so easily as Sweeps. Nevertheless, Joe was surprised. He had never seen anything quite like a Sweep. He was still trying to determine whether it was organic or not, when he saw it move. An odd, vertical movement, carrying it several inches into the air like very temporary levitation. Who would have guessed that this bounce, which was really little more than a nervous twitch, would later give rise to the fanciful claim that Sweeps can fly. Or that the Sweep would one day gain great wealth and influence through his internationally famous flying school, where he taught bouncing as the first stage of levitation.

But at this moment, Joe was not thinking about popular beliefs or the future fortunes of Sweeps. He was thinking about food. And he was not sure whether or not this peculiar creature, apparently composed entirely of dark, curly hair, was edible or not. He approached it cautiously with a friendly smile.

"Good evening," said The Sweep, nervous as a mouse in the shadow of an owl. "Eh, is there any particular reason you are gnashing your fence posts?"

"Gnashing my what?" asked the dragon, perplexed.

"I mean your teeth," said The Sweep. "Why are you gnashing your teeth?"

"I'm smiling, not gnashing," said the dragon. "It's quite different. But either way, I'm stretching my jaw muscles, which I suspect may shortly be getting some exercise. For is it not written in the scriptures that one should always stretch before exercising to avoid the risk of straining a muscle?"

Well, at least he is health conscious, thought The Sweep. But the monster also seemed hungry. To gain time, the prince laughed mysteriously, trying to appear casual and confident in the hope of confusing the dragon. In fact, he was so frightened he had to stick his knees together with a gobbet of honey to prevent himself from collapsing.

Most people panic when they meet a dragon. They lose their mental balance and try to run away, not much good when you are facing a monster that can fly. But The Sweep's extensive experience in sales and marketing had taught him to stand firm and persist, even when facing apparently hopeless odds. Trained to handle rejection, he stood his ground.

"Ah...exactly what kind of exercise do you think your jaws might be getting?" he asked, seeking the dragon's psychological weak point.

"The nutritious kind. I'll probably warm up with a little nibbling, then some snapping and biting to get the blood flowing, and then a steady routine of munching and chewing. Oh, and I'll finish off with the traditional crunching on the bones. I'm truly sorry to tell you that we're talking about your bones here, for I am a bit peckish and from where I'm standing, you look like breakfast."

"I wouldn't advise you to act on that impulse," said The Sweep, looking the dragon straight in the eye.

"Really? Why not?" said the dragon. "Underneath all that hair you look fairly tasty."

"Eating people is a sin. Aren't you afraid of going to hell?"

The dragon laughed. "Hell? I come from Hell!" He grinned, showing what looked like a thousand teeth, and shot some flame at an innocent bush that had never done it any harm. The bush squeaked in alarm and, inspired by The Sweep's apparent levitation, tried to bounce out of the way, but constrained by its roots, it sadly failed.

The monster paused.

"But seriously, I suppose that if hell existed I might be afraid to go there, but it doesn't so I'm not. Hell is an irrational superstition cooked up by the priesthood to intimidate the peasants and control the nobles."

So much for Maurice's brilliant theory of religious guilt. It seemed that The Sweep was dealing with an atheist intellectual dragon. Just to confirm, he asked, "So you're not a Christian?"

The dragon laughed again, a dreadful sound that made The Sweep think of an entire flock of rhinoceroses all trying to eat the same cabbage.

"A Christian? Me? I don't think so. Don't get me wrong, I like Christians. They're particularly good roasted in their armor with cranberry sauce—nice and crispy! And they are also quite entertaining when they run about shrieking before I catch them. Sometimes they are even kind enough to provide me with a horse for dessert. I believe this is what they call Christian charity. Now that I think about it, I suppose I am a Christian in a sense, for is it not said that 'you are what you eat?'" The dragon laughed again.

"But surely you must feel guilty after eating all those brave and noble knights?"

The dragon paused to consider this for a moment, then shook his head. "Nope. Can't say that I do. A little indigestion sometimes, on account of all the armor and weapons, but guilt? Never. And as for noble, don't kid yourself. We're talking about violent individuals here. Always showing off, charging around the countryside waving their swords, challenging people for no reason, picking on anyone smaller than themselves and trying to impose their illogical beliefs on everyone. Eating Christian knights is a public service. The morality of it is simple. They try to kill me. They're not very good at it, so I eat them. Should I feel guilty because of their professional incompetence?"

Since the religious guilt approach didn't seem to be working, The Sweep took another tack. "Leaving that aside for a moment, don't you know that eating meat is unhealthy? The European Surgeon General advises against the ingestion of too much red meat. Tell me, how much meat have you eaten this week?"

"Oooh, I'd have to think. Let me see now." The dragon began to count on his claws. "That would be one knight, one horse, four cows, a few dozen rabbits—they hardly count really, just snacks—a bear, twelve goats, and twenty-seven sheep. Oh yes, and one wolf, but that was an accident. It was wearing sheep's clothing. I wish they wouldn't do that. It tasted awful, ugh!" The dragon screwed up his face in disgust.

The Sweep was astonished, but he kept his head. "Twenty-seven sheep! My God! Anything else you want to tell me about?"

"Oh yes, and one ox. I forgot about the ox."

"You forgot you ate an ox? A whole ox?"

"Yes, of course, a whole ox. I wasn't going to leave half of it—that would be a waste. 'Clean your plate, Joey,' my mum used to say. 'Think of all the starving little lizards in Africa.' Anyway, it wasn't a very big ox. A bit underfed, if you ask me."

"That ox, what was his name?"

"How should I know? We weren't that close."

"So you don't even know his name. What about his wives? His sisters and brothers? His little baby oxlings? Do you think they miss their dad?"

The dragon shrugged his shoulders. "I guess so. I hadn't thought about it."

"And what about the sheep's friends, and the horses' mothers? Don't you think they are sad that their loved ones have departed forever for that eternal pasture in the sky? Don't you think their babies are wondering where their next meal is coming from?"

"So what do you want me to do?" said the dragon, irritated. "Start an orphanage for foals and lambs? Or maybe you think I'm going to break down and start crying? You've been reading too many fantasy stories. I've got news for you. Real dragons don't cry."

"Perhaps they don't, but you look like an intelligent dragon. The moral argument is simple but compelling. Given that we can't eat sand and sunlight like plants, we should always prefer the lowest life form when choosing food so that we cause the least harm."

"Great! Since dragons are the highest life form, I get to eat everybody."

"It's not that simple," said The Sweep, exasperated.

"But I thought you liked simple."

"Look, haven't you heard of karma? If don't stop all this killing and eating of people and animals, you're liable to be reborn as a flea on the belly of a leprosy-infested weasel in your next life."

"Sure, like I'm going to buy that. When are you humans going to stop trying to manipulate the rest of us with your religious gobbledygook. We dragons are far too smart."

"Well, I guess not everybody is mystically inclined. But if you were really that smart then how come you eat such a poisonous diet?"

"Poisonous diet? What are you talking about?"

"Do you know how much uric acid is secreted from eating a single ox? Gallons of the stuff. Don't blame me if you start getting joint pains in your old age due to an over-acidic diet. Have you any history of cancer or heart disease in your family? And how old are you anyway?"

Now the dragon was starting to look worried. "I'll be 9127 next Tuesday. Cancer? I don't really know. My father was killed in a ride-by-spearing—a professional job. They caught the culprit later, a vicious hoodlum by the name of George. But instead of punishing him they made him a saint! Can you imagine? My mother was so distraught she ran off with a dinosaur."

"A dinosaur?" objected Miranda. "Dr. Dogalogue, that's not possible. They've been extinct for sixty-five million years."

"Of course you're right, you clever girl," said Dr. Dogalogue. "But The Sweep was not about to argue with a live dragon about his mother's personal life, was he?"

"I guess not." Miranda frowned and added a note to her growing list of inconsistencies she'd detected in her favorite cephalopod's story.

Now that he had the dragon talking about his childhood, The Sweep felt that he was making real progress. After all, even a monster isn't going to eat you right after telling you about his mother, is he?

"I see you had a troubled youth. I may be able to help you with that later. But it's your *physical* condition I'm worried about right now. At your age you really have to take more care of your health. With a high-cholesterol diet like that you are at risk of developing heart disease—or worse still, of having a stroke and ending up half paralyzed. You're not going to look very scary trying to flap around on one wing. You'd be a laughing stock. My advice to you is to give up meat altogether before it is too late. You need to become a vegetarian."

"A vegetarian? You've got to be joking! What am I supposed to eat?"

"Why, vegetables of course."

"Vegetables? Where's the fun in that? They don't scream or try to run away. They just sit there looking boring."

"Not when *I* cook them they don't," said the Sweep firmly. "They don't dare. And at my uncle's castle we have the most amazing Chinese vegetarian chef. He'll design a menu just for you. Here's what I'm prepared to do. If you agree to become a vegetarian, I'll arrange to have special meals sent down to your cave every day from the castle kitchens. He can even make knights and dukes and so forth out of gluten or soy protein. They will look and taste quite real, I can promise you."

"Will they run away?" asked the dragon.

"Well, I can't promise they'll actually run, but if you push them they might stagger a little."

"Stagger? You say you're concerned about my health. What about my exercise, chasing down my food? I have to take care of my figure, you know."

The Sweep cast about desperately for a convincing response. Then he had it.

"Tennis! It's a fun new ballgame, invented by my uncle's sword master. I'll ask him to teach you. It involves lots of running and hitting and cursing—you'll just love it!"

"Well, it does sound like fun. All right, I'll give it a try. You're a capital fellow, Mr. The Sweep," said the newly vegetarian Most Fearsome Dragon in the Universe.

St. Lucifer: Space Insect

I think that's cool, the dragon giving up eating meat," said Miranda. She liked the dragon and didn't like the idea of him eating other animals.

"I wish all animals were vegetarians. I really hate it when you see them eating each other on the nature holograms. But how come the princess didn't just tell you Joe was a vegetarian? Then you wouldn't have had to go through that ordeal thinking you might get eaten."

"Iris had promised to keep it a secret," said the doctor. "She was protecting the dragon's reputation. And I'm pretty sure she was testing me to see if I had the courage to face the dragon. But now I have some important work to do with Lucifer in the navigation room. We have to make sure we actually get to your home planet, OK? There's human food in the fridge, and there are lots of books to read and holos to watch. If you really need me you can call me, but please don't disturb us unless there is an alien invasion or something. I mean other than you. You're a harmless kind of alien invasion."

"Don't be so sure," said Miranda, trying unsuccessfully to look menacing. "But one other thing I don't understand. How come you didn't just take a weapon with you, like a laser pistol? Then you wouldn't have had to be afraid of the dragon or anyone."

"We have strict rules against introducing advanced technology, especially military technology, to primitive planets like Earth. It can upset the entire process of social evolution and seriously disrupt the way a civilization develops. If the humans got advanced technology too early, before they had the spiritual and moral maturity to handle it responsibly, it could have resulted in a disaster. It would have been like giving a laser pistol to a child."

Miranda frowned. That was exactly what she'd been hoping to get for her eighth birthday. "But what about if you only kept a concealed weapon for emergencies? It would be really convenient in case you were about to get killed. You could have a rule that you could only use it when no one was looking."

"Not so easy. How would I explain that I killed a giant monster with a wooden spear? People would know that something strange was going on, and there's no telling where it would end. These things have a way of getting out of hand."

Lucifer had been watching silently, half hidden in a cupboard, parts of his spindly legs poking out, which made him look more like an insect than ever. Suddenly he spoke, causing Miranda to jump, unnerved by his thin and vaguely menacing voice. "Once one of our emissaries landed on a planet where they had not invented the wheel, and she forgot that she had a ballpoint pen in her pocket. She was playing with it at the dinner table, rolling it back and forth. A bright student observed it, conceived of the wheel, and before you knew it they had hip-hop music. Imagine that! An entire culture destroyed through a careless gesture.

"In another case, one of our chaps went to a planet where they had not yet invented the screwdriver. They had screws but no screwdrivers so they had to screw them in with their ears. The ear surgeons were running a roaring trade. All our fellow did was use his Swiss army knife once. An alien saw him and copied the idea. Within a year the entire medical industry was bankrupt, and within a hundred years they'd invented nuclear weapons and blown themselves to smithereens. All because of one little Swiss army knife. Imagine the long-term repercussions of knocking off a dragon with a laser pistol!"

Miranda moved behind the doctor and peered around him at Insect Man. "Dr. Dogalogue, is that true?"

"Yes, child, it is. And this seems like a good time to introduce you two formally. Space Nurse Miranda, I'd like you to meet my oldest friend, St. Lucifer."

"Charmed," said Miranda politely, trying not to shrink back in horror. Seeing him up close for the first time, she could see that he was a spindly creature, like a big spiky octopus, only less normal looking.

"Hey man, cool to meet a talking egg. Remarkable. Be careful or they'll put you in a circus." Exiting the cupboard, Lucifer stalked

around the lounge and finally occupied the entire couch with his legs splayed in seventeen different directions.

"I'm not an egg," said Miranda. "Didn't Dr. Dogalogue tell you? I'm a girl. A human girl."

"He told me you're seven years old, which means you're an egg. On Zondgraz we don't hatch until our eighth year, so technically you still belong in the shell."

"But that doesn't make sense. How can I be an egg? Look, I have arms and legs."

"Even more remarkable. A walking egg."

Miranda frowned but refrained from arguing further, not wanting to offend Dr. Dogalogue's friend.

"Lucifer is the one who stuck up for me when I was sent back to the training center for a thousand years," said Dogalogue. "He got in so much trouble that he ended up leaving the school altogether."

"Best move I ever made," said Lucifer. "While you were studying and undergoing impossible feats of asceticism, I was down at the beach surfing and working on my tan. Oh, and practicing my dance moves. Take a look at this."

He bounced off the couch and executed a dance that reminded Miranda of a sea turtle trying to fight off an attack of rabies while immersed in a bath full of malt syrup. As for the handsome tan, she couldn't tell how it had improved matters. She was pretty sure that if she woke up one morning looking like Lucifer she would want to stab herself to death.

"May I fetch you something to drink?" she asked sweetly, muttering quietly to herself, 'how about a nice vat of insecticide?'

Dragon vs. Cephalopod Round Two

After sharing a nice vat of tea with Joe I felt greatly refreshed, if a little bloated. The dragon lived alone in a huge cave complex. We'd passed several caverns and tunnels on the way in and it was hard to tell how many more there might be. Light streamed down from a deep fissure in the roof and lit the chamber we occupied.

"So who told you all this nonsense about me devouring maidens and violating by-laws?" asked Joe.

"It was the local council at Shaman's Refuge Village."

The dragon snorted—not something I'd recommend experiencing at close quarters, involving as it did prodigious quantities of smoke, flame, and coal-flavored mucous.

"Typical! Those stupid villagers always blame everything on the dragon. I never eat common maidens, only princesses, and only the nasty ones. The girls they were talking about were all young ladies who wanted to escape their boring little village. And who can blame them? It's foggy, witch-infested, and dull enough to give an enlightened Buddhist monk a death wish. Of course, being blamed for their disappearance does enhance my reputation as the most fearsome dragon in the known universe, so it's an ill wind that blows no one any good."

"That's true," I said. "Every cloud has a silver lining."

"Exactly. Water off a duck's back gathers no moss."

"Birds in the hand shouldn't throw glass houses."

The dragon bowed as we regarded one another with newfound respect.

"I'm honored to know you, Sir Dogalogue. I didn't realize that a mere knight would be so well versed in esoteric scripture."

I was equally impressed. "Likewise. I had not imagined that a mere reptile would display such deep knowledge of ancient wisdom."

"Let us call an official truce between locally based dragons and knights," he said.

"Excellent suggestion, but first I'd like to clear up a couple of rather delicate matters. The villagers, who we have agreed are completely unreliable, also claim that you steal and devour sheep and cattle."

The dragon snorted again, a terrible raucous sound like the banging of a thousand untuned trashcan lids.

"Those foolish villagers. I haven't devoured any livestock for at least two weeks. And if they think I live off their cattle and sheep, how do they explain my enormous supermarket bill? Every time a careless shepherd loses his sheep, or a cow walks through a poorly mended fence, they blame me. Ah well, I suppose I perform a valuable service as a universal scape-reptile." He hesitated. "Look, I'll let you in on a secret. I recently became a strict vegetarian."

For a moment I was too astounded to respond. I'd never heard of a vegetarian dragon. Perhaps that explained why Princess Iris was sure the dragon wouldn't eat me. She had probably known all along.

"Naturally no one believes I'm innocent," Joe continued. "Blame it all on the fire-breathing monster. Not that I'm surprised after observing human stupidity for ninety centuries. You would think that they would evolve but no sign of it yet. Anyhow, it keeps the riffraff away. Now if you're still considering trying to kill me, you can go ahead and try, but in all fairness I should point out that no human has ever killed a dragon in a fair fight. The only times human beings have got the better of a dragon was through cheating. Take Fafnir, stabbed unawares from below. Likewise Glaurung. Smaug was betrayed by a bird, and anyway it was an unfair fight with a hundred men ganging up on one dragon. The dragon the so-called 'Saint' George killed was in fact my own father, the victim of a cowardly professional hit—a ride-by spearing when he wasn't looking. Orm Umbar was defeated by magic, and Ancalagon the Black by an elf riding a giant eagle, not a human at all. For most dragons, knights coming to kill them are little more than breakfast with a little entertainment thrown in—or at least some mild exercise to stimulate the appetite. So I wouldn't be rushing to the betting office to put my money on a man."

Although not human myself, I felt this was unfair to the weaker species. "I suppose you call facing a five-foot man on a horse weighed down with forty kilos of armor and armed with a wooden spear a fair fight?"

"You do have a point there,' replied Joe, grinning yet eyeing my sword warily. 'No pun intended. Anyway, I see no need for antagonism. Let us be friends."

He stretched out his great paw with such an endearing smile that I let down my guard and shook with him. It was a moving moment, and one all these negotiators for peace would do well to take note of. An unprecedented pact between monster and non-monster, a triumph of goodness and reason over animality and senseless hatred, a glorious meeting of two sentient souls in camaraderie where once was only war and deceit, a miraculous transcendence of the destructive tendencies of human and animal nature in the light of love and friendship...

"OK, OK, OK, I got the point," piped an exasperated Miranda. 'You made friends with the dragon. For goodness sake, when are you two going to stop talking? I want to see some action"

Dr. Dogalogue looked offended but he continued.

The dragon was effusive in our newfound friendship.

"I say," he gushed. "You've been awfully decent about all this. I wonder if I could impose on you for just one more thing. You wouldn't have a spot of pizza on you, would you?"

Fortunately I had.

The Adventures of Supermouse

Mina darted down the hill, weaving her way through the towering grass stalks. Supermouse! she thought. I'll bet I'm the first-ever supermouse. I must not return without pizza and the dragon report. She'd never felt this important before. She was so excited that she even forgot about her nut.

When Mina reached the dragon's cave she found it vast enough for an entire mouse civilization. She was just in time to see the dragon's tail disappear around a corner further down the tunnel. Although she had only a very small brain, she deduced that a dragon's tail would most likely be preceded by a dragon, so she scampered after it. When she reached the corner, she took a deep breath and crept forward into the monster's lair, exactly as quiet as a mouse.

Passing deep into the mountain, she rounded another corner and found the dragon and the knight sitting at a table, debating the relative merits of dragons and humans. She crept up to the maroon curtain and hid herself in a fold of cloth. Exhausted from her stressful day she soon dozed off, dreaming a strange dream about a pizza with wings and a dragon and a mouse chasing after it. Suddenly she was awakened by a tantalizing smell. She sniffed deeply and her nose wrinkled with excitement, making her whiskers tremble, for there on the table was a glorious sight. A great golden brown lake of mozzarella cheese festooned with olives and tomatoes and rich with capsicum. Mina stared at the pizza as if in a trance. Her nut was a distant memory, her reason for being there at all gone from her mind. All she could think of was this glorious vision from mouse heaven.

Suddenly a demon in the form of a mouse appeared in a puff of crimson smoke.

"Look at all that cheese," hissed the sprite, indicating the pizza with its trident. "Doesn't it smell delicious? Better eat some now before that greedy dragon gobbles it all up."

Dazzled by the shining golden cheese, Mina's eyes glazed over and she began to climb up the curtain toward the edge of the table.

As she did, a white mouse in a flowing robe and a halo like an angel appeared, floating in the air. "Remember your mission, Mina. You cannot take such a risk. You have to tell the other animals what you have heard. Wait until the dragon is asleep and you can take some pizza crumbs. Don't let your greed get the better of you."

"Get lost, wimp!" sneered the mouse demon, brandishing his trident and poking the white mouse in the rump, sending her fleeing from the scene. "Mina!" he insisted. "Don't miss this opportunity. Aren't you supposed to be Supermouse? Now is the time to show your courage and seize your reward. Who else amongst all the forest creatures has ever dared to enter the dragon's lair? Why should you take the pizza to Brains? You deserve cheese, you need cheese—it is your destiny! This is the time to ask yourself once and for all: am I a man or a mouse?"

"Er...A mouse?" said Mina.

"Correct! Now think, what is the true destiny of a mouse?"

"Cheese!" This was one thing Mina was quite sure about.

The demon grinned and pointed upward. "That's right. And there it waits. Now go forth, brave Supermouse, and show the world what you are made of!"

"Cheese, cheese," Mina murmured, fully surrendering to her desire. Like a zombie on the trail of fresh brains she climbed up the curtain's edge, heedless of the danger, until she could see the pizza spread out before her, mozzarella dripping like a slow river of shining lava. Hypnotized by this vision of mouse Shangri La, she couldn't help herself. Closer and closer she crawled until she was able to take a little nibble at the cheese, lost in ecstasy, unaware of the great golden eye observing her.

"Hey, a mouse is eating our pizza!" roared the dragon, bringing his paw down with a crash and missing Mina by an inch. "Hey, where did it go?"

Mina had jumped just in time, landing in my beard with a death-defying squeak. It was soft and curly, and she thought it might make a fine nest, but I frowned and took her between finger and thumb.

"Little mouse," I whispered, "what are you doing in my beard?"

"I'm sorry, sir, but it seemed preferable to the wrong end of a dragon's gullet."

I felt sorry for the little creature. "How much longer do you plan on residing here?" I asked.

"Well, it's really rather comfortable. Do you think I could take out a long lease?"

"I'll have to think about that. But for the time being, just stay there. And don't distract me. I have to deal with this dragon."

The dragon and I were about to start on our super-extended family-size pizza when Joe remembered something. "What about the salad?" he asked. "It's not healthy to just eat pizza without salad. I have a nice salad in the kitchen. Would you mind fetching it while I cut the pizza?"

I headed for the far end of the cave. Just as I bent down to pick up the salad bowl, a nasty-sounding voice rasped, "Hello. I suppose you are my dinner." I jumped around in alarm to find myself face to face with another somewhat smaller but very fierce-looking dragon, crouching in a dark alcove, slavering hungrily and preparing to pounce. Evidently a less health-conscious dragon than Joe, it was not waiting for the salad.

I scuttled behind a rock pillar, my armor making an awful clattering noise. "Excuse me, Joe," I called. "Does our friendship pact extend to your protecting me from your carnivorous relatives? Or at least discouraging them from devouring me in your own house? After all, don't the laws of hospitality condemn allowing guests to be eaten?"

But Joe was so deeply absorbed in devouring his unfairly large share of the pizza that he didn't hear me. The new dragon started circling the pillar in pursuit.

"Help, Joe, I'm dinner! Quick! Help."

But Joe was still absorbed in the pizza. "Hmmmm, this is delicious." I could hear him muttering. "What's that? You need help? Can't you even find a salad on your own? I'll be there in a minute. Just let me finish this piece. Hmmmm! Pronto! Mama Mia! Fettuccini! Mozzarella!" He sighed happily and proceeded to steal the olives from my half of the pizza.

Meanwhile the carnivorous dragon was chasing me around the pillar, getting closer and closer with every passing moment due to my heavy armor.

Joe finished his half of the pizza and decided that it hadn't been cut properly in the first place. Obliged to correct this, he sliced an extra sliver to make it look more even and then another to hide the bits he'd accidentally nibbled. "Oh dear," he muttered. "Now it looks as if someone tried to take more than his fair share. That won't do at all. I'd better eat the whole thing and blame it on the cat."

"OK, that's it. Time for bed, Miranda," announced the doctor.

Miranda couldn't believe her ears. "What? You're about to be eaten by a monster! You can't stop there! No way! How can I sleep now? I'll have nightmares for sure! You can't do this to me. At least tell me what happened next. Pleeeeease!" She squirmed and gave him an anguished look.

"Sorry. It's past your bedtime. It says here in my book on how to rear earth children that they must go to bed early and all pleas and excuses to stay up late should be disregarded. What can I do? It's not my fault. I didn't write the book."

Miranda started to bite her pillow in anguish, shaking her head like a rabid dog. "Gnagnagnagnagnagna," she growled. "I'm going crazy. I have to know what happened next. This is unbearable. You must tell me, doctor. Otherwise I won't sleep well, and I'll be tired and impossible all day tomorrow, and I'll make your life a living hell. You know I can do it."

"Oh, all right. I'll tell you some more. But only two minutes—just so you sleep nicely and are perfectly good all day tomorrow."

"I will be, doctor, I will." Miranda smiled like an angel and curled up with her head on the doctor's lap, her eyes full of anticipation.

My next desperate cry of "Heeeeeeeelp!" finally caught Joe's attention. He jumped up and hurried to the kitchen just in time to find me flat on my back, about to be impaled by Fritz's claw. Joe shot out a tongue of flame that scorched my tormentor's rump. The nasty dragon jumped back in shock and turned angrily to Joe.

"What are you doing, Fritz!" growled the larger dragon. "This is my guest. You can't eat him! Now go to your cave and behave yourself!"

Fritz turned away with a snarl and slunk back into the darkness.

"I'm really must apologize for his behavior," said Joe. "I'm afraid he's from Australia. Total animal."

But despite his apology, Joe seemed quite unperturbed. Only when Mina pointed out that the pizza had disappeared did I realize that Joe may have been rather pleased by the distraction. Which reminds me of the wise saying: it's an ill wind that blows nobody any cheese.

"That worked out perfectly," said Miranda, yawning. "You didn't get eaten by the nasty Australian dragon, and the nice dragon got the whole pizza as a kind of advance reward for rescuing you. I think he likes you, which means that he may tell you the secrets of Atlantis." Her voice was fading. "Dr. Dogalogue, I'm so glad you're the one taking care of me." She sighed and snuggled up to him, drifting away into a dream where she was a princess and flowers laid bets on her bravery in a pizza-eating contest.

Dr. Dogalogue looked down at the delicate earth child in his lap, hardly daring to move lest he disturb her. An unfamiliar feeling, painful but piercingly beautiful, filled his alien heart. If anyone had been watching, they might have seen a single tear collect on the edge of a two-thousand-year-old eye-stalk and shimmer for a second, reflecting the light of the distant stars before it trickled down his cheek.

But no one was watching, so we'll never know if that really happened.

Post-Pizza Revelations

Since Joe had just saved my life, I made do with salad and did not mention the missing pizza. Our friendship had blossomed so quickly I was wondering if it was time to broach the delicate subject of the location of Atlantis. At least the princess had said it was a delicate subject. But considering that she'd described the dragon as "an overgrown earthworm," her reliability was in some doubt. I was eager to fetch the seed and get back to Zondgraz. To be honest, I was feeling a little homesick. Earth was quite pretty in places and I was meeting some interesting creatures, but it seemed rather dangerous, and having to pretend I was human all the time was exhausting.

To move things along a little I decided to risk telling Joe the truth about myself.

"Joe, I think you deserve to know who I really am."

Joe chuckled. "Well, you do have me wondering. You're the first knight I've met who can keep an entire family-sized pizza in his pocket without bending it."

I smiled. "Oh, that. That's an old trick where I come from. And where I'm from is somewhere you might not expect."

So I told Joe everything I'd told the princess—about the Zondgrazian School for Sadvipras, and the master, and my mission. The telling took a while and Joe had a number of questions.

"So my master sent me here to earth to find the last lost seed of the microvita tree for his mother's garden," I concluded. "And he said that the only ones who could help me find Atlantis are an ancient necromancer and the oldest living dragon. That is the real reason I sought you out. I know it sounds a bit extreme, my master putting me to all this trouble just to please his mum, but if you knew him you'd understand. He doesn't always reveal his true intentions but he always has a good reason for his actions."

"I once knew someone like that, long ago," said Joe, with a faraway look. "In any event, it seems that your master's intuition has served you well. It is uncanny good fortune that you came to me at this time. If you had come to any other dragon, or even to me but a few weeks ago, you would not likely have lived to tell the tale.

"You need to know what you are dealing with here. The microvita tree is no ordinary tree. It is a magical tree of such great power that it enabled the development of the Atlantis civilization. In fact, if it wasn't for the microvita tree, I wouldn't be here, for it was through the power of the tree that we dragons were created."

I was stunned. I'd suspected that there was more to this matter than my guru had told me, but this was really major.

"In the end, the tree was the cause of Atlantis' fall," said the dragon sadly. "An evil wizard, Nefarious, the creator of the dragons and most likely the very wizard your master referred to, was using the tree's power to build an empire that would have conquered the whole world. Rather than allow that to happen, the microvita tree chose to destroy itself and Atlantis with it. After that, Nefarious lost control of us dragons, and since then we have been the enemies of mankind."

He paused.

"In all my long life I have had no non-dragon friends, but now, within a few short days, I have three. It is very strange feeling."

"Three?" I said, relieved that he considered me a friend. I almost let on that I knew the princess, but I remembered just in time and asked him who the other two were.

"A brother and sister. One of them is the same princess you were supposed to be rescuing."

"I'm astonished," I lied. "So the seed is not really for my master's mother's flower garden, is it?" It was more of a statement than a question.

"I'd say not," said the dragon.

"I've been sent here for some greater reason, haven't I? This is not just an outing as a part of my college course."

"I very much doubt it."

I had a feeling that it wasn't going to be as quick and easy to get back to Zondgraz as I'd hoped.

Joe gave me a curious look. "Interesting meeting a being from another world. It seems you are considerably more developed than the humans. I'd place you somewhere between them and us dragons on the evolutionary scale."

I supposed this was meant to be a compliment.

"Now, we don't know exactly what your master really intends you to do with the seed once you find it, but you need to understand this: The microvita tree is designed to change worlds. By pursuing it you have entered into a very serious game with some powerful players, some of them a lot less kindhearted than I. Nefarious the necromancer survives. He was the one who first learned to manipulate microvita energy for his own ends. And legend has it that a terrible sea monster haunts the ruins of Atlantis, guarding the seed."

I didn't like the sound of this. "What kind of sea monster?"

"A really big one. And just finding Atlantis is going to be no joke. I have a rough idea of where it is, but we're going to need a map. And the only place I can think of where you might find such a thing is in the Cave of Stones. Fortunately it is not far away. It's beneath Duke Honk's castle."

We? Did this mean the dragon was considering coming with me? This was more than I'd dared to hope for. "What's so special about this Cave of Stones?" I asked. "Aren't all caves made of stones?"

"Not like these ones. This cave is constructed of stones brought from the temple of Atlantis and laid in a pattern of power beneath the earth. This was an important outpost of the Atlantean Empire long ago. It is one of the only locations above water where a portion of the microvita tree's energy remains active."

"Sounds like the place to start looking for more clues. So where is this cave? Can you guide me there?"

The dragon shook his head. "I am too large to explore underground. We will need help to find it."

Suddenly I felt Mina frantically taking notes in my beard, squeaking to herself in excitement. Of course! Mice are experts at exploring underground.

Later, as the dragon slept, Mina said, "So it's not a giant cheese."

"What are you talking about, Mina? I asked.

"We mice know about this cave. As children we were taught that the reason the animals around here can speak is because of a giant magic cheese buried there. But if what the dragon says is true, it's not a cheese at all. It is because of the stones of Atlantis, imbued with the power of microvita. This is going to be a major disappointment in some circles."

It occurred to me that the energy emanating from this Cave of Stones would also explain why my horse could talk. Interesting. I should probably explain this to the princess at some point, but not just yet. I preferred to let her go on thinking that I was the one who could grant animals the power of speech. After all, doesn't one good deception deserve another?

Swords vs. Butter Knives

A soft sound woke me.

"Shh! It's asleep, don't disturb it," said a feathery voice.

"What is it? Is it alive?" replied another like it.

"If it's sleeping, it must be alive," said the first.

"But it's made of metal. How can it be alive? Who ever heard of talking metal?"

"Look, it's moving. We have to deliver the master's message."

I opened my eyes and saw a cluster of floating dust motes shining in the broad beam of morning sunlight that lanced down from the fissure in the roof, whispering among themselves. Talking dust.

"Gosh," breathed the first mote in awe. "Look, it's awake. Go on, talk to it."

"No, you do it. I'm shy."

"Oh, all right. Since I already doing everything, I might as well do this, too. Infinity plus one is still infinity, so it really costs me nothing."

I eyed the hovering motes, curious.

One mote approached me and said, "Sir Dogalogue. I am Trond the dust mote. This is Fluff, my flighty sister. Dragon Joe, our master, asked us to assist you. We can direct you to the bathing facilities, and when you are ready he would like you to join him for breakfast at the front entrance of the cave. He also asked us to assure you that he has banished the other dragon to its own cave further up the valley."

"Thank you so much," I said to the dust particle. "I certainly like the sound of that bath."

"Please follow me, sir," said Trond.

The kitchen looked quite different in daylight. It was tidy and clean. No sign of last night's struggle or our meal remained. These dust motes ran a tight ship. Now that there was sufficient natural light from the deep set windows, the torches in their brackets on the stone walls had been doused. I stood my sword in its scabbard in the corner, along with my armor. I did not want the damp of the bathroom getting to the steel.

I peered warily into the tunnel mouth from which dragon Fritz had emerged the night before. There was no sign of movement, and I did have the dust mote's assurance, so I relaxed and looked around, admiring the facilities. Clay pots and dishes stood on wooden shelves; cutlery and utensils were neatly stowed in racks on the wall above a heavy looking workbench. It all looked well-used. Evidently the dragon was accustomed to entertaining.

I headed down the short passage into the spacious ablutions chamber. A warm bath awaited me, heated by stones. Next to it was a cozy fireplace. Thick mauve towels hung by the door, and there was even a window looking out over the valley below. I climbed out of my human suit and eased myself into the hot water, one tentacle at a time. Delicious! This dragon sure enjoyed a fine lifestyle.

Feeling fresh and clean after some well-deserved basking, I headed back toward the kitchen. But when I heard voices up ahead, I crept forward and stopped to listen at the door, peering through a crack in the wood.

"Look over there—a sword!" said a sharp voice. The speaker was a carving knife who was marching along the bench top as though he owned the place. He'd spotted my sword leaning against the wall in its scabbard.

"I wonder if it's real," said a gnarled fork made from an oak root, who was crawling out of the dish rack. Other items of cutlery clambered out of drawers and hopped off their hooks to discuss the new arrival.

"It's probably just one of those fake show swords," said the carving knife knowingly. "All handle and no blade. A bit like some people I know." He looked down his nose at the kitchen knife.

"It could be a whole sword," chipped in the cheese grater. "But one made of cheaper material, such as compressed dust, like that birthday cake we had to cut up last week."

Meanwhile my weapon had quietly woken in its corner, eyes glowering. Suddenly it sprang from its sheath and stalked across the floor towards the cutlery. "Who dares to mock me thus!" cried the sword, looking very real indeed.

The little gathering of knives and forks, spoons and corkscrews, scuttled into hiding, leaving the carving knife alone on the bench to face the irate sword.

"Oh dear, I am sorry, sir," stammered the knife. "We did not mean to offend you."

"I should hope not." The sword strutted up and down the room, lunging and parrying as it went.

"You're lucky you're just a carving knife. If you were more my size I'd have to challenge you to a duel for an insult like that." Excalibur paused and turned like a showman to the crowd of cutlery as they slowly emerged from hiding, overcome with curiosity. "And I don't often lose duels,' he smirked. "Perhaps you would like me to enlighten you regarding the way of the sword."

"Oh yes, please," gushed the female spoons and salad forks, emerging from hiding and batting their eyelids shamelessly.

"If you insist." Excalibur raised his chin and began to lecture the admiring utensils in haughty tones.

"Ours is a high and lonely destiny. The life of a sword is hard and adventurous. It requires courage and daring, discipline and loyalty. Every day we face challengers, defend the honor of ladies, and confront dastards and wrongdoers. It is a vigorous life, which is why we need to eat so much." He paused to devour an apple. "Notice how we never get fat. Look at these midriff muscles. Like steel." He laughed.

The cutlery rattled and jiggled in appreciation of his rapier-like wit.

"Excuse me, sir sword," said the butter knife. "Have you ever actually killed anyone?"

The sword adopted an air of great dignity. "Well, I do not wish to boast, but just let me say this: unless I have dispatched at least twelve enemies during the day, it is my habit to forgo my supper."

"Whom did you kill last month?" said a soup ladle. "Anyone important?"

"Important? Not really. Just a couple of kings, twelve princes, four earls, and a duke. I don't remember the rest. I don't bother to count anyone less than an earl. And don't ask me all their names; who has time for paper work? But I can tell you one thing. I definitely leave them dead."

"Tell us who you killed yesterday, at least? You can't have forgotten that already," insisted the skeptical ladle.

"Yesterday?" said the sword, glaring at the ladle. "Gosh, it seems so long ago. It was a busy day, a blur of fatal stabbing movements, deft parries, and narrow escapes. I do recall saving the life of my master twice and an image comes to mind of a huge mound of corpses. Ah yes, it's coming back to me now. Fourteen elephants, a couple of giants, a ghost, half a dozen witches, and an abominable snowman. Enough to deserve a modest meal for my trouble."

The utensils were wide-eyed and breathless. With the exception of the soup ladle, who said, "Doesn't sound like a very lonely destiny with all of those elephants about. Is that why you killed them all? You wanted to be alone? And where did you find elephants in England anyway? Did you visit the zoo?"

The sword looked flustered but he was rescued by the butter knife who asked timidly, "Do you think I could be a sword when I grow up?"

Grateful for the interruption, the sword spoke kindly. "Well, I'm not sure. Anything is possible. But it is rare for a butter knife to become a sword, you know. You have to prove yourself. It helps if you're of noble blood, but in your case you'd have to perform some notable deed in order to inspire someone to knight you."

"What kind of noble deed?" asked the butter knife, dreaming of greater things than merely spreading butter on a dragon's toast.

The sword leaned casually against the stone wall, resting its head in the crook of its arm, its ankles crossed.

"Oh, nothing too hard I'm sure. Any minor feat should do: capturing a band of ostrogoths, rescuing a princess from a monster, wounding a wyvern—anything like that."

"I'd have trouble wounding an earthworm," said the knife sadly. "I'd have to have a knight to wield me to do all that stuff you're saying, and what kind of knight is going to go into battle armed with a butter knife?"

"'Well, perhaps a knight whose opponent comes at him with a large slice of toast. In that case, a butter knife would be the ideal weapon," said the wooden spoon kindly.

The sword, irked by the interruption, ignored the spoon. "It takes many years of study to become a fully qualified knight's sword," he continued. "I had to learn to play the violin, inscribe *The Art of War* in Japanese on a tea leaf using a blunt axe, memorize the coats of arms of all the noble houses of Europe, acquire fluency in French, and learn court etiquette. And above all, I had to know whether I was confronting a noble or a peasant."

"What's so important about that?" asked the butter knife.

"If you're facing a peasant there are no rules. You can cheat, swear, and behave as crudely as you wish. You can even run away and look like a coward, because his opinion is of no consequence. But when you face a gentleman, it is another matter. There are conventions to be observed, challenges to be issued by personages of the appropriate rank, and rules of combat to be adhered to—a whole language of fine nuances that could mean the difference between honor and disgrace."

Having had enough of my sword's lies, I strode into the room. "A fine example of honor you are, my pretty little weapon of mass destruction. It would appear that while studying the rules of chivalry, you were learning to lie and boast and exaggerate. You ought to be ashamed of yourself, befooling these simple working cutlery."

I snatched up the sword, slid it back into its scabbard with a click, and turned to the startled utensils while a series of enraged squawks emerged from the scabbard at my side. "I'm afraid I must advise you to disregard my sword's fanciful stories." I glanced at the scabbard. "He's a braggart and a liar and I intend to confine him to this sheath until sundown tomorrow in order to teach him a lesson. Elephants! He wouldn't know what an elephant was if he found one in his porridge."

Turning from the disappointed cutlery, I donned my armor and headed for the front entrance of the cave. My breakfast awaited.

15

The Treasure Raiders

The little constellation of glowing dust motes drifted ahead of me through the tunnel. We passed an archway to a spiral stone staircase that descended into darkness. The sign above the arch read: "This way to Dragon Joe's Treasure Cave. Don't even think about it."

If they didn't want anyone to think about the treasure cave, then why mention it at all? It was like telling someone not to think of a bottle of white worm's sweat—it's all they're going to think about. Earthlings can be pretty illogical sometimes.

Suddenly I heard a faint clattering from the archway, like a kitchen accident in a distant echo chamber. It was followed by a curse that wound its way up from the depths, twisting and turning through unseen tunnels until finally, gargling with fatigue, it staggered over the threshold and collapsed at my feet. "Careful, you moron! Keep silent! Do you want to be roasted and served on toast for the dragon's breakfast?"

"Sorry, boss." The reply came close on the heels of the first voice in an earthy whining tone like an old dry root with whiskers.

The dust motes bristled and arrayed themselves in attack formation before the archway.

"What's that?" hissed Trond.

It seemed pretty obvious to me what it was, but these motes were not the sharpest cards in the deck. "I do not wish to be overly suspicious," I offered, "but it sounds to me as though somebody is helping themselves to your master's treasure."

"I fear you are right, sir knight," said Trond grimly. "We must stop them. We are charged to guard our master's treasure with our lives."

I looked doubtfully at them. "Exactly how were you specks of dust planning to do that?"

"Senseless gratuitous violence is our preferred initial response," said Fluff with the enthusiasm of a zealot. "We employ the ancient martial art of Yubby Wuzza, enabling us to turn our enemies strength against them. Yubby Wuzza is the perfect form of defense for a dust mote. It is the great equalizer. The stronger our enemy, the more danger he is to himself."

"Only if our Yubby Wuzza fails us do we resort to diplomacy or rational persuasion, tactics we find morally abhorrent," added Trond. "And if even that fails, we inform our master the dragon, or in his absence we raise an army, calling on the help of any honest-looking passing knights."

Another clattering sound echoed up through the stairwell, and the motes turned as one in the air to stare at me meaningfully, like a tiny flight of avenging angels. They addressed me formally. "Someone is robbing our master. We appeal for you, good knight, to aid us in apprehending these criminals."

I was loath to get involved. Surely this was a matter for the police. The last thing I needed was to get caught up in a territorial dispute with local law enforcement. On the other hand, there didn't seem to be anyone else around, and I did want to earn my way further into the good graces of the dragon. So I tried to sound as though I fitted the job description.

"By the Rood, right willingly will I offer my sword and come to the succor of noble Dragon Joe and his wealth." Grabbing the hilt of my vorpal blade, I made to sweep it out, ready to add a defiant yell for dramatic effect. But the sword did not budge. It appeared to be stuck. I gripped the scabbard with my left hand, grasped the hilt, and attempted to wrest the weapon from its housing, but to no avail. "Come out of that sheath, curse you!" I muttered through my teeth. "By Zond, why does this have to happen at the worst moments?"

From the stairwell came a muffled clank of metal on stone. The looters were approaching.

"Shhhh!" hissed the whiney voice. "Don't make so much noise. Do you want to alert the guards?"

"Don't complain," growled the deeper voice. "I'm doing all the work here. I'd like to see you drag a sack of treasure bigger than your house up a flight of stone steps without making any noise."

What kind of invincible creature was this that dared to raid a dragon's hoard? What fearsome strength must it possess to drag so large a trove up all those steps? Fear filled my alien heart and I began to tremble. The very stone walls appeared to be sweating. Even these hardy minerals shared my trepidation.

Cloon the chief dust mote stared at me quizzically. "What's the delay, sir knight? You have not drawn your sword, and you appear troubled. Surely you are not afraid?"

"Me afraid?" I laughed. "Ha ha. What an absurd idea. I'm just having a little philosophical discussion with my sword here. I never like to pass up an opportunity to expand my learning and flex my intellectual muscles. Life isn't just about fighting and rescuing princesses, you know. A holistic knight must also maintain a sharp wit."

A horrible rasping breath cut through the cool air that wafted up from the treasure chamber. The enemy was almost upon us. I wrestled desperately with the reluctant blade. "Come out you woebegone weapon, you. This is your chance to fulfill all your boasts!"

"Did someone say something?" came a sleepy voice from the scabbard.

"Wake up, dromedary. We have to defend ourselves. There's a monster approaching! Quick, get yourself unstuck."

"I'm not stuck," said the sword in a dignified tone. "I'm resting."

"Resting? For Zond's sake, this is an emergency! This is what swords are for — dealing with emergencies. Where did you get your combat license, on Betelgeuse?"

"I'm merely obeying your own orders. Just moments ago you insulted me and unjustly exiled me to the inside of this scabbard. I am simply observing discipline like any good soldier."

"Well, hello! I've changed my mind. Now I'm ordering you to come out and help me fight."

"Hmm," said the sword, furrowing its brow. "This is a complex matter. Your original order did not allow for any change of plan. Yet now you attempt to countermand your own previous instruction. There is no provision for this kind of whimsical leadership style in my sword obedience manual. To which of you do I owe the greater loyalty: your former self or your present self? I know of a philosopher whom I can consult on this matter. Unfortunately he is dead, but in about fourteen years his son will be grown and I can consult him. He will know what to do."

"I'll philosopher you, you metallurgical mesodorf! Get out here at once!"

The sword drew itself up to its full height, quite an achievement when one is inside a scabbard. "So, now I get the picture. Back there in the kitchen you didn't need me, so you felt free to abuse me and punish me cruelly. But now that you need my help you expect me to forget your wicked deed and leap to your defense. I think a little repentance might be in order."

"I'll make you repent you were ever forged, you iron-brained idiot. I'll melt you down, so help me."

"Well, I'm sorry to see that you are too proud to admit your error. I think I'll just catch up on a little more sleep. I'm feeling quite fatigued. Dispatching all those elephants yesterday rather took it out of me."

"There weren't any elephants," I hissed. "You made them up. You're so deluded you believe your own fantasies! Get a grip on reality, for Zond's sake."

"Reality? You're the one who thinks he's talking to a sword," said the weapon archly.

As I stood there grinding my teeth, trying to figure out how to strangle a sword, the dust motes were flitting about in agitation as the sound of the mysterious thieves drew closer. The gloom in the cave deepened and a chill ran up my spine.

"Quick," whispered Cloon, "get ready. They're approaching."

I could hear heavy breathing and growling. Zond! These creatures must be at least twelve feet tall. Maybe they were dinosaurs from the ancient world, spawned anew in the darkness beneath these hills. Ever growing in a lightless chamber under the earth, devouring any unfortunate explorers who wandered there, awaiting their moment to unleash a living nightmare upon the world of light. What a horror! The hissing breath, the sickly green scales, their noisome underbellies leaving trails of slime as the monsters emerged from their dark pit of decay. I heard a snuffling from the darkness. Zond save me! They have smelled my blood and now seek their next victim! I didn't stand a chance, especially with my sulking sword refusing to cooperate. Paralyzed with fear, I could smell the monster's feisty breath and I thought I caught a glimpse of horrid teeth and slavering jaws, dripping as they anticipated feasting on my warm flesh.

Not knowing what else to do, I tensed my muscles, preparing to spring on the creatures as soon as they appeared. Clutching my reluctant blade in its scabbard, I tried to compose some poetic last thoughts. I didn't expect to survive, but at least I could make a good showing. That way the dragon might think better of me posthumously.

A small grey-and-white-striped nose appeared near the base of the archway, poked cautiously around the corner, sniffed, wrinkled itself, and withdrew. It did not appear to notice me, half hidden in the shadow of a pillar.

"Oh, all right, I'll come out if you insist," said my sword suddenly, sliding smoothly into my hand. "See how cooperative I am, despite your mean behavior? You owe me big time."

Two small furry creatures appeared in the archway, walking backwards, dragging a heavy-looking sack.

"Well, we made it this far," said the larger of the two creatures, the owner of the striped nose. It was about the size of a medium-sized dog. It looked over its shoulder and started as it spied me.

Upon discovering the diminutive stature of my enemies I suddenly felt a great deal braver. I strode forward with a stern expression on my face. "That treasure is not yours. Hand it over, thieves."

Brains the badger and Maurice the mole ignored me and started to drag their weighty sack of loot toward the cave entrance.

Brandishing my sword, I accidentally struck the wall in a shower of sparks.

"Yeooww! Watch what you're doing!" cried Excalibur. I wasn't listening. I was too busy falling over. With the momentum of my ill-aimed blow I lost my balance and crashed to the floor where I lay for a moment, steaming in my heavy armor, wondering how to get up. The fleeing thieves glanced over their shoulders in surprise and hurried away with their sack as fast as they could, leaving the dust motes twittering in agitation.

I rolled back and forth on my back like an upturned cockroach, weighed down by my armor and unable, for the moment, to rise to my feet and pursue them.

"Hey, stop," I called after them. "You're under arrest. Hello! Don't leave. I'm apprehending you. Why aren't you listening to me? I'm a knight, you know."

The thieves disappeared around the corner.

Cloon, floating above me, raised an eyebrow. "That wasn't terribly impressive. You're not very good at this, are you?"

Fluff was hopping about in the air in agitation. "You let them escape right under your nose! What kind of a knight has so much trouble apprehending a badger and a mole? I never saw anything so pathetic!"

"Stop hassling me and keep an eye on where those two went with the loot," I gasped, finally struggling to my feet using Excalibur's scabbard as a prop. "They can't get far with all that heavy treasure."

I charged after them down the corridor as fast as I was able, the motes floating about my head. With my long legs and my prey so burdened with their loot, I cornered them just before they reached the cave exit. Refusing to release their sack, the badger and the mole turned to face me, teeth bared and claws out. I advanced, uncertain what I was supposed to do. I certainly didn't actually want to strike one of these little animals with my sword. I might injure it. Instead I bent and reached for the badger with my free hand, trying to grab it by the scruff of the neck. "Come with me, little creature. I'm not going to hurt you. I just want to talk to you."

The badger dodged away but the mole was not so quick. As I moved forward I tripped on my scabbard and staggered, waving my arms and accidentally catching the mole on the back of his head with my armored fist. The poor creature collapsed and lay still.

"Now look what you've done, you oaf!" cried the badger. "You've killed him!"

I was mortified. I bent down and reached out to touch the unmoving mole. "Oh dear, I'm ever so sorry. Do you really think I've killed him? I didn't mean to hurt him." I removed one gauntlet and felt through the black fur for a pulse. The little animal was soft and warm with squinty eyes and a strange puckered mouth. It was kind of cute. I didn't feel much like fighting anyone any more. I wondered whether a knight could be a pacifist. Then with a flood of relief I sensed the creature's life force and felt a heartbeat.

"It's OK," I said. "He's alive. He's just stunned. Listen, I don't want to fight with you little animals, but I've promised to help guard the treasure. I'm sure we can sort this out. Don't worry, I won't let anyone hurt you."

Brains looked at the unconscious mole. "Really?" he said doubtfully. But he was so relieved that his friend was alive that he agreed to cooperate.

I took the mole in my hand and stroked his little head. Meanwhile Fluff was flitting up and down with excitement. "Prisoners! Great! How do we tie them up?"

"With porridge," said Trond, with the air of one who is experienced at this kind of thing.

"That's a good idea," said Cloon. He looked thoughtful for a moment. "How do you tie someone up with porridge?"

"Tightly," said Trond. "Especially if it is runny."

"I bags first go at torturing them," cried Fluff. She floated up beside Brains's ear. "You'd better hope I don't get you alone," she whispered. "I took a course in torturing captives. I was top of my class!"

Brains glared at the mote.

I decided it was time to take charge. After all, I'd provided the necessary muscle to capture the burglars. Without me the dust motes couldn't have done much except complain.

"Listen. No one's torturing anyone or tying anyone up with porridge. These are my prisoners and they're under my protection."

I shooed Fluff away. "Cloon, help me interrogate the captives. The dragon will return soon and we need to sort this out before he gets here. And as for you, young badger," I said, turning to Brains, "from what I hear of dragons and their attitude to people who try to steal their treasure, you'd better have an unbelievably good explanation for what you did."

"But we didn't steal it. We were just borrowing it. We fully intended to pay it back."

Maurice stirred and moaned. His little pink tongue came out and licked his lips.

"'This is all terribly embarrassing," continued the badger. ""I've never done anything like this before. My family are known as upright and trustworthy citizens. Why, I am the elected mayor of the valley. But this was a matter of life and death."

The motes hovered closer. They loved adventure stories, especially ones featuring death.

"You see, recently I lost rather a lot of money on a bet."

Fluff laughed out loud. "It's really not your week, is it? Losing a bet and getting caught stealing from a dragon." But her elders shushed her.

"I'm sorry to hear that," I said. "Do you bet often?"

"No, sir," said the Badger, his snout drooping to the stone floor. "But I was unwise enough to take the advice of a flower and open a betting shop, and my customers were laying bets on a fight between a dragon and a knight."

This was interesting!

Suddenly Maurice sat up and started speaking quickly, looking a little dazed. "Look, he's not explaining the story right. Let me tell it. It's really quite simple. It all started with these crazy flowers, you see. One of them was trodden on by an overweight horse and it had a brain-wave that our great entrepreneur here turned into a complicated equation that none of us understood, except for the part about the Italian sauce recipe, so we had to ask the snake and we fed it a magazine for my cousin, and the crazy dragon didn't even put up a fight so the customers were really upset, especially this dreaded lemur clan who want to kill us. I mean him." He nodded toward Brains. "I'm just helping my friend. They aren't going to kill me. I hope."

Poor little creature. His brain was quite addled from the blow on the head. "Hush now," I said. "Why don't you lie down? You should get some rest after that nasty bump on your head."

Maurice obediently lay down and closed his eyes.

"Now badger, finish telling us what actually happened."

"Well, it's sort of like the mole said. We were laying wagers on a fight between a knight and a dragon, but they unexpectedly made friends instead of fighting. Now our whole betting operation has been sued for fraud by our clients. The problem is that the people I owe the most money to are a notorious gang of African ringtail lemurs."

"A lemur clan?" sneered Fluff. "I'm so scared!"

"No one in their right mind," said Brains, glaring at Fluff, "messes with these lemurs. They're killers, absolutely ruthless. They didn't go into much detail but they did mention that if I failed to pay up by tomorrow they would put me in a pizza and bake me crisp, and they will do the same to all my ancestors and descendants for seven generations, which adds up to rather a large number of badgers, this being a Catholic country, you'll remember. So in desperation I decided to ask the dragon for a small loan. But when I got here, he was out, so I thought that since we were here already, the dragon wouldn't mind if we saved ourselves an extra trip and fetched the necessary amount. We could sort out the paperwork later."

"So, sneaking into Dragon Joe's cave with a sack and a mole is your way of asking for a loan?" I said. "Some people might consider that a little, er... informal."

"This dragon loves informality," said Brains. "Look at how he annexes kingdoms. He just zooms in and burns everything and eats everyone. He doesn't bother with building permits or health regulations, he just does it. He is our role model. Anyway, we couldn't wait around to ask him. We've got this lemur-style deadline, remember?"

Trond chuckled. "Deadline, good one. Get it? Dead line. Wednesday he'll be dead. Get it?"

Cloon sat on him.

"Let's have a look at what they've taken," said Cloon. "We need to evaluate the magnitude of the crime."

I approached the sack and removed the contents carefully, placing each item on the stone floor in the brightest spot beneath the skylight. There were eleven gold plates and four goblets, a jewel-encrusted scabbard that Excalibur eyed greedily, a finely engraved dagger with a huge emerald set in its pommel, several glittering necklaces, a bag of coins, a scepter, a couple of crowns, onyx medallions, garnet broaches, a casket brimming with gems of all shapes and sizes—rubies and opals, emeralds, sapphires, diamonds, pearls—and a fabulous crystal chandelier, slightly bent after being dragged up the stairs in a sack.

"That's quite a haul for an unsecured, unconfirmed, unapproved 'in a sack' type loan," remarked Excalibur, dazzled by the sight of such wealth.

"There are a lot of those lemurs," said Brains, sounding defensive.

But I was unimpressed. All this fuss over a pile of crockery, glass baubles, and gaudy ornaments. These earthlings were very strange.

"Let the court come to order," declared Cloon. "For the case of Brains the badger and Maurice the mole, charged with purloining excessive amounts of treasure from Joe the dragon. How does the defense plead?"

"Not guilty, your honor," said Brains. "And may I add that I'm impressed by the highly professional way you run your court. You inspire confidence that justice will be done."

"That is not relevant," said Cloon, glowing with pleasure. "This matter will be tried now. Bail is set at one sack of treasure."

"May I approach, your honor?" I asked.

"Very well," said the mote.

I spoke in a low voice. "Look, firstly they are animals and therefore, according to your theology, have no understanding of the concept of good and evil and therefore cannot sin. In addition to that, they didn't mean any harm. They were just afraid of the lemurs. They are not habitual criminals, the dragon has plenty of extra treasure anyway, and frankly I think I should decide what happens to them since I captured them. Plus the mole got hit on the head, so why don't we just let them off with a warning and not mention anything to the dragon who already has enough problems? What do you think?"

Cloon nodded slowly. "What you say makes a lot of sense, good knight. And we recovered the treasure, so there's no harm done. Let's call it quits."

He turned to the badger. "Since the treasure is intact, just let me remind you that crime doesn't pay and you shouldn't do it again. You and your friend are free to go."

Brains was overcome. "Why thank you, your honor, and you, sir knight. We will not forget this."

"How about you stay for breakfast while your friend rests?" I said. "And we can think about what to do about those rascally lemurs."

The mole chose this moment to wake again with a start. "Free at last!" he cried, leaping to his feet. He turned to face me in my full armor.

"Away, foul friend in human form," he squeaked, staggering back.

I stood my ground, unsure how to react to this bizarre challenge. Mina, awakening in my pocket, intervened.

"Maurice, I think perhaps you mean '*fiend* in human form.' 'Friend in human form' doesn't make much sense."

This struck me as uniquely ironic. "You know, normally it would make no sense, but just this once it actually does since I persuaded the judge to release the mole."

Maurice looked disappointed. "Is that all? I thought we might be awarded something more along the lines of a free holiday for two in the Bahamas."

"Don't push your luck. But you have been invited for breakfast."

"Breakfast?" said the Mole, "Great! I'm hungry."

Everyone headed for the picnic zone at the cave entrance.

I glanced at the sack, lying partly open on the ground. As I reflected on the folly of the earthlings' preoccupation with treasure, something caught my eye. I bent down and picked up a silver amulet studded with rubies. I held it up to the light and examined it carefully. I could scarce believe what I was seeing. Glancing about to ensure that I was unobserved, I slipped it into my pocket, alongside supermouse.

Even Dragons Have Birthdays

We emerged from the cave and stood blinking in the sunlight. Our small party now consisted of one stressed space alien, one pocket-occupying mouse, one anxious badger, one still-dazed mole, and three highly disciplined dust motes. Just then we were joined by a battalion of kitchen utensils. They laid out a picnic cloth upon which they deposited a pile of emotionally unstable pancakes. Breakfast had arrived.

We were about to sit and eat when Joe appeared in the sky, the sun shining behind his wings so that they spread like golden fans. On his back rode a small figure. The dragon circled in closer and I saw that the rider was Princess Iris.

Was this the same girl who had claimed, "Well, he's not exactly my friend; he's more like my employer"? Add it to the list of odd things that I'd encountered this morning. Gullible kitchen utensils, martial arts experts in the form of dust motes, kleptomaniac rodents. And what about the mysterious amulet I'd "borrowed"? I just hoped that all that I had heard about dragons and their attitude to treasure theft was just an exaggeration. But I couldn't help feeling a hollowness in my stomach.

"There's something funny going on," I whispered to Mina. "This princess is not what she appears to be. She has already deceived me twice. First she pretended she was a witch. Then she neglected to tell me that the dragon was a vegetarian. And now after claiming he is not friendly to her, she is behaving as if the monster is her long-lost pet. When she was encouraging me to go and fight the dragon, she said it was fat and lazy, not much more than an overgrown lizard. This monster is about the over-grownest lizard I've ever seen! Next she'll be telling me that Dracula only drinks wheat grass juice."

"I heard she is planning to sue a bunny rabbit," said Mina.

"Did anyone ever tell you that you're a funny kind of mouse?"

"Of course. I'm a Super Mouse."

I was beginning to think she just might be.

The dragon swooped right over our heads, his armored underbelly reflecting the light. Then he veered and swept in low, cupped his wings, and stalled perfectly, landing on all fours on the stone platform. Iris clapped her hands and leaned forward to pat Joe on the back before sliding off to the ground.

"Top o' the morning to you, sir knight. I trust you slept well," said Joe. He lay down on the warm rock, sighed with pleasure, and glanced around at our company. "Won't you introduce me to your friends?"

I couldn't help thinking about the stolen amulet in my pocket. Feeling as nervous as a bunny being sued by a witch, I tried to keep my cool. "Why yes, thank you, I slept perfectly. Your dust motes are excellent hosts. Allow me to introduce Brains the mouse, I mean the badger, I mean Mayor Brains, and Maurice the lizard, which is to say the smartest mole in moledom, and these motes who would never think to disturb your peace of mind with any fanciful tales about anyone having designs on anyone's valuables, for they are your dedicated servants."

Joe raised his eyebrows. "What are you talking about? Are you all right, Sir Dogalogue? You need to relax. Why don't you take your armor off and make yourself comfortable."

He turned to address us all, shining turquoise with pleasure. "Come friends, enjoy the repast my kitchen utensils have prepared for you. Until yesterday I was on a raw food cleansing diet, but I'm done with that for now, so I'll be joining you. Allow me to introduce you to my public relations secretary, Princess Iris of Navarre." He smiled fondly at the princess.

"Charmed," she said with an elegant curtsey. She gave me a quizzical, what's-the-matter-with-you look.

"This," said Joe to Iris, "is Sir Dogalogue, the brave knight I told you about who dared to challenge me in combat yesterday and was the first ever to survive such a confrontation." The dragon laughed. He was evidently in very fine spirits.

Iris clapped her hands again. "I have a special announcement to make."

Everyone turned to her, all attention.

"Today is Dragon Joe's 9128th birthday. And to celebrate I have a special gift for him.

She beckoned to the kitchen utensils who wheeled in a large gift-wrapped package, about the size of an adult human. Everyone gathered around, curious.

She looked at Joe. "Well? Aren't you going to open it?"

Joe reached out with a claw and delicately removed the wrapping to reveal a life-sized chocolate princess! This was even better than the tofu knights from the Duke's kitchen.

"Just what I've always wanted," he said happily, carefully lifting the chocolate princess and standing her upright.

"Be careful not to melt it," said Iris. "No breathing fire near the chocolate."

I removed my armor and sat down at the table. I was hungry but I was too nervous to eat much. It was probably my imagination, but the stolen amulet felt warm in my pocket. It was not that I felt guilty, I was just afraid of getting in trouble. After all, he had stolen his hoard in the first place. I doubted that this particular item even originated on earth.

I prodded my pancake absently with my fork. Everyone else set to eagerly and the pile of pancakes dwindled quickly, followed by slices of chocolate princess. I left the table and stood at the cave's entrance, looking out over the valley. The sun was a blur of brightness, relentlessly dissolving the mist so that it rose in fuzzy tendrils from the stream like a many-armed ghost. Mina crept out of my pocket. I set my plate of pancakes down before her and fed her a piece. She smiled up at me adoringly. Great. My first earth fan was a mouse.

Iris appeared and sat next to me. "You're not eating. Is something wrong?" she asked.

"Just some personal problem." I still hadn't decided if I could completely trust her.

"Congratulations on the way you handled Joe. He likes you. I told you he wouldn't eat you."

"Yes, well you had the advantage of knowing in advance that he was a vegetarian."

"I'm really sorry I couldn't tell you about that, but the dragon swore me to silence. I said as much as I could. I thought I stretched it pretty far saying he only eats meat on Fridays and that he was giving up fighting knights."

"Even so, confronting Joe believing he might eat me was not an experience I would want to repeat."

"I see you're still angry. Isn't there something I could do to make it up to you?"

Her expression reminded me of an owl, and since I'm so fond of owls, I melted a little.

"As a matter of fact, there may be something," I said. "Since you seem to be such close friends with the dragon, I'm wondering if you might be able to persuade him to part with a little of his treasure for a good cause."

I told her about Brains and his lemur problem.

The princess furrowed her brow. "That is a noble idea, but it will take some diplomacy. I don't know if the dragon will listen to me. However, I'll do my best. Treasure is a famously sensitive subject with dragons. But as you can see, Joe is a very unusual dragon, so maybe we can do something."

"I don't know much about dragons but he does seem very odd."

"Indeed. Just this morning Joe was telling me in great detail of all the knights who tried to steal his treasure and how he roasted and ate every one of them. He was quiet for a while after that. Not depressed—more thoughtful. But moments later here he is, the jolly birthday dragon. He's difficult to predict."

"Perhaps he's going through some kind of existential crisis. He just became a vegetarian, which is a major lifestyle change for a marauding monster, and just last night he told me that the two of us and your brother are his first non-dragon friends in nine thousand years."

"What's an existential crisis?"

"A temporary psychological condition usually brought on by a sudden change in circumstances or a critical phase in the individual's psycho-spiritual development. Until now, eating Christians was his main reason for existence. Now that he's given that up, he doesn't know what to do with himself. He has no sense of higher purpose. Perhaps he's even feeling guilty about all the people he's killed, though I doubt that. He doesn't strike me as the remorseful type."

"Gosh," said the princess, "you sure know a lot about thoughts and emotions. You sound like a shaman, except that you actually make sense."

"I studied alien psychology in college."

Suddenly we were startled by a terrible sound, as though a thousand rabid otters armed with trumpets were fighting over a single fish.

Miranda laughed. "That's funny. Think of all those otters." Then she looked worried. "Poor otters. Most of them would have to go hungry." Then she giggled. "But then I could feed them and they would all be my friends. Dr. Dogalogue?"

"Yes, child?"

"I'm glad you decided to trust Princess Iris. I really like her. I think it's great that you totally made friends with her."

"So am I. She was a wonderful friend. But do you remember what we agreed about California-speak?"

"Whoops, I said 'totally' again. Sorry. I know loony Lucifer doesn't like it."

"He's not a loony, Miranda. He is actually a great hero."

"Really? I find that hard to believe."

"Just because you're smart doesn't mean you know everything. He was the one who saved the dragons."

"What? Old spider legs? Gosh." Miranda loved the dragons, or at least Joe. She was not so sure about the meat-eating ones. Lucifer was really spiky and sarcastic and kept calling her an egg. But if he had really helped Dr. Dogalogue save the dragons she might have to decide she liked him after all.

Possessed by a Christian

"HAAAAWWWAAAAH! ARRRRGGGHH! GNNNRAAAAFFFGLE!"

The dragon cried out in agony. Iris ran to him as I leapt to my feet in alarm, scrabbling for my sword.

"I wish you wouldn't do that every time something unexpected happens," said Excalibur. "Try to be graceful but alert like a proper knight. Assess the situation calmly, and if you deem it necessary, draw me, your faithful weapon, and dispatch your foe. Maintain the demeanor of a gentleman in preference to that of a highly strung rodent."

I can't say I was thrilled to be receiving instructions in knightly conduct from a petulant piece of metal. Still, he had a point. Oh dear, unintended pun.

The dragon moaned again. "OOOOOHHHHH! NNNNGGGGRIIIII!"

"What's wrong, Joe dear?" said Iris anxiously. "What is it? Did you bite your tongue?"

The monster's face was all crumpled like a 3D map of the north of Spain. I winced at the thought of all those teeth biting his poor tongue.

"It's my tooth," moaned Joe. "It sometimes hurts when I bite on the left side. It makes a strange clanging sound, and I keep hearing a terrible voice in my head muttering religious curses and dangerous Christian spells such as "Mother Mary, have mercy on my soul," and "Help me, Jesus." I fear I'm possessed by a Christian. Perhaps the spirit of a knight I ate is seeking vengeance. I think I need to see an exorcist."

"You see?" Excalibur whispered. "The dragon has a toothache. No cause for alarm and probably no less than he deserves. Now, please try to keep your head and put me back in my scabbard."

"Sounds like you need a dentist as well as an exorcist," I said to Joe. "It's better not to leave these things too long, you know. They only get worse." I wondered where on earth we'd find a dentist willing to treat this monster. We'd have no problem finding an exorcist, however. Medieval Europe was infested with them.

"No problem," said Iris brightly. "I read a book about dentistry once. It looks pretty easy."

"That's very commendable," I said, "but hadn't we better find a professional? Joe, you don't have a regular dentist, do you?"

"None of them want to treat me," said Joe, looking annoyed. "They're all complete cowards. Generation after generation it's the same. Each new batch refuses to stick their heads inside my mouth. I haven't had a checkup in 197 years."

"Do you have dental insurance?" said Brains.

"Not any more. I let it lapse a hundred years ago. It didn't seem worth it at the time. Now I regret not keeping up the payments."

"There's your real problem," said the badger. "Those dentists are not afraid you'll eat them. They're afraid they won't get paid!"

"I have a passing knowledge of amateur dentistry," said Iris. "Let me at least have a look to see what the problem is, and if needed we'll find a dentist. As for the exorcist, we can easily rustle one up. Eleven of them pestered me on the way here."

Parinte Sinistru, the Romanian exorcist, was not having a good week. His first case had been complicated—a donkey apparently possessed by the spirit of an aardvark. And it wanted to pay in manure. Now he was broke.

"It's a simple casting out of an evil spirit," Iris told him. "A Christian spirit, nothing dark. Run of the mill job. I must ask you to come to the client. He is not fit to travel. He is just nearby, outside his cave."

"That'll be one gold piece," said Parinte Sinistru, assessing her net worth with a practiced eye and adjusting his price accordingly. He wanted to settle the mode of payment first this time.

"No problem for this client, I assure you. But I'm curious. What happens if someone can't pay for the exorcism? Do they get repossessed?" She giggled.

Parinte Sinistru turned to her with a baleful stare. "Yes," he said, unsmiling.

"That was a joke. You don't seem like a man who laughs a lot," said Iris as they walked the short distance to the dragon's cave.

"I laugh at jokes that are funny. Your joke was of the non-funny variety. Plus I've already heard it three times today. There are not many exorcism jokes, so each one gets more than its fair share of repetition."

Iris tried to pretend that she had just been awarded a Nobel prize for funny jokes about exorcists. "Ah yes, well, that would explain it. But enough about me. Let me introduce you to my friend Joe."

She led him around the corner to the cave entrance.

As soon as Parinte Sinistru spotted Joe he dived for cover behind a thorn bush. "Quick," he hissed. "Hide, there's a dragon behind you!"

"As I was saying," Iris continued, "let me introduce you to my friend Joe. He's the one who needs your help."

"The dragon is the patient?" said the exorcist, trembling in his nest amongst the thorns.

"Yes. He's afraid he is possessed by a Christian. You can come out. I promise he won't bite."

Parinte Sinistru emerged timidly, dusting himself off. "Well, here's something new. I don't normally do dragons. My fee will be double, with no guarantee of success. Dragons are themselves all too often agents of the Enemy."

"You mean Satan's forces?" said Iris in awe.

"No, I mean the Danish," said Sinistru. "They keep trying to invade England. They're real pests. With huge axes."

He turned to address the monster. "Now to business. Mr. Dragon. First, I must ask you some questions. Are you allergic to anything, Bibles, for example?"

"Of course I'm allergic to Bibles," said Joe, turning dark red. "Let's try and guess why. Maybe it has something to do with the fact that the last four hundred people I met who were carrying Bibles all tried to impale me with a sharp spear. But no, I'm getting carried away. That couldn't possibly cause any emotional trauma in a dragon child, barely out of the egg, helpless and alone, who's just lost his friends and watched his home get blown up by a volcano and then sink into the Atlantic Ocean."

Parinte Sinistru used his quill to place a tick on the form he was filling out. "We'll count that as a yes. Can you please give me the address of your nearest living relative?"

"No, I can't. Now get on with the treatment before I decide to supplement my regular diet with a little fresh exorcist."

Parinte Sinistru quickly packed away his forms and papers. "Why yes, of course. At once. Come, Madam, let us embark on our little adventure into the dragon's gaping maw. I must ask you to accompany me as insurance against the dragon closing his mouth."

I'd been trying to sense the exorcist's personality, but something was blocking me. It was as though he wanted to open up to me but at the same time he didn't. I'd never encountered anything like this before in any creature's mind. Iris beckoned me to accompany them.

"OK, Joe," she said, "now open wide and no sudden closing of your mouth. Don't worry, we're just having a look. We won't be doing any extractions or wrestings or stuff like that. See? I'm leaving my crowbar behind."

"Mbggggh," said Joe, jaws agape, his anxious eyes looking down at us.

I had an uninterrupted view of Parinte Sinistru's pantalooned buttocks as I followed him up the ladder into the monster's mouth. My finely tuned instincts told me there was something not quite right about this man, but I could not place my finger on it. Superficially, all seemed in order. He was as bald as an orange but blessed with a thick black beard. And judging from the tufts of curly chest hair poking out of the neck of his doublet and the wrists of his jacket, his body was as furry as a gorilla. The grotesque hunch in his back, the disfiguring scar running from ear to jaw, laying open the lower left side of his mouth in a constant hideous leer, the smell of rotting death wafting from his slime-encrusted black jacket with its fake brass buttons, the spine-chilling croaking tone of his voice were all what one would expect in a genuine exorcist. He seemed perfect. Almost too perfect. Could we be dealing with another imposter?

I took a deep breath and stepped off the ladder into the cavern of the monster's mouth. Iris followed me. A gust of peppermint-scented wind swept over me as the dragon exhaled. So it was true, dragons do brush regularly. I peered about, trying to orient myself. There in the distance were Joe's tonsils, and emerging from the darkness was his tongue like a living lava flow, forked at the tip. A row of huge curved teeth hung above us. To the left, I could see something protruding from the fence-like structure. As I struggled along the mountain range of the lower jaw, I tripped over a rabbit.

"Here, watch who you're tripping over," said the rabbit.

"What are you doing here?' asked the princess in surprise.

"Taking a nap, what do you think?" said the rabbit.

"Has no one offered you somewhere safer to sleep?" I asked, concerned.

"I was being sarcastic, you idiot," said the rabbit. "Look. I'm stuck." It was true. He'd gotten himself wedged between an incisor and its neighbor.

Balancing precariously on a tooth, Iris and I reached down and grabbed the rabbit's ears. As it struggled, we tugged and tugged and suddenly it popped free. The three of us fell onto the dragon's palate.

The rabbit recovered first. "Thanks a lot. May your ears grow ever longer," it said, and hopped off.

Sinistru had gone further into Joe's mouth along the left jawline. "Ahoy!" he called up into the gloom. "Anyone up there? In the name of Jesus Christ, our savior."

"Thank the Lord! A Christian soul," came a voice from aloft. As the dragon opened his mouth a little wider in surprise, we saw a pair of armored legs sticking out from between two giant molars."

"By the Rood! This infernal reptile has a Christian stuck between his teeth!" exclaimed Sinistru.

"Praise be to Mary, Mother of God," said the Christian knight from his aerie.

Reaching into his backpack, Sinistru drew out a rope woven of human hair. He swung it expertly, deftly lassoing the knight's feet, and pulled the rope tight.

"Hey!" said the knight. "What are you doing?"

"Just hold on, brave sir, we're rescuing you. Here, give me a hand here, will you," said Sinistru as Iris and I approached. We all pulled together and suddenly the knight came free, plummeting to the ground with a crash.

"Oof!" came a voice from within the armor.

"Are you all right, sir?" asked Sinistru.

"By the blood of Christ, if I get my hands on the idiot who did that I'll have his head, I swear it!" said the knight in fury, his face still hidden behind his visor.

We backed away nervously. "I think he's OK," said Sinistru.

"He doesn't seem very grateful, does he?" I said as the armored warrior rose to his feet cursing. His helmet was out of place and he was blinded by his visor. He cast about with his sword in anger.

"Grateful? No, not very," said Iris. "Let's leave."

"Good idea," said Sinistru. Iris and I raced for the ladder with Sinistru just ahead of us. Suddenly a human figure appeared from behind the row of teeth.

"Hellooo," he said.

"Sweep!" cried Iris. "What in the world are you doing here?"

"Everybody's got to be somewhere," said The Sweep reasonably.

"You live here?" I asked in astonishment.

"Sure, let me show you my place. It's quite comfortable." The Sweep led us further into the darkness.

Suddenly the dragon's mouth contorted and his booming voice came rushing up his throat on a great wind, "I ing hoo eeee ou o ere. I eeer I oin oo oh!"

"What's that? What's this crazy dragon saying?" I asked.

"Perhaps he's just hungry and is suggesting that we go for pizza," said Sinistru. Dragons are always thinking about food.

"Good idea," I said. "I could use a pizza myself."

"Uuuiii uh, i aaaah ooo iih u onga." The dragon's voice sounded more urgent.

"He sounds anxious," said The Sweep. "He must be really hungry."

The knight strode up, snorting with anger and menacing us with his sword. "Forsooth, I deem you are the very brigands who brought me crashing to the ground on my head just moments ago. Defend yourselves, cowards!"

"We were just trying to rescue you, sir," I stammered, backing away. I looked around but Sinistru had fled. Big help.

"God's blood, miscreant. Draw your weapon." The knight advanced, brandishing his blade.

I drew Excalibur. "I don't think you want to fight this guy," said the sword. "He has the look of an expert swordsman."

I couldn't help admiring the knight's style. "I say, sir knight. You seem to be rather good at this. Any chance you could give me lessons?"

"Impertinent swine! I'm going to teach you a lesson you won't forget!" The knight lunged forward and I barely managed to dodge and parry with Excalibur.

"Wow!" I said breathlessly, skipping out of the way as he slashed at my legs. "Could you show me how you do that, but a bit slower so I can follow? It was really impressive."

The knight hesitated, looking bashful. "Oh, all right. Now watch carefully. It's like a dance. Place your feet thus." He demonstrated as he explained. "Balance on the balls of your feet so you can move quickly in any direction. Then sweep out your blade in a single fluid motion, just so." He swept his sword from the scabbard in a graceful arc. "Then you slickly weave it through the air, thus!"

He delicately wove a pattern in the air with the heavy blade, using its weight and momentum to keep it moving with minimum strain, and ended with a flourish.

"Now that's what I call a brandish!" I said, clapping.

"Yes, well I was a noted brandisher in knight school." Suddenly he straightened and took an aggressive stance. "Aha, demon spawn! I see what you're doing—using flattery, the wily devil's own favorite trick, to allay my righteous wrath. By the Rood, I am not one to forgive such an indignity easily." He advanced upon me.

Joe could hold it in no longer. He let out a mighty sneeze and blew us all out of his mouth. Being a well-brought-up reptile, he covered his mouth to prevent the spread of disease and caught us in his paw. All of us save the unfortunate Christian knight who shot between Joe's claws and landed head first in the increasingly popular thorn bush. This was really not his day.

Joe set Parinte Sinistru, Iris, The Sweep, and myself down on the ground carefully. We stood gathering our wits and checking to see that no parts were missing.

"Blaggarts!" came a now familiar voice. "I suppose you think this is some kind of a joke!" The knight's armored legs waved in the air, the pointed toes of his metal shoes jerking about in frustration.

His legs were his most attractive feature, which is fortunate since they featured so prominently in his public life.

"A joke? No, no, not us," gasped Iris, rolling on the ground, trying to control her mirth. "At least, not me. My brother is laughing, though. He has no respect."

But The Sweep was already wrestling with the thorn bush to extract the poor knight. After a moment he freed him and removed his helm.

When Iris and The Sweep saw his face they cried out in unison, "Uncle Honk!" and ran to embrace him. The Sweep took his uncle's hand. "Allow me to introduce Duke Honkobeefiac, lord of the nearby castle. He is our uncle on our mother's side and our host while we are in this foreign land."

"Why, Lord be praised," said the Duke. "You're alive after all, my little Iris. I was so worried. Everyone was saying you'd been eaten by the dragon. By the Rood, your poor mother thinks you are dead. I must send her a message at once telling her you're alive after all. Then you can marry one of those nice rich kings they've arranged for you. Won't you like that?" He patted her affectionately on the arm. Iris scowled but held her tongue for the moment.

"I've got it!" said The Sweep suddenly.

"Got what?" Sinistru said, looking nervous.

"I've figured out what the dragon was trying to say when we were inside his mouth. When he said 'I ing hoo eeee ou o ere. I eeer I oin oo oh!', he was trying to tell us, 'I think you should get out of there. I'm going to sneeze'."

"Who's your brilliant friend?" said Sinistru.

"He's my brother," said Iris.

"Sweep," said Duke Honk, "this dragon tried to eat me. He seems to be friendly, but are you sure he is safe?" He peered doubtfully at Dragon Joe whose great eye loomed above us.

"My apologies, sir knight," said Joe. "I am relieved to see that you were not in fact my last human meal. And doubly so since you are kin to my dear friends Princess Iris and Prince The Sweep."

Parinte Sinistru fingered the gold coins in his pocket as he made off down the path. Not bad pay, he thought. Very fair. But not as much as the evil necromancer Nefarious will give me for this information. He smirked and slimed his way back towards the secret entrance to Nefarious's cave.

THE FALL OF ATLANTIS

As soon as Sinistru left, Iris approached the dragon. I could almost see the lightning bolts shooting out of her brain. She seemed all spiky, like a puppet made from fishhooks. Joe, all glowing golden, unaware of his impending storm, sang a little song he'd composed to celebrate the fact that he was no longer possessed by a Christian.

Lo, a Christian not I be
Look between my teeth you'll see
No Hindu, Muslim, Druid or Jew
'Cause that's not what I do.
Look inside and all about
Of biblical verse you will find naught
Of dogma I'm completely free
Excuse me while I dance in glee.

The Sweep bounced, his body's default reflex when exposed to bad poetry. His sister, however, was in no mood for entertainment. "Hey you, dragon! Stop that silly singing and listen up." She stood with her hands on her hips, glaring up at Joe, her slight figure dwarfed by the huge animal.

The dragon had been hoping for another birthday present but when he looked down at Iris he sensed that this probably wasn't it.

"I've had about enough of you and your nasty eating habits," snapped the girl. "How dare you try to eat my uncle? Some vegetarian you are! Any more of my friends and relatives you'd care to regurgitate?" She stamped her foot in impotent rage.

"I wish I was a knight with a big pointy spear. I'd teach you a lesson."

"Hell hath no fury like a woman's corns," murmured Brains to Maurice, trying to look wise.

"What are you *talking* about?" said Maurice. "That's ridiculous. How can a callous on someone's foot have emotions?"

"It's a wise saying," said Brains. "When you're quoting wise sayings, you don't have to know what they mean. It is sufficient merely to say them. And I feel that a wise saying is fitting at this juncture."

"Is it really possible that you are attempting to quote the *actual* wise saying, which goes, 'Hell hath no fury like a woman's scorn'?"

"How about that!" said Brains. "That does make more sense. I always wondered why I got strange looks whenever I said that."

Maurice shook his head in wonder.

The fury of a woman was a new experience for Joe. He eyed the princess warily. "I'm pretty sure I didn't eat any more of your relatives, at least not the local ones. I actually prefer foreign food."

From the deepening of Iris's already crimson complexion, Joe concluded that this was not the answer she was looking for. She grabbed a branch and struck him on the foot, looking frustrated. It was all she could reach. "Humans aren't food, you wicked dragon!"

She turned away. "I don't think I can ever be your friend. You're just a monster, inside and out." She burst into tears and ran off upstream toward her own cave.

Joe turned a deep blue. "Does your sister often behave like this?" he asked The Sweep.

"She's rarely this angry. I'm afraid you've really upset her, eating our uncle."

"But I didn't even chew him! I just snapped him up as he rode by. It was a reflex, an old habit. He's fine. Look." Joe indicated with a claw.

Duke Honk was happily gorging himself on pancakes.

The Sweep nodded in sympathy. As both the master and victim of his bouncing reflex, he could quite relate.

"It didn't seem like a big deal at the time," the dragon continued. "How was I supposed to know he was her uncle? She's the first princess I've ever actually spoken with. Though I suppose it wasn't really their fault, the other princesses, I mean. I ate them before we had a chance to get acquainted. But Iris is different. We were getting along so well."

"I wouldn't worry too much," said The Sweep. "I'll go find her and explain to her what happened. Don't worry, I'm sure she'll calm down soon."

As The Sweep headed up the path, Joe's golden glowing scales faded like a dying sunset. "Oh dear," he said. "Just when I was beginning to make a friend. I didn't even know that I could like people until a few days ago, and already one of my new friends hates me."

"You can count me as a friend," I said. "Although we've only just met, so I suppose I'm what you'd call a fast friend."

"I say," said the dragon, smiling in spite of himself. "That's rather clever. Mind if I use it?"

"You're welcome," I said, hoping that this might be considered of some value against my item of pilfered dragon treasure.

"What ho, by the Rood," said the Duke as he marched up. "It's getting a bit hot out here in the sun. What do you say we all retire to that glade by the stream and sit under the birches."

"Good idea," said Joe. So we descended to the glade and made ourselves comfortable in a little circle on the grass amongst the silver tree trunks, listening to the finches and robins as they sang their accompaniment to the perpetual gossip of the stream.

I wanted to ask Joe about the amulet but I had been feeling nervous and my human suit was responding with all kinds of stress-inducing hormones. It was most uncomfortable. Finally I couldn't bear it any longer. "Perhaps while we wait, I could get something off my chest," I blurted out.

Mina knew all about the amulet in my pocket. After all, they were roommates. She shook her head at me and ran her paw across her throat. I wondered what she was going on about.

"So what is it you wanted to tell me, my fast friend, Sir Dogalogue?" said Joe with a wan smile.

I could feel my fingers tingling. "Not to put too fine a point on beating about the bush here," I said. "I have to say something about what can only be described as nothing other than... your treasure." I offered up my spirit to Zond.

"My treasure?" said Joe mournfully. "You know, I've been wondering about all that hoarded wealth. Now that I'm entering the last phase of my life, considering that I might only be around for another couple of thousand years, I've been wondering what my treasure is good for. I mean what can you actually *do* with diamonds or gold brooches or jeweled necklaces? You can't eat them. You can't even cut vegetables with them. And it's a huge bother, paying security guards, insurance premiums, constantly counting everything to see if any items are missing, other dragons pestering me wanting to swap pieces. My nephew Fritz has been trying to assemble a complete collection of crowns of Abyssinian kings for two hundred years now. He's obsessed. I have four and he keeps asking to exchange something for mine. But he's too new at the game to have anything I really want. Still, his sincerity makes up for a lot. It is enough to make an uncle proud. He sacks castles with enthusiasm and never lets a good pillaging pass by. At the rate he is going, in a few hundred years he'll have a respectable hoard. But for now he doesn't have anything unique to offer me. I mean, who needs another set of gold crockery or jewel-encrusted amulets?"

"Right," said Maurice. "It's just a lot of useless, boring junk."

"Actually, I could really use some of that boring junk," whispered Brains but Maurice hushed him.

"I've been reading some of the human philosophers," said Joe. "For primitive folk, they have some real insights regarding how you can't take your wealth with you when you die and how it is better to focus on building character and pursuing wisdom and enlightenment rather than worry about money, especially when you already have more than you can possibly use. It makes a lot of sense. You can't spend treasure you know. Have you ever tried getting change for a priceless ruby? The minute you attempt to buy anything with it, everyone assumes it's stolen and wants a ridiculous discount to fence it for you. Everyone thinks that having treasure will solve all their problems, but actually it's a real pain in the neck."

Joe did have a very long, large neck so it must have been most bothersome. This seemed like good news. If the dragon was not so fond of his treasure perhaps he might not miss a small amulet. I stole a glance at the mole and the badger and could see that a similar thought had occurred to them. They looked like they hoped the dragon would help them out with their lemur problem.

Just then Iris and The Sweep reappeared. The princess was dressed as if for a journey, in riding breeches, light boots, and a cape, with a satchel over her shoulder. She wore a short sword by her side and looked very smart. She marched up to the dragon. "Ok, Joe, I forgive you. My brother explained everything. But you have to swear never to fight or kill any more knights or humans."

Joe seemed faintly bemused at how quickly this girl's moods changed. He glanced at The Sweep, who nodded his encouragement. "Very well, princess, I so swear."

Iris reached up and kissed him and the dragon's color shifted to olive green.

Fluff floated up, followed by some towels and a rather excitable tea set that poured tea for everyone, spilling a fair bit in the process and finally setting itself down on a smooth rock near the stream. The new arrivals settled into the circle in the dappled shade. The aroma of herbal tea mingled with the spruce and pine and the scent of wildflowers on the gentle spring breeze. A bee paused to watch us for a moment and sped off to tell its hive of the odd gathering.

Joe, still more green than golden, continued. "Sir Dogalogue, you were about to ask me something about my treasure."

I didn't know what to say. Mina whispered to me, urging me not to confess. The badger and mole gesticulated wildly with their eyes, probably worried that I'd mention that they'd tried to walk off with a sack full of the dragon's treasure. I had no intention of getting them in trouble, but I had to unburden myself. I brought out the amulet.

"Joe, can you please tell me where this came from?"

The dragon stretched forth a claw and took the object from my outstretched hand. "Interesting. As you know, this comes from my treasure hoard. I might ask you how it got to be in your pocket, but I'll let that pass for now. Tell me, what interests you about this particular item?"

I hesitated but I was committed now. I had no choice but to go ahead. "I must beg your pardon, for you are of course correct, the amulet comes from your hoard. But I felt compelled to ask you about it. When I saw the inlaid emblem, two serpents entwined about a staff, beneath two wings and a star, I could scarce believe my eyes, for I recognized it instantly. It is the emblem of my spiritual master."

It takes a lot to surprise a dragon, but this revelation did the trick. He examined the amulet with new interest and a shining yellow sheen spread over his scales in a wave. Everyone, even the trees, held their breath in curiosity.

Joe looked at us in silence for a moment before speaking. "I think the time has come to tell all. This amulet is an artifact of Atlantis. But it depicts a symbol of Sir Dogalogue's home. I'm mystified about this connection but it is surely significant. It surely has to do with the history of Atlantis and the first dragons, a story which I will now to relate to non-dragons for the first time."

"This had better be good," whispered the badger to Mina. "I'm supposed to be umpiring a football game for my nephew. I'm already in hot water with my mother."

"I was born on the island of Atlantis," began the dragon. "In those days that was where all the dragons lived, for that is where we come from. But when I was just a few years out of the egg, not much bigger than a horse, that all changed."

"How cute!" exclaimed Maurice. "It's a wonder your parents didn't lose you down a crack."

The dragon ignored him.

"This was nine thousand years ago and Atlantis was the heart of the world. It was the center of beauty, culture, music, and learning. Wise philosophers gave discourses in the squares and musicians plucked Aeolian melodies on their harps on every street corner."

"Sounds a bit boring," interrupted Brains. "I don't know if I'd want to live in a place where all everyone did was sit around talking about philosophy and playing the harp."

"It was not boring," said Joe with a stern look. "It was the global center of commerce, culture, and industry and the number one destination for merchants and tourists. Atlantean ships plied the Mediterranean from the pillars of Hercules to the gardens of Phoenicia, and the empire's power extended far into the lands beyond. Our city was a Mecca of learning. Why, on her streets you could hear every language of the world."

"That must have been pretty confusing," said Maurice. "How did people understand one another?"

"Hush, you guys," said Iris. "Let Joe tell his story."

Joe gave her an appreciative smile.

"The true source of Atlantis's power was known to only a few. The main temple was on a hill above the city, and in the courtyard at the heart of the temple stood the microvita tree. Now the microvita tree was no ordinary tree. Only one of them can live in the world at any time. When it is a thousand years old, it finally blossoms and releases a great flow of spiritual energy. This microvita energy lies dormant within all living things but when the tree blossoms, the microvita within everyone on the planet awakens, ushering in a golden age of peace and harmony. If the microvita tree were to blossom now, this world would become a heaven on earth."

The Sweep bounced. Everyone started asking questions all at once.

"Would people stop being mean to mice?" said Mina.

"Would it make Brains smarter?" said Maurice. "That would improve my life immeasurably."

"Would those pesky trees next to my castle stop growing their roots through my drains?" said the Duke.

"I'm not sure about all that," said Joe, "but I do know that everyone would be a lot kinder to everyone else. Microvita energy helps us to sense our connection to all life. Remember, this is the same power that dwells in the nearby Cavern of Stones that enables all of you animals to speak."

"Maybe that is why you became a vegetarian," said Maurice. "You've been living so long here in this valley, near the Cavern of Stones. Maybe that's why you're different from other dragons."

Smart mole, I thought.

Joe looked surprised. "By Cuernnos, that never occurred to me."

"Gosh," said the Sweep. "If that's true, it's thanks to the microvita that I'm still alive."

"Me too," said the Duke Honk, adding as an afterthought, "by the Rood."

Joe looked uneasy. "That would also mean that I'm not as free-willed as I thought. I'm not too comfortable about that. In any event, it is important to understand that this microvita energy has influenced all our lives. And don't forget, Iris and The Sweep are the living descendants of the last kings of Atlantis, the home of the microvita tree."

"That's really weird," said The Sweep. "All these events seem to be connected somehow."

I was thinking the same thing. I sensed the hand of my master.

"You know how they say that truth is stranger than fiction?" said Maurice. "This is stranger than either."

"So what happened, Joe?" said Iris. "What happened to the heaven on earth? How come Atlantis was destroyed?"

The dragon's color turned a dark green.

"The beginning of the end came with the arrival of the dark wizard, Nefarious. At first he appeared in the guise of a wise teacher. He revealed much about the tree and how to use its energy to enhance their powers of mind. He gathered a group of scientists and priests and they initiated a great experiment: using the power of microvita for the development of new species. Their first big breakthrough came when they created the unicorn. They gave a baby unicorn to the emperor's daughter. She loved it and that was how the necromancer won his way into the emperor's heart."

"Dr. Dogalogue," said Miranda. "Are there still unicorns on earth? I think I need a unicorn really badly."

"There may be," said Dr. Dogalogue, "but I never heard of one. But your planet is a big place. Who knows, perhaps there are unicorns somewhere in a hidden valley."

"I really hope so!" said Miranda.

"But the necromancer's experiment didn't end with unicorns or flying horses or centaurs. When he saw the amazing new creatures, the emperor realized that this technology could be used to enhance his power and a dark desire awoke in his heart. He commanded his scientists to create beasts that might be used for war. So then they created the chimera, the harpy, the minotaur, and the manticore, a hideous blend of lion, human, and scorpion. Finally the necromancer himself set his sights on the most ambitious goal of all: the creation of the great dragons. There were many attempts and several failures. First was the wyvern, a kind of half-dragon, pathetic creatures with no back legs. There were never very many of them and they quickly died out. They were such an embarrassment that the Atlanteans issued an official statement declaring them mythological.

"Griffins came next. They showed more promise, physically at least. But they were conceited creatures, forever boasting how they were featured in the coat of arms of the Duke of Norfolk, so insufferably vain that no one wanted to work with them. Few tears were shed when they finally became extinct.

"But after much toil and many trials, Nefarious's team produced the first of the great dragons, Dragon Bert, my grandfather; then Dragon Jane, Dragon Fred, and Dragon Martha."

"How come the dragons all have such ordinary sounding names?" said The Sweep. "All the dragons in the stories I've read have exotic names like Fafnir or Glaurung."

"It was intended to keep us humble," said Joe. "Since we were already the most intelligent, powerful, long-lived creatures in the world, there was a danger that we might become too proud, so Nefarious gave us all very plain names. We liked having names that are easy to remember so we've continued the practice. Just because Nefarious was evil doesn't mean he never had any good ideas."

"Does it work?" said Brains.

"Does what work?" said Joe.

"Does it keep you from being proud?"

Joe somehow managed to look proud of his humility. "I believe it does. It serves as a valuable reminder of one's humble origins."

"I don't think it's working," whispered Brains.

"Clearly not," murmured Maurice.

"We dragons," said Joe, "were the necromancer's crowning achievement. Even an average dragon possesses awesome strength. He can fly like an eagle, breathe fire, live for thousands of years, and reason at least as well or better than a human. We also possess a dry sense of humor and excel at word games. When the king realized this, he became afraid. He commanded the wizard to cast a spell on each dragon as it was born, binding it to obedience. And so we became the slaves of the necromancer, never knowing the true meaning of freedom.

"As the empire spread, serious differences developed between the two most powerful groups of Atlanteans. One group held that since Atlantis had such a superior culture, it was their duty to impose their ways on all other peoples in their empire. They felt they should all be required to speak only the Atlantean language and adopt Atlantean lifestyle. To them other races were children who needed their guidance. This group was known as the Verticalists. They loved tall trees, standing at attention, and impressive monuments.

"I know a few animals like that," said Brains bitterly. "Giraffes are the worst."

"You've never even met a giraffe," said Maurice.

"I've read about them. They're clearly textbook fascists."

Maurice rolled his eyes. "I'm sorry to be the one to point out to you that a 'textbook fascist' is *not* a fascist that you come across in a textbook."

"Oh. Well, why do they try to confuse us by using the term?"

"You don't have to be a giraffe to be a fascist," said the Sweep. "Royalists can be just as rigid and domineering. Believe me, I know. They are the main reason I decided to leave the palace and become a hermit."

"I'm pretty sure at least one of the creeps I was supposed to marry belongs to this authoritarian Verticalist Party," said Iris in distaste.

"The second party," said Joe after everything quieted down, "were known as the Horizontalists. They believed in free will, long holidays, and freedom of expression. They held that if the Atlantean culture was truly superior, other peoples would adopt it of their own choosing. They loved flounder, grass snakes, and poorly designed buildings that collapsed immediately upon completion, thus not requiring one to strain one's neck looking up at them."

"You've got to wonder if this lot ever actually got anything done," said The Sweep.

"That's the exact philosophy of my other nephew," said the Duke, "and pleasant as he is, I have to say, I don't exactly see him as a potential world savior."

"Hmmph," said Iris. "I wouldn't trust one of those Horizontalists to manage my broom cupboard."

"So let me get this straight," said the mole. "The Horizontalists are a bunch of hippie poets and the Verticalists are all aspiring fascist dictators. I'll bet I know what happens next. The cunning wizard plays them off against one another and gains power."

"You're pretty sharp, Maurice," said Joe.

Maurice squirmed modestly. "It's standard mega-villain tactics. Mole evil geniuses do it all the time."

"Anyway," said Joe, "matters really came to a head when the emperor died and there were rival claims on the throne. Tension between the two groups escalated rapidly, bringing Atlantis to the brink of civil war. Each party sent representatives to the necromancer, demanding that he support their claim to the throne with his army of dragons but he secretly agreed to supply fighting dragons to both parties—for a price. And so the two armies fought for control of Atlantis. The destruction was terrible and both armies were decimated. When the two camps had fought one another to a standstill, the necromancer commanded the dragons to return to him and became the undisputed ruler of Atlantis and its empire. Then he set his sights on world domination."

"Ambitious fellow," said Maurice.

"Very!" said Joe.

"One thing," said Maurice. "I can't help wondering how come you don't mention moles even once in your whole story, not even as a joke."

"I don't mention sea anemones either," said the dragon, exasperated. "Anyway I don't know any mole jokes."

"Well, don't you think it's about time you learned some?" the mole insisted. "Not everyone is a warrior or a king or a wizard or a great dragon you know. And when you consider biomass, the total weight of all members of a species, dragons don't even feature. Ants are number one."

"Really," said Iris, staring pointedly at Maurice's somewhat rotund figure. "Given your current dimensions I thought it might be moles."

"Yes, really," said Maurice, putting his paws on his hips. "Not only that. As the earth's temperature increases, ants breathe faster since their metabolism speeds up, and that increases the level of carbon dioxide, which increases the temperature even further, which makes them breed even faster. Before you know it they will take over completely."

"Oh no!" cried Brains. "It sounds like one of those vicious bicycles."

"It is," said Maurice. "So don't underestimate the importance of us smaller animals."

"I knew that!" said an ant, popping its head up from its assigned path following the scent of the ant in front of it. He was a small black ant on a mission to retrieve a piece of dead leaf for his queen. He did not question why his great leader needed the dead leaf, nor who had killed it. He was simply proud to be serving his queen. He'd never met her personally, but he did have an extensive collection of ant postage stamps displaying her likeness.

"Of course, I knew that about ants also," said Joe. He didn't want to give the impression that he lacked the common touch. People always brought up stuff like that when it came time to elect the Top Dragon. Concerned that he was losing his audience, an inspiration struck him, causing his skin to glow silver. "I have an idea," he said. "Everyone who listens properly to my tale will get a reward."

This got everyone's attention.

"What kind of reward?" asked the badger, thinking of Joe's treasure.

"It's a secret, but I can guarantee that you will really like it."

"Oh goody, I love surprises," said the mole.

"Do I get a reward too?" asked the ant hopefully.

"Of course not," said the mole. "You just gatecrashed our party. No one invited you. Weren't you on your way somewhere? Hurry along now. Go on, shoo!"

"All right," said the ant, who sadly made to slink off.

"Don't be mean, Maurice," said Iris. "Here, little ant." She carefully picked the insect up in her hand. "I'm inviting you to stay and listen. And I'm a real princess, not just a common mean old mole. I'll ask the dragon to give you a reward too. But you have to listen to the tale carefully so that you can remember it."

"Thank you," said Harvey the ant, faint with gratitude at being in the hands of a real princess.

The Duke spoke up. "I've been thinking about this problem of the ants weighing so much. I can recommend a good weight-loss program. See here in this magazine. A simple regimen of healthy eating, regular exercise, yoga, and these rare herbs only found in the Amazon rainforest and available exclusively from this multi-level marketing company, Slimant, Inc., will have them trim in no time. And it also represents an amazing wealth-building opportunity. If you get two million of your little ant friends to sell this to just one thousand friends each, why within five years you could own the Himalayas."

"Why would an ant want to own the Himalayas?" said the Sweep. "Why would anyone want to own the Himalayas? The insurance premiums alone would bankrupt a small kingdom. And can you imagine the maintenance headache? Anyway, ants only live about two months. Five years is not going to work for them."

But Iris was interested. "I think the idea of all those little ants doing yoga is quite charming."

Mina was thinking deeply. Here finally was someone smaller than herself. "Little ant, I seldom get the opportunity to talk to your kind, so I want to tell you how I admire you. I've always been impressed at how you ants always seem so purposeful, as though you know exactly where you're going and why."

"Thank you for saying that," said Harvey. "But the truth is, half the time we don't have a clue where we're going. We just act as though we do because it makes us feel important and intimidates our enemies."

Joe had gone to take a drink. He crawled down to a spot where the stream formed a medium-sized pool and sucked up the water with his lips like a horse. His color shifted to a healthy shade of bluish green with silver highlights.

"Oh, how beautiful," cried Iris. "I'd love a dress like that. So Joe, where were you during the conflict?"

"I was just a kid, remember? During the fighting we'd hardly been allowed out. But once it stopped I was able to enjoy a rare day with my friends. We were down by the ocean when one of the mermaids cried out and pointed to the mountain behind me. I heard a roar and turned to see lava pouring down the slopes. Cracks opened up in the distance, swallowing people and horses and buildings. It was awful! What I later learned was that the microvita tree, rather than allow Nefarious to use the dragons to conquer the earth, used its power to destroy itself and Atlantis with it. The mermaids were terrified. They headed for deep water and I flew off to find my mother. As I flew I could see the lava reaching the ocean. There was a terrible hissing sound and huge clouds of steam billowed up. My beautiful home, the island of Atlantis, began to sink into the sea.

"I was crying so hard by then I could barely see but finally I spotted my father and Grandpa Bert beside a collapsed tower. It had fallen on Grandpa's wing and my father was trying to free him. I landed and tried to help but it was no use. His wing was broken. 'You'll have to leave me,' he told us, gasping for breath. 'I was trying to save the eggs. They're in that building. Take them and flee for the mainland.'

"My father had no choice but to do as Grandpa asked; otherwise we would have been destroyed ourselves. He motioned for me to go collect the eggs, but Grandpa asked me to stay so that he could talk to me. I was very fond of my grandfather. He had been my teacher since I was an egg. He had always seemed so wise and strong, I'd never imagined that anything could defeat him. But now his left wing was bent at an odd angle and he grimaced with pain. He blessed me and bade me farewell and I will never forget his last words. 'Joe, today you are the youngest, but in the future you will be the oldest. Then it will be you who will have to save the dragons.'

"My father returned with the eggs and we had to leave my grandpa behind. Once we took off, many humans cried out to us, begging us to save them, but we could not carry both them and eggs. At that moment my father discovered that he was free to choose. In his first act of free will he took the dragon eggs and abandoned the humans and we flew away to safety. But Grandpa Bert, the first dragon, could not follow.

"Eventually we caught up with my mother and made it to the Iberian coast, the longest journey I'd ever flown. When we made land there were many other dragons there along with hypogryffs, flying horses, and other winged creatures, many of them bearing humans to safety."

Joe paused, moved by the memory. His scales now a dark blue.

"What happened then?" said Iris.

Joe took a deep breath. "When the microvita tree was destroyed we were released from the necromancer's power. We understood for the first time how we had been controlled to further human ambitions, especially those of Nefarious. After that we swore an oath that we would never make war on each other again. From then on we hated humans and hunted them, considering them a blight on the world. But above all our anger was directed at Nefarious, who had created us to be his slaves."

"Some of those human survivors must have been our ancestors," said The Sweep. "What happened to Nefarious?"

"I heard that he survived. But he would be ancient now, even for one of his long-lived race. And with the destruction of the tree he lost much of his power. We dragons no longer fear him."

Joe turned yellow and laughed. "I just remembered something that may amuse you all. Another wizard put a curse on Nefarious that forced him to always introduce himself as 'The Evil Wizard, Nefarious, Scourge of Atlantis'."

"That could be very awkward at parties," said Brains.

"It gets better," Joe said, laughing. "If he tries to explain himself, he is compelled to say things like, 'What do I do? Oh, I betray people and manipulate them, guiding them to their own destruction.' Wizard humor."

"Neat spell," said Mina.

We pondered the dragon's story in silence. I watched the stream, quick as silver, amusing itself composing little waltzes and minuets, unconcerned with the turbulent history of men and beasts. The water wove its own magic, singing its tinkling song as the day lengthened, flashing in the sunlight, feeding the slow-thinking trees.

Then the sound of one hand clapping broke the silence. "That's an amazing story," said a sardonic voice. "It would be even more amazing if it were true."

19

THE VAMPIRE'S TALE

We all turned around in surprise to see Parinte Sinistru, the Romanian exorcist, standing on the other side of the stream.

Everyone spoke at once: "What are you doing here?" "What do you mean it's not true?" "Are you calling Joe a liar?" "What's that strange smell?"

The decrepit priest smiled his crooked smile and hunched his hunched back and jerked his head in a spastic manner, as though he did not have complete control over his own body.

"I am not accusing Joe of deliberately lying," he croaked. "I am merely pointing out that though he may believe this version of events, it may not be the *true* story of the fall of Atlantis. His tale was entertaining, to be sure, but where is the proof? All we have is what Dragon Joe remembers of what the older dragons told him nine thousand years ago. *They* may have been lying, making themselves out to be the good guys. Has it occurred to you that perhaps Nefarious used his magic to control the dragons for a very good reason? Hello? Because they're DANGEROUS MONSTERS."

Joe took a breath, about to protest, but hesitated. After all, what the exorcist said was sort of true.

"You creatures of various permutations sit here, fat and full of pancakes, listening like lemmings to a self-confessed mass murderer who but a few weeks ago would have devoured you all without a second thought. He tells you how he and his kind were wronged long ago by the supposedly evil necromancer and the supposedly corrupt Atlanteans, and he justifies his crimes as a war of revenge. But what kind of war was he waging? He's eaten countless innocent princesses, brave warriors, and helpless sheep. They were not the ones who wronged him and his kind."

"Did he just call me a permutation?" muttered Brains. "I don't have to take that from a mere exorcist. I'm a real mayor, you know."

"Peace, badger," said Maurice. "The time for vengeance has not yet come."

"Then suddenly," said Sinistru, "when Joe learns that his cholesterol is a bit too high he conveniently decides to become a vegetarian and promises not to kill anyone, and you embrace him like a long-lost friend. In spite of the fact that he gobbled up the good Duke. Why in the world would you accept his version of events that occurred thousands of years ago? If you're interested, I could tell you the true story of the fall of Atlantis. But maybe you'd rather go on believing this unlikely yarn related by your buddy, the man-eating monster."

"Why should we accept your version?" said Iris. "You weren't there. What's *your* source of information?"

"A fair question," said Sinistru. "There are only two living witnesses to the destruction of Atlantis. You heard the story from Joe. I heard it from the only other remaining survivor, the necromancer, Nefarious."

Everyone gasped.

"You met the necromancer?" asked Iris.

"Indeed I did. And to me he seemed like a far more reliable witness than your dragon friend."

"How come he didn't turn you into a newt?" said Brains.

"Because I am his student. In fact, he taught me how to turn badgers into newts."

Brains shrank away but Harvey pricked up his antennae. "Do you think he might turn me into a newt?" he whispered to Mina in excitement. "That's my life's dream. It's all very well for you mammals with your warm blood, going around suckling your young all over the place, but for me to become a newt would represent an unimaginable evolutionary leap. Just think—no more exoskeleton, replacing these crazy confusing compound eyes with bifocal vision, free at last from this autocratic, rigid social structure—it's more than an ant could hope for."

He tried to catch Sinistru's eye, but the exorcist appeared to be focusing on the mammal demographic.

"I don't see why we should believe you or your wicked necromancer," said Iris. "We don't know anything about you, except that you associate with evil spirits, overcharge for your services, and smell bad." She turned up her nose.

Parinte Sinistru seemed to shrink into his hunch and began to turn away. "If you don't want to hear what I have to say, I'll be on my way. I will tell my tale to those who want to know the truth."

"Wait," said The Sweep. "Iris. I think we should hear him out. He may have information that can help resolve this mystery. I, at least, am more than curious to know the true history of our ancestors."

Iris bristled but before she could reply I interrupted.

"Peace, Iris. The Sweep has a point. Perhaps we should listen to the decrepit hunchback's story. What do you say, Joe?"

Joe seemed to have taken Sinistru's remarks to heart. "Do whatever you want," he growled, looking at the ground, his scales turning grey.

"In the interest of fairness, I think we must hear him out," I said. "Come and join our circle, Parinte Sinistru, and tell us your tale."

"You mean we have to hear the whole story over again?" said Brains.

"If this Sinistru guy doesn't stop jawing soon I'm going to strangle myself to death," whispered the mole. "I can't stand this. First chance to escape I'm out of here on the first vulture."

"Me too." Brains shook himself and tried to stay alert. "Thinking makes me so sleepy."

Sinistru hesitated for a moment, then sprang across the stream, surprisingly agile for one so bent. He took a seat on a fallen log, keeping as far from Joe and Iris as possible.

"The basic story Joe told you is undisputed, of Atlantis and the tree and the empire and its fall. But who conspired to rule, and who was responsible for the eventual catastrophe? That is the question. What I heard was this, that when the Horizonalists and the Verticalists approached Nefarious for support, he refused. He loved his dragons like his children, and he had no faith that the Horizontalist and Verticalist extremists would not put his creations in harm's way. The Horizontalists were insulted and laid siege to his temple, but the necromancer's dragons defended his home and none dared come against them. Then the Horizontalists and

Verticalists denounced one another as traitors. The Horizontalists tried to seize control of the army, but the military leaders' loyalties were divided and the Verticalists declared martial law. Civil war broke out and the island descended into chaos that spread across the empire.

"The necromancer had the power, through his dragons, to determine the outcome of the war, but he was reluctant to get involved. But then a group of dragons conspired with some Atlantean priests to remove the necromancer's spell. They allied themselves with the Horizontalists, and the Verticalist army soon collapsed. Then the Verticalist priests appealed to the necromancer in desperation. Seeing the slaughter of so many innocents, he agreed. His dragons were launched in the Verticalist cause and the Atlanteans' worst nightmare was realized—dragon fighting dragon. That's when the microvita tree, seeing its power abused and helpless to stop it, despaired and destroyed itself and Atlantis along with it."

Parinte Sinistru stopped and looked around at the circle of eyes, eyes that reflected a lot of confusion. Where did the truth lie? Were the Horizontalist rebels and the dragons responsible for the destruction of Atlantis? Or was it the manipulative Verticalists, insisting on their right to rule? Or was it, as Joe claimed, the fault of the necromancer?

We all looked at Joe for a response. "Go on, Joe," urged Iris. "Aren't you going to defend your kind? Tell us it's not true."

But Joe was unwilling to argue. "You've heard my tale," he said sadly, "and I believe it to be accurate. But the Parinte Sinistru creature is correct in saying that I was just a child at the time. It is possible that my parents told me a distorted version of events or omitted vital details. Now you will please excuse me. I need to think."

Joe's scales had turned a dull metallic gray. He turned away, and with a scraping sound of scales dragging over the rocks he crept into his cave.

"What about the surprise he promised?" asked Brains.

"Hush, don't be so insensitive!" said Maurice.

I called Iris aside and whispered to her. "Iris, go after Joe and get him to come back as soon as Parinte Sinistru is gone. We need to talk this over privately."

"I'm on it," she said, slipping away after the dragon.

I turned to Sinistru. "We will consider this new information and decide what to do. Please leave us alone so that we may discuss this in private."

Sinistru bowed. "As you wish. If you have more questions for me, I reside in another cave lower down the valley. The princess knows where to find me."

We watched his decrepit figure lurch away, following the path by the stream that led down into the valley.

"Well," said the mole, "talk about a party pooper! Did you notice that he did not once mention the role of moles in world history? His story was even more depressing than the dragon's. I was really enjoying myself until he came along. Surely we aren't going to accept his slimy word against the word of our nice friend the dragon?"

"I don't like the smell of that exorcist," said Brains the badger. "It may be true that Joe has killed many people in the past, but they were trying to kill him. And he's turned over a new leaf. I say we should accept his repentance."

"First we need to come to a common understanding," said the Duke. "I mean we've only just come together as though by accident. This story concerns the ancient history of my family, but apart from that I don't see how solving this riddle is going to help with our practical problems? For instance, how is it going to help with the infernal plague of garlic salesmen who keep bothering me at my castle?"

"I think there is a lot more at stake here than we realize," I said, wondering if the Duke had recovered from those bumps on the head, but I was not quite ready to tell my own story.

"What are you getting at?" said the Duke.

I was spared having to reply by the Sweep's interruption. "I've known Joe longer than any of you, and I'm inclined to trust him. The exorcist does not exactly have the most endearing personality or confidence-inspiring demeanor, you know. But I think we have to give this matter careful consideration. In one point Parinte Sinistru is correct. Joe was a young dragon at the time of the fall of Atlantis. Even Joe accepts that. For all we know he is just repeating what he was told by the older dragons. Naturally they would see things from their own point of view, and they may have fed their younglings a colored view of events."

"Good point, Sweep," said the Duke. "Perhaps we should reserve judgment on the matter."

"What about you, Sir Dogalogue?" said Iris.

"Well, I like Joe too, but I do think that the undeniably slimy Parinte Sinistru showed great courage in coming forward and challenging the dragon's story, while admitting that he is a disciple of the necromancer. Why would he take such a risk? What does he have to gain from it? I am inclined to believe Joe's story, but I'm mindful of The Sweep's points. I think we should call Joe back and tell him that although the past is unclear, he was obviously not involved since he was a child, and that we trust that he will do as he has promised. We'll see where that takes us."

We all agreed and settled down to wait for Iris to return with Joe.

"I still don't understand what in the world garlic salesmen have to do with anything," grumbled Brains.

I Will War No More Forever

Dragon Joe lay alone in his cave, his head resting on his paws. Since dragons cannot sit in the lotus posture, this is their favorite meditation pose. Immersed in his contemplation of the unchanging truth of the universe, he didn't notice a slight figure entering the chamber and taking a seat next to him.

Iris watched Joe as he gradually changed color from greyish green through aquamarine to cobalt blue. The longer he sat, the brighter the blue became until gold flecks began to appear, a dazzling mixture of gold and a rich azure that Iris had not seen before.

Finally, Joe stretched and open his eyes. "Ah, little princess. Were you meditating with me?"

"Not really," said Iris. "I was just watching you change color. You look much happier now."

"I was reconnecting with my inner dragon nature. It calms me and gives me clarity when I need to make important decisions."

The princess climbed onto his paw. "What decisions?"

"Most of my life I believed that eradicating humans was a form of community service and I was proud of how good at it I was. But if Sinistru is right, my original motive was based on a lie. It seems I may never know whether or not the adult dragons were telling the truth. Maybe some of them really were trying to seize power in Atlantis. Nevertheless, that was all so long ago I'm not sure how much it really matters. I am who I am now, and I need to make my decisions based on the present, not some ancient tragedy I can't change. And right now I'm feeling pretty good about my new lifestyle. I think I'm on the right path to becoming a better dragon."

Iris kissed him on the paw. "You're so wise, Joe. I think I could learn a lot just listening to you. Of course, you really ought to be wise at your age. It would be pretty embarrassing if after nine thousand years contemplating the meaning of existence, you couldn't come up with anything more original than stealing treasure and eating princesses."

The dragon chuckled. "Good point. I'll use that in my next debate with the other dragons. I'm going to have my work cut out for me explaining my new world view to that lot. Anyway, I intend to give a good part of my treasure away. I don't want to go to extremes. I might regret that. But I really don't need most of it, so what's the harm in giving away a few cartloads to people who need it more than me?"

"That sounds like a wonderful idea," said Iris. "Joe?"

"Yes, child."

"I'm sorry I was so angry at you earlier. I was actually upset with my uncle, too. You can't imagine how it feels, being married off for political convenience. And just when I was feeling free for the first time in my life, Uncle Honk had to go and spoil it. As soon as my mother gets his letter telling her that I'm alive after all, she will start looking for another ogre for me to marry. My life will be ruined."

"I thought your plan to fake your own death was really quite ingenious," Joe said. "It's a real pity your uncle had to go and spoil it. Would it help if I were to eat him again?"

Iris hesitated for a moment and then shook her head. "No, you'd better not, but you are a dear for offering." She hugged his paw. "If I can't find someone else to marry before my mother tracks me down, I'll just have to get my own ogre suit so that I'll be well matched with my husband."

"If he treats you badly, I don't care who he is, I really will eat him."

"Joe, I'm beginning to wonder just how serious you are about giving up eating people."

"I wouldn't have to swallow him. I could just chew him up a bit and spit him out."

Iris giggled. In spite of herself she was beginning to appreciate dragon humor.

When Joe and Iris rejoined their companions the dragon was a deep orange color that went very well with the spring greenery.

"Joe has an announcement to make," declared the princess in what she liked to think of as her most dignified regal voice but which her brother called her 'bossy voice.'

Now that the sun had shifted behind the hills, the heat was gone. Half the glade was in shadow. The Duke had been giving me a lesson in swordplay while we waited and the motes were carving their names on a rock face in the hope of being remembered by future generations. But when Joe reappeared we quickly gathered around to see what he had to say.

Joe seemed calm. I thought he must have made peace with his inner demons, which I imagine is easier for dragons than for most of us since the demons were surely terrified of him and therefore more than willing to agree to whatever terms he proposed, such as, "bother me again and you're toast."

"You know," said the dragon, gazing into the distance as though recalling some ancient memory. "I've been thinking a lot about my life and I can't help wondering if it hasn't all been a bit of a waste of time. I mean what have I achieved? OK, I have a mountain of treasure, I've laid a dozen empires to ruin, and I've lost count of the kings I've devoured, but have I really made the world a better place? I haven't noticed any marked improvement. Have any of you?"

Everyone shook their heads dutifully except for me. I could not reasonably be expected to offer an opinion, having just arrived on the planet. But according to all reports, progress was slow at best.

"Even before I gave up eating people I was beginning to feel that something was missing in my life. I've slain thousands of obnoxious humans but today there are more of them than ever. And they're better armed. Did you know we have a team of one hundred dragons answering calls 'round the clock to exterminate troublesome knights, and we can't keep up with the demand?"

"I know what you mean," said Brains. "We have a cockroach infestation in our den. No matter how many we gobble up, there seem to be more than ever. And now some of them are carrying Bibles."

The dragon frowned and the badger shrank back into a nook between two rocks from where he blurted out, "Uh, but of course that has absolutely no relevance to your story. Please do go on. It is most instructive."

"Indeed," said Joe with a sigh. "Take a look at my to-do list for a typical day: 1. Find and toast one Christian knight spotted near the edge of the forest. He is wandering about boasting to anyone who will listen that he killed you already. 2. Fly three hundred miles north and dispose of a king and his small army who has sworn to destroy all dragons. 3. Check on a report of two escaped knights hassling a lizard colony in Dorcester. And all of that is supposed to happen before noon, at which point I check in for my afternoon assignments. When am I supposed to practice the piano?"

Brains whispered to Maurice. "He plays the piano? I thought he was a singer."

"I heard that he ate his piano teacher and it's been a bit of a sensitive subject ever since," said Maurice. "He also ate the piano."

"Most of you," said Joe, "have very brief lives. I thought to end war by destroying warlike humans, but today there are more wars than ever. And despite its magnificence, my treasure has brought me no lasting satisfaction."

The dragon raised himself up and turned a deep dazzling golden color. In a solemn voice he declared, "Though the history of my race be clouded in mystery, of one thing I am now certain: I will war no more forever."

Gathered in that little vale, acknowledging this auspicious declaration, we all bowed our heads. Even the mole felt the moment too sacred for jest. The breeze dropped and the golden birch leaves overhead hung still, as though holding their breath. The stream alone kept up its soft tinkling, oblivious to the tides of history.

Now that the oldest of the dragons had renounced war forever, I wondered what would become of his ancient kind. From my studies of other planets and their evolving civilizations, I knew the way of it all too well. Whether the monsters attacked humans or not, a time would come when the humans, with their deadly opposable thumbs, would invent terrible weapons capable of destroying the dragons. I suddenly became aware that Joe was watching me thoughtfully. His color had shifted to a lighter gold and a strange light burned in his eyes but he said nothing.

The Duke drew a deep breath. "Noble words, O dragon. Surely now the time has come to make peace between our races. The great wrong my people did to yours was long ago. The bones of the perpetrators have moldered into dust and five hundred generations of my people have come and gone. You are long lived, with long memory, but if you can forgive and make peace, then surely others can, too. As you have pledged yourself to peace between our kinds, so do I pledge myself to do all I can to bring a lasting peace between our species."

"I, too, am deeply touched by your auspicious declaration," said The Sweep. "So much so that I would like to offer to clip your hedge."

"How kind," said the dragon. "But I must warn you, the lands to which I lay claim are quite extensive. They include hundreds of miles of hedges. But I'd be grateful if you just clip my favorite hedge. Its name is Pedro, and even though I am now a vegetarian, I will never eat it."

Suddenly The Sweep bounced. "I have a win-win idea." he said excitedly. "Why don't you set up a dragon wellness clinic and convince all the dragons to become vegetarians and give up eating people? If dragons are no longer dangerous, then people will stop hunting and fighting with them."

"Hey, that almost qualifies as a cunning plan," said the badger.

"Except that it's not very cunning," said the mole. "Just because you don't eat people doesn't mean they won't kill you. Look at elephants. Elephants don't eat people but humans hunt and kill elephants."

"The dirt eater has a point," said the dragon. "Now perhaps you're beginning to understand why we dragons decided to hunt and kill people in the first place. But I think The Sweep's idea still has some merit."

"So now is it time for the dragon to give us our surprise?" said Mina. "Maybe it's some cheese. I could really use some cheese."

The dragon smiled at Mina. "Yes, little mouse, now is the time for your surprise." He looked around at us all. "A wonderful surprise that I have for all of you."

Brains nudged Maurice with an eager grin. They both loved surprises, so long as they did not have too many teeth.

Joe raised himself and started downstream along the path. He glanced over his shoulder with a grin. "Well?" he said. "Aren't you coming?"

Miranda furrowed her brow. "Your dragon friend seems very philosophical. I never thought a reptile would have such a rich contemplative life."

"Do not think of Joe as a mere reptile," said Dr. Dogalogue. "Dragons were created with the energy of the microvita tree. They have powers we still do not fully understand. As for his being unusually thoughtful, at that point in his life he had a lot to think about. He was going through some enormous changes. He'd just become vegetarian, he'd befriended his lifelong enemies, and he was wondering if the Cavern of Stones had been interfering with his free will. Plus, since he'd just given up his main form of entertainment—eating Christians—he didn't know what to do with himself. What was he supposed to do on weekends?"

"You mean once he'd sworn off eating Christians, he needed a new hobby?"

"Exactly."

Miranda thought for a moment and then said brightly, "Why didn't you suggest that he take up collecting foreign stamps?"

The Cavern of the Sales Pests

The dragon, with Iris walking by his side, led us down the path beside the stream. The dust motes floated in the air by Joe's head like tiny beacons, trying to look important. The Sweep and his uncle came next, followed by the mole and the badger. I brought up the rear. Mottled shadows played on our faces as the sunlight filtered through the gently dancing leaves. The dragon's frequent passage had worn the path as wide as a road. An outcrop of smooth rocks appeared on our left, and there, sunning themselves as though they owned the place, a crowd of lizards lay about like a tiny dragon's brood, soaking up the warmth, paralyzed with pleasure. I gazed about as we walked, drinking in new discoveries with each step. To my alien eyes everything still seemed so new.

After hearing the Atlantis story, I finally understood that the quest my master had sent me on was not going to be a relaxing holiday. This microvita tree business was a much bigger deal than I'd thought at first, and finding the seed was beginning to look really hard. First I had to find the map in the Cave of Stones. That should be doable, with a bit of help from the mole or Mina. But the next part looked tricky. The dragon had hinted that there were powerful forces ranged against us who also wanted the seed. I was bound to come up against them at some point and I didn't like my chances against a giant sea monster or a wicked enchanter. The dragon turning out to be vegetarian was a huge stroke of luck, but I couldn't count on being that lucky twice. And how in the world was I supposed to locate a single seed on the bottom of the ocean, even with a really good map?

I wondered if my master would mind very much if we returned and said that we really tried, but we couldn't find the microvita seed and would he like in its place a nice collection of other seeds from unique earth species. But I knew the answer to that. My master was always saying stuff like, "Failure is not an option," and he meant it. He'd probably banish me to the unpopular planet Sand Food, where the most sought-after cuisine was concrete flake ice cream.

We passed a sign reading, "*This way to Dragon Joe's Treasure,*" depicting a pile of jewels and an arrow pointing down the path.

"Hey Joe," called The Sweep. "You've got a pretty funny idea of security, advertising your treasure cave like that."

"It's not a problem," Joe chuckled without turning his head. "No one dares try to steal it. They're afraid I'll eat them."

The path curved to the right around the grassy hill where I'd first seen Joe and came to a cave with a large sign on the wall: *Dragon Joe's Treasure Cave. Souvenirs and refreshments available. No fishing in the lake.*

A vole stood at the entrance behind a counter marked *Entrance Fee: One Copper Farthing*. When it saw the dragon, it bowed and greeted us. Joe glanced at the sundial by the entrance and halted abruptly. "Oh," he exclaimed. "Is that the time? I forgot about my music and poetry lessons. I have to go. I don't want to be late. Listen, why don't you all explore the cave complex and I'll meet you here in three hours. My motes can guide you. You'll find plenty of entertainment inside. And if you're hungry I recommend the artificial treasure nuggets."

The dragon hurried off down the path, leaving us guests a little bewildered. "What's three hours?" said Brains.

"Search me. I don't even know what *one* hour is," said Maurice.

"I like the sounds of those treasure nuggets," said The Sweep. "I'm feeling a bit peckish."

The motes happily stepped into their role as hosts and led our little company through the cave entrance.

As I crossed the threshold I sensed a presence, as of some entity lurking nearby, waiting for me. With a growing sense of foreboding I followed the others beneath the archway into the darkness, through a broad tunnel that abruptly opened out into a great cavern. When I emerged from the tunnel everyone was staring upward. My eyes followed their gaze and I saw why. Above us, thousands of blue lights adorned the rocky ceiling, forming unfamiliar constellations.

"They're so beautiful, like stars," Iris whispered, as though reluctant to disturb something sacred. "But what are they?"

"They're glowworms", said the mole. "The lights lure small insects. Some get caught on a sticky thread and the worm devours them."

I wished he hadn't told us that. I know that beauty can be deceptive, but sometimes I prefer to be deceived. The pretty blue lights now seemed cold and ruthless.

The luminescent walls shone faintly, illuminating a dangerous-looking spiral stairway that climbed upward and disappeared into darkness.

"That's the route we took back from the treasure cave to the dragon's home where we met you," said the badger. "We didn't realize there was an easier way out. Be thankful you don't have to climb up all those steps carrying a heavy sack full of treasure."

"I thought Maurice carried the treasure," I said.

"He did," said Brains. "But I carried Maurice."

A faint echo of dripping water reached our ears. It was coming from somewhere up ahead, perhaps from the lake mentioned in the sign.

We passed the foot of the spiral stairway and entered a maze of spectacular natural architecture. Pillars of limestone, fused stalactites and stalagmites, formed flying buttresses that leapt from floor to ceiling. The flowering stone cast shadows like wings, as though the rock had been frozen in a spell. We had entered a living mineral world where love-struck stalagmites awaited their lovers' touch, reaching upward through the years with a yearning only matched by that of their beloved stalactites reaching ever-downward. Drip by dream-filled drip the two fingers of stone approached one another in a slow-motion dance whose steps were measured like the movements of the stars.

It reminded me of my childhood on Zondgraz with my brothers and sisters when we used to play by the seashore, dripping wet sand carefully through our tentacles, building fabulous structures, pillars and spires, bridges and castles, that were all too soon washed away by the tide. But the limestone structures in this cavern were built to last, one drop at a time, with the patience of stone.

We advanced deeper toward the mountain's heart and found ourselves in an eerie world of half-seen crystals, looming slabs of stone, and fantastic shapes rearing up in the faint light. We crept on past sleeping cliff faces, towering structures of ancient quartz, always aware of the huge weight of rock hanging above our heads, separating us from the world of greenery and light. Who knew what ancient secrets slept here in the darkness, what forgotten mysteries, what lost treasures? Here, in the depths of the dragon's great lair there was no wind, no laughter, no friendly voice. Only silence and the slowly growing rocks.

"Pssst. Want to buy a replica stalactite?" I looked down in surprise to see a beaver carrying a tray of souvenirs. "Clay glowworms, bottled lake water with miraculous healing properties. Cures wooden legs," the rodent said, rattling off his list of wares.

"Really?" I was intrigued. "That sounds handy. How much for a bottle of that lake water?"

Mina poked her head out of my pocket and addressed the beaver. "Go away and leave us alone, sales pest. We are on an important mission. We have an appointment with the dragon."

"Of course," said the beaver smoothly. "I understand completely. But this will only take a moment." He turned to me again, "Only one silver coin and I'll throw in a free vulture ride." The sales creature frisked about, unable to contain its enthusiasm at the mere thought.

"It really does sound worth it," I said to Mina.

She ignored me and addressed the beaver again. "Get lost, varmint. We're busy."

Undeterred, the beaver approached Brains. "How about you, sir? You look like the adventurous type. Wouldn't you enjoy a scenic flight around the cave on the back of a vulture?"

"First, there aren't any vultures in England," said the badger. "And second, if there were, I would like a ride on one only slightly less than I'd like a strange dog to pee in my suitcase."

This all seemed quite harmless, if a little commercial, yet I still felt uneasy. There was something weird about this place. Beyond the fact that it was completely weird already. Something weird and scary. The feeling of an unknown presence was growing stronger.

Up ahead The Sweep was bargaining hard with a sales pest. He came away with an extra-large bottle of lake water and a giant pizza.

"How much would you expect to pay?" The Sweep declared proudly.

"I haven't the faintest idea," I said. I was quite certain about this, as I was still trying to get my head around the concept of money.

"I offered to clip her hedge and she was so happy she said I could have as much pizza as I could eat at her shop for an entire year."

"Poor woman," cried Iris. "Little did she know that she was talking to the All-Europe Pizza Eating Champion of 1337."

"What are we supposed to do while we wait to see the treasure?" growled the badger. "It's getting late, and I'm hungry too, and badgers don't eat pizza."

The vole reappeared like magic. "As I was saying before SOMEBODY"—she glared at the badger "fobbed me off: cave refreshments; chocolate stalagmites, candied glowworms, magic stalactite drops, lake juice, assorted artificial treasure nuggets: only a farthing a bag."

"Oh all right," grunted the badger. "I'll take a bag of those nuggets."

An orange dog appeared, carrying a tray of souvenirs. He approached the princess. "How about you, fair lady? Wouldn't you like a little model of Atlantis as a present for someone special? Perhaps you have a secret sweetheart who would appreciate such a gift." The creature lolled its tongue cheerfully.

The dog could hardly have chosen a more provocative sales line. "Even if I did have a secret sweetheart," snapped Iris, "I'd hardly be likely to tell a talking mongrel!" She turned away. The poor animal looked a little hurt. After all, it was just trying to make a living.

The vole had more arrows in her quiver. She approached The Sweep, who by his dress was clearly a hermit with disposable income. "How about this special rare item, sir? Genuine microvita tree seeds, fresh from the ruins of Atlantis. And I'll throw in a free toy dragon. Only five copper pieces."

This certainly got my attention. I grabbed the vole by the shoulder. "What are you talking about? Where did you get those seeds?"

The vole looked abashed. "No need to get so excited, sir. I won't lie to you. They're not really microvita tree seeds. But they will grow into fine silver birch trees if tended properly. By which time I will be long dead of old age, so it remains a solid business plan."

I was disappointed to hear this, but Iris wanted to know more. "How come you know so much about Atlantis?"

"You don't know? This whole county was an Atlantean outpost. Legend has it that there is a cave around here permeated with the energy of the microvita tree. That's how come we animals here can talk. In the deep caverns there are even rocks that can talk. Unfortunately they never have anything interesting to say, so it's not really much use."

"That's right," said the orange dog. "I keep meeting people who claim they're from Atlantis, which is very annoying because I really *am* from Atlantis myself, and I know they're mostly fakes."

"What do you mean you're from Atlantis?" said Iris. "Are you some kind of underwater dog?"

"Not generally, no. It's my ancestors. They were the official hounds of the Atlantean king."

"You're from Atlantis?" said the vole. "Me too! Which temple did your ancestor attend?"

A lonely worm perked up in excitement. "Well, what do you know? Another Atlantean. I myself am descended from a long line of Atlantean Druids!"

"Druids! Pah!" spat the beaver. "Druids are trouble, they are, casting evil spells and bothering nature spirits. Don't talk to me about Druids."

"They were very inoffensive Druids," the worm said, saddened that her attempt at gaining acceptance in this elite social circle was foundering so quickly.

A portly fox with a thick Welsh accent waddled up. "Atlantean Tarot Cards. Predict your future. Curse your enemies. Beef up your Druidic charms with a dose of microvita energy. Bargain prices. Or why not gaze into this Atlantean crystal ball and peer into another world? Or try this amazing Atlantean amulet guaranteed to bring success in matters of business and love? And check out this top quality Atlantean sword, guaranteed to never rust."

"Atlantean peanut butter," whispered the worm, intimidated by the fox, but anxious to sell something so it could feed its family. But amid the din nobody even heard.

"Let me have a look at that sword," said the Badger. "Here, see this!" He pulled the sword out of its scabbard and showed it to us all. "Of course it won't rust - it's made of wood! And I'll bet my last whisker it's not from Atlantis!"

I edged away from the invasion of sales pests. "Sir Dogalogue," said Mina. "Can we get away from here? I'm fed up with people claiming they are from Atlantis. So far as I am concerned, they are all phonies."

The orange dog approached me and said, "If you want to find the treasure, you'll be needing a guide."

"The badger is our guide," I said.

"You can't be serious. No self-respecting knight would keep a badger as a guide. Especially one—and I hope you'll forgive me saying this—who could not find his way out of a paper bag. You are worthy of someone more fitted to your high station. What you need is a deluxe guide. I offer a lifetime money-back guarantee, entertaining anecdotes about badgers and moles, and lectures on the history of this cave in fourteen languages. All for only one silver piece!" He ended with a flourish.

"Furthermore," said the dog, "I am orange."

I saw that the badger had finished the bag of nuggets and was asleep at the foot of a forlorn-looking stalagmite. That didn't inspire much confidence. I decided to go with the dog. After all, it was orange.

"Very well, I'll hire you for one silver piece," I said. "But no lecture. I need to think. And just one language." A sudden hope came to mind. "You don't speak Zondgrazian do you?" A yearning welled in my heart to hear my own tongue spoken by a living creature.

"Sorry, no. I can do Welsh..."

I demurred and followed the dog along a curving line of dark stone that outlined where the lake met the water. Thousands of glowworms gazed down at their own images reflected on the flawless surface. We passed seven oriental tourists sitting on the rocks before easels, painting the scene. They nodded to us and smiled politely.

The next sign read: *Dragon's Treasure this Way. Wheelchair Accessible. No Free Samples.* A little further on we found a pleasant spot to relax and have a nibble while we waited for the dragon. I lay back, resting my head on my folded cloak, and reflected on our situation. Why would an orange dog want to speak to me in Welsh? It seemed very odd. Wasn't Welsh the preferred language of dragons? Or was that Welsh people? I was unsure. I needed more information about this planet. I didn't even know the whereabouts of the nearest decent vegetarian restaurant. Perhaps my new guide dog would know.

One by one my companions dozed off. But I was restless and could not shake my sense of mounting unease. This place felt unfriendly to warm-blooded creatures. It was too quiet. In the silence I became aware of the presence of skeletons from ages past, undisturbed by any but the very deepest roots, probing the darkness so slowly they could crack stone.

The blue lights of the glowworms high above watched the still water like scattered stars. A drop fell and struck the lake with a ping that echoed and faded. The tranquil surface became a pallet of widening rings, the reflected lights rising and falling as the ripples passed. Gradually the water returned to stillness and the silence swallowed our little company as we waited in the silver-lined darkness.

The Mother of all Treasures

"Wake up, wake up," cried Fluff in excitement.

We all sat up.

"Dragon Joe is waiting for you at the Treasure Cave. Follow us."

Fluff and Trond led us around the edge of the lake and into a wide-mouthed tunnel. Along the way we passed a series of notices:

This way to priceless dragon hoard.

Come and help yourself to Dragon Joe's wealth. Everyone else does.

Just kidding. Thieves, please bring your own coffin.

And finally above an elaborate stone archway, etched into the cave wall:

Welcome to Dragon Joe's Treasure Cave. No smoking. No consumption of food or beverages. Don't even think about pocketing anything from this hoard. Thieves will be tracked down by Dragon Joe personally and burned to a crisp. Have a nice day.

"Well that's pretty clear then," said The Sweep. We looked about for Joe but he was nowhere in sight.

"Do you think we are allowed in?" said Brains.

Iris was impatient. "I think Joe has made us wait quite long enough. I'm not standing around here."

She turned and marched under the archway and we followed. The entrance was designed to impress. Carved stone gargoyles stared down at us with malicious grins. The tunnel dwarfed us as we tiptoed forward into the gloom. Breathless with anticipation, our nerves on edge, we stumbled on, but we did not have to go far. After a couple of turns we saw light ahead. Rounding a corner we entered a huge cavern.

The treasure chamber was more brightly lit than seemed likely. Clusters of glowworms, strategically positioned, cast a bluish light.

Walls of phosphorescent stone lent a shimmering ambience, and daylight lanced down from a shaft cut high into the rock, reflecting through quartz crystal windows, artfully placed to display the shining hoard to optimal effect.

None who entered that chamber could be unmoved by the sight, for this was no ordinary treasure. Here lay the accumulated wealth of Joe, the Most Fearsome Dragon in the Universe, dreaded above all of the winged beasts of Atlantis, devourer of kings, conqueror of empires, slayer of all who dared bear arms against him, top monster of the ancient world. Before us lay the fruits of his reign spanning nine thousand years.

Gold coins spilled carelessly from shelves and ornate chests. Racks displayed the crowns and scepters of forgotten kings in ordered rows and sets. Necklaces festooned the walls that had once adorned the lovely necks of princesses whose beauty had long since melted into the earth. There hung amulets and rings, bracelets and broaches glittering from the shadows, each with its own story of loyalty or betrayal, defiance and courage, attachment, love, and loss. Precious goblets and golden plates from the banquet tables of emperors now dust lay strewn about. Coats of cunningly crafted armor inlaid with swirling patterns and magical devices to protect the bearer displayed emblems that proclaimed the glory of forgotten realms. Yet no matter how sharp the sword or how mighty the arm that bore it, no matter how cleverly wrought the armor or how potent the spell that protected its wearer, none had prevailed against the power of the dragon.

Caskets of precious stones lay open so that the many-colored faceted gems spilled out and shone with their own light. Strewn about as though in contempt of the kingdoms of men and their fleeting dynasties were piles of bloody rubies, smaragds and sapphires, priceless diamonds and gold—gold, everywhere, malleable, incorruptible gold, lovingly beaten and crafted with clever fingers into a thousand forms: antlers and leaves, floating birds, entwined lovers, flowers and angels, crucifixes and hoary occult symbols, flowing streams and branching trees bearing the faces of goddesses.

The reactions written on the faces of my companions ranged from shock to rapture, and even I, of alien mind and body, was not altogether immune to the treasure's spell. We stood for a long time, drinking in the beauty and power that all this wealth represented. And whichever way we looked, there was more.

Finally a shadow fell across the floor and we heard the tread of heavy feet. Our enchantment shattered, we looked up at Dragon Joe, mounted on a high step, staring down at us amid his priceless treasure. One great taloned foot rested on a small hill of gold coins that gleamed in the soft light. But rather than pride, there was a somber expression on his face. We waited for Joe to speak.

"When you look on this treasure," the dragon said, "you do not see what I see. Over there is a sword decorated by the finest craftsmen with gold filigree and precious gems embedded in its hilt, but where you see beauty I see war. You see a gorgeous crown. I see the brave king who died wearing it. In the past I didn't care for humans. To me they were a blight on the world but now they are my friends. Now when I look on all this wealth, I wonder what it is really worth."

Joe took a great breath, as though bracing himself for something he was unsure of. Then his face turned a pale gold. "But that is all in the past. I cannot bring back the dead, and I cannot rebuild what is destroyed. But I am no longer ruled by hatred and greed. This treasure no longer has any power over me. My new delight will be to give it away."

This was the moment we'd been waiting for. We looked at one another, waiting for someone to say something. The Sweep took the floor. After all, he was a real prince.

"Dragon Joe, the day we met, you chose to forgo your breakfast rather than eat me. It was a moment I will not forget and, it seems, it was a significant turning point for you. You have revealed a previously unknown side of dragon nature. The noble side. The generous, kind side. I name you the greatest dragon of our era, not because of your strength and power, but because you alone have willingly turned your back on the path of death and are ready to make amends. That day when you spared my life, and ceased eating not only humans, but all creatures, I knew then that I was in the presence of greatness. Today you have gone even further and given up that which you have held most dear. You stand as a shining beacon, an example for all dragonkind."

We all clapped and Joe turned pale pink, which, when mixed with the light gold, made him look like a very large piece of expensive girl's jewelry.

Iris ran up to Joe and reached up to embrace him. A few tears and several kisses later, Joe turned to us and smiled. "And now the part you've been looking forward to. Your surprise. I want to begin by giving each one of you, my first non-dragon friends, a gift. You may each select one item from the hoard to keep as your own."

Everyone started thanking Joe and talking excitedly, looking around and discussing with one another what they should pick.

"Come along, don't be shy. Feel free to explore and choose carefully. There's no hurry." Joe appeared to be enjoying himself immensely.

And so we all started clambering about in the treasure room, seeking some special item that spoke to us. It was the mother of all treasure hunts. As for myself, I already had what I wanted. The stolen amulet with my master's emblem was mine, so I just watched the others. While I could sense that the treasure held sway over the minds of my friends, I was bemused by their intense reaction. I couldn't quite see why it was such a huge deal. Some of it was beautiful, and some of the design and craftsmanship was exquisite, but much of it looked fairly ordinary to me. But one item did catch my interest. Toward the back of the cave, in a small out-of-the-way alcove, stood a magnificent golden harp. I sensed its powerful magic and greatly desired to hear its voice. I tried to speak to it with my mind, but it seemed shy. I saw that Iris had noticed it, too, and was making her way toward it.

Meanwhile, the others were choosing their gifts. The Duke was torn between a magnificent sword and a fine crown. In the end he picked the sword, saying that he felt that having a crown, even if he didn't wear it, was a bit above his station.

Fluff held up a tiny necklace of fine wrought silver, studded with sapphires that glittered in the darkness. "This will make me look so beautiful," she twittered.

"Why do you want that, you foolish kid," Trond scolded his sister. "It's hardly worth anything. Go for diamonds, rubies—big, flawless ones. And never pick silver instead of gold! Have you no sense? I should have left you at home. Girls are never practical!"

Iris glared at him but resisted responding. I think she did not want to spoil the mood. "Come here, little Fluff," she said. "I'll help you choose. We princesses know a fair bit about jewelry."

Mina had been running around the pile of treasure but came back to me empty-pawed. "I didn't see anything I wanted," she said. "There was no cheese and no nuts."

"Ah, Mina, you're such a sensible little mouse. How about we let the Duke choose something for you, and if you ever need any money he can give it to you. He's very honest and he understands how to manage such things."

"OK," said Mina. She nibbled happily on a nut from the bag I'd bought for her from the vole sales pest. She deserved it.

With Iris's guidance Fluff stood up to her brother and chose a silver-colored necklace, though I did notice that she switched the sapphires for diamonds, and I had a suspicion that it was not silver but white gold. Not such a dumb kid after all. Her brother, ever practical, chose a valuable crown set with rubies and diamonds. He was clearly planning on cashing in.

Amazingly enough, The Sweep had come across a pair of golden hedge clippers and was quite taken with them. Maurice chose a gorgeous emerald necklace for his mole sweetheart.

Brains approached Joe timidly. "Er, Sir, I mean, Dragon Joe."

"Yes?" said the dragon who, from his radiant rose and gold color, was obviously in the finest of moods. His new role as benefactor seemed to suit him.

"I've got a bit of a problem. I had a spot of bad luck in a bet and now owe rather a lot of money to someone. I need to appease a particularly vicious pack of lemurs."

"Really. What were you betting on?" Joe enjoyed games of chance.

"Er, nothing important, that is to say, nothing so important as to command the attention of someone as important as you."

Joe, by no means a stupid dragon, understood that the badger didn't want to disclose the nature of the bet, which of course made him even more curious. "Well, if you won't tell me the details, I don't see how I can help you."

"Very well," Brains said, looking embarrassed. "We were betting on the outcome of the fight between you and Sir Dogalogue." He glanced at me, then proceeded to tell the story of their betting shop and the disastrous outcome.

Joe laughed loud and heartily. Everyone turned in surprise as the monster guffawed as though freeing himself from all the cares of the past few weeks, his huge body shaking with mirth.

When the dragon recovered his composure, Brains continued, "Er, so I need something of value that would satisfy a family of two dozen lemurs. Which means I'd have to give my present away, which would leave nothing for me." He looked about as pathetic as a badger can look.

"So you're saying you want an extra gift," said Joe. Brains nodded in shame. "In my former life I would have simply offered to toast the lemurs for you, but that would hardly be fitting, given my new resolution. So I'll tell you what, badger. Your story of your betting shop made me laugh more than I have in years. How about I engage you as my official jester. I will give you an advance on your salary and with that you can satisfy the lemur clan and put something aside for your retirement at the same time."

Brains was overcome. "Thank you, Joe, for your great kindness. It's not often that anyone helps me when I'm in trouble. Being mayor and all, people are always coming to me for help, but it seldom goes the other way. You have a good heart, Dragon Joe. I won't forget it."

"Just don't forget that you're my jester. You have to make me laugh at least once a day. Otherwise I will dock your salary."

Brains went for value and selected two magnificent crowns. Way nicer than those dastardly lemurs deserved, in my opinion.

We all showed one another our choices and Joe gracefully granted the gifts. When I showed him the amulet there was a twinkle in the monster's eye but he said nothing.

I felt something move at my hip. I looked down and found my sword jiggling in its scabbard. I quietly slid the weapon halfway out.

"What is it?" I hissed. I didn't think it would be polite to wave a sword about after Joe's pacifist-style speech.

"Ahem," said the sword and paused in a pregnant manner. I'd never seen Excalibur at a loss for words before. Then I understood. "You want a present, too? Is that it?"

"Well," said the sword, "one doesn't wish to presume, but one might be forgiven for hoping that one's past service deserves a small token of appreciation, and the fact that some may take the view that one is somewhat inorganic, and therefore unqualified for a reward that hitherto has been bestowed only upon the living might be overlooked, especially in light of the fact that there is a precedent, notably the case of these two dust motes, who barely qualify as living beings either."

"So you're saying you want a present?"

"If one were pressed one might agree to accept a modest gift," said Excalibur with a pleading look.

"OK, I'll ask the dragon, but first I need your promise that I'll have no more nonsense from you. No more refusing to come out of your scabbard when I need you, sleeping on the job, and so forth."

The sword hung its head. "I'm sorry, Master, it won't happen again."

Joe frowned when I asked him. "Your sword? Isn't that the same vorpal blade you threatened me with only yesterday?"

"Yes, but he was only doing his duty. He's had a change of heart. He was deeply moved by your speech," I lied. "I thought you'd understand."

Joe nodded ruefully. Changes of heart were something he understood very well right then. "Of course. Now what kind of gift could a sword use?"

"I think he wants one of those lovely jeweled scabbards."

So Excalibur became the proud owner and occupant of a beautiful emerald-studded scabbard. He looked extremely pleased.

Only Iris had yet to declare her choice. When Joe saw her resting her hand on the golden harp, he frowned. "My princess, that is a dangerous choice. None have dared to play this instrument for an age, for it is a magical harp under a powerful spell. Allow me to read you the warning I inscribed upon it:

> Who plays me right
> Will see the light,
> Who plays me wrong
> Will be impaled on a prong,
> Sorry about this pathetic song."

The Sweep bounced in alarm. "That was a really horrible poem," he muttered. "There are too many syllables in the fourth line, which completely spoils the rhythm. The choice of words is infantile, and the message is vague and silly. I deem it worthy of consideration for the worst poem ever penned by a giant reptile."

Joe coughed self-consciously. "Please forgive my clumsy verse but do heed the warning. But if by some chance you do fancy my poetry, I have collected my works in a small book that you may purchase from the vole by the cave entrance. To be truthful, I must admit that I have only sold three copies in the last four thousand years. I've written a lot of poems, an entire cave full in fact, and none of them have rotted even after all these years. The mold spores and silverfish are so offended by my syntax they won't even eat the paper. My poetry books remain perfectly preserved like a monument, mocking me for all eternity." He grinned sadly.

"I say, Iris," said Maurice softly. "I think this dragon friend of yours has problems."

"He's going through a personal crisis," said Iris. "He's not normally like this."

"What he needs is a nice hobby," said the mole.

"He had one before," said Brains. "You know, killing people and stealing their treasure. But now he doesn't want to do that anymore."

"Why doesn't he collect cheese?" said Mina. "That would be a good hobby for a dragon."

"Or worms," said Maurice.

"Or dead beetles from exotic lands," said Brains.

"I'd rather not be the one to suggest to him that he collect worms," said The Sweep. "He might think you were trivializing his personal problems."

"Worms aren't trivial," said Maurice. "They are the means of sustenance for moles throughout the world."

"Yes, I know. No offense intended. But what is a dragon going to do with a bunch of worms?"

"What is he going to do with a bunch of treasure? It just sits there. By comparison, worms are exciting. You can race them or stroke them. They like being stroked."

The Sweep was not convinced. "I'm not confident that, in terms of excitement, stroking worms is going to serve as a substitute for overthrowing empires and devouring kings."

"Oh, I don't know," grumbled Maurice. "Some worms can be quite vicious."

But Iris was no longer heeding them. She'd gone to comfort Joe. The rest of us followed her.

"Joe," said Iris gently. "I think it's a lovely poem. And this harp is my choice, if you, in your generosity, are willing to part with such a marvelous instrument."

Joe looked worried. "For you, of all people, I would willingly part with anything, but this particular gift I am reluctant to put in your hands. Why do you not heed the verse? What if you were to play a wrong note? I don't think I could bear it if you were impaled on a spike."

"There are worse things than spikes. When my parents tried to marry me to a disgusting ogre I prayed that someone would impale me on a nice spike. Anyway, I've been playing harp for years. I won't make a mistake."

"It's true," said The Sweep. "At first she sounded awful. I had to invent special wax earplugs and issue them to the entire palace population, but after a while she became really good. Now everyone loves to hear her play. Sadly my patent on the wax earplugs is now worthless."

Suddenly The Sweep stooped to get a closer look at the harp. "Look here. There's another inscription, engraved in tiny letters. But the letters are strange to me. Can anyone read them?"

We all gathered around to peer at the letters but no one could decipher the strange script. None, that is, but me, but I was astonished and held my tongue. The writing was in Zondgrazian and it bore the mark of my master. I did not share my knowledge, for what was revealed there seemed too extraordinary, and I needed to ponder its meaning.

We all stood back. The dragon sighed in acceptance. "Very well, Iris. Play the harp. But please, child, do be careful. The last thing I need is to lose my new human princess friend."

The Music of the Spheres

While we gathered around the princess and made ourselves comfortable, I remained at the back and considered the Zondgrazian inscription I'd read on the instrument. It read: *Zondgrazian Spiritual-Trance Inducing & Life-Purpose-Finding Harp Model Z14. Please note: no one really gets impaled on a spike. We just say that to deter amateurs.*

Could this really be one of the legendary Z14's? The Z14 was an early experiment with microvita energy designed by the master himself. Properly played, it could induce in listeners a profound spiritual realization. Its undoing was that it worked *too* well. The Zondgrazian Council of Sadvipras had banned its use. They argued that the device made spiritual enlightenment too easy. They felt that this wasn't fair to all the people who'd gone through lifetimes of fasting, meditation, and selfless service. Only three Z14s were ever produced and they were supposed to have been destroyed. But it looked as though the master had secreted this one away on earth, and it had ended up in the dragon's hoard. If this was the real thing, these earthlings were in for a mighty big surprise.

Dragon Joe focused his gaze on the princess. He'd never heard the harp played. "Listen well, all of you," he said. "Legend holds that this harp was crafted long ago by a wizard from another world and that its music can change people in unpredictable ways, awakening deep feelings and rekindling forgotten dreams."

All eyes were on Iris as she sat before the harp. She closed her eyes, took a breath, laid her hands on the strings, and began to play.

The first note, hesitant as a fawn, peered out and stepped into the silence, followed by another, and another, until a little group of them ventured forth, their delicate hooves barely touching the ground. Then suddenly, like the last snowflakes of winter, a fresh flurry of younger notes sprang from the princess's fingers, drifting downward before melting into the sun-warmed earth. Iris, unmindful of all but her playing, seemed lost in her own world.

The power of the music mounted, as a spring stream fed by melting snow swiftly grows from a tiny rivulet into an eager brook, the freezing water ringing like crystal on the lingering icicles, filling the forest of our minds with wonder. The instrument's power came into full focus, as though the spring rain, touching at last the earth it loved, was eager to feed the thirsty trees and course through the veins of the living once more, moving ever downward, rushing around rocks, diving over waterfalls to land in pools in foaming eddies, spinning and shining silver. The cascading notes leapt and shattered like a spray of ice into a thousand shards.

The music rushed through us like a reckless river crashing down a mountain slope, fanning into waterfalls, leaping out to fall down, down, down in a curtain of cataracts made of light, falling into a seething cauldron, a roaring confusion far below, then relaxing at last as the waters spread outward and this wild army of harmonies found their common theme, the melodies weaving together and flowing on with a gentler strength.

But the music was not done yet. Not until it reached the great sea of forgetfulness that lies at the end of every journey. The many waters formed a single river, a musical theme so strong and broad that all parts merged into one thrumming bed of rhythm. Across its surface flew a new melody, pure and simple, like a bird of gladness, carrying our spirits the last distance to the boundless ocean. We lost ourselves in the vastness, endless, silent, blissful. A place beyond the world where each of us came to know our heart's desire. Until the music stirred again, like gentle waves on an endless sea, drawing us back to what we knew. Finally we emerged, as from a blissful dream, as though seeing the world for the first time. I opened my eyes to see the faces around me shining with a new understanding.

As the last note faded into silence I felt extraordinarily lucid, keenly aware of my connection with the infinite and with all life, as though tendrils of consciousness joined us, allowing energy, feelings, and thoughts to flow freely between us. Our little group looked at one another shyly, checking to see if this common understanding was reflected in each other's eyes: that we were part of a greater plan, players in an unfolding dance.

During my brief stay on this planet, these quaint, short-lived earthlings had come to matter to me more than I could have imagined. Now I was here not simply because my master sent me here on a mission but because I wanted to help them for their own sake. To my surprise, I was now a fan of loyal mice and dull-witted badgers, of clever moles and passionate princesses and eccentric Sweeps, and of mighty dragons. I had come to love the quiet trees and talkative rocks, the fanciful flowers and carefree streams. And I was deeply moved by earth's painful but beautiful history, its wars of power, the towering and crumbling ambitions of men, for even there I sensed the invisible power that flowed through all life, the spirit in its endless quest for enlightenment.

I had read of a rare kind of human called a bodhisattva, the embodiment of self-sacrifice, for a bodhisattva renounces enlightenment in order to serve all the living beings of the universe. For the first time, I understood why someone might make such a choice.

Suddenly a vision appeared before me, a great city by the sea, a city with skyscrapers and helicopters, shipping docks and freeways. As I watched, the ground trembled and shook. Buildings toppled as fire rained from the sky and the sea rushed in, flowing through the streets and washing over the fleeing crowds. Cracks opened in the ground, fanning out across the land as the cataclysm spread across the globe.

I knew that I was being shown a possible future of this planet, a future where humans had developed advanced technology before they grew in love and wisdom. Like giving laser pistols to children.

I had heard stories of planets where this had actually happened. To prevent this was the very reason our master had established the Sadvipra School, training and sending out emissaries to worlds in need. This was what might happen if we didn't get there in time.

But then I saw a fresh vision of a tall tree bursting with white blossoms, growing in a green valley surrounded by mountains. A powerful wind arose. Petals and flowers flew into the air in a swirling cloud, and the tree began to radiate an invisible power that spread upward and outward over the world in a continuous stream. Those it touched gazed about in wonder, as though newly awakened, and I knew that the dawn of a new era had begun.

The next instant I found myself alone with my master. My eyes filled with tears. I'd missed him so much. He smiled at me and spoke.

"Now you understand. I did not send you to earth to collect a gift for my mother. You must find the microvita seed and plant it in the Valley of the Snow Monkeys in the Himalayas by the light of the full moon of May. My first attempt to use the microvita tree to establish a spiritual civilization on the earth failed. We have one more chance. This new tree that you will plant will blossom at the critical point in the future when humanity develops the technological power to command their environment. Through the power of the microvita tree they will develop spiritual wisdom and awareness and will learn to live in peace with one another. An idyllic civilization will emerge."

"Once you plant the tree, you must hide it. The snow monkeys will be its guardians. This is our chance to save the earth for future generations."

He then told me something personal that I cannot reveal but which filled me with inspiration. He didn't ask me whether or not I was ready accept the mission. He didn't need to.

The vision faded and I found myself sitting on a pile of gold in a cave surrounded by a very odd collection of creatures.

This changed everything. Major mission upgrade! It still sounded hard, but Eikelbohm would know what to do. I couldn't wait to tell him.

Padre Sinistru crept through the tunnel as softly as a ghost. Though there was no need, he kept silent out of habit. The habit of a spy, a sneak, one who is not as he appears to be. Long ago, when he was fresh in his role as chief secret agent of Nefarious, he had relished the feeling of being party to secrets. Then it made him feel important. Now he just felt lonely.

His master had been pleased with his report on the conversation with Sir Dogalogue and his companions and had rewarded him with gold. But it brought Sinistru no satisfaction. Spying and sneaking about just didn't give him the same thrill it used to. After nine thousand years the novelty was wearing off.

He heard music in the distance, coming from deeper within the cave complex. It was unlike any music he had ever heard, like water dancing over crystal, like sunlight lancing through the darkness that had crept into his heart. A long-forgotten feeling stirred deep within him. He stumbled like one entranced, unable to help himself, drawn by some deep longing.

Hearing the harp music, Sinistru fell into a trance that took him back to the early years of his life, to Atlantis before the Necromancer had enslaved his will, when he was a scientist in his own right and desired to create some beautiful new life form with the newly revealed power of microvita. A barrier in his mind fell away and his long-suppressed memory suddenly returned. He remembered who he was.

Master and Hench-Wizard

Eikelbohm leaned on his sword, breathing heavily and looking sternly at Nefarious, the old wizard who groveled before him, begging for clemency. Overpowering the old fellow hadn't been hard. He was clearly well past his prime. But now that he had defeated him, Eikelbohm faced the more difficult task of deciding what to do with him.

"Dr. Eikelbohm," croaked Nefarious. "You are indeed powerful for one so young. But do not kill me too hastily. I have a proposal that might be to your great advantage."

"What is it?" said Eikelbohm, gruffly.

"You are an impressive wizard, but I can show you how to gain more power than you ever dreamed of. With my training you could become invincible. I am old. I need a successor to whom I can pass on my knowledge. Let me teach you how to realize your true potential so that you can rule the earth after I am gone."

The sorcerer bowed to Eikelbohm.

"I get it." Eikelbohm's response was typically blunt. "I know the routine. I've heard all the stories about evil sorcerers corrupting zealous young magicians and turning them to the dark side, so you can dispense with the niceties. Relax, I'm in. I'm the perfect candidate for dark-side seduction. I'm strong, ambitious, resentful of authority, impatient, emotionally needy, determined to get what I want by any means, and I love power. I have no interest in going through another couple of hundred years of humiliation and study at the wimpy Sadvipra School for stupid Saints and mediocre Messiahs. All to become a goody-goody World Savior who is never allowed to actually use his power when it is most needed. I could do a lot more good by acting directly rather than by lurking about trying to implement some fanciful thousand-year plan centered around a temperamental plant! So you won't get any arguments from me. I assume it's the standard deal, right? I become your apprentice and have to obey you? In return you teach me to develop my powers, make me evil like you, and I become your successor?"

The Necromancer clapped his hands in glee. "Why, you're perfect! What happy chance brought me such a ready-made disciple? But you are almost too good to be true. How do I know you are sincere? Perhaps in your heart you are still loyal to your old master."

"Me, loyal to him? I don't think so! I know that at this point it is traditional for you to test my sincerity by ordering me to eat a decaying rat or to disembowel my best friend, but in my case I don't think that is really necessary. Anyway, I don't have any friends. You want to know why I'm such an easy convert to the dark side? I'm a natural sociopath, a classic maladjusted individual. It started while I was still in the test tube. I was a total loner. I couldn't even get along with the other test tubes. Then I had a terrible relationship with my father, who was also a test tube, by the way, so go figure. Never knew my mother. Bullied when I was young, so I bullied others when I grew bigger. Grew up with a Napoleon Complex, an Oedipus Complex, Tourette's syndrome, schizophrenia, paranoia, all the famous psychological disorders. I'm your textbook psychotic evil dictator, except that in real life I have seventeen tentacles."

"Why, I really do believe you are perfect," crowed the wizened sorcerer. He rubbed his hands together and gargled with glee. For a moment Eikelbohm thought he would start crying but then he remembered that he was a homicidal maniac.

"By the whiskers of Zond! I am tempted to cry 'calloo, callay, oh frabjous day, come to my arms my beamish boy,' but I will not, for I am no benevolent king. I am Nefarious the Wicked and it would ill befit me to speak in such a childish manner. People might talk, and then I'd have to turn them into beavers and they would be compelled by their detestation of the sound of running water to dam up every stream in the world. There would be a great flood and a drought and a calamity and a catastrophe and everyone would blame it on me as usual, so I'm not about to make that mistake again, am I?"

He paused for breath. Eikelbohm just stood there, bewildered.

"Well? Am I?" Nefarious urged, thrusting his beard forward and raising his eyebrows in a terrible arch. Eikelbohm shook his head.

"So instead," concluded the sorcerer, stabbing the ground with his staff in his dastardly style, "I will adopt you as my new apprentice and together, as master and hench-wizard, we shall dominate the earth!"

Mission Improbable

"Wow," breathed Maurice. "That was so cool! It was like I was chief mole of the whole world! And I was really brilliant at it!"

"And I really *was* supermouse," whispered Mina. "It was just like I've always imagined!"

"Let's do that again!" said Fluff.

Iris rose from her seat before the harp, a challenge in her eyes, willing me to speak of my mission. Her music was a pretty hard act to follow but I'd just have to do my best.

Joe too looked at me, expectant, his golden eyes shining in the darkness like lava. I found his ancient alien mind particularly hard to read. Now he was blue and silver and purple, making his luminescent serpent body seem more magical than ever. So much of my mission's success depended on my companion's response to what I was about to say. I really needed their help, so I had to inspire them to join me on my quest, especially Joe.

"I think the time has come," said Joe, "to learn what really brought us all here together. Sir Dogalogue, tell us your story. What was so important that you undertook your great journey between the stars?"

"I'd like to know more about you, too, Sir Dogalogue," squeaked Mina. "You look like a human but I know you're not because you're too nice and you smell like a fish." She hid her nose in my hand, abashed at her own outburst.

I cleared my throat and faced my odd group of new friends. The mystical music had created the perfect mood for my message.

"You already know the story of the microvita tree and how its power was used to create dragons, and how that led to war and the destruction of Atlantis. Our lives are bound up in that continuing story. This land is infused with the memory of the microvita tree. It enables animals and even dust motes to speak and think as humans do. But this is just an echo of the living tree's power. The very future of the earth hinges on the microvita tree. That is why I am here."

I saw Iris's and The Sweep's eyes glowing with excitement. It was working! I was giving a motivational speech!

"Now you may be wondering, 'what has this to do with me?'"

"Not really," said Brains. "I was wondering what it has to do with *me*."

"That's what I meant," I said. "When I said me, I meant you."

"Then why didn't you say so?" said the Badger. "I wish you'd say what you mean. Don't confuse us!"

Iris turned on the Badger. "Why don't you shut up? We want to listen to Sir Dogalogue, not you!"

I gave Iris a grateful look. "If you're wondering what this has to do with *you*, then listen carefully and don't interrupt. This is very important."

It certainly was. So much depended on my ability to inspire them about my mission. Talk about pressure. What is it all those speaking gurus tell you to do before giving an important speech? Relax. That's a laugh. I read a crazy earth book about how most people are more afraid of speaking in public than they are of giant spiders eating their eyeballs. Anyway, this was my moment of doom, like it or not, so I took a deep breath and jumped in, back-to-front feet and all.

"As some of you know, I do not belong to this world. I come from the planet Zondgraz in the Arcturus star system."

The Duke crossed himself several times and made as though to speak, but Iris put her hand on his arm and whispered to him and the old man settled down.

"This human form you see is a kind of costume I wear to conceal my true body, which to you might look like a large and handsome octopus."

The Duke crossed himself again, looking a little pale, but said nothing.

"On my planet I am a student at the Zondgrazian Sadvipra Training Institute for Saints, Messiahs and World Saviors. Our master is the very same wizard who planted the microvita tree in Atlantis all those millennia ago. Now he has sent me, together with another student, on a mission to earth."

"There's another alien?" Iris was so curious she forgot not to interrupt. "Where is he now?"

"I wish I knew. I'm actually quite worried about him. He was supposed to meet me in Honk Village two days ago."

"Gosh," said Maurice. "There are some tribes out there who eat octopuses. Do you think they've eaten your friend? That would be really gross."

I shook my head. "Hardly possible. When he's on earth he doesn't have tentacles like me. He has the power to shape-shift, to change his body into a human body. Plus he's a great fighter who is able to throw energy bolts at his enemies. Save your concern for anyone who tries to eat him."

"Maybe he's late because his horse got sick," said Brains.

"He doesn't have a horse," I said.

"How come he doesn't have a horse?" asked Maurice. "You have a horse. That doesn't seem fair."

"He has a spaceship—er, a kind of cart that can fly through the air at great speed. I got the horse."

"Ah," said the mole. "Smart fellow."

"If he can shape-shift and throw energy bolts, how about you? What can you do?" asked Brains.

"Sir Dogalogue can talk to everything," said Mina proudly.

"To birds and flowers and trees," said the princess.

"I say," said the Duke. "That's a handy talent. I have a couple of trees in my garden that keep growing their roots through the drain pipes. Do you think you might have a word with them?"

"If I get the chance, right willingly," I said. "But you know, it's not always so handy, knowing the thoughts of so many creatures. I get to listen to my horse's incessant complaints and birds twittering nonsense and flowers gossiping about their neighbors. Sometimes I just have to switch it off to get some peace."

"What a letdown," said the mole. "You finally get to find out what other creatures are really thinking and talking about, and it's just a bunch of mundane rubbish. I thought they'd be expounding on the wonders of nature and the folly of man, and philosophizing about the meaning of existence."

"What do you expect?" said Iris. "Most of the stuff humans talk about is rubbish, and going on my experience so far I'd say the same is true of moles. Why would you expect a bug or a bird to do any better?"

"What does this other alien, this friend of yours look like?" she asked. "Is he tall and swarthy, of proud and stern visage, keen of eye and deft of hand? Black of hair, clean-shaven and square-jawed, wearing a silver embossed doublet and a carrying a doughty firkin?"

"Why yes," I cried in astonishment. "In his human form, he appears exactly thus. How did you know?"

"I didn't. It was just a wild guess." Iris snapped her mouth shut the way princesses do when they don't want to say anything more. She was beginning to behave strangely again. How in the world could she know what Eikelbohm looked like? No time to wonder about that now, however. I had to finish my motivational speech, if I could ever get this rabble to keep quiet.

"I do so love stories," sighed the dragon. "Especially when no one interrupts!" Everyone fell silent, looking a little guilty.

"As I was saying," I continued, "my fellow disciple Dr. Eikelbohm and I were sent to earth on a mission by our master to recover the lost seed of the microvita tree. My master first planted this tree in Atlantis, hoping to create the earth's first spiritual civilization, but as you know, that didn't quite go as planned. So now he has sent Dr. Eikelbohm and me to find the lost seed and plant it in the Himalayan mountains. When we landed we divided forces. Eikelbohm went to locate and interrogate the wizard, and I was tasked to find the dragon and discover the location of Atlantis."

Maurice raised his paw. "So let me get this straight. You got a horse and had to extract information from a fire-breathing, man-eating monster that can fly, and your friend got this cool-sounding flying cart and all he had to do was beat up an old man?"

"I'm afraid that is about it," I said, feeling a little foolish to hear it put it like that.

"Just checking," said Maurice.

I drew a deep breath and jumped straight to my call to action, as prescribed in the latest motivational speech training books. "For thousands of years humanity has been plagued by war, ignorance, and injustice, causing untold suffering and destruction. If this mission succeeds, the power of the microvita tree will set in motion an enormous evolutionary leap in human consciousness. It will end this destructive cycle and usher in a new era of wisdom, peace, and prosperity. To recover the lost seed and plant it in the appointed place is a daunting challenge. I cannot do this alone. I need your help. Who among you will aid me? Who will join me in this noble quest to save the earth?"

Dead silence. Hardly daring to look around, I glanced first at Iris. Her eyes were glowing in admiration. That was encouraging. Joe was a golden shade I'd never seen before. Even better. Maybe he'd help me after all. Then he winked at me with a great shining eye and relief flooded through me. I knew everything was going to be all right.

Mina broke the silence. "When I heard the princess play the harp," she said in her tiny voice, "I realized that Sir Dogalogue is the first person who was truly kind to me. I would give anything to help create a world where everyone treats everyone else with kindness and respect, no matter how small they are. I know I'm not really a super mouse, but I'll do whatever I can to help Sir Dogalogue on his mission."

She stopped and looked around nervously, twitching her nose. This was the longest speech she'd ever given in public.

"Count me in for sure," said The Sweep. "I never saw much point in training to be the next king of Navarre, so I tried becoming a hermit, but I was only doing that because I didn't have anything better to do. This is a no-brainer for me. By helping Sir Dogalogue to save the earth I'll finally have a life purpose that actually makes sense!"

Iris hugged her brother.

The Duke rose to his feet, his armor and his old bones creaked slightly. "Ah, to be young again!" he said, beaming. "This is a fine quest and I'm greatly honored to be invited." He paused to bow to me. "It warms the cockles of my heart to see you young people inspired to follow our family tradition, embarking on quests, rescuing helpless maidens, fighting dragons. Present company excepted, of course." He bowed to Joe now. "How I wish this offer had come during my own youth. Why, I would have leapt at the chance. Saving the world, eh? Who would have thought it? When I was a lad all you had to do to be a hero was put out a burning barn or rescue a cat stuck in a tree."

He smiled fondly and shook his head. "Sadly, I cannot accompany you. I know I don't look it, but I am in my autumn years. Furthermore, I carry the burden of high office. I have to take care of the drains, as I mentioned, and I have to deal with a veritable plague of marauding dragons, which I'm hoping our peace-loving friend of that reptilian persuasion will advise me upon. Such are my obligations that they do not allow me the leisure of going on such a lengthy journey."

He shook his head in genuine regret, then brightened. "However, I will provide you with whatever you need in terms of provisions and financial management. You have no shortage of funds," he said, laughing and looking around at the small ocean of gold all around us, "but an operation like this needs organization, budgeting, accounting. I'd be honored to provide logistical support."

I bowed and nodded my thanks.

Brains and Maurice had been whispering together. Maurice rose, wearing a tuxedo and bow tie, and read from a scrap of paper. "So moved were we by the princess's enchanting music and Sir Dogalogue's memorable motivational speech that Brains and I have composed a small poem to express our feelings, which I will now recite."

He stood up straight and began to read in his best literary manner:

Yon Knight's Request

This eager crowd yon knight addressed
Upon his shield shone Zond's fair crest
Those wicked foes we must arrest
Even though our brains be stressed

A quest works best when pointed west,
Embarked upon with fullest zest,
Sign up for this brave knight's request
And join us in this scary test

Brave badgers yearn to fly the nest
They bow their knees and clean confessed

Their hearts of courage full possessed
Their shoes all shined, their shirts well-pressed

We'll best the obnoxious sales pest
His every ruse and ploy and jest
From monster's grasp the seed we'll wrest
And so at last the quest successed.

Everyone stared at the mole in silence.

"That's it?" said The Sweep.

"Wasn't it long enough?" said Maurice. "I have more verses. Here, just wait a moment." He rummaged in his satchel.

"No, no," said the Sweep hastily. "It was the perfect length. And it is over, and that is a good thing. By which I mean it feels complete and fitting to the moment."

"What's a 'successed'?" whispered Mina.

"It is a special word that only exists for the purpose of completing a dreadful rhyme," Iris explained to the mouse.

"Why did you want to arrest the wicked toes? said The Sweep. "Aren't they attached to someone's foot? If so, I'd have thought that if someone's toes were wicked, the rest of him would be wicked. And if the rest of him is not wicked, then his toes would not be wicked either."

"Not wicked toes," said Maurice. "Wicked foes. You know, enemies."

"Ah," said the Sweep. "Now it makes sense, sort of."

"With due respect," said the Duke, "I have to say that the whole poem sounds like it was written by someone who just wanted to rhyme everything and nothing else mattered, such as the poem making sense, using actual words, or sounding any good."

"That's sort of what happened," said Maurice. "It's an adaptation of a poem I wrote a while ago when a troll gave me a list of words rhyming with zest and told me that if I didn't write a poem utilizing at least sixteen of them by nightfall, he'd beat me up."

"That sounds pretty unreasonable," said The Sweep.

"Trolls aren't reasonable," said the mole darkly.

"Anyway," Brains said, clearing his throat. "This is a quest, right? We badgers" ("and moles", hissed Maurice). "Er, we badgers and moles, we do quests. Quests is what we do. Are what we do. Anyway, we're in."

He sat down abruptly. We didn't know whether to laugh or to cheer. Maurice whispered furiously to Brains. Brains rose again. "Furthermore we'd like to acknowledge that perhaps we've underestimated the mouse. I can't put it better than she did—what she said about kindness to small creatures and all that. What Mina said rocked."

This time everyone cheered and Mina hid her nose in her paws in an ecstasy of embarrassment. Iris came up to me and clasped my hands in hers. "Oh, Sir Dogalogue, what you said was wonderful. You know I've already pledged myself to your mission but now we have a whole team!"

Still holding my hand she turned to the dragon and looked up at him beseechingly. "Dearest Joe, greatest of dragons. You know this all depends on you. You know where Atlantis is. You have the strength and wisdom to make this mission a success. Are you ready to truly forgive the humans with all your heart and help us to secure their future?"

Joe looked down on her kindly. "Little Princess, set your mind at rest. You and your brother were my first human friends. Even if I were not inspired by Sir Dogalogue's fine speech, I'd help just because you asked."

Maurice nudged the badger. "Get me out of here fast. I'm afraid I'm going to cry. I'll ruin my reputation."

Joe addressed us all. "I, too, was deeply moved by Sir Dogalogue's words, for is this not the theme of my life? The power of microvita flows in my veins. It created me but it also destroyed my ancient home. I know its power for good and for evil. I am deeply honored to join the great mission of the microvita tree. I vow that I will see it through to the end or die in the attempt."

"Damn," whispered Maurice to Brains. "I wish I'd said that. We could have put a whole thing about dying in our poem. It would have made us look awesomely brave!"

"But I don't want to die," said Brains. "It's all very well for Joe. He's had a nine-thousand-year life already, and I suspect that he is secretly suicidal half the time anyway. But I'm only three years old. I want more."

"Just because we put it in the poem doesn't mean we actually have to really die! It's just a poem. It's like an advertisement or an election promise. No one expects you to actually deliver."

"Can I come too? I am also ready to die for your cause," came a whining voice. No one had noticed when Sinistru joined us. He hunched beneath the archway at the cave's entrance, cringing like a dog unsure of its welcome. "Dying for causes is my favorite thing."

"Why are you always spying on us?" said Iris, her face showing her displeasure.

"And why would we want you to join our mission?" said Brains. "You told us yourself, you're a disciple of the probably evil necromancer. I doubt that he is our friend."

"And there is this to consider," said Maurice, his voice full of scorn. "Saying you're ready to die for our cause is unoriginal. You're just copying the dragon. What a loser!"

"Yeah, what a loser," said Fluff the dust mote. "Why don't you get lost? This is a private party. Who invited you?"

"I'm inviting him," said The Sweep. Everyone looked at him in surprise. "At least give him a chance to explain himself. We all listened to his story when we were together by the stream and it sort of made sense. He may have useful information for us. And we should not be too hasty to judge him simply because of his disgusting manner and hideous personality."

Iris looked as though she were about to say something but hesitated and glanced at me. Joe lost much of his shine but also waited for my lead.

Sinistru addressed The Sweep. "Indeed, I could aid your cause. It is true, until recently I was an agent of the necromancer. But when I heard your magical music, Princess,"—he bowed to Iris, who scowled at him in return—"I was freed at last of the necromancer's spell. The scales of forgetfulness dropped from my eyes and my memory returned. I remembered that I too lived in Atlantis. I was a disciple of the dark wizard and learned much of the lore of creating creatures with microvita energy. But when he started making monsters for war I left him. Unfortunately he captured me and I was forced by... er... circumstances, to swear fealty to him. I have been his servant ever since."

"I am eternally grateful to you, Princess, for reawakening my true self. I feel so happy. I don't even want to be a vampire any more." He halted abruptly and glanced around nervously at the shocked faces. "Whoops. I didn't mean to say that."

Everyone save Joe and I backed away from him, their eyes full of fear.

"Cursed creature of darkness," cried the Duke. "So, you're a vampire who drinks the blood of mortals in the night. Deathless, evil, one who turns innocent virgins into monsters like himself."

"Actually, there's been a bit of a shortage of innocent virgins lately," began Sinistru, but they were not listening. Iris stared at him in horror. Brains and Maurice and The Duke had their weapons drawn. Even The Sweep seemed unsure where he stood.

"I think you'd better leave," said the princess stiffly.

Sinistru nodded to me and The Sweep and left the circle, head bowed, accompanied only by Harvey the ant.

I slipped away and followed him until we were out of hearing and I called to him. I was not afraid of him. I wasn't even sure if I believed in vampires.

"Listen, Sinistru, we need to talk. I may be ready to accept you as part of our company. After all, I need all the help I can get. Obviously, the others aren't too keen, but in the end it's up to me. This is my mission. Let's meet privately tonight and we'll figure out what to do."

Sinistru bowed in gratitude and slipped away into the darkness.

When I returned our group headed for the exit. Joe, The Sweep and I lingered behind, pausing by the lake. The great monster gazed at the lights reflected in the water.

"I wonder what will become of my kind," he mused. "I fear that we will not survive on this planet for much longer. Humans are already beginning to invent terrible weapons capable of killing us. Bows and arrows were never a big problem but now they have cannons. I don't know exactly what will come next but one thing is for sure: humans are really good at inventing ever more powerful killing devices."

"I'm afraid you are right," said The Sweep. "But surely there must be something we can do." He looked at me as though expecting an answer, but I was otherwise preoccupied.

The dragon did not reply but I got a rare glimpse of his mind. As he watched the blue lights in the water an idea dawned on him. Was it possible? He hardly dared to hope but he knew that he must. In that moment he made a vow to himself and to the mysterious secret God of the dragons that would change the future of dragonkind forever.

I excused myself before we reached the cave exit. "I think I'm going to take the opportunity to brush up on my Morris dancing," I said.

"Morris dancing? At this hour? Where?" said The Sweep. "Hadn't we better make preparations to leave for Iberia?"

"I saw a sign back there offering free lessons. I may never get another chance," I said hurriedly, turning back. "See you later."

I could feel curious glances on my back, but no one followed me. Which was just as well, for I was about to keep an appointment with a vampire.

The Magician's Labyrinth

I found Sinistru waiting for me in the shadows at the base of the spiral staircase. He greeted me with childlike warmth, which seemed a little incongruous coming from someone who lived on blood. Not that his unorthodox diet concerned me personally. After all, no human blood flowed through my veins. But the idea of actually drinking blood seemed kind of gross, even to me.

"Thank you so much for giving me a chance to help you on your mission," said Sinistru.

"You're welcome," I said. "If I might make a suggestion, you could use some advice from a PR professional. The Sweep and I might have brought the others around but then you had to go and mention that you're a vampire! You must know that humans love vampires even less than Visigoths."

"I know, I blew it," said Sinistru, "but try to imagine what kind of day I've had. Only hours ago I awoke from a spell that had kept me ignorant of my identity for nine thousand years. I'm still in shock. I had completely forgotten who I was. It's like suddenly being a different person. I don't even know if I can stop being a vampire. I mean, I want to stop, but I have no idea if I can actually do it. For starters, what am I going to eat?"

I'd actually been considering this. I happened to know that the molecules of chlorophyll and hemoglobin are very similar, and that ingesting chlorophyll builds hemoglobin. "Have you considered wheat grass juice?" I suggested. "It's basically the same as blood. I know a hermit who lives on wheat grass juice. He is sort of greenish and very bad- tempered, but he's really healthy."

"What are you talking about! A vampire can't live on wheat grass juice! It tastes awful, and all the other vampires will make fun of me."

"OK, maybe not. It was just an idea. We'll have to think of something else."

Sinistru shook his head in disgust "Wheat grass juice! Bleccch! Anyway, that's my problem. Listen. I've got to tell you about Nefarious's true intentions. I was his only confidant and I know many of his secrets. He desperately wants to get his hands on the microvita seed. He hopes that with the help of the dragon you will succeed where he has failed. He will help you to recover the seed, but he plans to steal it from you. I think he hopes to convince you to become his disciple."

This felt a bit like being told that a homicidal rhinoceros, intent upon world conquest, wants to marry you and have your babies.

"By the whiskers of Zond, that wily rascal," I said. "Thanks for warning me. But if he is so treacherous, why do you think I should seek his help?"

"If anyone knows the exact whereabouts of Atlantis, it's him. He's been seeking it for centuries. I think you should meet him. When he tries to convince you to become his disciple, just play along and let him believe you are considering it and I'm sure he will help you."

This made sense. It also explained the lurking presence I'd sensed from the moment I first entered these caves. The necromancer had been observing me. "Can you take me to him?" I asked.

Sinistru shuddered. "I dare not go near him again. Not yet. I have not learned how to hide my newly awakened awareness. He may sense that I am free of his spell and entrap me again. But I can give you directions. He has a secret hideout in this very cave complex. He's been using it to spy on the dragon for years."

"How will I find you again?" I said.

"Don't worry, I'll be nearby. I know how to stay hidden. I'm a vampire, remember? I can transform into a bat and even follow your dragon when he is flying."

"Well, thanks so much for your help. I'm so glad you are free of that nasty spell."

"Good luck," said Sinistru. "And remember, don't let the necromancer know what you're thinking. He can be very charming, but he's ruthless. He'll try to manipulate you. You mustn't trust him. Once you have the seed he will try to take it from you."

Sinistru led the way around the east edge of the lake and pointed to the entrance of a tunnel that I'd not noticed. "To get to his cave you follow that tunnel and keep to the right. After two hundred yards you'll come to a small waterfall. Turn left there, and it will take you to a larger cave, the magician's lair. You can't miss it."

You can't miss it! My least favorite human phrase, because I invariably missed the elusive "it." I don't think Sinistru had ever given directions to an alien like me before. I felt very shy about my dyslexia. Here I was, an alien from an advanced civilization, capable of navigating the stars, and I couldn't find my way through a few simple tunnels. I've known very dim fish who knew the difference between left and right.

Too embarrassed to admit to my disability, I said, "That sounds simple enough. Thanks again and farewell."

I hadn't wanted to prolong the conversation with Sinistru, not only because of the urgency of my mission but also because I badly needed to empty my bladder. Under normal circumstances this would have been no problem. Zondgrazians are equipped with all kinds of tubes and reservoirs which make this sort of operation a minor inconvenience. In addition to possessing a mechanism that is not laughter inducing, we are blessed with bladders substantial enough to rival the anatomy of the queen of England. Zondgrazian anthropologists postulate that this was an adaptive response to lengthy space journeys in cramped quarters, before the development of modern spaceships. However, I was wearing that cumbersome human suit. This made the whole procedure far more complicated and placed me at risk of exposing my Zondgrazian body, which would have inspired more than mere curious glances.

I passed through the narrow entrance into the tunnel, which wound like a worm into the hill, and after a few moments I found myself by the tiny waterfall where I was able to safely divest myself of the annoying human suit and relieve myself. When I was ready to continue I saw two passageways leading in different directions. Sinistru had said I should keep to the left. "Er, Mina, which way is left?"

"What's a left?" said the mouse.

Surely mice aren't dyslexic too? More likely they just don't learn about left and right in school.

I looked one way, then the other. "We'll just have to guess," I said. "We have a 50 percent chance of being right, and if we don't find the way out soon, we can just come back and take the other way, which we will then know is the right way."

"I suppose so," said Mina doubtfully.

We took one of the options, to this day I could not tell you which, and after a short distance we came upon another fork in the tunnel. I stopped and bit my lip. "Hmmm. I have a feeling it's this one." I pointed with my northeast tentacle, I mean paw.

"That would give us a 25 percent chance of being right," said Mina. "How about we go back and try the 50-percent chance fork?"

"No, I'm sure it's this way."

Unfortunately my chronic dyslexia was often accompanied by fits of unwarranted confidence. Ten minutes later we didn't seem to be any closer to our destination. "Our odds are now down to 0.84375 percent," said Mina. She was sometimes smarter than any mouse has the right to be.

"I think we might be lost," I admitted. I was getting worried.

I chose a tunnel at random, my default navigational technique. "I sure hope this leads to an exit, Mina old girl. Otherwise I don't know how we'll ever find our way out of this labyrinth."

Suddenly I felt something in my pocket. I took out a ball of string. "That's odd. What is this ball of string doing in my pocket?" I wondered aloud.

"I put it there," said Mina. "In ancient times people used balls of string to find their way out of labyrinths."

"Brilliant!" I cried in relief. "You clever little Mina! What foresight! You've saved us!"

I examined the device, turning it over in my hands. "How do you switch it on?"

Mina sighed. "You're supposed to start using it before you get lost, not afterward. You unravel the string as you proceed and leave a trail from the beginning of your journey. Then you can use it to retrace your steps. The Greek hero Theseus used it on the advice of the king's daughter when he went to fight the minotaur."

"So you're supposed to start unraveling it at the beginning of your journey?"

"That's right."

"What a pity no one thought to do that earlier. Can we go back to the beginning and start over?"

"Are you familiar with the expression, 'closing the stable door after the horse has bolted?'"

"Is that a proverb? I'm fond of proverbs."

"Yes, Sir Dogalogue," said Mina. "It's a proverb. And in this case it signifies that we truly are lost."

"Perhaps I can be of some assistance." I spun round and found myself facing an old man.

The word old was scarcely adequate. Ancient as stone, wizened like a prune that has been stored in an Egyptian pyramid for millennia, his skin looked dry as dust. The man's features were so crinkled it was impossible to tell whether he was smiling or glaring.

We stood open-mouthed. I pulled myself together first. "I'm Sir Dogalogue, knight errant and emissary of truth."

The ancient wizard, for such he seemed to be, judging by the wizard costume he was wearing and the pointed hat on his head featuring embroidered stars and planets, and the staff he bore, engraved with runes and mystic signs, and the big label on the front of his robe reading 'Top Wizard Award 1196,' replied in a friendly tone. "I'm delighted to meet you, Sir Dogalogue. And what a sweet little mouse you have there. Here mouse, may I offer you a free subscription to *Atlantean Artifacts Monthly*, a popular magazine for amateur conspiracy theorists?"

With admirable aplomb, Mina managed to turn her wince into a grateful bow.

"Sir Dogalogue," said Mina softly. "I don't like this old man much. He smells like a rancid sea-elephant."

Obviously the wizard was Nefarious, but just as obviously I knew I shouldn't let on that I knew this.

"So, I understand that you seek Atlantis. Do you mind telling me why?" he said.

"I'm not at liberty to say," I said. "But it is a very important and noble mission, and I entreat you to help us. So many people seem to have heard of Atlantis, but no one knows where to find it."

"Good! At least you have the sense not to blab about your mission to every stranger you meet. But there is no need to worry. I know you have been sent to retrieve the microvita seed."

I feigned surprise. "Can nobody around here keep a secret? How could you know this?"

"Do not be alarmed. I, too, was a disciple of your master long ago." He held up his hand, displaying an ornate signet ring, and when I looked closely I saw to my amazement that it bore my master's symbol.

"I will help you fulfill the mission he has given you. I am old and my powers are waning, but I still have my wisdom and know much that will be of value to you."

"Why, thank you. I could certainly use some advice. I met this dragon who says he comes from Atlantis. He has been very kind and even showed us his treasure. But I'm not sure if what he told us about how Atlantis was destroyed is entirely true."

The wizard looked at me sharply. "Listen, young Dogalogue. I know you are no man, and you are not young by earth standards but I am ancient by even the standards of you Zondgrazians. I know much of the history of this world. Because of my faith in your master, I am going to reveal to you secrets known to none. You have seen the treasure of Dragon Joe, the greatest in this world. But how would you like to see the *real* treasure?"

"Great galaxies, you certainly know how to make a cephalopod curious. But I'm not sure exactly what you mean."

"If you wish to understand, come. Time is short."

We followed the old wizard through twisting passages, climbing ever higher until we came to a great chamber with an opening high above that admitted daylight. The cave smelled musty and seemed to be the abode of numerous spiders, for the rocky room was hung all about with dusty curtains of web. All about us I saw withered documents, scriptures, hundreds of books ordered in shelves or stored in chests bound with silver, and faded maps on parchment displayed on the walls or stacked in scrolls.

"Here lies stored much of the ancient wisdom of Atlantis," said the wizard gravely. "More precious than the wealth of a thousand kings, for here is the knowledge that gave the Atlanteans the power to rule over nature, to cure disease, to create flying beasts, monsters and miracles, to give and take away life and to communicate telepathically over great distances, for so they ordered their empire. The one who commands this knowledge possesses the power to rule over all. But I cannot use it. I have lived beyond my time and am not long for this world. Soon I will have no more use for this treasure trove of wisdom, but I can help you interpret it. I can teach you how to harness the power of those ancient people. I feel in my heart that fate has guided you to me. No ordinary earthling is capable of receiving this mantle of knowledge. They are too short-lived and stupid. You wonder why I offer it to you? You forget too easily how vastly superior you are to the earthlings. You mingle with them and let them treat you as their equal, but you should be a god among them. And equipped with this treasure of knowledge, why, you could do anything, overcome any obstacle."

"Do you know what this is?" The old man's eyes glowed softly as he held up a fragile volume. "In this book is the secret formula for a potion so powerful that he who takes it will never again feel fear. He will be able to face any challenge undaunted. He will be a hero such as this world has never known. Men have wasted cities and stormed castles in search of this book. Yet here"—he waved to the library of wisdom—"it is but one of many such treasures. No one knows of this but we two, and only I know how to utilize it. I am loath to allow my knowledge to die with me. Become my disciple and you can have it all."

This was a lot to take in all at once. In truth, though I knew I could not trust Nefarious, I was sorely tempted. It seemed like the opportunity of a lifetime. Armed with this wisdom I'd be much better equipped to carry out my mission. The problem was, I was on a deadline. We had to plant the seed on the third day of the waxing moon. If I chose to study with the wizard I could be delayed for months.

"You are very generous," I said, "but I came to earth to fulfill the mission assigned to me by my master. I cannot turn aside from my task. But once my mission is over, may I return to take you up on your offer?"

Nefarious sighed and spoke reasonably. "I see you are determined and loyal. Exactly the qualities that make you such a promising student. But if you are set upon pursuing your mission first, so be it. And if you prove successful, by all means return, but I cannot promise I will still be alive. My life force wanes daily. If you should change your mind, do not hesitate to seek me out. But do not ponder over long. It would be a terrible loss were this knowledge to die with me."

"I will think upon your words," I said gravely. "If I reconsider, where am I to find you?"

"For now, I live here. But don't worry. We are destined to meet again, young Dogalogue. And even if you will not be my disciple, I will still help you with your mission, for I too pray for the day when the power of the microvita tree returns to the world. I have an excellent map showing the exact location of Atlantis. Now let me see, where did I put it?"

He turned to the piles of scrolls. "I seem to recall that it smelled of cheese."

Mina perked up her head. She sprang to the floor and began scuttling from one scroll to another, sniffing intently. Within moments she let out an excited squeak. We hurried to the spot and there Mina crouched proudly before a scroll so decrepit and aged-looking that I was loath to touch it lest it crumble in my hands.

The wizard carefully unrolled it. Sure enough, there before us was a map of the Iberian coast and some two hundred miles out in the Atlantic, the island of Atlantis. I stared at it in awe, memorizing every detail, for I was afraid the old map would not survive a journey. Then the wizard rolled it carefully and passed it to me.

"Now you have the map you will need to fly to Iberia, take a ship, and mount a diving expedition." Suddenly he stiffened in surprise. "What do you have in your pocket?"

"A ball of string and sometimes a mouse," I replied, wondering what this had to do with anything.

"You also have an important artifact," he said.

Of course, the amulet. He sensed its presence. I drew it out from my inner pocket.

"Do you know what this is?" he said.

"No, but as you can see, it displays our master's symbol, so I kept it, figuring it must be important."

"This is the key to the hidden Chamber of Stones that lies nearby. I've sought this key for many an age. You have uncanny luck, that's for sure. Where did you find it?" He gave me a strange look.

"I found it in the dragon's treasure trove."

"He gave it to me," I added, a little defensively.

"No wonder I never found it. That dragon doesn't care for me, and I'm certainly not going to pick a fight with him. Anyway, in the Chamber of Stones you will find the original talking stones from Atlantis, guardians of the secret way to the microvita seed. Knowing the whereabouts of Atlantis from the map is not enough. You need a way to find the seed's location in the ruined city under the water, and once you have it you must get out of there as fast as you can. They say the seed is guarded by a dreadful sea monster who devours anyone who even thinks of stealing it. What you need is an iPoss."

This was getting complicated. First I just had to find a dragon and make it talk. Then I needed a map. Then a ship and some kind of diving equipment. And now I had to use this magic key to talk to a bunch of tedious stones and on top of that, an iPoss, whatever that was.

"What's an iPoss?" I asked wearily.

"A small creature not much bigger than your forearm. It is mystically linked to the microvita tree. If you follow the map you will come to the coastal kingdom of Navarre. From there the iPoss will guide you."

"Navarre?" I said. That was where the princess and her brother were from.

"Navarre was built by the survivors of the ruin of Atlantis, the ones who escaped with me, riding on the dragons."

I had no need to feign fascination. "You were there, nine millennia ago? You witnessed the fall of Atlantis?"

"Indeed I was. Haven't you guessed? I am the wizard who created the dragons of Atlantis."

Even if I had not been forewarned by Sinistru, I think I would have figured that out by now. I had to make some show of surprise, however.

"I suspected as much. So you are *that* wizard."

"I believe my assistant, Sinistru, has already apprised you of my perspective on events leading to the destruction of Atlantis," he said evenly.

"Yes, he has." The old fellow seemed friendly and helpful. I found it hard to imagine that he was as dastardly as Joe's story made out. "Tell me one thing. Did you meet my companion, Eikelbohm? He was supposed to seek you out and er… request your assistance in our mission."

The wizard laughed. "Yes, he found me, and after his own fashion he requested my assistance. He is a young wizard with much energy and felt the need to prove himself. We fought and he bested me nicely, for as I told you, my powers are waning. In truth, I haven't had so much fun in years and we parted friends. I agreed to help him with the information he needed, and he was kind enough to spare my life. That is one reason I am helping you now."

"Do you know where Eikelbohm is now?"

"He did not tell me of his plans. He is slow to trust."

The old man looked sad and lonely and I felt a pang in my heart.

"One more word of advice, if I may," he said. "The dragon, Joe. You say he is your friend."

"That's right. I went to fight him, and he ended up inviting me for pizza."

"Hmm. Well, I know dragons better than anyone. I do not wish to say too much, but you must remember that they are complex creatures and very intelligent. I must warn you to be careful."

"I'm sure I'm safe. He recently became a vegetarian." The words came out before I was able to catch myself. The wizard's eyes gleamed with pleasure and I kicked myself for my foolishness.

"Oh, that is good news," he said. "You know, if you want to gain Joe's trust, I think it best you don't mention you met me. We really never got on. I was like a father to him, but the older dragons turned him against me when he was too young to think for himself and he has regarded me as an enemy ever since. But you're definitely going to need his help if you want to recover the seed. You're going to need all the help you can get."

"How do I address you?" I asked after a short pause. "You haven't told me your name."

"I'd rather not say if you don't mind. Can't we make do with a 'hey you' or a simple throat clearing or a grunt or a nudge?"

"That won't do at all. I have a mental complex about not knowing what to call people. It all started when I was in school, and my mother, in spite of being a kind of test tube, taught my class for a year. I never knew what to call her in front of the other kids. I couldn't call her Mrs. Dogalogue, that felt way too weird. And if I called her Mum in front of the other kids I'd have been a laughing stock. It was the most awkward school year of my life. I really must know what to call you if this relationship is to go anywhere."

"Oh, very well, if you must know. My name is Nefarious, Architect of Evil. And lest you think this is some sort of joke name,

I am bound to assure you that it is not and that I am genuinely evil and you should not trust me or believe anything I say."

"I think I can understand why you did not wish to tell me that," I said, suppressing my laughter.

"But don't jump to any conclusions. This name was imposed on me as a curse by my archenemy, Insidious. He is the real evil necromancer but he calls himself *Puppy Dog Eyes the Kind - All Loving Saint and Planetary Savior*."

"Well, I must say, that doesn't seem very fair. But why don't you just change your name to something more appealing, like Geronimo the Gentle, or Waldorf the Wise."

"Or Prospero, Protector of all Small Beasts," said Mina. "Then mice would like you."

"The curse does not allow me to change it or lie about my name or use a nickname. Insidious is a very powerful wizard."

"So he compelled you to introduce yourself as Nefarious the Evil?"

"Yes, and that's not all. The worst part about this curse is that whatever I say to explain the curse and my admittedly suspicious-sounding name, ends up sounding like a pathetic lie and gives people the impression that I really *am* an evil necromancer just making excuses."

"I'm sorry to hear that," I said. "And it works, too. Your story is quite unbelievable and does sound exactly like a pathetic lie. That wizard who cursed you really knew his spells. But I'm not going to let him fool me with his tricks, no sirree! I've decided I'm going to trust you and take you at your word, if for no other reason than to spite that nasty fellow who placed this awful unfair curse on you."

"I want to thank you from the bottom of my black heart. You see? There it goes again, the curse forcing me to say silly things that give the impression that I am a knave and a dastard who will stop at nothing to seize world power, when in fact I'm innocent, just like a little child."

At this last utterance the ancient magician's voice cracked. He cackled and his fingers hooked and curled. His back hunched, his eyes became red, and his body emitted a hideous stench like that of rotting flesh. And just in case that was not convincing enough, his features transformed into a grotesque caricature of innocence.

"Now that's what I call an impressive curse," I said backing away.

Nefarious recovered in a moment and I was left wondering what kind of other terrible powers the dreaded *Puppy Dog Eyes the Kind* wielded. I was certainly going to keep an eye out for that guy!

"Anyway, never mind my troubles," said the wizard. "Let's get back to your mission. Your next step is to find the talking stones. When they learn of your objective they may well give you the iPoss—if they decide to trust you. Here is the entrance to the passageway. This leads out of the valley and connects with the dungeons under the castle of Duke Honk."

He stopped before the wide tunnel. The air from it was cool and a little damp.

"I can go no further. I cannot roam freely in the realm of the dragon. Just follow this tunnel straight until you come to a stairway. At the bottom of that stair is the entrance to the Cave of Stones. Oh, and one more thing. You might want to steer clear of the castle glank. Farewell, Sir Dogalogue, and may Zond watch over you on your mission."

"Hey, wait a minute," I called. "What's a glank?" But the wizard was already leaving, so I called out my thanks and turned towards the tunnel. What in Zond was a glank? I knew I could not trust the old rascal, but I could not help but feel grateful. I drew the amulet from my pocket. It shone blue with excitement in the dim light, as though sensing that it was returning home.

The Speaking Stones

The passageway headed straight for the Duke's castle. I knew this, not because I had suddenly miraculously developed a sense of direction, but because I was standing in front of a big sign that read, 'Duke's Castle This Way.'

"Well, that was pretty easy," I said. "We're making progress at last, Mina. And who would have thought it? All thanks to Nefarious."

"Don't forget what Sinistru said about his true motive," said Mina.

Sometimes Mina was sensible to the point of being boring.

The tunnel burrowed through the rock, and we followed it straight and level for at least a mile. Here the rock became black and shiny, like melted glass—volcanic obsidian.

Suddenly Mina wriggled and sniffed suspiciously. "What's that sound?" she squeaked.

"What's what sound?" I halted and grabbed the hilt of my sword, glancing anxiously up and down the tunnel.

"I thought I heard something up ahead."

I listened but neither of us could see or hear anything more. As we went on, I couldn't help wondering whether or not glanks are fond of seafood.

The tunnel turned left and we came to a halt at the top of a spiral staircase, just as Nefarious had described. I paused to remove a fresh torch from a wall bracket and lit it from my own. Very considerate of somebody to provide light for visitors. I descended the steps, my armored feet ringing on the stone. Suddenly I stubbed my toe on a jutting rock. Fortunately this did not hurt as I was protected by my armor, and even if I hadn't been, I was wearing my human suit. The suit did have certain advantages. It wouldn't even have mattered much if someone cut a finger off. At least not until I got the repair bill. Not that I was volunteering or anything like that, but it was nice to be so insulated from this hostile planetary environment. Anyway, you can hardly stub a tentacle. They're too squishy — virtually unstubbable. A compensation for being squelchy and repulsive to look at. That's right, deep down inside, we cephalopods know that we are a hideous, disgusting sight. We pretend that we think we're attractive to look at, not because we're stupid or bereft of good taste. We're just in denial.

So when I stubbed my toe I was unhurt, though someone else was.

"Ow!" said the rock. "Watch who you're stubbing there with your nasty metal-plated foot."

"How come you're talking?" I said.

"I didn't say anything," said Mina.

"I'm not talking to you, Mina," I said. "I'm talking to this talking rock."

"What talking rock?" Mina seemed confused.

"Me. Hello!" said the rock. "Sir knight of the formidable toe. I think your mouse can't hear rocks speaking. Don't worry. It's normal for rodents. It's not a disability or anything."

"There's nothing wrong with my mouse," I said defensively.

"I know that," said Mina, "but I'm beginning to think there is something wrong with you! Why have you stopped?"

"Hush, Mina," I said. "I'm talking to this rock."

"I can only conclude that you've finally lost your last marble," said Mina, irritated.

"Why am I talking?" said the stone. "I talk. That's what I do. Usually no one listens though. See? Your mouse is not listening right now."

"What's the use of talking when no one is listening?" I said. Wow, what a great line for a song. I wanted to write it down before I forgot it, but I didn't have a notepad. As a result it would not be turned into a key line of a hit song for another 650 years. Which goes to show, it always pays to carry pen and paper.

"Are you one of the talking stones of Atlantis?" I asked.

"If anyone else around here claims they're from Atlantis, there's going to be trouble," growled Mina. She seemed upset at being left out of the conversation.

"You know, it's funny you should ask that," said the rock. "As it happens, I once occupied a rather important position on that blessed isle. I am Sigurd, the talking rock, named for the famous dragon slayer. I am noted for my courage and eloquence, which, I might add, runs in my family. One of my ancestors, an igneous boulder of some repute from the Cretinous Era, was prone to dispatching hideous monsters in his spare time. But forsooth, judging by the glazing over of your eyes and the snores of your diminutive rodent friend, I fear I digress and my famously active tongue runneth away with me."

My attention was indeed beginning to sag.

"To address your question," continued the garrulous mineral deposit, evidently a close relative of my sword Excalibur, "I am a solitary outrider, a brave guardian of the way to the sacred cave. Fending off vandals and spies, alone and unaided for nigh on nine millennia. And yet I suffered not a scratch, so doughty is my prowess. To get to the holy stones you have to continue to the bottom of this stairway, then pass through the locked door. My job is to act as a guard and to guide visitors. And also to warn off the tourists before the glank gets them."

"The glank?" The stone had my attention now. "What is a glank?"

Right on cue a dreadful sound echoed up the stairwell, a drawn-out howling, as though twelve walruses were responding to the news that they were required to eat only sand-flavored ice blocks for the rest of their days. The wail lingered, rising and falling, rebounding from the walls of the labyrinth and causing all with teeth to wish they had none.

"You were asking about the glank," continued the stone. "That is the sound the glank makes. You definitely don't want to run into him. He is big and hairy and hates tourists. He's on his inspection round. His job is to keep the castle free of intruders."

"So we're under the castle already?" Amazingly I'd managed to follow the directions that involved walking down a straight tunnel. This would have been excellent news, were it not for the fact that I was about to be devoured by this awful glank thing.

"Only just. This tunnel runs under the edge of the Duke's castle. The glank considers it his duty to secure the entire area. He is, I'm afraid, a little over-zealous about his duty."

"C'mon Mina, let's get going," I said, "I think it better we get into the Chamber of Stones before the glank finds us."

"Hey, don't rush off," called the stone. "We were just getting acquainted. Why don't you stay for a nice game of noughts and crosses. Then we could each tell our life story."

That's the problem with stones. They either don't talk at all or they won't shut up.

"Sorry. Must go. Planet to save. See you later." Before the stone had a chance to respond, I hurried on down the spiral staircase. At the bottom stood a heavy-looking oak door. It was locked.

The glank's wail rang out again, sounding closer. I fumbled with the amulet and searched for a keyhole. There was none. I began tapping and poking at the door, seeking some way to open it. "By the tendrils of the Space Ghost, how do you open this thing!" I muttered, beginning to panic. I thought I could hear the echo of heavy footsteps.

"What's up?" Someone yawned. "What's happening? Oh sorry, I must have been asleep. Did you want to come in?"

It was the door. A talking door, naturally.

"Yes, I'm rather anxious to avoid being eaten by this glank. I have the key. See this amulet. How do I open you?"

"Why, this is a very special occasion. It is many an age since anyone came here with a genuine amulet key. This is quite an honor."

"Thank you, but how do I use the key?"

"Oh sorry, it is so seldom used that I've gotten into the habit of keeping the keyhole closed. It keeps the dust out."

A keyhole, just the size of the amulet appeared on the left side of the door.

"But wait. Before you can use the key, it is customary to answer some riddles."

"Riddles? What kind of riddles?"

"Difficult riddles," said the door.

The heavy tread of the monster was quite clear now and getting louder.

"Is there any way we can postpone the riddle part? I can answer all the riddles you want once I'm inside."

The door laughed. "Ha ha, that's what they always say, but once they've got what they want, they're nowhere to be found. No, sorry, it's a strict regulation. But since you're in a hurry, I'll just ask one, instead of the usual forty-nine."

I looked around for a place to hide. This had better be a really easy riddle or we'd have to get out of sight. "OK, then, what's the riddle?"

The door recited in a sing-song voice:

> Greater than God,
> More evil than Satan
> The poor have it
> The rich don't need it
> Eat it and you die.

The door was right. This riddle seemed a little tricky, and I certainly couldn't think clearly with a damned glank breathing down my neck. Mina tugged at my pocket. "Not now, Mina, I'm trying to think." I stuffed a sock on her head and tried to concentrate on solving the riddle.

Greater than God? That made no sense. It was some kind of trick. It was probably one of those children's riddles where the answer turns out to be bananas or something silly. But bananas weren't more evil than the devil. At least most of them weren't. And you wouldn't die if you ate a banana, unless someone had poisoned it. This was hopeless. The footsteps sounded really near. Time to hide.

I left the doorway and hurried to crouch unseen in the darkness by the stairs. No sooner was I out of sight than a huge shadow fell on the wall. Into full view swung one of the most mournful-looking creatures I've ever seen. It was big, very big. Its eyebrows hung from its brow like twin bears, so shaggy I wondered how it could see at all. They shaded a pair of large, sad eyes set in a massive, drooping face with jutting teeth and a head like a melon. Its huge hands ended in long claws. Its protruding lower jaw boasted two upward jutting tusks, giving it a permanent moronic expression. It walked upright on two legs but stooped, its arms swinging to the ground like those of a monstrous ape. It was entirely covered in matted black hair and held a watering can in its left paw.

I could feel Mina cringing and shivering in fear. I, of course, was not shivering, being a cold-blooded animal, but I could still have used some of that fearlessness potion Nefarious had mentioned.

The glank bent down to spread something on the floor of the cave. When it stood back I saw to my horror that the ground was covered in large spiders. The monster was giving them food! Then it picked up the watering can and proceeded to water the hinges of the door, singing a tuneless song:

> Rust, rust, rust and dust
> Water the hinges, that I must
> Decorate with rhinoceros tails
> Feed the beetles, worms and snails
> Spread the fungus and paint with slime
> Make all look old and guard the grime
> Dangle spiders' webs about
> Howl and sing and growl and shout
> Water the mold and moss and fern
> So the nosy tourists learn
> To leave and follow a different route
> 'Ere I throw them down my garbage chute!

This was certainly the oddest monster I'd ever come across. When it had finished watering the door hinges, it crouched down and began petting the spiders and singing to them.

> I love you little spiders, you're so cute,
> Not like the nasty human brutes,
> Don't you worry I will take care
> To keep you safe in my lovely lair.

This song was not factually correct. The spiders were not little. They were about the size of my hand, which for a spider is way larger than necessary. Nor were they, by any stretch of the imagination, cute. They were hairy, with sharp fangs and clusters of malevolent eyes. A less cute creature is hard to imagine. But they seemed to adore the glank creature. They clustered around him and I could hear them muttering, competing for his affections: "Pat me," "No, me" "I'm his favorite, get away." No accounting for taste. The glank was also seriously not cute, so perhaps it was a kind of hideous critter bonding thing.

The monster rose to its feet, picked up its bag, which appeared to be stuffed with still more spiders, and lumbered back the way it had come, still humming its spider song. I waited a couple of moments to let the footsteps fade away completely and emerged from my hiding place. The spiders turned to me in suspicion, some of them adopting a terrifying defensive posture, crouched back on their hind legs, forelegs and fangs upraised, ready to strike. I kept my distance.

"Well, I never saw such odd behavior from a monster," I murmured. Mina wriggled in my pocket. First, I must figure out that pesky riddle. Now how did it go again? More evil than Satan? That could be the person who invented this dumb riddle. But why would the poor have such a person? It didn't make sense."

Mina wriggled violently in my pocket. "Oh, all right!" I removed the sock. "What is it, Mina! How can I figure out this riddle with you chattering all the time?"

"It's nothing," said Mina.

"If it's nothing, then why in Zond are you bothering me? I must say, that's a pretty silly reason to make such a fuss, wriggling about and interrupting my thinking!"

"The answer to the riddle. It's nothing."

"What do you mean, nothing? There is no answer? I don't think so. I'm sure this nice door would not have given us a riddle with no answer."

"No, no. Listen. The answer to the riddle is NOTHING. Nothing is greater than God. Nothing is more evil than Satan, the poor have nothing, the rich need nothing and so on: the answer is nothing."

Oh, gosh. How clever. I felt mean and stupid. "Oh, Mina, I'm so sorry. I should listen to you more. I promise I'll make it up to you, Ask for anything you want." I picked her up and stroked her head.

"How about we get rid of the sock?"

So we fed the sock to the spiders, who fought over it with enthusiastic delight. I wondered what they could want with a sock. Perhaps they were just fighting for the fun of it. I could not see how they were planning on wearing it. After all, a spider would need eight socks. And then it would have to get some shoes as well, which was going to prove very expensive at four pairs per spider. But they started tearing the sock to pieces and scuttling off with tufts of wool into the darkness. I could hear them twittering excitedly about lining their nests. These were going to be some mighty warm spiders. Unfortunately, that also meant they were breeding. The glank would be pleased.

The Chamber of Stones was the quietest place in the world. The dome of the cave formed its ceiling but this was no regular cave roof. It was lined with phosphorescent blue stone, inset with thousands of glittering white crystals like stars, arranged to represent the night sky as seen from this spot eons ago. Beneath that glittering dome was a stone garden surrounded by a large hexagonal star. Within the star were a series of concentric rings of arches and pillars, sculptures and mosaics. And at the heart of it all, seemingly growing out of the very rock, was a tree of polished marble, its hues shifting from coral pink to tourmaline. The marble tree shone softly from within, microvita energy pulsing through its veins, imbuing all around it with intelligence and awareness where once there was none.

As we walked the winding paths to the center of the pattern, a faint sound came from all around the chamber, like a whisper of the distant ocean. Slowly I became aware that I was hearing the soft muttering of a sea of voices, a host of stones conversing through thought. I'd heard a stone speak but this seemed more subtle and intelligent. A chorus of voices that rang as they spoke, sometimes in unison, now in harmony. These were not uncultured, wild stones, spouting random thoughts and foolish words. This was the ancient outpost of a great civilization at the zenith of its power. Yet all was still, as though all these mysterious minds were frozen in a dream where nothing ever changed.

"It's so pretty," said Mina softly, gazing about in awe. Finally we'd found something to impress my mouse.

I needed to get the attention of the stones. Or at least one of them. I certainly didn't want to talk to all of them. That could take a while. One would be just fine. It just needed to be the right one. I sent out a gentle thought, like a whisper, not wanting to wake them all at once.

"Stones of Atlantis, can you hear me?" I felt rather foolish. At least I didn't have to say it out loud, so Mina couldn't hear me.

"Hey, what's that?" said a sleepy voice. "You're not a stone."

"No, but I am a friend of all well-meaning stones. I seek knowledge of Atlantis."

The stone came fully awake now. "Oooh, Atlantis, those were our glory days and that's the truth. The fresh sea washing away our molecules to make them sand, the call of the gulls, the masterful kings… until…" Then the stone fell silent.

"Good sir," said another stone. "Please spare us the sorrow of this memory. We would rather not speak of that which is lost forever, lest it break our hearts."

"And our hearts are not easy to break," said another. "As you might have guessed, they are made of stone."

"But my mission is to restore those wonders that are lost," I said. "If you help me find Atlantis I will plant the microvita seed again."

"How do we know you are not evil, like that nasty necromancer who sneaks around these tunnels," said the second stone.

"But he could not speak our language and hear our voices like this creature," said the first.

"Anyway, we are right pleased. You are our first visitor in three thousand years."

"And the last was just a rat that had lost its way, asking for directions."

"This new one seems to be some kind of shellfish."

Then an authoritative voice joined the conversation, and the other stones fell silent in deference. "This creature has come from the stars. His arrival is of import to the Great Dream of the Microvita Tree. See, he bears the amulet of the master, and he can hear our thoughts."

"Greetings, O Queen of Stones," I said, a little unsure of how one addresses a chief stone. "I am Dogalogue of Zondgraz. I bring a message from my master, who planted the microvita tree in fair Atlantis long ago."

"Welcome Dogalogue of Zondgraz," said the queen. "We stones of Atlantis have long waited for this. This was the northernmost outpost of the Atlantean Empire. We were brought here from the blessed Temple of the Microvita Tree itself where we bathed in its radiance for centuries and became self aware."

"That's right," said another stone. "Not all stones can talk like us, you know."

"We can still speak and hear one another because we are stones, and stones don't forget."

"Sometimes they do," said the first stone. "You forgot our wedding anniversary four hundred times already."

"Ah yes, well, I didn't claim to be perfect." The stone subsided in a pool of embarrassment.

"Oh, c'mon," said a deep-voiced stone. "You guys are getting carried away, romanticizing the past as usual. Atlantis wasn't so great for all of us."

"It was paradise compared to this dump," said the first stone, "sitting around in the dark for hundreds of years having to listen to you loonies arguing."

"It was OK for the fortunate few," said the deep voice. "Like you, or our queen stone, perched atop the archway over the palace courtyard. A nice view, a cool breeze, it was a cushy number. Me? I was underneath, face down in the dirt for 340 years with horses treading on my back every morning. The stupid mason put me upside down so that I couldn't see anything. I suppose it would have been even worse to have the horses tread on my face. I hadn't thought of that. Either way, it was not much fun, I can tell you."

"Luxury! What are you complaining about? At least the sun wasn't in your eyes. You could get a nice tan and you had a regular relaxing back massage. Some folks are never satisfied. Now, we, on the other hand, had it tough! Somebody ground part of me down into dust with a nail file in order escape from his dungeon."

"A working-class hero, no doubt," said the deep voice. "Or an unjustly imprisoned proletarian poet or radical thinker who dared to challenge the fascist monarchist dictators. It just goes to show, it doesn't matter how fancy they dress up the ruling class, they always exploit the weak and the workers. What we need now is a common stones revolution to set things right."

Fascinated as I was to meet my first Marxist mineral deposit, I thought I'd better get to the point.

"Listen," I said. "Your discussion is most engaging, but my mission is urgent. My master sent me from our distant world to recover the lost seed of the microvita tree and plant it to grow anew in the mountains of the east that touch the sky. The fate of your world depends on my replanting the seed so that it can restore harmony on the earth. I need your help to find the seed."

"We would like to help you," said the queen stone. "However, there is one small problem. Please allow us to confer privately for a moment."

A few minutes later the stones were back.

"Alien wizard, you must understand that even I, queen of the stones, am bound by our laws. We have tried to come to a collective decision. All the stones in the discussion are agreed that we should help you, with the exception of one small pebble who is sleeping. Unfortunately, this means that we cannot do anything because our constitution stipulates that all decisions must be unanimous."

"Can't you wake the pebble? Surely she would agree."

"That is not likely. This particular pebble has been possessed by a demon and always disagrees with everything we say. That is why we cast a spell on her to make her sleep."

"But you're the queen. Do you really have to make all of your decisions by consensus? It must be incredibly difficult to get anything done."

"Tell me about it," said the queen in a bitter tone. "We were doing fine until the Athenians came along with all their talk of democracy. Now every pebble with a lonely brain cell thinks its opinion should carry the same weight as that of a trained administrator with a degree from Oxford. We haven't been able to make a single decision since 483 BCE. It's driving me nuts."

"Me too," said Norman, a particularly unimportant stone. "And I was already nuts, so now I'm two nuts."

"There must be some way around this impasse. It seems so silly."

"It is silly," said the queen. "It is an incredibly silly rule and should be ignored. That is why you have to arrest us."

"What?"

"If you charge us with idiotic obstruction of important world-savior-type activities and arrest us all, we will be compelled to obey you and answer your questions. It is the law."

"Well, I don't like to compel anyone against their will, but since you seem to want me to, I suppose I could do it."

"You misunderstand. We are not saying we want you to arrest us. Only a crazy person would want that. But we are prepared to allow you to arrest us on one condition. You must teach us Morris Dancing."

"What?" These stones were crazier than I'd expected.

"Actually, that was a little joke." All of the rocks were giggling and rocking with mirth. "Ha, ha! Whoever heard of stones Morris Dancing? How absurd." The queen stone composed herself. "No, what we really want is that you to teach us to play chess."

As if that made more sense. These stones were really peculiar. I suppose it is to be expected after sitting around for thousands of years with nothing to do. I figured there was a better chance of teaching them chess than Morris Dancing, particularly since I had no idea how to Morris Dance myself, so I accepted their bizarre offer.

"All right, it's a deal. Are you ready for me to arrest you?"

"No, never," said the queen stone firmly. "Let the record state that we hate to be arrested."

Then she whispered. "Now, go ahead and arrest us. It has to appear to be against our will; otherwise it might look as though we arranged it and it might be judged unethical."

Appear to whom? Who was watching? I was bewildered. But what the heck. I declared loudly, "I arrest you all in the name of the law."

"Oh woe, what will my mother say!" cried one stone.

"My life is ruined," wept another stone. "Now I can never marry that very respectable stone who is the son of an altar stone and is so wealthy and intelligent. Tonight I will attempt to stab myself with an escaped goldfish."

"That was perfect," the queen stone said. "Now that we are all in your power you can demand that we tell you about Atlantis."

"But I feel terrible. I've made you all so unhappy."

"Oh, they're just being melodramatic. They haven't had this much fun in centuries. They'll be fine once they figure out that it makes absolutely no difference to a stone whether it is arrested or not. Now, before we get to your mission, how about that chess lesson?"

So I taught the stones the basics of chess. I reasoned that they'd have plenty of time to work on strategy, so I only had to make sure they were clear about the rules. For pieces we used little black and white pebbles of various shapes and sizes in a courtyard paved with square tiles. The stones used their latent telekinesis to move the pieces. It was eerie to watch the little pebbles move by themselves as the stones ordered them, queen to king's rook four, and so forth. I felt proud as my new students vied with one another for supremacy on the field of strategic combat.

When the lesson was over, the queen Stone spoke. "Very good, boys. I do believe you've got it, and that is because you have an excellent teacher. I want you all to thank Sir Dogalogue."

They thanked me in chorus.

"And now," said the queen stone, "let us turn to your mission to replant the microvita tree. I must warn you, you will face many dangers. Our scripture contains an ominous warning about a mysterious creature that haunts the drowned ruins of Atlantis. A many-tentacled sea monster in appearance but possessed of a spirit more malevolent and powerful than a mere beast. For this creature is a manifestation of the collective hatred of all the extremist Atlanteans and will not die until that old feud is ended. It covets the microvita seed and has laid a curse on any who try to steal it. This monster is known by many names: The Mysterious Guardian, The Obnoxious Slime Thing, The Deranged Leviathan, and the Fantastic Many-Tentacled Spirit of Doom that can Hold its Breath for One Hundred Years. And some would say, a good thing, too!"

"I'm not bothered by such stories," I said. "They always put that kind of thing in prophecies to keep the tourists away. If they didn't make it sound scary, why, everyone would go off on quests and adventures and there'd be no one left to weed the vegetables. Manufacturing ominous myths is essential to the medieval economy." But beneath my bravado I was worried. This sea monster sounded formidable.

"I see you are determined, despite the risk," said the queen. "That is good, and we will help you."

An exquisitely carved box floated into the air and came to rest on the stone table before me.

"In this casket is a mysterious being that can lead you to the microvita seed. It is a cross between a possum and a thought wave, called the iPoss. For centuries we have kept it safe against this moment. May it aid you in your quest."

"Is that an Australian possum or an American possum?" I asked.

"An American possum?" sneered a rough-looking boulder. "No self-respecting stone would be seen fraternizing with an American possum! No, no, no. We're talking about the cute and furry Australian possum." He subsided, muttering, "American possum? Pah!"

"My oafish friend is correct. It is part Australian possum," said the queen stone. "Now use your amulet to open the box."

This amulet was sure good at opening things. I opened the box but it was empty.

"Don't worry, the iPoss is sleeping," she said. "It is only corporeal when it is awake, and then only when it is in the right mood. It can materialize and de-materialize at will. It does not eat. It doesn't even need the box really, but we stones enjoy putting things in boxes, so there you are."

Just then something white and furry began to appear, lying on the blue velvet lining of the box. A pair of large, gentle eyes opened and came to rest on me. I could feel its spirit but no clear thoughts. It was more of a quiet presence, sensing those around it and responding, but not fully self-aware. I reached my hand out slowly. The creature glided out of the box and onto my hand. It wound itself around my arm and ended up perched on my shoulder, its furry tail wound around my neck. Its touch was as soft as air.

"What a beautiful creature and what an invaluable gift. I cannot thank you enough, O temple stones."

"May Zond speed you on your mission," said the queen stone, and I heard all the voices of the temple singing together like a chorus of carved angels. Then the temple faded from view, and I found myself outside the door in the corridor where I'd seen the glank. Evidently these stones weren't into long sentimental goodbyes.

"Well Mina, that was an experience and no mistake," I said.

"I couldn't hear the stones talk," she said, "but I loved the stone garden and I like your new pet. It seems to be friendly to mice."

"It's called an iPoss. It won't harm you. And it will lead us to the microvita tree." I paused for a second. I was picking up a mental message from the iPoss. "Well, that's a bonus! It knows the way out of this labyrinth!"

Questionable Premonitions

"Hey, look who's back. Sir Dogalogue. How was the Morris Dancing?" said Brains.

"More fruitful than I expected," I said. "I'll tell you all about it in the morning. Let's all get a good night's sleep. We have a long journey ahead of us tomorrow."

As the others were settling for the night, Iris took her brother aside and said, "Last night I had a strange dream. I saw a dark castle on a hill, above a village. It was windy and a storm was brewing. It began to thunder and lightning and I saw a man walk into the village. I could not see his face but he was tall and had the gait of a warrior. A group of old men were gathered in the central square and he spoke with them for some time and then continued up a winding path that led to the castle gate. He blasted down the castle gates with occult fire and once he was within the walls he confronted an ancient wizard. The air was filled with flame and energy bolts as they fought but in the end the young warrior prevailed and the old man knelt before him in supplication. But then I caught a sly smile on the old man's face. After that the scene faded and I awoke. You know, I think he was Dogalogue's friend. Remember when I asked him what Eikelbohm looked like? It was a perfect match."

"That's true," said The Sweep slowly. "That was more than uncanny. But look, Sis, isn't it possible that your husband-search problems are influencing your vision? Perhaps this phantasmagoria is just the result of wishful thinking."

Iris stamped her foot. "Why will you never take me seriously? I know the difference between a mere whimsical dream and a dream of significance. I'm sure this has some importance to our mission."

"OK, you're probably right. Perhaps your intuition really did enable you to farsee Sir Dogalogue's friend beating up the old necromancer."

"But what about the old man's sly smile? I felt he was somehow entrapping the warrior. That's what really worries me."

"I don't know what to make of it, Sis. Clairvoyance and farseeing are your department. Let's just keep it in mind and perhaps the meaning of the dream will become clear as events unfold."

"I was sort of hoping they'd become clearer before events unfold. Otherwise, what's the use of having a vision?"

By the Rood

The others were soon snoozing, but I had much to ponder and my mind would not let me rest. The fire had sunk to a bed of embers, occasionally flaring up halfheartedly, the little fingers of flame no taller than a toadstool. A modest chorus of frogs sang their chirping love song over the unending tinkle of the stream that in the darkness seemed louder than usual. Night had fallen and the twittering and chirping of the diurnal birds was replaced by the soft, eerie voices of night creatures. An owl hooted into the darkness, passing deadly intelligence from one hunter to another. Mina shuddered and crept closer to me, her nose twitching. I took her in my hand to comfort her. I was coming to love this place. Not just this charming valley where I'd found such good friends but Earth, the planet, was growing on me.

The next morning, before we readied ourselves to take flight, we held a war conference.

"Last night when I spoke with the stones of Atlantis they gave me two gifts. The first was this map that shows us the location of Atlantis in relation to the Iberian coast."

Of course I was lying about how I got the map, but I was not quite ready to tell them that not only was I buddies with a vampire but that an evil necromancer had adopted me as his favorite future disciple. I spread out my map so all could see and everyone gathered around in excitement.

The dragon studied the parchment closely, which unfortunately involved the close proximity of his enormous nose. "This is wonderful, Sir Dogalogue. See? We can fly to the seaside town of Mondragon today and obtain a ship to sail to

Atlantis. From there, given the right weather, it is less than a day's journey."

"Isn't it very deep?" asked Iris.

"In my natural form, without the encumbrance of this human suit, I am a good diver," I said. "And my comrade Eikelbohm is even better."

"But how will we find a single seed in the ruins of a drowned city?" said Maurice.

"I'm glad you asked that question," I said.

Trying to appear nonchalant, I brought out the box containing the iPoss and opened the lid. The wispy white creature was awake. It emerged from its casket like a spirit, floating and furry, its black eyes reflecting the dawn sky. I felt its mind immediately, more alien than any earthling, a being of pure microvita energy created with only one purpose—to bring the dream of the microvita tree's blossoming to fruition. I sensed a moment of uncertainty when it was not sure whether to remain visible or not but then I felt it touch each of our minds briefly. Reassured, it chose to stay.

"This is the iPoss. It is connected in some mysterious way with the microvita seed. It will sense the seed when we are close and guide us to it."

"Oh, how adorable," exclaimed the princess. She reached out to the iPoss and the creature glided over her hand and up her arm to rest on her shoulder, its long, furry tail curled about her neck. She stroked its head carefully. The creature seemed quite contented, and so Iris became the caretaker of the iPoss. I was only slightly jealous and it seemed like a good idea to have something to take her mind off her family problems.

The duke then unrolled two large maps of his own.

"You'll want to follow this route. Head for the cliffs of Dover, then across the channel to Northern Gaul. Avoid all towns and especially any castles. Most English castles are equipped with anti-dragon cannons these days, and if they don't have cannons they'll have crossbowmen."

"I don't like crossbows," said Joe. "Those bolts can really sting."

"You'll have to purchase a ship in Mondragon. I have given Iris enough gold coinage from the treasury to cover any expenses, so you should have no problem with finance. But if you want to have any dealings with the coastal folks you'll have to keep Joe well out of sight.

They are very superstitious about dragons. They will have nothing to do with you if they know you are associated with one. After you launch your ship and you're out of sight of the coast, the dragon can fly out and join you. Now, who is going to captain the ship? Prince Sweep, you must have training in the seafaring arts. Can you handle it?"

"No problem," said The Sweep, who had no such training at all. He'd spent all his maritime training time reading comic books in the cabin.

"Although, sadly, I cannot accompany you on your quest," the duke continued, "I can furnish you with some sound advice. I happen to be a bit of a quests aficionado, you see, having embarked upon several in my youth. The best kind of quest does in fact proceed to the west, just like in the song."

"You see?" said Brains to everyone and no one. "Not such a stupid song, after all." He proceeded to burnish the small shield he'd picked up somewhere along the way.

"Now there are quests that proceed to the east, but they are generally of the more mystical kind, rather than the adventurous kind, and I'm not well-versed in that type of quest."

"They may not even qualify as true quests," said Brains, now assuming his own air of authority. "Consider this. East doesn't rhyme with quest. That would be more of a *queest*, which sounds more like a new kind of washing powder or a dreadful disease."

"But *queest* rhymes with beast and least and yeast and feast and priest and questing beast," said Maurice, "so it might be possible to compose a song about a *queest*."

"Except for the fact that there is no such thing as a *queest*," said the exasperated duke. "And anyway, this quest does go to the west and the number one rule of quests is that moles and badgers are not allowed to participate unless they are gagged and chained to the mast." He glared at the animals, who fell silent.

The Sweep was studying the map closely. "Actually, the latter part of our quest does take us east to the Himalayas." At a stern glance from his uncle, he hastily added, "but let's worry about that when we've completed the west part of the quest. I'm sure that's best. For now, let's put that matter to rest. It's a later test."

"Will you shut up!" said Iris. "Uncle is trying to explain important stuff here. Please go on, Uncle Honk. I will personally ensure that anyone who interrupts you has to walk the plank."

"Thank you, Iris," said Honk. "Now every quest must have a leader. You, Sir Dogalogue, are the leader of this quest. But I understand that your colleague Dr. Eikelbohm is in fact the commander of your mission, so once he rejoins you, he will be the leader. Tradition holds that anyone who disobeys the leader has to adopt the life of a beaver and commit to sleeping in a pond and eating tree bark for the rest of his life."

"Wait a minute," said Joe. "I do not know this Eikelbohm. I pledged my allegiance to Sir Dogalogue and his mission, not to a stranger."

"Me, too," everyone said in chorus, except for me of course because I was Sir Dogalogue, and I would look pretty silly pledging allegiance to myself.

"That should not be a problem," said the genially bossy duke. "So long as you understand that Dogalogue will be under the command of Eikelbohm once they're reunited. Now, you need someone to be in charge of supplies. Who'd like to volunteer?"

I really didn't mind him taking charge of my team like this. I'd never much enjoyed managerial positions, and he understood much more about what it took to mount an expedition on his planet. The money thing for example. I would never have thought of that. Anyway, he'd be left behind shortly, and I'd be free to assert my authority if I wanted—which I didn't.

"I would rather like to manage the supplies," volunteered The Sweep. "As the educated among you will know, some time ago I invented breakfast. This will be an opportunity to test my recent breakthrough, the radical *Two-Bowl Theorem.*"

"But you're the captain of the ship," said Brains. "You can't do everything. You need an assistant at least."

"I'm well-versed in the art of breakfast," said Maurice. "I could be Prince Sweep's assistant."

"Very well," said the duke. "The chief navigator will, of course, be Sir Dogalogue. After all, he claims to have found his way here across the vast expanse of space. Finding a mere microvita seed should be a doddle."

"Except that he is dyslexic in three dimensions," said Iris. "I think that Joe and I should take care of the navigation."

"As you wish. So I think you're all organized now. This is a really stripped-down team. Normally on an expedition you'd have lookouts, scouts, bosuns, bosons, research assistants, language experts, branch managers, animal handlers, gaffers, mission directors, secretaries, lawyers, accountants, feng shui experts, architects, bridge builders, negotiators, telephone sanitizers, vice presidents of marketing—in short, an entire quest bureaucracy. But I think this particular mission needs to be lean and agile."

"Plus, we're all we've got," said the mole. A fact of which I was very glad.

Early the next morning, before everyone else was awake, the duke took me aside, seemingly ill at ease. "That Sinistru fellow," he said in a low voice. "I'm guessing he was the one who helped you obtain the map and the iPoss creature. I fear you trust him too much. He's supposed to be an exorcist, but he didn't seem like a priest to me. Do you know he told me he hasn't even read the Bible? Said he gave up at page four because it was boring. I do not believe he is even a true Christian."

He stared at me intently. "Now it occurs to me that I really know very little about you, and I am allowing my young niece to accompany you on this quest. So I'd like to know, how about you? I certainly hope that *you* believe in Jesus Christ our savior?"

I found this confusing. Sensing trouble, I began to edge away. "Er, no thank you, I've already got one." I was afraid he was trying to sell me something.

"What the devil do you mean? I'm asking about your faith, man. What do you say? Do you believe?"

"Believe what exactly?"

"God's blood! Am I hearing this right? Do you believe in our savior Jesus Christ, Son of God? Answer me, man!"

The duke moved toward me as I backed away. He had become quite red in the face. Despite his age, he was a formidable swordsman.

"Well, I'm not exactly a man, as you understand the term. And I'm really not sure what I believe right now. I'm afraid I've been a bit busy since I arrived here so I haven't had the leisure to study much of your holy literature."

"For the last time, do you believe in Jesus Christ?"

"I suppose I believe that Jesus Christ existed. I mean, it's part of your history, isn't it? Will that do?"

"By the Rood, I've taken off a Saracen's head for less, but since you are a friend of my nephew I will forgo that pleasure. Your level of faith is hardly sufficient to save your immortal soul, but at least you appear to be honest. I will pray for you."

The Sweep hurried up to rescue me.

"Uncle, leave Sir Dogalogue alone. Where he comes from they've probably never heard of Jesus Christ."

The duke snorted. With some measure of expertise, I noted. He must have been taking lessons from his horse.

"And another thing. You don't really expect me to believe you come from another world, do you? It's an original story, to be sure, but I wasn't born yesterday. Now, don't get me wrong. If a man wants to conceal his identity it's not my business to pry. Plenty of good men don't want to be known. You could be an escaped lunatic, or an assassin, or a kidnapper of goats, or a mass murderer. There could be any number of innocent explanations, all of which are far more likely than the one you insist on."

I was about to explain that Zondgraz is in another solar system and there aren't any goats there to steal, but The Sweep was shaking his head, so I tried to simplify things.

"I'm from a place called Zondgraz. We don't have any of your religions there. It's a very long way away."

Suddenly I felt terribly homesick. I wondered what my friend Lucifer was doing. I could just picture him dancing on the beach in a foolish manner, or shaving himself in a taxi, terrorizing the other passengers. Little did I know that at that very moment my friend was gazing at the night sky thinking, That loony Dogalogue, I'll bet he's living it up having a holiday on earth; I wonder what the surf is like there.

The duke seemed to suddenly remember something, as old men are wont to do. "And another thing. You're not going to want to marry my niece or anything like that, are you?"

"Out of the question," I answered, relieved to have some good news for him. "Of course, she is a very eligible girl, for the right entity. But I am rather too old for her, being born around the time of your ancestors from Sumeria. And an ideal mate for me should possess at least fourteen legs, so your niece is twelve legs short, which would seem to present an insurmountable obstacle. So no need to worry on that count."

"I'm not a count, I'm a duke. Much more important."

"So sorry, my mistake." I had no idea what he was talking about, but I was not going to question this guy.

"Good. I'm glad that's settled. Having one loony in the family"—he nodded towards The Sweep—"is quite enough. Anyway, romance always complicates quests. Believe me, I know. In my youth I tried to woo a fair princess at the same time as undoing a spell that had turned her into a dangerous witch. I ended up almost marrying the witch by mistake, and the princess ran off with a richer knight who hadn't lifted a finger to help her. Ever since then I've made a point of keeping my love life and my work separate. I recommend you do the same."

"Thanks for the advice, I'll take note of it," I said, much relieved that we seemed to have left the subject of the duke's religion behind. "I wonder if I could trouble you for some more advice. Have you ever heard of a glank?"

"Yes, of course. I have one in my employ. Does an excellent job of keeping the castle scary. Howls nicely, never forgets to water the hinges, takes care of the spiders, he is most diligent. Glanks are quite the fashion these days, very popular with castle lords. We don't see our glank much, but occasionally he howls and frightens everyone, just to let us know he's on the job. Why do you ask?"

"Oh, nothing important. It's just that last night it almost ate me."

The duke laughed. "I seriously doubt that. Our glank is a vegetarian. All howl and no devour. He lives mostly on miso soup. Wouldn't harm a fly. Though I couldn't vouch the same for his pet spiders, ha ha."

Duke Honk wandered off in the direction of breakfast. "Thanks, Sweep, for saving me from your uncle," I said. "He is a bit intense when it comes to talking about his religion."

"I'm sorry about that. Yes, he's rather old fashioned on matters of faith. He's not the only one. You'd do well to remember that roughly 98 percent of the population of Europe feel the same way."

"Oh dear. And what about this Bible they keep on about? I mean, I know the basic story, but have you actually read it? Is it any good?"

"Not really my cup of tea," said The Sweep. "There aren't any jokes in it. I kept falling asleep around page four. But better not to mention that to my uncle."

We both laughed.

"I think you should just tell Uncle Honk that you found the Bible a gripping read and you think Jesus Christ is a capital fellow and his life story is an inspiration to all species."

"OK. But just between us, I honestly can't get too excited about the crucifixion part. We students at the Sadvipra school on Zondgraz have to practice crucifixion as a part of our messiah training and nobody likes it very much."

The Sweep bounced. "Better not mention that. Just say that you'd like to invite him to visit your homeland."

"Do you think he'd accept? I mean, he has a lot of responsibility here on earth? Oh, you mean your uncle. I thought you meant... never mind."

Actually, that wasn't a bad idea. There was someone on my planet I really wanted Jesus to meet.

We said farewell to the good duke, and the motes, and I spared a thought for the lonely Sinistru. And so we set off with our brave crew of seven on a mission to determine the future of planet Earth. As Joe took off in the chill air with us seated on his back, I still sensed a faint presence, difficult to pinpoint. Someone, or something, was following us. It looked like Sinistru was on task.

By the time the sun stood high above us, we had left behind Not Enough Hugs Valley, the dragon's caves, and pretty much all I knew of this planet, and had reached the chalk cliffs on the southern coast where we stopped for a short rest. We then left the shores of England and climbed into the air above the English Channel, which the French called the French Channel in order to confuse people. I sat astride the great dragon's body, feeling its power pulse beneath me, carrying us out over the shining sea spread beneath us in a great sheet of blue silver. I looked back at white cliffs receding behind us and noticed something most curious. Carved into the face of the cliff in huge letters were the words, "No Vultures Admitted".

"Joe," said Iris. "How many other dragons are there?"

Joe had settled into a steady rhythm, staying high out of bow range as he flew, favoring forests and fields and avoiding human habitations. This was way better than riding a horse, exhilarating, in fact. The ride was a lot smoother and you could feel the amazing power of the dragon's muscles as he beat his way through the air with little effort, riding on the wind. "There are only 159 dragons left in Europe," said Joe. "We were never many and our numbers increase very slowly. We don't breed easily, you see. Our metabolism is not completely suited to your planet, so fertile eggs are rare. And since the invention of cannons, two dragons have actually been killed by humans! It's unprecedented."

"So what are they like, the other dragons?"

"They're OK, I guess." Joe's color dimmed a little. "You know we dragons are solitary creatures."

"How come?" said Brains.

"Well, I don't like to complain, but dragons are pretty difficult to live with. At least the others are. Believe me, I know. I've tried it."

Iris smiled and said, "But you are so kind and sophisticated and funny. Aren't they like you?"

Joe turned a warmer shade of orange. For such an intelligent creature he was absurdly easy to flatter.

"Yes, I suppose there are some fine thinkers and musicians amongst the Germans and Italians. The Australians on the other hand are complete barbarians!"

"What's an Australian?" said Iris.

"Ah, I forgot. You humans have such short memories. Australia is a vast dry island far across the world. It was discovered by Vikings way back in 1129. The Icelandic ship returned after many months with only one survivor. He told dreadful tales of beer-drinking demons who slur their words and curse, and huge garish-colored insects roaming the wilderness in droves. The rest of his crew were apparently eaten by poisonous snakes and spiders and vicious crocodiles and perverse animals that keep their young in their pockets. Upon hearing this, everyone agreed that Australia was a bad idea and promptly forgot about it. Everyone, that is, except us dragons. Some of us were curious and set up a colony there, a move the rest of us have regretted ever since."

"It sounds like a harsh place," said Maurice.

"Very. The dragons there have become wild and uncouth. They eat knights with their mouths open, they forget to say grace, they boast, they maltreat crocodiles, step on snakes, tease tourists. Bruce the Strongest Dragon in the World shows off by juggling poisonous reptiles—it's embarrassing. And they're annoyingly good at sports. If you are rash enough to invite one to a respectable social occasion, they're as likely as not to go on a drunken rampage and leave a mess of bodies and ruined villages behind them. You can't take them anywhere. Total *animals*!"

"They sound dreadful!" said Iris.

"Worst of all is when they eat the wrong food. Feed onions or garlic to an Australian dragon and you've got real trouble on your hands. Then they go completely antipodean."

Everyone shuddered, including me. I did not know what an antipodean was but it sounded awful.

30

LUCIFER, MASTER STORYTELLER

Dr. Dogalogue's Spaceship
Five days out from planet Earth.

Miranda was up early. The doctor found her sitting in the lounge gazing at the starscape on the viewfinder and playing with some rocks on the table, holding one of them up to her ear with her eyes closed.

"Dr. Dogalogue, could you really hear what the stones in the cave were saying?"

"Yes, but it's not like they were talking out loud. I could pick up feelings and thoughts. Remember those stones were charged with microvita. Because they were from the very castle that housed the microvita tree for hundreds of years, they were far more sentient, with higher consciousness than regular boring stones."

Miranda looked at the stones in front of her. "I think I know what you mean. These ordinary stones are really boring. I felt quite sorry for them."

"I don't think they actually suffer. So far as I can tell, they are remarkably content."

"You really don't understand what sarcasm is, do you, Doctor?"

Dogalogue raised his eyebrows, which, incidentally, were a kind of symbiotic seaweed—that's how Zondgrazian eyebrows work. He looked up to his left and pursed several of his lips. "Nope, can't say that I do. Why do you ask?"

Miranda shook her head, smiling. "Don't worry about it. It's a human thing. Can you also talk to the stones and molecules on Zondgraz?"

"No. The microvita energy of our planet is so intense that in order for anyone to manipulate the natural order by reading minds or transforming matter their own mind has to be extraordinarily strong. Our powers don't work so long as we remain on Zondgraz. My master says this helps us, as it forces us to develop great strength of mind so that on other planets we really are like super beings. But at home we are quite ordinary. He says it is the perfect training environment since most of us are such immature idiots that if we developed powers we'd just make a tremendous mess and it would all go to our heads and our egos would get out of control."

"You mean like, if you're on a planet with a strong gravitational field, you won't be able to run and jump easily, but you'll develop such strong muscles just from walking that when you go to an ordinary planet you'll be able to jump like a grasshopper?"

"Exactly. Good metaphor."

"He must be very wise, your master. What about him? Does he have powers on Zondgraz?"

"Sometimes he does things that would be impossible for any of us, but he doesn't like to talk about it. If anyone asks him, he usually yells at them or scolds them."

"I want to be like Princess Iris when I grow up. She's so brave and smart and even funny sometimes. And she loves animals. I think she is the dragon's favorite. Don't you?"

"Yes, I suspect so. She was always kind to him when he was sad. I think that meant a great deal to Joe. Iris somehow represented all the princesses he'd eaten, and Joe was especially grateful because she forgave him for eating them. I think he instinctively wanted to make it up to her by giving her his special love and affection. Now are you going to continue to plague me with questions or can I take a little time off from storytelling to help Lucifer with the preparations for the final jump to the Sol System?"

"I wish you could tell me more right now," said Miranda, "but I guess you'd better make sure we actually get to Earth. But you have to finish that stuff as quickly as possible so you can do important things like answer my questions. Tell Lucifer that a mad earthling has invaded your spaceship and that she demands your presence."

She gave him a quick hug, trying not to step on his tentacles, and then headed for the kitchen to raid the refrigerator.

As Dogalogue squished his way along the corridor to join Lucifer on the bridge he reflected on the fact that Miranda had indeed invaded not only his spaceship but his heart. Since her arrival in his life, his days had revolved around her. Feeding her, comforting her if she was sad, telling her the story of his trip to her home planet long ago. He found himself distracted during his work, looking forward to getting back to her bright little face, worrying in case she was bored or lonely. What was wrong with him? Perhaps it was some kind of alien virus from earth. He had been trying to avoid thinking about what would happen if he had to leave her on that planet. When, not if, he reluctantly corrected himself. He couldn't keep her as his ward forever. She didn't belong on Zondgraz. He really must find out how to return her to her parents, whoever they were, if they were still alive. Or at least some relative or human who could take care of her.

After lunch, Dogalogue was free to continue the story and this time Lucifer joined them. Miranda had been struggling to like Lucifer. He was Dr. Dogalogue's best friend, so that was a huge point in his favor. And they were all stuck with each other on the ship, so she wanted to make the best of the situation. Trying to be civil to Lucifer made her feel very mature, but it wasn't easy. Perhaps his prickly exterior was a ploy, hiding a heart of gold. She decided to officially like him unless he did something really awful.

"I think it is high time," said Lucifer, gathering his tentacles and settling onto the couch, "that somebody sensible told this tale the way it ought to be told. Dogalogue is far too sentimental. If you really wanted to know the truth you'd ask me to take over the storytelling."

"I like the way Dr. Dogalogue tells it," said Miranda. "And anyway, you haven't even been to earth."

"Actually, Miranda, he has," said Dogalogue. "After I returned to Zondgraz, he went there on a secret mission at the request of the master. Look, how about I finish this part, and we ask Lucifer to tell the next bit?"

"I guess so," said Miranda, "but only if I'm allowed to stop him if I don't like the way he's doing it."

Into the Atlantic

Later that day, Sinistru and Harvey landed in Iberia. The Iberian immigration officer examined Harvey's documents and regarded him gravely.

"Insect, are you aware that last time you came to Iberia you overstayed your visa by four days?"

"Four days?" Harvey tried to appear nonchalant. "Ah well, that's water under the bridge. What's a few days between arthropods, eh?"

"It can amount to quite a lot actually," said the officer. "Consider for instance that a butterfly only lives for an average of four days."

"That is misleading," said the ant. "In its caterpillar stage, the butterfly lives for months. Anyway, what difference could it make if I set foot on Iberian soil? I'm hardly going to sink the continent."

The officer turned to Sinistru. "Your friend does not seem to appreciate the seriousness of the situation."

"Please officer," said Sinistru. "He's only an ant."

At this the officer drew himself up and looked even more grave, if that was possible for a person who already looked as if he'd just been presented with genetic proof that his ancestors were cockroaches. "That's how it begins," he said in an ominous tone, "but ants are not so incidental as they might appear. It is a little known fact that ants weigh more, in total, than any other species on earth."

"Not quite so little known as you seem to imagine," said Sinistru. "Listen, I have a suggestion. How about you let the ant through, and in return I will refrain from sucking your brain out of your head through a straw?"

He made a face so scary that the officer blanched and stamped the paper.

"Thanks, great Sinistru," said Harvey, once they were out of earshot. "You were awesome."

"Think nothing of it," said Sinistru, who had thoroughly enjoyed himself. "If you want, we can go back and do it again."

The waves rocked the Dodecahedron gently, her sleek hull creaking against the wooden dock. She was a fine-looking ship with three cabins and a foredeck large enough to accommodate one dragon. Her modern rigging would enable her to sail as close to the wind as any craft on the sea. Built for speed, she carried no cannon, and thanks to our stash of dragon gold we'd been able to purchase her outright. None of the local ship owners would have been willing to hire a ship to us on such a risky venture anyway.

The Sweep was organizing the sails and rigging. It looked very complicated to me, as though fifty Zondrazians had gotten all their tentacles tangled, but The Sweep insisted that it would be no problem. Iris told me privately that she couldn't recall The Sweep ever sailing a ship before, but he claimed that he had done it when he was away from home and she was in school with the nuns.

It didn't take long to load since we only needed supplies for a few days. We were due to sail within the hour to catch the ebb tide. I took up my post by the gangplank, waiting for Iris, the last of our crew, to arrive. She had gone out to purchase medical supplies, "just in case." This town, Mondragon, had some bad history with dragons and we didn't want to alarm them, so Joe was laying low. He would fly out to join us once we were out of sight of the harbor.

A small crowd of curious locals had gathered to see these crazy foreigners who spent gold like it was going out of fashion and knowingly risked death by seeking Atlantis and trying to steal from the fabled sea monster. Suddenly there was a commotion in the crowd. A tall figure pushed his way to the front and hurried towards me. He was square jawed and strong, running with a spring in his step like a warrior. He wore no armor, just a sword at his side, and leather gauntlets on his hands.

"Eikelbohm!" I cried in relief. "You just found us in time. We're about to set off for Atlantis."

We embraced like long-lost brothers, the pommel of his overlarge sword digging into my side painfully. Then Iris arrived. I introduced them and she looked strangely at Eikelbohm. At that moment an old crone stepped out the crowd and began to speak in a loud voice with an air of authority. She raised her shriveled arms in the air, fists clenched.

"Brave but foolish strangers," she cackled. "Repent of your rash quest before you meet your doom."

I silently mouthed the lines as she spoke. It was straight out of our *Zondgrazian Prophecy Writing Manual.*

"And while we're on the subject of rashness," she gargled, spittle flying from her horrid lips as everyone backed away, "I be wondering, where did you young people come across all that gold? There's a mystery that answered might answer a good many other questions. It be no business of mine, of course, but we wouldn't want to be harboring no thieves in our town, now would we?"

People stepped even further away from her, whether out of fear or respect or aversion to witch's spittle, I was uncertain. I wondered if every town had a hideous pessimistic crone as a standard fixture. I supposed it was a form of entertainment when there was nothing else of interest going on.

"We're not thieves," said Mina angrily. "A nice dragon gave us the gold."

"Mina! You're not supposed to talk," said the badger. "Ooops. Nor am I!"

Great! I thought. Never depend on the discretion of a rodent.

Now the townsfolk backed away from *us*, muttering in fear. I overhead words like "witchcraft" and "devilry." The crone cried out, "They be powerful witches it seems. A talking mouse and a talking badger and claims of dragon gold."

The men gripped cudgels and knives and began edging towards us. This was looking ugly. But then the Mayor stepped forward and held up his hands, shaking his head. "Look," he said. "We don't want any trouble, and we appreciate your generous spending in our town. But it is well that you were on your way. And might I suggest that if by some miracle you survive both the ocean and the monster, you land in another town. Wizards and witches are not too popular around here. And dragons are openly disliked."

"As you wish," I said. "We mean no harm. Just let us leave in peace and we will not disturb you again."

The villagers kept their distance and began to settle down. I overheard talk of betting on our chances of survival, but a church elder spoke against it, so people began to leave the square in ones and twos, pausing to stare back at us in none too friendly a manner. I thought I glimpsed a hunchback hobbling away, but when I looked again he was gone.

"The old crone has a point, you know." One old gaffer had remained behind, the very fellow whose ship we'd purchased. He was more friendly than most, and seemed unconcerned about the talking animals. The large pouch of dragon gold he'd received in exchange for the ship had probably improved his mood. "The weather out at sea is very unpredictable in this season," he said. "A storm from the north can blow up in the blink of an eye. I urge you to get this trip over as fast as possible."

I thanked him and the mayor and boarded our trusty vessel, the Dodecahedron.

Eikelbohm's Tale

We sailed out into the Bay of Biscay and turned west before a light wind. The Sweep and Iris seemed to be handling the ship without any problem, so I took the time to bring Eikelbohm up to date on our situation.

"Zond's eyes!" said Eikelbohm after hearing my tale. "I must say, you seem to have done rather well, finding the iPoss and that map, and even recruiting the dragon. You've got everything we need to recover the seed."

"I had some lucky breaks," I said modestly. "But tell us how you fared with the evil necromancer!"

I had told no one of my own meeting with Nefarious. Eikelbohm sat down with a glass of wine while the rest of the crew gathered round.

"After we parted a week ago, I flew to the village where I'd heard the old wizard might be hiding out. He has quite a reputation, so it wasn't hard to track him down. He was living in a castle on a hill above the village. The streets were deserted when I got there. I didn't see anyone until I reached the main square. In front of the church there was a priest and six well-dressed men who appeared to be waiting for me. The oldest of them approached me with his hand outstretched. 'Welcome to Bedrock, sir,' he said. 'Pray come and sit with us and take some refreshing ale. We are eager to hear any news from the wider world. We see precious few travelers here.'"

"'Why, thank you,' I said, and we all sat at a table and drank one another's health. When I told them I was seeking the wizard they told me that he lived in the castle. 'He has ruled this land for centuries,' they said. 'He controls everything that goes on in this village and discourages visitors. He is wicked, powerful and fearsome and that's the truth. Unless you plan to offer your services to him, I advise you to depart at once and not return. He is a great enchanter, and as you can see, will stop at nothing.'"

"'What do you mean, "as I can see?" Your village seems quite peaceful, though I don't see many people about. I get that the castle is a bit daunting and gloomy looking, but what harm has the necromancer actually done to you?'"

"'Open your eyes, man! Look at us! Once we were men like you, able to stand and speak and bear ourselves with dignity. But ten years ago the wicked wizard turned us into beavers and we've been like this ever since.'

"None of them looked in the least like a beaver. They all looked like perfectly normal men. 'And what else did he do?' I asked."

"'Look around you, man. Once this was a handsome town. Now it is nought but dust and rubble.'

"'Aye,' said another man. 'Dust and rubble, nought but rubble and dust, as far as the eye can see.'

"I gazed about at the fine city buildings and the tidy houses with their neatly tended gardens. No one in their right mind would describe this as rubble."

"'And devils. He's infested the village with devils and demons that torment us so that we cannot sleep. I myself have not slept in two hundred years,' cried the priest."

"It was clear that this wizard had done something terrible to the minds of these poor men to make them believe all this. 'Well, if I can do it, I will bring this tyranny to an end,' I declared, 'for I am also a sorcerer and a warrior, and my hobby is besting and expelling tyrants.'"

"'Ooh no, ooh no,' chorused the men who thought they were beavers. 'That's very risky,' said one elderly man. 'Many a knight has tried it before, but they all ended up mad or as slaves or even as corpses like me. I used to be a young, handsome warrior. I challenged the wizard fifty-eight years ago and look what he did to me. He cast a terrible spell on me and now I've become so old that I'm dead. And I'm a beaver as well, so my prospects are not good.'"

"'Double trouble,' murmured the others."

"'Look,' I said, 'I appreciate your concern, but I really must try and get rid of this fellow for the good of everyone. Please just point me to the road up to the castle and if I beat him I'll be back in time for lunch.'"

"'Oh, it grieves me sorely to see another young life thrown away like this,' said the head beaver. I mean, man. 'There's nothing we can do to change your mind?'"

"'No. I am bound by my oath of service as a knight.'"

"'Very well, but at least let me offer you something to help you.' The priest took from his neck a talisman on a chain and gave it to me. 'This is the tooth of a dragon. It repels spells of certain kinds, such as the spell of premature aging, the spell of warts, and the spell that causes a man to imagine that he is a beaver.'"

"'And you're sure it works?' I asked."

"'Definitely. I used it to repel a spell intended to make me imagine that I'm a beaver and it worked perfectly. Unfortunately, now I really am a beaver so even this wonderful talisman cannot help me.'

"As soon as I rounded the corner and was out of sight of the old men, I tossed the talisman into the gutter and made my way up the stony path toward the castle. I didn't plan on employing any fancy tactics or mounting a surprise attack. I was confident that I could overwhelm the wizard with raw power. After all, our master would not have selected me for this task if he was not confident that I could beat up an old man."

"A young soldier stood guard at the castle gate before the raised drawbridge. 'What can I do for you?' he said."

"'I've come to see the wizard. I have a question for him.'

"'What kind of question?'

"'The kind that I address to powerful wizards, not to their minions,' I said."

"'He's busy.'

"'OK. I'll wait.'

"'He'll always be busy.'

"'In that case I may become impatient.'

"'You'd better leave. He only sees people he has personally summoned.'

"'Not today,' I said. I raised my arm and blasted a hole in the raised drawbridge and the iron portcullis behind it. Then I pushed the terrified young man out of the way, grabbed his pike, and used it to pole-vault over the moat and through the hole. Armed guards ran into the courtyard to meet me. 'Who are you who has entered so violently into our castle,' their leader said nervously, 'and what do you want?'

"'I want to talk to the wizard and I don't have time for underlings. Take me to him at once if you don't want to end up like your gate.'

"The guard was shaking but he stood his ground. 'Please do not do anything hasty, sir,' he said. 'I'll fetch my master, if you don't mind waiting here for a few moments.' He turned to one of his men and said, 'Here you! Fetch a stool and some wine for our guest while I call the master.'

"After a few minutes Nefarious approached, leaning on his staff. He was the picture of a venerable enchanter with a tall pointed hat and a long dark robe that swept the ground, all emblazoned with stars and planets. He had a gnarled staff with a red jewel set in its tip, a long beard, white hair, a craggy, ancient face, and eyes that glittered with power. But what really impressed me was his gait. He walked slowly and with great care, as if a slight misstep might lead to disaster, yet he seemed calm and fearless.

"He looked me in the eye with an air of amusement and said, 'Your demonstration of occult power appears to have convinced my men of your worth. I have never heard of you, but you seem to be a wizard of some strength.'

"'I can do a whole lot more than fool a few ignorant peasants into thinking they are talking beavers. I've come to challenge you. It's time for you to release the villagers from your thrall and retire gracefully. If you give me the information I need, I'll even spare your life. What do you say?'

"'What a hasty young man you are,' he said with a chuckle. 'You're not from Australia by any chance, are you? No? Well, I suppose I was like that when I was your age. I must for the present decline your offer of sorcerous combat. I've just had lunch, and I fear it would disturb my digestion. Perhaps you would like to come indoors out of the sun so we can talk. I will ask my cook to prepare some supper for you.'

"The old rascal was playing nice. I decided to go along with his game, but as I followed him down the castle corridor a trapdoor suddenly opened beneath my feet and I fell into a deep oubliette.

As I tumbled into the darkness I heard the necromancer shriek with laughter, classic evil-genius style. But it takes more than an oubliette to get rid of me. Like a striking snake, I grabbed a passing bat and clung on with both hands. This was no ordinary bat, mind you. It was a giant, man-eating bat especially bred to terrorize the dark wizard's enemies. We landed in a noisome cell, but it didn't take me long to blast my way out and confront the wizard once again. This time I did not waste time listening to his excuses. I challenged him face to face and soon bested him. Within minutes I had him on his knees, at my mercy.

"'Tell me why I shouldn't kill you,' I said, 'after you tried to kill me in your oubliette.'

"'But I'm evil,' he squawked. 'It is my nature. You're only starting out. You don't want to go down this road, believe me. It's hard having to think of new evil things to do all the time. It's downright exhausting. Anyway, you shouldn't be too hard on me. At least I offered you dinner. OK, I see you're still upset about the oubliette. But try to see my point of view. I knew you would beat me in a fair fight but I couldn't just give up without even trying. My men would have lost respect for me. Think of it all as a test of your worthiness. Although I'm old, I have much knowledge to offer you. I have little strength left now. When I was in my prime you would never have gotten past the front gate, believe me. But my life force is almost spent. I have been searching for a worthy successor for centuries to no avail, but seeing you so vital and clever, so strong-willed and determined, inspires me. If you're going to kill me, at least let me teach you something first so that my knowledge is not lost forever. Then you can kill me if you wish. It would be a relief to not have to get around on these aching old bones any more. My best days are gone. All I have now are memories.'

"'Memories of Atlantis perhaps?' I said.

"'What do you know about Atlantis?' he asked, with a coy look on his face.

"'I know that you were there, and some say that you were the cause of its downfall. I seek its whereabouts.'

"So to cut a long story short, he spilled the beans and agreed to help us. I didn't have to torture him or threaten him at all. Bit of an anticlimax really."

"So what happened to the necromancer?" growled Joe.

"After I'd extracted the information I needed, I forced him to release the townsfolk from his spell and then I set him free. I didn't have the stomach to kill him. He was old and quite harmless compared to what he used to be. Now to business. We have a fine wind and a mission to fulfill. What's the status of the ship and how does the weather look? What's your report, Captain Sweep?"

"I'm glad you asked that question," said The Sweep. "I have decided to use my newly patented weather-detection device. Allow me to show you how it works."

He produced a circular chart with weather symbols at various points around the circle. "First you ask the local self-appointed weather experts for their opinions about the weather for the next forty-eight hours. You then record them using these symbols and conduct a meta-analysis, taking the average of all the predictions. Then—and here's the really unique feature of my invention—you rotate the center of the chart to show the exact opposite of what they all predicted. Since everybody knows that weather forecasts are always wrong, it stands to reason that if you take the opposite you will be right. I'm currently in negotiations with the Earl of Sussex for the manufacturing rights of my new navigational device."

Everyone shuffled close, eager to hear more, except Eikelbohm. "Thank you for explaining that," he said with a dismissive air. "As commander of this mission I am relieving you of your duty as Captain. I will captain the ship myself. You will handle the rigging."

Eikelbohm took The Sweep's circular chart, ripped it in half, and threw it overboard, then turned away as though all was settled.

"Er..." said The Sweep.

"No time for that," said Eikelbohm brusquely. "Get the spinnaker up. Let's take advantage of this fine tailwind."

"But..." said the mole.

"No time for that, either. You're our new lookout. Climb up to the crow's nest and watch out for anything unusual. And don't come down unless you're called, even if we forget you ever existed."

"We could have used a bit of this kind of authority to shut the mole up earlier," said Iris softly to Joe, but the dragon eyed Eikelbohm with dislike. I remained silent. I was not comfortable with Eikelbohm's overbearing manner but I thought it better to have a word with him privately. Then I could point out that appointing Maurice as lookout might not be the best possible utilization of his talents.

Fired by an Egg

Saint Lucifer scowled at his movie script, silently willing it to wither and die. Writing this stuff was way harder than it looked. He'd recently secured a contract to write the script for a big-budget movie. Which would have been great news if he'd had the faintest idea of how to actually write a screenplay. Unfortunately he had exhausted his supply of creative ideas writing the résumé that secured him the job.

Still grappling with the problem, Lucifer stalked onto the bridge to find Dr. Dogalogue ready to continue telling his own story to Miranda the Egg. The sight irked him mightily. As a high-profile creative writer he could not, in good conscience, allow this to continue.

"OK, Dogalogue, you can step aside. The cavalry has arrived. It's time for a professional to take over the storytelling. I might just be able to fit it into my busy schedule as I'm working on my major motion picture."

Lucifer coughed modestly.

"You got that job?" Dogalogue was incredulous. "That's amazing. Whatever gave them the idea that you know how to write a film script?"

"Well, I may have exaggerated a little in my résumé. But I have watched a lot of vampire movies."

"I've watched the Galactic Games pretty often too, but it doesn't mean I'm a champion pole-vaulter. Ah well, I'm just glad it's not my money. So what's your great movie about?"

"Oh, it's nothing that would interest you," said Lucifer, his tentacles scurrying to hide behind one another.

"C'mon, you can tell us. What is it?"

"Just some silly story about a guy who goes to another planet to rescue some dragons. Kid's stuff."

"It's about you! They're making a movie about you! I knew you had it in you! There you were, Mr. Self-Effacing, and all along they're going to make you a galactic hero. That's fantastic! There will be troupes of dancing cephalopods and presidents begging to shake your tentacle."

"Not that. We saints work in secret and our heroism is never acknowledged. We are the silent world saviors, like shadows. No one ever learns our names and we lie in unmarked graves."

"Except when they make movies about you."

Lucifer gazed out at the stars, adopting the classic "noble heroic stick insect pose."

Miranda giggled. She was finally beginning to like Dr. Dogalogue's friend. Lucifer took this as an invitation to begin his stint as chief storyteller.

"So, listen up ladies, gentlemen, and eggs. You are about to witness the slickest presentation of facts in the history of fact presenting. But be warned, I'm not going to cut out the gross or scary parts. Don't expect a romanticized picture of Dogalogue as the fearless hero, and don't expect any talking flowers or entrepreneurial badgers. My story will feature entire fleets of vultures on holiday, and evil laughs so evil they could pickle a persimmon. We're entering into the realm of fear and danger, death threats, true wickedness, and spiritual corruption of the most dastardly kind."

Miranda sat forward eagerly.

Lucifer licked his thin lips, all twelve of them. He'd successfully created a sense of anticipation in his audience, as advised in chapter one of his new book, How to Write a Hit Movie Script in Seventeen Minutes. *But he hadn't read chapter two, so he had no plan for the next part. He was, however, a great believer in spontaneity. He glanced sideways at his audience and continued.*

"First, let me explain that the highly esteemed Dr. Dogalogue, although he means well and is the hero of our story, has an unusual weakness. He is dyslexic in three dimensions. Not only can he not tell left from right, he doesn't understand the difference between up and down."

Miranda sat up straight. "Really?"

"No, not really," said Dogalogue, looking annoyed. "Lucifer is just being a loony. Again."

"OK," said Lucifer. "Let's see who's the loony. Tell us all, Dogalogue, which way is up?"

"Hmm, let me see now, that's a tricky one. Let me see." Dogalogue glanced about warily. "Now first we divide everything by the square of the hypotenuse and then, how does it go? Ah, that's right. Every obstacle has an equal and opposite optimist. Hmm. It must be... that way?" Dogalogue pointed toward Lucifer's lair down the corridor.

Lucifer chuckled. Miranda squealed with delight. "It's true. You really don't know up from down. That's awesome!"

"Darn it, Lucifer," said Dogalogue. "Why did you have to tell the egg?"

"I'M NOT AN EGG! Even you are calling me an egg now. That's not fair. You're supposed to be on my side."

Dogalogue patted her on the head. "It could be worse. I have a friend who is dyslexic in four dimensions. Not only can she not tell left from right or up from down, she can't distinguish between past and present. It's quite awkward. You can't take her anywhere."

"Or any-when," giggled Miranda.

"May I continue my story?" said Lucifer tapping his ninety-seventh sucker so that it made a scary squidging sound. Dogalogue and Miranda sat up at attention.

"So the hero of our tale is our well-meaning wimp, Dogalogue. Eikelbohm, on the other hand is a serious bruiser with muscles like watermelons."

Miranda was wide-eyed. She whispered to Dogalogue, "Like watermelons? Is that possible?"

"Well, er."

"I heard that!" snapped Lucifer. "If you don't believe me, check out this hologram. See the muscles. Are they or are the not like watermelons?"

Miranda had to concede that they were indeed remarkably like watermelons, including the seeds.

"Listen. I can't tell this story properly if you're going to go fact-checking everything I say with Dogalogue, the most unreliable source of factual information since the Intergalactic Planet Smoking Corporation hired scientists to prove that smoking planets is good for the health of the inhabitants. What's the matter? Don't you trust me?"

"Of course I trust you, Mr. Lucifer, and I think you're a wonderful storyteller." Miranda smiled so sweetly that even Lucifer was mollified.

"As I was saying, Eikelbohm of martial-arts repute was a formidable fighter from an early age."

Miranda couldn't resist interrupting again. "I knew it! I knew Eikelbohm was mean from the moment he took the comfy spaceship and made Dr. Dogalogue go and fight the dragon on a horse."

"Now, Miranda," said Dogalogue. "That's not fair. Be reasonable. He was not a disciple of the necromancer at that point."

"Eikelbohm was a scrapper from the outset," said Lucifer. "Why, even when he was still an egg himself, he used to roll aggressively at the other eggs and bump them. I remember him terrorizing us younger students in the training school. And he was no pansy when it came to psychic powers. He could heft fireballs and shoot laser beams from his fingers with the best of them, and he wasn't too particular about fighting fair. No one in their right mind was ready to take him on. Most of us assumed that our master sent him on the mission to add some brawn to the team but I suspect he had another motive. He knew Eikelbohm was trouble and just wanted to get rid of the guy. I never trusted him. If I had been there it would have turned out very differently. I'd have set the dragon on him."

Miranda gasped.

"That's right," said Lucifer grimly. "Even Eikelbohm with his karate chops would have had trouble dealing with a live dragon. But here you see a perfect example of Dogalogue's fatal wimpiness. He considered that unfair or dishonorable. And look at the result—a disaster."

"But I'm getting ahead of myself. Let me start from the beginning."

"In 1357 AD, planet Earth was a mess. Of course, it had always been a mess, but it wasn't getting any better. Since Earth was not a priority project, our Zondgrazian council decided to send two trainee world saviors on this special mission. The assignment was hardly demanding. All they had to do was:

1. *Travel thirty-seven light years to Earth in a wooden bathtub.*
2. *Fulfill a few standard prophecies that foretold that Dogalogue would be the world savior. You know, routine stuff: simulate a virgin birth, arrive just in time for an eclipse, hire half a dozen wise men on camels to come and read his astrological charts and announce that this remarkable youth will change history.*
3. *Challenge a fire-breathing dragon, armed only with a wooden stick.*

4. *Locate and recover the microscopic lost seed of the microvita tree last seen sinking in the conflagration of Atlantis nine thousand years earlier.*
5. *Plant the seed in a hidden valley in the Himalayas and train a tribe of monkeys to take care of it and keep it safe while it matured during the next eight centuries.*
6. *Use the master's unsquidulizor machine to shift the valley into another dimension so that no one would find the tree by accident and chop it down for firewood.*
7. *Return home with his companion disciple Dr. Eikelbohm and the unsquidulizor machine all intact.*

"Now what could be simpler than that?"

"Yeah, what could be simpler than that!" laughed Miranda, poking Dr. Dogalogue.

Dogalogue smiled a long-suffering smile.

"You already know what happened when Eikelbohm met the necromancer. He volunteered to become corrupted in about thirty seconds flat," said Lucifer.

Miranda nodded eagerly.

"But remember, our squishy-bodied hero, Dogalogue, only knew what Eikelbohm told him about that encounter, conveniently leaving out the part where he turns traitor and aligns himself with the necromancer."

"Well, obviously," said Miranda. "Of course he's not going to tell Dr. Dogalogue that."

"What you don't know, oh too-clever-for-her-own-good egg, is that the old wizard liked being beaten up by Eikelbohm. It was the most excitement he'd had in centuries. Plus, he was secretly delighted to have discovered this powerful young wizard on a mission to recover the microvita seed. This suited the wicked old goat's plans perfectly. For, you see, much of what the wizard told Eikelbohm and Dogalogue when they met in the caves was true. He was indeed so old that his powers were waning, and he knew he did not have much time left. But what he kept secret from all, hidden in the deepest recesses of his mind, was that the seed was his one hope of extending his life. By absorbing its power he could rejuvenate his body and live another nine thousand years. With his vitality restored he could then rule over the earth. He had no intention of handing over power to an untested young scrapper like Eikelbohm.

He just wanted to use him to get the seed. He was looking forward to the moment when he'd regained his strength and would be able to give Eikelbohm a demonstration of power he would never forget!"

Miranda gasped. "He's so horrible and selfish! He was going to let the whole world go on suffering and just use all the seed's energy for himself? Dr. Dogalogue, how could you even pretend be friends with him? Couldn't you see what Eikelbohm was really like?"

"All of this was unknown to Dogalogue," said Lucifer. "When Eikelbohm appeared at the docks, Dogalogue, in his innocence, was hugely relieved. If you want to see how naive he was, just listen to what happened next."

"Zond, am I glad to see you!" said Dogalogue. "You can't imagine what I've been through! I've been deceived by a temperamental princess and discouraged by a pessimistic witch. I've had to face down a terrifying monster and keep company with a cowardly horse, an eccentric prince constructed out of human hair, and a psychotic man-eating dragon! What a relief to see another Zondgrazian again! These earthlings are crazy. Most of them are not even people. They're beavers and mice and moles and mobsters, I mean monsters. It's bizarre. And there are rats! You know I can't stand rats! And now I have to walk around with one in my beard or my pocket or somewhere."

"Sorry to hear that," said Eikelbohm. "I'm rather enjoying this planet myself."

"Dr. Dogalogue doesn't talk like that!" said Miranda. "And Mina's a mouse, not a rat. You're telling the story all wrong."

"She's right, you know," said Dogalogue. "I never said that stuff."

"I know, but you should have," said Lucifer. "Anyway, it's true. Earthlings are crazy. And the place is infested with rats and monsters and beavers. You never let your true feelings out, Dogalogue. That's your problem. You're a repressed individual. My version of the story is where we get to know what you're really thinking."

"I'm pretty sure I never thought those things."

"Of course you did. It's only now you're able to block it out after hundreds of years of therapy."

"I don't believe you," said Miranda. "I want Dr. Dogalogue to tell the story from now on."

Lucifer sighed. "All right, little egg. Have it the boring way, if that's what you prefer. The wimp Dogalogue version. Guaranteed pathetic. But I'm warning you, it won't be nearly as exciting or as funny. But, if you want a bland story, it's up to you."

"That's exactly what I want," said Miranda. "You're fired!"

"Fired by an egg. How humiliating. This is going to ruin my résumé." Lucifer shrank into himself and withdrew to his lair to work on his movie script.

Dogalogue Revealed

Iris blinked as the spray hit her full in the face, but she didn't flinch or turn away. She gripped the smooth rail, resting her weight against it to counter the rise and fall of the deck. All night the *Dodecahedron* had run before a brisk westerly wind, leaving the coastal town of Arrasate-Mondragon far behind. Now as dawn approached, Neptune seemed done with buffeting and the ship moved to a gentler rhythm.

As each surging wave lifted the ship beneath her, Iris felt a thrill, sensing the power of nature flowing through her body. The foam highlights on the crests caught the light of the fading stars. So many stars, floating in frozen shoals on the ocean of night, the Milky Way stretched above her like a flying silver dragon. Since Sir Dogalogue had explained to her that stars were distant suns, many with worlds of their own, she'd looked at them with new wonder. Were those worlds inhabited by alien beings like him? Thinking creatures with strange bodies, gazing up at our sun, wondering about beings like her? A great longing arose in her heart to explore this endless universe of worlds.

Above her on the bridge The Sweep manned the wheel, a proud silhouette against the lightening sky. An albatross wheeled and soared above the main mast, never settling in the rigging as a gull might but never far away. Watching this loneliest of birds, her heart ached. What in the world was she doing here in this watery desert with a group of creatures not even her own species, embarked on what was surely an impossible mission? How were they supposed to find a single seed in this endless ocean, thousands of feet below the surface? What if it really was guarded by the mother of all sea monsters? That was worrisome, even with Joe to protect them. She was not sure how good Joe was at fending off ginormous aquatic beasts. Water was clearly not his favorite element; there he was right now, sleeping fitfully on the foredeck, looking a sickly green. Getting mixed up in a madcap adventure like this was typical of her crazy brother, but Iris was generally more level-headed. She sought adventure but not the impossible-to-achieve, certain-death variety. But then, she'd witnessed so many impossible things during the last week that she was trying to suspend judgment. Or maybe she was just trying not to think about it.

The Sweep, on the other hand, considered nothing impossible. She envied him his irrepressible optimism. Though she would never admit it, Iris was enormously proud of her fearless brother. She would never forget how he'd risked his life to help her to fake her death. But she worried about him and did not always appreciate his unhesitating readiness to volunteer in the face of danger and so she hesitated to praise him openly for fear of boosting his already exaggerated self-confidence. Anyway, it didn't seem to make any difference to him what she thought. She knew he loved her and would do anything to protect his little sister, but she still felt that he didn't take her as seriously as he ought. Still, if she could find a man half as good as her brother she would marry him in a flash. Though perhaps someone just a little less eccentric would be nice.

As the bright edge of the sun appeared on the horizon, she saw Eikelbohm emerge from below deck. As she pretended to be gazing out at the waves, she noticed how at home he seemed aboard ship, pacing with the grace of a panther across the swaying deck as he strode up to The Sweep and took his place on the bridge for the morning watch.

The Sweep strolled down to where Iris stood and leaned his elbows on the rail beside her. "So, how're you feeling, Sis? Any more strange dreams?"

"No," she said. "These days I get enough weird experiences just staying awake. I'm not so sure I'm making the right kind of friends," she said, wondering whether there was any chance her brother would take her man- finding problems seriously.

As she talked to her brother, Iris continued to study Eikelbohm, wondering how strong his alien body really was. If it wasn't for the fact that underneath that human suit he was a bundle of slime and tentacles, he might make a decent prince. She almost laughed out loud at the thought. Then she remembered what Sir Dogalogue had told them. Eikelbohm was a shape shifter. He wasn't wearing a human suit. Interesting. Though if the Bible was anything to go by, it was probably better not to think too much about that.

"We need to do a test dive," Eikelbohm said, addressing Joe and me. "Dogalogue and I are new to this environment, and we've never teamed up with a dragon before."

Joe was still looking seasick. "Good idea," he said. "I'd be happy to get off this ship for a spell."

"I'm up for that," I said. "It'll be a relief to get rid of this human suit for a bit and have a swim."

I handed The Sweep my sword and went below deck where I removed my human suit and stowed it carefully. I'd been dying to show off my elegant Zondgrazian body so that the earthlings would understand that I was not a somewhat less-good-looking human, but a beautiful Zondgrazian. I'd been anticipating this moment and wanted to savor it.

But when I proudly squelched up on deck and my friends saw my true squishiness, my writhing tentacles, slime ducts, and abundance of eyestalks for the first time, their collective gasp disappointed me. Iris actually suppressed a scream, which I thought was uncalled for. Even The Sweep bounced slightly.

"That's what you look like under your human suit?" Brains exclaimed.

"Well, that's certainly different," said Maurice.

"On Zondgraz, he is considered rather handsome," lied Eikelbohm. I was astonished. He'd never shown any kind of sensitivity before, ever. I guess he felt that we Zondgrazians should stick together. Whatever the reason, I felt enormously grateful to him at that moment.

"I guess I can sort of see that," said The Sweep slowly, turning his head sideways as if viewing me from an odd angle might improve matters.

I swallowed my chagrin and proceeded to the gunwale. This was no time to get self-conscious. We had serious work to do, preparing for our momentous dive. Nervous, I looked down at the water. The sea was choppy, the water deep blue. I spotted the iPoss darting about impatiently just below the surface like a flash of silver.

Eikelbohm appeared on deck in his shorts, looking like a body-building champion. "Sweep, keep the ship turned into the wind and try to stay in the same area so we can find you. We're going down pretty deep to see how our Zondgrazian bodies handle it. It's just a test. We shouldn't be too long."

He leapt onto the rail and executed an elegant swan dive into the waves. I followed less gracefully by slithering under the rail and landing in the water with a plop. But once immersed I stretched my many limbs and shot downward effortlessly. This was more like it. I glided and turned like a dancer, reveling in the cool embrace of the sea.

From beneath, I could see the ship rock as Joe took off and landed in the ocean, the water hissing in a great commotion of steam when his body hit the surface. Joe poked his head underwater, grinned at us, and turned turquoise. "This is not usually my favorite medium," he said, "but today it is pleasantly cool."

Eikelbohm and I each clutched one of the curved spikes running down Joe's back. Taking an enormous breath the great dragon dove beneath the surface and swam downward with powerful strokes of his tail, trailing a stream of bubbles. I clung on easily now that I could use my tentacles. It felt wonderful. This was definitely my element.

Iris paced the deck of the Dodecahedron, peering over the side, seeking some sign of us returning to the surface. The Sweep was at the helm, keeping the ship into the wind, as instructed. Suddenly Iris noticed him stiffen and stare intently to the east. Following his gaze she saw why. A long black cloud spanned the horizon. It was spreading and approaching fast, preceded by a bank of thick rain. The wind became restless, whipping off the tops of the waves in sudden gusts so that they tossed and plunged like frightened horses. A cold burst of spray caught them by surprise.

"Brains! Maurice!" yelled The Sweep. "Get up here."

But our trusty lieutenants were on deck already. They'd sensed the weather shifting and rushed to the bridge.

"That doesn't look like much fun," said Maurice, frowning at the charging clouds.

"That old gaffer in Mondragon was right," said Brains. "He warned Sir Dogalogue about sudden weather changes."

The wind was stronger now, coming from the northeast. The rigging snapped and flapped like a cloud of butterflies in a wind tunnel. The Sweep's instincts kicked in. He grabbed the wheel and turned us away from the wind. "We have to run before it, it's our only chance. Iris, keep only a bare minimum of canvas. We just need enough to maintain way. That won't take much in this gale."

"But Eikelbohm said to remain stationary, into the wind." Iris had to yell as the wind whipped her words away as soon as she uttered them.

"Not possible in this squall. If we don't run with it we'll capsize."

Iris ran to do his bidding. Brains and Maurice joined her and together they wrestled the flapping sails and flying ropes and took down enough sails to make the ship manageable, at least for the moment.

The sky, clear and blue just moments ago, was now filled with racing dark-gray clouds. Water spouts danced in the distance, the advance party for the downpour, and the waves were roiling in confusion. The pulse of the rollers ran westward but the mounting gale cut across them at an angle, pushing them into increasingly irregular shapes. The ship was forced by the wind to turn southwest, so that now instead of pitching and plunging, the hull stretched in a sickening corkscrew motion as she cut across each wave at an angle to the wind. Then as she plunged down the slope of a huge roller, the fierce leading edge of the rain hit the stern on the starboard side. The ship twisted, the deck shuddering as she threatened to capsize altogether. Iris screamed and Mina, clutching the edge of her pocket, squeaked in terror.

As the ship righted herself, The Sweep gripped the wheel and wiped water from his eyes. "I don't know if she can handle many more like that," he said.

Iris stood beside him, clinging to the rail with both hands, staring eastward with her eyes squinting against the wind. "How in the world will they find us when they come to the surface in this storm?" she said.

"Don't worry," said The Sweep. "Sir Dogalogue will hear our thoughts and Joe will fly above the sea and come to us. They'll take one look at the storm and laugh and say, 'Is this the worst you can do, great Neptune? Why, this is nothing!'"

Our test dive went smoothly. My natural aquatic form and Eikelbohm's now semi-aquatic human body performed perfectly, even at some depth, and we'd determined how far the dragon could comfortably dive. As we neared the surface again I looked up. The sun was no longer visible. The water above us was grayish blue and the Dodecahedron was nowhere to be seen. "Hello, the ship's gone," I said.

"The weather looks bad," Joe said. He paused in his ascent. "It looks like a nasty storm has come up while we were down there. The ship could have been blown some distance. I think the only way we can reach her is for me to fly. It's going to be pretty bouncy flying in a storm. Hang on tight!"

One great advantage of Zondgrazian physiology is that with fifteen tentacles with suckers on them, hanging on tight is what we are best at. Plus you can do all sorts of amazing party tricks. I latched onto Joe's back like a limpet. The great dragon lashed his huge tail from side to side and we sped horizontally through the water for a few seconds. Then in a surge of power he broke the surface and with exquisite timing took off from the crest of a mountainous wave, opening his wings and springing upward into the wind.

The second we burst free from the water, I understood how a banana feels when it is thrown into a blender. The sudden transition from the silence of the deep to this whirling madness of howling air and threshing water hit me like a shockwave. Visibility was a joke. I could barely see Joe's wings for the water blasting into my eyes. I couldn't even figure out which way was up. Which was actually quite normal for me, only this time it was official. For once no one could make fun of me for being disoriented.

Joe struggled against the sudden gusts that sought to toss him up or down or both at once, fighting to gain altitude. Eikelbohm's face was set in a grimace and his hands were red with strain as he clung to the dragon's back.

Puny human, I thought, secretly delighted that I'd finally discovered an arena where my physical powers surpassed Eikelbohm's.

Suddenly a gust caught us from the side and Joe lurched, veering over to his right. Eikelbohm lost his seating and with a yell swung outward, clinging onto a dorsal spine with one hand. This called for Dogalogical action. Clinging firmly to the dragon's body with eleven tentacles, I leaned down and stretched out with four limbs, catching Eikelbohm's arm in a glue-like grip just as his hand slipped and he fell. For a moment I was stretched like a rubber band, hanging from the dragon and supporting Eikelbohm's weight as he swung beneath me. Then Joe righted himself and Eikelbohm clambered up on to his back again, gasping out his thanks.

Joe fought on, up through the roiling air, peering down through the rain, searching for the ship. I reached out with my thoughts. For a moment I could sense nothing other than a great many disoriented fish. Our friends must have been out of range. It wasn't going to be easy to find them in this storm. I tried not to think about the possibility that the raging waves had engulfed the *Dodecahedron* while we were still in the deeps, and that the reason I could not pick up their thoughts was because there were none.

But then I caught the touch of a mind saying, "This is nothing." It could only be The Sweep.

"That way," I yelled to Joe, directing him due east, the opposite direction from where we actually wanted to go. There was no helping it. This wild wind carried everything before it, ever further from our goal. That included our friends, the *Dodecahedron*, and us.

Following The Sweep's thoughts, we soon saw them, bravely battling the giant seas in the small ship. With the precision of a master, Joe landed on the tossing foredeck, narrowly avoiding the swaying masts and flying ropes. We jumped down from his back.

"You're safe!" Iris cried, wrapping her arms around one of Joe's toes, her tears mixing with the rain.

"Well, my toe is safe at least," said Joe, smiling.

"Hey, what's that big turquoise dragon doing here?" I said, staring over Iris's shoulder.

Everyone turned to look blankly at the waves as they charged like mountains, drawing our brave ship down into a valley of dark water. The *Dodecahedron* shuddered and shivered her way out of the trough, groaning, now lower in the water with the dragon's weight.

"What are you talking about, Dogalogue?" Eikelbohm said. "I don't see anything but this storm from hell that is likely to sink us at any moment."

"It was only there for a second," I said, "flying through the rain and curving like a big opalescent snake."

Iris and Joe were both staring at me now, looking worried. "Are you feeling OK, Sir Dogalogue?" said Iris.

But I never got a chance to answer her question. Suddenly a blurred shadow appeared above us, like a serpentine body swimming through the air. Then it shot into the heart of the storm and the wind and rain appeared to follow it, leaving us in an abruptly calm ocean. Then a dozen water spouts shot out of the sea around the ship and raced north, against the direction of the wind. All was a blur as the blinding rain whipped into our faces. I felt helpless seeing how our proud ship could be tossed about so easily by the power of nature.

Just as suddenly the gale dropped. The rain lifted and the wind settled back into a steady breeze, blowing westward, out to sea. The tumult of confused waters drew back and we found ourselves rising and falling to the gentle rhythm of the rollers. We stared at the sea around us and at one another, breathless with shock, relieved but utterly bewildered.

"What just happened?" said Iris. "Did one of you aliens cast some magic spell on the weather?"

Eikelbohm frowned. "Some wizardry to be sure. But from where and by whom I do not know."

"Maybe it's a boon from the sea god, Neptune," said Mina. "Did anyone rescue a dolphin recently?"

"I keep telling you," I insisted. "I saw a thingy like a dragon, only I didn't see any wings. A pretty turquoise one."

But no one else had seen it, and they were all giving me sideways glances when they thought I wasn't looking and talking behind my back.

"Planning on any more test dives then, Captain?" said Maurice.

Eikelbohm didn't have the energy to respond. He just shook his head ruefully.

Atlantis: The Guided Tour

The iPoss was going positively nuts with excitement, dancing about like a vampire who's just been handed the keys to a blood bank.

"I guess that means we've arrived," said The Sweep.

Eikelbohm and I were already preparing to go over the side again. This time it was not a test.

The weather had been getting calmer from the moment the storm mysteriously vanished. By mid-morning the wind barely ruffled the surface and the waves were little more than a gentle swell. I stared over the side, trying to see into its depths. A flying fish looked up in surprise at the dragon's tail trailing over the edge of the deck. It had never seen a dragon's tail before. In fact, it'd never seen any part of a dragon at all.

The wind in my face felt fresh on my eyestalks. Ah, this was the life.

"Are we there yet?" Maurice yawned as he emerged from the cabin. I'd noticed that moles tend to sleep whenever they get the chance.

The Sweep manned the helm while the rest of us gathered on the foredeck with the dragon and studied the map one last time. Joe peered down at it, his hide shimmering azure with pleasure as the sun warmed his scales.

"Brains, take a sounding," commanded Eikelbohm, still staring at the map. The badger, pleased at being called upon to perform such an important task, took the heavy sounding weight and threw it over the side with a splash. It disappeared in an instant.

"What about the string?" said Maurice.

"The string? It's right here in my hand," said Brains proudly.

"You idiot," said Maurice. 'You threw the sounding weight into the water without tying on the string. How's that supposed to tell us anything?"

"Oh, dear," said Brains sheepishly. "I remember now. I was using the string last night to play cats cradle with the iPoss and forgot to reattach it."

"You nincompoop!" Eikelbohm glared at him. "I've a good mind to throw you overboard to find it, except that you might float. Get something else we can use as a weight and be quick about it."

We all watched as the fresh sounding weight—which was, tragically for Brains, his favorite pet rock—sank rapidly and the attached string hissed out of its basket, measuring the depth. We all prayed it would stop soon. If the water were too deep for diving we might not be able to reach the bottom to recover the seed.

The string stopped paying out and the badger went forward and drew it taut. "Two hundred and twenty fathoms, Captain," he called.

It took me a second to figure out what that came to in Zondgrazian eye-stalks, our standard unit of linear measurement. It was a lot.

Eikelbohm looked worried. "I think that's close to the limit of the depth pressure we can tolerate on this planet," he said to me quietly.

It sounded like the extreme limit to me, but I didn't see a lot we could do about it. "I guess we'll just have to try," I said. "We'll have to get in and out fast. Anyway, we want to be quick. The sooner we get away from here, the better chance we'll have of avoiding the guardian monster."

"If it exists."

"That raises another problem. If it doesn't exist, how do we avoid it?"

"I hadn't thought of that." Eikelbohm frowned. "That is a worry."

Eikelbohm turned to address the crew. He was kind of bossy but I sure was glad he was coming with me on this journey down to the ocean floor. He was the kind of guy you wanted on your side when you're about to steal a dangerous sea monster's favorite toy.

""Let's make sure we're all clear about the plan. Dragon Joe will carry Dogalogue and me, and we will follow the iPoss down to the maximum dragon depth of forty fathoms. Joe will wait there for the two of us, since we have to go much deeper. On our test dive we reached one hundred fathoms with no problem. We are naturally aquatic and should be able to handle the pressure at the full depth."

So we hoped.

Eikelbohm continued with his instructions. He really liked giving orders.

"You all remain on deck and watch out for us coming back to the surface. We will want to set sail for Iberia as quickly as possible. Now that the wind has swung around to the west, we won't even need to tack home. Iris, make sure you have your harp ready and tuned. If the monstrous guardian of the seed pursues us, we may need the music to enchant it."

"If we get that far," muttered the badger.

"Got something to say, badger?" said Eikelbohm.

"Yes, I suppose I do. What if you don't make it back to the surface? Are we supposed to jump in and dive down and try to find you? I can't even swim."

Maurice turned on the badger. "Don't even contemplate failure, you pessimist."

"Yes, you bigamist," said the mouse.

"That's right, you botanist," said Maurice. "You always want to imagine the worst."

But Eikelbohm interrupted them. "Brains raised an important point. You need to know what to do if we don't return. If we do not come back to the surface within three hours, you must take the ship and sail for land. If we cannot save ourselves there will be nothing you can do for us."

This underscored the degree of danger involved in this dive. I rated the odds of returning alive with our prize at around eleven percent. And that was assuming that the sea monster did not exist.

Eikelbohm thrust his chest out and said, "Thus we embark on the adventure of a lifetime. By the Grace of Zond, we will be successful!"

We dove in with the iPoss speeding down ahead of us at a steep angle, shining silver with an inner light, easily visible in the deepening blue gloom. The dark shape of the *Dodecahedron* grew smaller, floating high above us, the sun flashing and dancing on the surface. The dragon's tail, all turquoise and white, drove us with powerful strokes, ever deeper into the eerie silence of the abyss. He was saving us a lot of work, carrying us on the first stage so that we could conserve our strength. A shimmering shoal of fish swam past us and upward, like an endless ribbon. In spite of the danger, and the responsibility of our mission, I felt quite relaxed. Being back in the water, free in my natural body, boosted my confidence. Just imagine. We were actually going to see the Atlantis of legend and, hopefully, recover the microvita seed at last.

As we dove deeper I sensed the tiny minds of fishes, large and small. The great school, now barely visible in the distance, was a mass of flitting sparks and fleeting thoughts, appearing and disappearing, so alike it was hard to tell one from the other. I was floating in the moment, riding the wave of the now. I felt bemused by my euphoric mood for a moment and then I understood. I was sensing the presence of the seed, an invisible source of light and love, attracting me, illuminating my mind from within. This was what the iPoss was attuned to. It felt magical.

But then I sensed another presence. In the depths far below us something enormous stirred. A mind so alien I could not fathom its intent. It lurked, ever watchful, powerful, protective, guarding the seed. I felt none too comfortable wondering how it would feel about us making off with its treasure. And there was something else. Another mind I could not easily read, but which filled me with dread.

Joe slowed his strokes and leveled out, hovering in the water. We were near his effective limit. We signaled our thanks and continued the descent, Eikelbohm and I following the iPoss down into darkness. I noticed that Eikelbohm's fingers and toes were now webbed and that he had gills on the sides of his neck. Kind of gross, but a very neat trick. The sun was still faintly visible far above, but around us was a blue gloom. Hideous yet beautiful luminescent fishes with long transparent fangs floated by. I could hear their pitiless thoughts, waiting for their prey, hunting one another in the endless night. I could still sense the evil presence, but at the same time the power of the microvita seed filled this ancient submarine world.

Soon I saw vague forms below us. We had reached the sea floor, flying above it like underwater birds. I could discern ghostly shapes in the gloom, the ancient remains of a ruined city, barely discernible lines that might once have been walls circling the top of a hill. We had found Atlantis at last.

We descended toward the hilltop, my body tingling in awe. My master had come here long ago, full of hope. Perhaps this was the very hill where the temple had stood, where the microvita tree once grew. But there were probably many hills and walls. This had been a vast city, the heart of a great civilization. I felt sad to think that this was all that remained of those who'd lived here long ago. The remnants of a broken dream, their story blurred by weeds and time. It was a silent place. Little moved here, save the kelp and sea grass stirring in the gentle current. And pale worms and fish with lighted lures, beacons set above their jaws, inviting the curious to a swift death.

"What are you looking so depressed about?" a voice said in my head. A deep sea angler fish stared at me.

"Oh, hello," I said, momentarily startled. "It just seems a bit gloomy here. I mean this used to be a city of light and learning. Now it's just a ruin, all covered with barnacles. That thought rather gets me down. And there's one other thing: there is a possibility that very shortly I will be eaten by a monster."

"You surface creatures are all the same, coming here with your high airs, lamenting the past, talking about light and learning. What's wrong with how it is now? Look around. Where else would you find a nice soft bed of slime to rest on? And where else are there so many innocent little fishes to gobble? If you're ever bored, you can go look at the statues. They're perfect for a romantic rendezvous, if that's what you fancy. It's a veritable museum here, all free of charge."

"Statues?" I asked. "Where are they?"

"The good ones are deeper down where there's no current. But there are a few bits and pieces up here. Just keep going straight ahead. You can't miss them."

"Much obliged. I'll try not to make disparaging remarks about your lovely home in future."

"Thank you. Spoken like a true gentle-fish. You are a polite one. Most surface visitors won't even talk to me."

"You've had other visitors? I wouldn't have thought you'd get many tourists down here."

"Not tourists, thieves, after the sacred seed. None of them returned to the surface. The mermaids captured them and fed them to the monster. Which works out well for us anglers. We get to feed on the scraps. A rare treat, a bit of fresh surface food. The few who escaped the soldiers were taken by the mermen hunters on the way up."

I sure didn't like the sound of that. Our odds seemed to be getting worse all the time. Eikelbohm was impatiently signaling me to hurry. He was right, of course. We couldn't afford to linger.

We swam on above the city. Eikelbohm pointed at something below us and signaled to me to follow him. We swam over a ridge, and to my astonishment, there on the sea floor, lay the bodies of seven humans. They seemed strangely fossilized, perfectly preserved in some kind of crystalline casing.

"This is remarkable," said Eikelbohm. "I wonder who they were."

I nodded. "Very remarkable."

One of the bodies sat up and looked at us.

"Look," I said. "That one is so well preserved it's still alive."

"You're right," said Eikelbohm. "It's a living fossil!"

The fossil stood up and came toward us carrying a large spear and looking very annoyed. It didn't look like it wanted to talk so we sped away over the ridge.

"What do you think those fossils were doing there, lying on the sand like that?" said Eikelbohm.

"I suppose they must have been sunbathing," I said. There seemed to be no other logical explanation.

We continued to follow the iPoss, gliding above the sea floor. I began to think that we might actually succeed in this daring task. Suddenly Eikelbohm slowed and stared. As I came level with him and saw what he saw, I felt hope die in my heart. There ahead of us a sleek shape hovered above the sand, waiting. An aura of menacing power surrounded it, darker even than the inky sandscape.

A traffic shark.

It was too late to flee. The shark, equipped with the latest in-shark technology, had already spotted us. Powered by highly efficient engines, once a traffic shark has seen you, there's no chance of escape.

"Halt," commanded the traffic shark as we approached. The faint blue light of the sun glinted off its armored fins. It swam lazily, graceful and powerful, remaining in place in the current. I sensed coiled energy, eager and ready to pursue any prey. Before this magnificent specimen of marine biology we must have looked bedraggled and disreputable. At least I'm sure I did.

'Ello, ello, what's going on then?" said the shark.

Eikelbohm cleared his throat, clearly unnerved. We'd not anticipated this. "Er, nothing, nothing. We were just going for an evening stroll to digest our dinner."

"At this depth? A couple of surfacelings?" said the shark. "What do you take me for, a fool? You top-side folk are all the same; wandering around thinking you can just go anywhere without a permit. Didn't you see the sign? This is a one-way ocean! You aren't allowed to swim in this direction."

To our dismay we saw that he was right. Right below us was a one-way sign pointing back the way we had come.

"But this is crazy," I blurted out. "We're in a desolate seabed in the midst of a million square miles of open ocean. What in the world is the need for a one-way sign?

"It's the law," said the traffic shark firmly.

"Shut up, you fool," Eikelbohm hissed at me. "Don't you see? If we go the wrong direction in a one-way ocean, we could cause a serious accident."

"But there is no traffic for hundreds of miles. And we're moving in three dimensions. An entire school of fish could pass over my head and no one would be bothered. Anyway, this is a virtual wasteland. What on earth is a traffic warden doing here? This whole thing makes no sense."

The traffic shark and Eikelbohm gave one another a meaningful look. Then together they jumped on me, tangled me in a net, and stuffed me into a burlap sack. They filled my mouth with sand to muffle my yells and Eikelbohm sat on me to suppress my struggles.

"I'm terribly sorry," came the muffled sound of Eikelbohm speaking to the traffic shark. "My friend has recently escaped from a lunatic asylum. I am trying to rehabilitate him."

"No doubt a dangerous anarchist. Keep a sharp eye on him. I see that you respect rules. I respect that. As of this moment I'm engaging you as my assistant. You must deliver the prisoner to the Atlantean traffic headquarters. As my henchman I'm giving you this special pass allowing you to move freely, even against the traffic signs. Report back for duty at dawn tomorrow."

The officer turned away, his razor-sharp intellect already focused on his next vital mission—redirecting the course of an escaped sea slug who appeared to be considering ignoring a no-right-turn sign a couple of sand dunes away. The traffic shark surged north fearlessly.

As soon as he was out of sight, Eikelbohm released me from the sack. "Sorry about that. I had to come up with a quick way to get past the shark."

"No problem," I said, stretching. "Your solution was remarkably creative. I'm impressed by your ability to focus on the mission, regardless of how much humiliation or inconvenience it might involve for the other members of your team."

The iPoss appeared up ahead, wriggling with impatience. A huge dark shape loomed up from the seabed ahead of us. As we glided closer, I saw it was a rocky outcrop, shaggy with weeds and pockmarked with holes and grottos, populated with nameless hungry worms and slimy things. I felt drawn to it. This was the kind of environs favored by my tribal ancestors. I could not resist exploring.

I swam down to the base of the great rock and peered beneath an overhang. Hidden there in a cave of rough stone thrived a colorful community of soft corals and small fish. And there in the furthest corner huddled something that looked very familiar. Its large round eyes regarded me solemnly and a voice spoke in my mind.

"Go find your own lair. This spot's taken."

As my eyes adjusted to the darkness, I saw tentacles and suckers and, yes, I was in the presence of that most noble of earthly mollusks, a giant octopus.

I withdrew slightly to avoid crowding her. "It is an honor to make your acquaintance, O Queen of Cephalopods," I said. "I am Dogalogue, a cousin from Zondgraz."

"Never heard of it," grumbled the matriarch, but she did not seem altogether displeased. "What brings you to these parts?"

I thought fast. What could possibly impress a giant octopus? Then it came to me. Of course!

"I'm researching intelligent invertebrate behavior. I wondered if you'd consent to an interview for my feature article in *Cephalopod Monthly*."

The octopus' knobby skin changed color to a pinkish hue. Octopuses, like dragons, can change color. But while a dragon's color changes according to their mood, these remarkable eight-legged mollusks can shift hue at will. I don't mean to imply that octopuses are kind of like me and are in some ways superior to dragons or anything—I'm just saying.

"I suppose I could spare a few moments," said the octopus coyly.

"Excellent. Why don't you start by telling me about yourself?"

The huge creature emerged from her hole like animated ooze, and I sensed a greater degree of trust from her. "My name is Lithmus. I come from a long line of Welsh octopuses who migrated here generations ago. I'm an average twenty-foot-long sole survivor from a batch of seventy thousand eggs that hatched on a distant coral reef. I pretty much dominate the food chain around here, along with a certain homicidal shark. We don't count the sea monster. She's not indigenous, and anyway, she sleeps most of the time."

I was fascinated to learn more about this alien species, outwardly so like my own, but I sensed Eikelbohm waiting impatiently above me so I sent him a mental message to bear with me for a while.

"You're an intelligent, well-educated animal, capable of extraordinary dexterity. How come the humans have become the dominant species on earth, and not cephalopods? I mean, look at you. You could gobble up a human in a moment. You have eight powerful limbs to their four. Your eyes are the best in the world. You can even change color! It seems to me that in the evolutionary struggle for supremacy, you have significant advantages."

Lithmus blushed pink, and then became serious.

"Dogalogue of Zondgraz, you are not the first to make this observation. A few years ago a group of us, noting what a phenomenally bad job humans were doing of governing the planet, figured that we could hardly do worse. So, fully confident of our natural superiority, we decided to take over. It shouldn't have been a problem. After all, as you say, we are bigger, stronger, smarter, and we have more limbs. And they've never dreamed of such a possibility. We would take them completely by surprise. These humans make me laugh, with their opposable thumbs and no-longer-prehensile toes. You want dexterity? Take a look at this!"

She reached out with a tentacle and performed open-heart surgery on an unsuspecting sea-urchin. "If you ask me, rigid, internal skeletons are overrated. See how I can squish my entire body through a hole the size of a cuttlefish's eye. I'd like to see a human manage that! The only reason the human race, despite their intellectual inferiority, got to inherit the earth instead of us is because they know how to get along with one another."

"They do?" This was a surprise. "I've noticed them fighting wars and exploiting and enslaving and oppressing one another."

"Yes, but they do it in teams! Look at us. We are total loners. Can't stand being in the same area of reef together. As a result, we can't pool knowledge, form communities, or specialize and develop technology. Community is a prerequisite for the evolution of a culture. Even the greatest octopus geniuses don't stand a chance because every one of them has to start the entire learning process from scratch. Dolphins were another contender for top of the food chain, but they have a different problem. They are sociable and intelligent in a childish sort of way, but they cannot build anything because they have no tentacles. They don't even have opposable thumbs. Their dreams of world domination were nixed the moment they traded feet for flippers."

"They don't even have *non*-opposable thumbs," I said.

"Tragic but true," the octopus said, nodding gravely.

"You know," mused Lithmus. "I think that the real reason humans hate us is because they are jealous. A classic case of tentacle envy. If you want to know what I mean, you should see me play the piano!"

"I think I have tentacle envy," said Miranda, looking sadly at her meager allotment of limbs.

Dr. Dogalogue stroked her hair affectionately. "Never mind, child. If you're very good, maybe next lifetime you'll be born as a cephalopod with a set of tentacles to call your own."

"Really?" she said. "I think I might like that."

"So what happened with your plan to take over the earth?" I asked.

The poor creature twisted its squishy features into a lopsided, rueful grimace. "Our invasion plan started very well. We attracted thousands of recruits. We devised a brilliant strategy. First we would take Spain and from there overrun Europe. Once we'd secured the continent, our Pacific division would come ashore in China and capture all of Asia in a massive two-pronged attack. From there it would be child's play to capture the planet."

Lithmus gazed into the distance with a dreamy look. She started strutting up and down the ledge of the cave like a general before her troops.

"Cephalopods of the universe, unite! That was our slogan. Ah, how I remember those glory days: the flags rippling in the current, our massed spears glinting in the sun. We seemed invincible."

She paused. "And we would have been, but for one small problem."

"What was that?"

"Remember how I said we can't cooperate? I thought that if we had a mission statement, it would build unity. Bad idea. Some of us thought that the mission statement should come before the vision statement. Others insisted on the reverse. Most didn't understand the difference. We argued about that for months. By the time we got to a disgruntled consensus, we couldn't stand the sight of one another and several of our most senior generals had died of old age. Finally the splintered factions of our magnificent octopus army glared at one another one last time and went their separate ways in a huge cloud of angry ink. It was an effort that was doomed from the outset because we just couldn't get along."

I didn't know what to say. Lithmus had turned quite gray. She withdrew into her cavern without another word. The first-ever media interview with this giant of the deeps was over. We were never to meet again.

I departed with some regret. Who knew? Perhaps the cephalopods would have made better planetary custodians than the simians. We tentacle types had done all right on Zondgraz. But, I had to remind myself, Zondgrazians, though genetically related to earth's cephalopods, were very different psychologically. Like in form but not in nature. Appearances can be deceptive.

The Microvita Seed

Not one to dwell upon his past crimes, such as stuffing one's companion into a sack and sitting on him, Eikelbohm was intent upon the task at hand, following the iPoss as it flitted above the sand ahead of us. I realized that he possessed an unusual capacity for filtering out self-doubt. The concept that he might have done something wrong seemed entirely foreign to him.

The iPoss stopped. In the gloomy distance I could just make out several humanoid shapes, hovering between the stumps of two huge pillars. We approached cautiously, keeping out of sight behind the rocks and weeds. But the stupid iPoss swam right up to them and then back to us, dancing about with excitement and giving away our position. The humanoids, alerted, approached us. I saw that they were mermaids. They stopped before us, floating horizontally with spears leveled. On top of the fact that they were part fish, there was something very peculiar about their bodies. When viewed from below or above they looked like mermaids, but from the front they did not appear to have any depth. Their bodies were entirely flat, making them look like mermaid-shaped pieces of paper.

"Surface creatures," said one. "What are you doing here and what is your business? And how did you get past the traffic shark?"

Of course, they were thinking, not speaking. You can't speak underwater. Try it sometime and you'll see what I mean. In other words, we were being challenged by a large sheet of telepathic paper.

"With this!" Eikelbohm brought out his traffic pass with a flourish.

The mermaids bowed, clearly overawed by both dimensions of the pass.

"We seek the microvita seed," declared Eikelbohm. "Our spiritual master on Zondgraz sent us to replant the sacred seed so that in the future the tree will blossom and regenerate spirituality and universal love on the earth."

"Ah yes, we've been expecting you," said one of the mermaids, lowering her spear. "Miriam," she commanded her companion, "go and fetch our supervisor."

Miriam the mermaid swam off. She cut a curious figure, half human, half fish, half playing card, which did not make mathematical sense but was a fair description, yet another unnatural result of the microvita energy experiments on ancient Atlantis.

"You've been expecting us?" I said. "We didn't expect to be expected."

"It's all in the prophecy. You're right on time. Would you like to know what happens next?"

Eikelbohm looked eager. "I sure would. Any chance I could get a look at that prophecy?"

The mermaid smiled at him and from then on ignored me. He was very handsome, after all, and he appeared to be buying into her prophecy nonsense. I, on the other hand, resembled a pot of overcooked, skeptical spaghetti.

"It is engraved in the sacred stone in the temple, but you have to get special permission to view it."

The mermaid smiled at Eikelbohm again. "But no matter, I have it memorized. I can recite it for you if you wish."

This maiden was proving very cooperative. Sometimes it's useful to have a good-looking companion.

"You are most kind, we would appreciate that," said Eikelbohm. "Allow me to introduce myself. I'm Doctor Eikelbohm from Zondgraz, and this is my companion Dogalogue."

"Oooh, you're a doctor!" the mermaid purred. "I'm Aphrodite. My duty is to guard the temple of the microvita tree and uphold the ideals of the Mermaid Horizontalist Party."

She led us toward the spot by the two pillars where she'd been waiting when we arrived. As she swam, her ribbon-thin body undulated through the water, reminding me of a painted lady sea slug. I wisely decided not to mention this.

"The prophecy goes like this," she said, barely able to contain her excitement. "It says that on this particular day two strangers will arrive from another world on a special quest, sent by their spiritual guru to recover and replant the microvita seed, just like you said. I'm not supposed to tell you any more, but since you seem so polite and nice, perhaps I just might."

"So, what else does the prophecy say?" said Eikelbohm.

"It predicts that two aliens, a tall, strong, handsome leader and a squishy subordinate who looks like leftover cuttlefish will descend from the surface world, guided by the iPoss and seeking the microvita seed. They will then sign an affidavit absolving us from any further responsibility for the seed and produce two forms of ID showing their current address."

"So this is no harder than getting a library card?" I said.

"Is that bad?" she said.

"Well, I don't know," I said. "I mean, it is the only microvita seed on earth, and it was responsible for both the rise and the fall of Atlantis, the greatest civilization in the history of humanity, and it has the potential to revive the planetary spiritual culture in the future unless it falls into the hands of someone evil, in which case it will probably mean the end of the world. So yes, I think there might be a bit more importance attached to it than 'two forms of ID and an affidavit!'"

"Look, do you want the seed or not?" the maiden retorted. "Do you want to know why we make it so easy? My tribe has been guarding this thing for nine thousand years, and, quite frankly, we're sick to death of it! In fact, we're dying to get rid of it. If I had my way, I'd donate it to the nearest passing sea turtle. Do you have any idea what it is like having to remain vigilant for your entire life? Continuous guard duty, emergency drills, being yelled at by psychotic sergeant types. If it didn't mean my hide, I'd pay you to take it away."

"Excellent," said Eikelbohm. "So let's get the seed and leave." He hesitated for a moment. "Of course, I'd love to stick around," he said, smiling at the slightly forlorn-looking mermaid, "but higher duty calls."

He raised his chin, trying to look noble. I thought he looked quite ridiculous, but the girl was agog. She seemed bright enough but was clearly quite helpless when it came to resisting Eikelbohm's charms.

"I understand," she said sadly.

Miriam reappeared, undulating toward us, accompanied by a merman, a portly, at least wide, if not deep, genial-looking fellow dressed in red. "Greetings, surfacelings. I'm Captain Simeon. I say, you look just like the description in the prophecy. This *is* exciting news. To think this is happening in my lifetime and on my shift, too! There will be celebrations in Atlantis tonight! We just need to sort out the paperwork, and then we can go ahead and surrender the microvita seed into your custody. Could I just have two forms of ID? One of them should specify your present address."

We looked at one another in dismay. "Er," said I, "I don't actually have any ID on me. I left it on the ship. And there's only one of it and it doesn't have any address on it."

Simeon frowned. "How about you, Dr. Eikelbohm?"

"All I have with me is this," Eikelbohm gave Simeon his spaceship license. Where there should have been an address, it just said, 'Somewhere in space.'

"No problem, it's perfect," said Simeon, hardly glancing at it before he returned it. "Now, if you'll just come along with me, we can proceed to the sacred circle where the seed is kept in its magic casket."

It seemed all too easy so I decided to keep a wary eye out for trouble. The mer-people seemed tense. They hurried us past occasional murky looming shapes, the blurred remains of the ruined city.

"This was the site of the main temple of Atlantis," said Captain Simeon in a perfunctory manner, quickly pointing out landmarks as they urged us to move faster. "Here was the residence of the necromancer himself, the head of the priest order. There on your left were the stables, and further down the hill, where you see a couple of symmetrical rocks, was where the dragons and other artificially created species were housed. Except for us mer-people. We had our own quarters on the coast."

I swam up to Miriam. "Er, do you mind if I ask a personal question?"

"Not at all. My favorite kind of question."

She, at least, did not reserve her conversation for magazine models with biceps the size of cantaloupes.

"I am familiar with the legend of mermaids, but you don't look quite as I expected. I couldn't help noticing that you are all sort of flattish."

"That's because I'm a Horizontalist. Horizontalists value equality, fairness, justice, love, peace, and the Atlantean Way. We believe that everything should be on the same plane and we live by this principle." She indicated her horizontal body proudly. "Unlike the disgusting Verticalists," she said with a shudder.

"Verticalists?" I said, glancing about uneasily. "What are they? Are they dangerous?"

The mermaid lowered her voice. "They are the other team of mer-people guardians. We hold joint responsibility for the security of seed. But they are quite unlike us Horizontalists. They believe in discipline and tradition and dogma and are, frankly, major party killers. Verticalists just LOVE rules, and they will insist on the two real forms of ID and a whole lot of other bureaucratic stuff."

Captain Simeon broke in.

"Now we come to the council chamber and the laboratories. In the center of this circle grew the microvita tree itself." He was trying to show a brave face, but he was clearly nervous. With good reason, I thought. First there was the danger of the sea monster turning up, and now I was hearing about these difficult-sounding Verticalists. Nor had I forgotten the nameless malevolent presence I'd sensed earlier. We needed to retrieve the seed and get out of there post haste. His commentary, however, enabled me to picture the city as it once stood, just as you might look at a sky full of stars but only understand the constellations when shown the drawings of the zodiac figures on a star map.

We entered the circle. In the center stood a smaller circle of freshly hewn stones. Within that sat a large casket with a plaque that read:

"This is to certify that this is a genuine microvita tree seed and has been designated a national treasure by the Atlantean Heritage Act of 7427 BC. It is the only one like it on the planet and is not one of the cheap imitation knockoff souvenir microvita seeds manufactured for tourists by underpaid Minoan artisans. The penalty for removing this seed without authorization is death by sea monster. Permission to remove it may be obtained by first entering the Official Bureaucratic Nightmare from Hell Building number thirteen and applying in triplicate to the Atlantean committee of 197 elders whose original signatures are a must and whose names are listed inside the casket, which is to be kept locked at all times. Copies of documents are not acceptable—originals are a must. If these individuals are all dead, tough luck. In case you are considering registering an official complaint, you should know that the last person who tried this spent his entire life working on the project and never even secured the first level of permits and authorizations. He died a frustrated pauper. Have a nice day."

"They can't be serious," I said in dismay.

Simeon laughed a hollow laugh, looking over his shoulder anxiously, which was quite a feat for a two-dimensional creature; it involving his twisting himself into a spiral.

"Oh, don't worry about that. No one cares about that stuff anymore. The authors are long dead for a start. Let me show you how it works." He stared at us both for a moment, frowning. Then he turned to me. "You, cephalopod creature. Reluctantly, I give the key into your care, for that is what the prophecy instructs, though I would personally rather give it to your captain"—he cast an admiring glance at Eikelbohm—"as he is clearly the more worthy of the two."

As leader of the expedition, Eikelbohm looked rather put out that Captain Simeon was obliged to choose me to take care of the key, but he couldn't very well say anything without looking like an arrogant, egotistical megalomaniac.

Simeon handed me the key with a warning. "This casket has some special magical properties."

"How come it's so big?" I asked. "There's room for a wolfhound in there. Exactly how large is this seed?"

"It is no larger than Eikelbohm's smallest fingernail, but the casket also contains many important documents."

"What sort of documents?"

"Prophecies. Lots of them. You see, in this box we have prophecies for every contingency, reaching far into the future. The ones that turn out to be true remain in the box, together with the ones that are still possible. Any that turn out to be wrong we feed to the sea monster as punishment when she snores too loudly. We update them every month. It's a brilliant system, don't you think? Our philosophy is that prophecy is an art best practiced with the benefit of hindsight."

Eikelbohm and I glanced at one another, trying not to laugh out loud. Simeon didn't seem to notice.

"That box looks heavy," said Eikelbohm, ever practical. "Can't we just take the seed and leave the heavy box full of papers that are mostly incorrect prophecies?" He smiled ingratiatingly at Simeon. "You can keep them. Consider it a birthday present."

"Oh no, that would not do at all. The seed likes living in the box," said Simeon.

"And it needs some reading material," pointed out Aphrodite reasonably. "How would you like to be shut up in a box for nine thousand years with nothing to read?"

"You must understand how this box works," said Simeon. "If you take the seed out, the box will not like it. It will feel lonely. So someone has to stay in the box to keep it company until the seed is replaced."

"And not just any old somebody," Aphrodite added. "The microvita seed replacement must be handsome and engaging and capable of holding up his end of a thousand-year-long conversation with an empty box."

"Fair enough," I said, trying not to look as though I thought they were all suffering from a mental disease.

Simeon glanced about and leaned forward. "You may have noticed that we're in a bit of a hurry," he said in a low voice. "The other party of mermaids, the Verticalists, are rather, er, rigid regarding the interpretation of the rules. They might not exactly agree with me telling you that you don't have to bother about the permits and ID and all that. They do so love their paperwork. My party, the Horizontalists, who, luckily for you, are on guard duty today, have a different view. We prefer to observe the inner spirit of the law. It is also our opinion that the sooner we can get rid of this wretched seed the better. There are many tribes of merpeople in different locations, but they all originated in Atlantis. We're the only ones silly enough to stay here for nine thousand years guarding this seed instead of outsourcing the work and repairing to the Bahamas where we can sleep in the sun. Now we must hurry before the Verticalists get wind of what is happening. They're bound to cause trouble."

"One thing," I said.

"Yes, yes, what is it?" Simeon was still looking at Eikelbohm. He didn't seem much interested in listening to me.

"We heard some silly rumor that there is a ginormous sea monster that might not take kindly to our procurement of the seed. Any thoughts on that matter?"

Simeon frowned. "Oh, so you heard about that, did you? Yes, well, that's one of the risks you run, I'm afraid. Fortunately for you today is Sunday and since she is a good Catholic, she is resting. She doesn't like to eat anyone on her day off, so you may be in luck."

I never knew that sea monsters took days off, but when you think about it, it makes sense. Everyone has to take a break sometime. You can't expect a monster to be on guard twenty-four-seven. The monster unions would never stand for it, and you'd have monster strikes all over the place. Where would that leave us? But I was not so sure about the sea monster being such a good Catholic as Simeon claimed. I'd distinctly sensed her stirring in the depths.

Suddenly, a different kind of merman appeared above us. Large and flat but standing vertical, like a playing card on its edge. "What's going on here?" he demanded, looking more than suspicious. "Why are these strangers here in our sacred circle? Why were we not informed?"

The Horizontalist mer-people looked guilty. One of them tried to bury herself in the sand like a flounder. Captain Simeon spoke up querulously. "Get lost, Grend's smaller brother. This is none of your business. What you don't know can't hurt you."

"Yeah," chipped in Aphrodite. "Sticks and stones can break your bones, but if you tell anyone what you saw here, I'm going to make you sorry you were ever squished flat by nine thousand years of dogmatic insistence on a bunch of meaningless rules!"

"You're giving away the seed without following all the protocol," cried small Grend. "Traitors! My big brother will put a stop to this!" He fled.

Simeon looked grim. "We have to move fast. Big Grend is big trouble."

If my intuition was worth anything, Big Grend was the least of our worries.

The little troop of Horizontalist mer-people helped us carry the casket back along the route we'd just come. Now that we were traveling in the correct direction, the traffic shark waved us through, no questions asked. There was no sign of my octopus friend at her rocky outcrop. But just beyond her lair, we were forced to halt. Our way was barred by a gang of mean-looking Verticalists led by one huge club-wielding merman.

The sand quaked as Grend stepped forward, flexed his muscles, and dealt us a proud glance. Grend's minions broke into song.

"Grend, his skin is like ebony, his teeth are white, as he gnashes them angrily and looks for a fight!"

"I am Grend, war leader of the Verticalist hero types," declared the merman, brandishing a spear large enough to impale an orca. The Verticalists were much bigger and fiercer-looking than our Horizontalist friends, half of whom were girls. We seemed to have formed an alliance with the Hippie Party.

This would have been a lot scarier if it were not for the fact that Grend spoke in a high, squeaky voice. A voice like that seemed like a major disadvantage for a ruthless tough guy. I actually found him quite charming. After all, not many professional enforcers have a theme song of their own. I thought it significantly raised the general standard of thuggery and intimidation.

After his classy entrance, Grend seemed uncertain what to do next. I thought we might be able to work with this guy. But when I saw his controller my heart sank.

"Excuse me," said Grend. "I have to consult with my cunning advisor."

A vague-looking shadowy figure drifted up beside Grend. They conferred for a moment. Then Grend turned back to us.

"I hope you don't mind my asking, but are you the famous alien thieves, one handsome and heroic, the other squishy and repulsive, who have stolen our sacred microvita seed with the aid of the treacherous Horizontalist defectors, exactly as predicted in one of the more unlikely of our large array of prophecies?"

I'd never met such a polite hit man. He was the kind of thug you would hire to beat up your grandmother. His advisor, on the other hand, gave me the creeping horrors. His outline was indistinct and I found it difficult to get a clear idea of his appearance. Every time I tried to look at him, a large luminous fish swam in front of me. It was incredibly distracting. He seemed to be manipulating my mind, but even that was hard to think about. And I was pretty certain that the fish was his special pet mental-interference fish, which you have to admit is mighty suspicious. Who *was* this guy?

Meanwhile the confrontation escalated.

"Where do you think you're going with that casket?" demanded the brawny Grend, scowling meaningfully.

"Who wants to know?" said Eikelbohm, flexing his own not-inconsiderable muscles, reminiscent of a certain popular fruit.

"I already told you who I am, plus you got to enjoy my song," said Grend. "Weren't you listening?"

"You'd better just listen to this," snarled Eikelbohm. "Get out of our way, we're coming through!"

"Wanna make something of it?" growled Grend.

"I reckon I can," said Eikelbohm.

"Over my dead body!"

"If you insist."

"You and whose army?" sneered Grend. He leaned forward to get a better look at Eikelbohm. "I say, are you by any chance from Australia?"

"No," said Eikelbohm. "I'm from Zondgraz."

The advisor slunk up behind Grend. "Stop fraternizing with the defectors!" he hissed. "You're setting a bad example for the minions."

"Sorry, master." Grend turned back to Eikelbohm, looking embarrassed. "My apologies, but I must get back to my duty and insult your mother."

I decided to address the advisor directly, since he was obviously in charge. "Excuse me, but I'm wondering if you're acquainted with a friend of mine, Nefarious the wizard? I just thought you might know him."

The vague figure spat in disdain, an impressive move underwater. "Nefarious? That wimp! Tell him from me that the hatred of Insidious the Dark abides and that I plot his untimely death nightly. And as for you, any friend of his is an enemy of mine. One more reason to destroy you, thief!" My attempt at name-dropping as a form of defense didn't seem to be working very well.

Insidious leered and flexed his bony hands, cracking his knuckles, a habit I've always found incredibly annoying. Feeling like a mouse facing a poisonous snake, I drew my umbrella. "Back, minions," I cried. "Plus Grend," I added as an afterthought.

I opened the umbrella. The mermen had never seen such a fiendish device before, leaping from one dimension to three in an instant. They fell back in fear.

"Keep away," I cried, "lest I strike you with my arcane weapon and you become three dimensional and turn into helpless globular mer-people that float to the surface and bob about waiting for a seagull to peck you and pop you."

If I found this image amusing, the Verticalists did not. They shrank back in horror. Nothing like a little creative lying to deflect your enemies.

Eikelbohm swept out his sword and sliced a couple of living playing cards in half. I made a mental note to ask him for lessons on how to ruthlessly beat people up. He was really very good at it, though I did think it was a little harsh to actually cut them in half. But there wasn't any blood and the severed cards really didn't seem to mind. They just carried on as before, except in two parts.

Melon-man hefted the casket onto his shoulder and nodded to me to follow. With a spring he shot straight upward. This took these two-dimensional thinkers by surprise. I made to follow, but something seemed to grab me by the brain. I felt as though a clutching claw of evil spite had seized my head in a vice and was dragging me across the sand. I tried to scream, but just as in space no one can hear you scream, neither can they underwater. All I could manage were a few bubbles as transparent fangs penetrated my brain. I could feel them injecting neurotoxins as the claws pierced my heart, sucking out my life force.

Insidious had me in a death grip. The tendrils of his mind entered mine like slivers of magnetized steel, forcing poison through my nervous system. It was even less pleasant than crucifixion practice, which is really saying something. I was really beginning to hate this guy. I fought to escape with all my might but I had lost control of my body, and my mind was going the same way. I couldn't see how to get away from this pitiless, unrelenting creature. My energy was fading fast. As the brain poison took hold, the pain faded and I stopped struggling. I began to feel quite relaxed and carefree, somehow glad to be donating my life force to this evil being. Yet a part of my own will remained, and with it a faint sense of sorrow that after all I'd been through, just when we'd succeeded against all odds in retrieving the microvita seed, I was going to die a horrible death. What a drag. My last thought was one of mild disappointment.

Suddenly everything exploded in shards of light. I felt the monster's awful grip slacken. His fangs withdrew and with a last effort I wriggled free. Eikelbohm seized my arm and dragged me to safety.

"C'mon, Dogalogue. Let's get out of here."

What a guy! He'd come back for me and blasted the evil wizard creature who made Nefarious look like a garden gnome. Eikelbohm was definitely the kind of friend you wanted with you when you had to fight bad guys at the bottom of the ocean!

Grend and his gang looked dismayed to see their evil leader stricken down. They pursued us halfheartedly as we swam upward. Eikelbohm threw a lightning bolt back at them, a small one, just enough to frighten them off. He had to conserve his strength. "That should give them second thoughts about pursuing us," he said with a grin. "By the way, who was that guy?"

"Not a very funny man," I said. "He bit me on the brain."

I caught a malevolent thought below us from a mind as evil as any I'd come across in my short life. It had turned toward the leviathan, willing it to pursue us. Oh Zond! He was waking up the sea monster. This ought to be fun, I thought cheerfully as we sped toward our rendezvous with the dragon. I was in an excellent mood, oblivious to the poison still flowing in my veins.

Joe was waiting faithfully where we'd left him. We mounted his back but as we sped swiftly toward the surface, the dragon's scales shining brighter with each moment, a hideous form stirred in the depths and a pair of malevolent eyes turned toward us glowing with strange desire. The guardian shot forth in pursuit.

I saw it first, a great shadow, blacker than the murky deep. I could sense its desire to clutch us in its many tentacles. Joe struggled to swim faster, but he had been underwater too long and was straining to hold his breath. I watched in amusement as the monster rose beneath us, rapidly closing the gap between us, its wriggling bulk dwarfing our brave dragon.

"Nice Mr. Sea Monster," I said. "I'll bet it will behave itself if I give it a chocolate fish." I was feeling quite lightheaded. I didn't see how such a pretty sea monster would want to do us any harm.

"Very funny," said Eikelbohm. "I'm going to deliver a thunderbolt right between the eyes before it gets any closer."

He braced himself against the dragon's dorsal spines, drew one arm back and with a throwing motion cried a ruinous spell. This was no warning shot. A bolt of energy flew from his palm and struck the monster with a great flash of light. The creature recoiled and writhed in pain, creating a shockwave that passed over us so that we had to cling to the dragon's back.

"Oh dear!" I cried. "Poor monster. She's got a sore nose."

I wanted to dissuade Eikelbohm from hurting the monster again, but I was laughing too hard. I found it difficult to take any of this seriously, especially the idea of dying, which seemed extremely hilarious right then.

"What's gotten into you, Dogalogue?" Joe said, frowning.

"Isn't life strange?" I began to sing, trailing off as we neared the surface. "Hey, look at the dancey waves. We should do this every day."

Meanwhile the iPoss slept through the whole thing, happily curled around the handle of the casket.

Love, Leviathan Style

We gathered on the foredeck, the casket of the microvita seed in our midst. Eikelbohm sat on a barrel, his shoulders slumped with exhaustion. First the dive and then the energy blasts had really taken it out of him. I felt a bit strange myself. I had this weird idea that an evil underwater wizard had tried to kill me and had almost succeeded. Which was silly, of course, but still I sensed that all was not as it should be. Somebody was out to get me, I was sure of it, but who?

"Well," declared Eikelbohm, leaning on his sword, "We did it. Here, finally, is the microvita seed, above water for the first time in nine thousand years."

"That old weedy box?" said Brains doubtfully. "This is what we went to all this trouble for? It doesn't look like much."

"None of us are going to look like much if we don't get out of here fast," said Eikelbohm grimly. "That monster is sure to be back. Let's get the ship underway. Sweep, set course for Iberia!"

As everyone else hurried about the business of setting sail, I approached the casket. "Let's clean this box up a bit," I muttered to myself. "Here, let me scrape the slime off with my umbrella." I looked about. "Hey, has anyone seen my umbrella? Iris? I don't suppose you have my umbrella, do you?" The whereabouts of my umbrella suddenly took on enormous importance in my mind.

Iris did not seem to share my concern. "No," she said. "What would I want with your umbrella? Perhaps you dropped it during your escape from Atlantis."

This was a real blow. That was a top-quality umbrella and we were thirty-seven light years from the nearest decent department store. There was no helping it. I had to get it back. I squelched over to the gunwale and leapt into the water.

Everyone rushed to the rail. "Are you nuts?" Eikelbohm yelled. "What in Zond are you doing? Haven't you had enough swimming for one day?"

"I'm just going to fetch my umbrella," I called. "I won't be long. Just relax." I'd noticed that Eikelbohm was a very tense person.

"You're out of your mind! It's hundreds of fathoms down. The place is swarming with angry Verticalists and we're about to be attacked by a sea monster. Get back on the ship immediately!"

"But it was a special umbrella. I don't want to leave it in the hands of those rough Verticalists. They might break it. Where am I going to get a replacement in this galactic backwater? What am I supposed to do if it rains? I might catch cold. Be reasonable."

"You lunatic! If we get out of this alive I'll buy you fifty gold-plated umbrellas. Now get back on the ship immediately, and that's an order!"

"Ah," I said, "an order! That's different. Why didn't you say so before?" Besides being compelled by the order from my superior, I was sorely tempted by his generous offer of fifty gold-plated umbrellas. I'd never had a gold-plated umbrella. I swam back to the ship, squelching easily up the side of her hull with the suckers on my tentacles.

Eikelbohm was behaving very strangely. He had a wild look in his eyes and kept clenching and unclenching his fists. I thought that perhaps the water pressure had affected his brain. Maybe he was already regretting his extravagant promise of so many gold-plated umbrellas. I wondered how long it would take him to procure them and what I was supposed to do in the meantime if it rained. I glanced at the sky. Just a few white clouds. We should be fine for now.

Iris was watching me. "Sir Dogalogue, what's wrong with you?"

"Me? I'm fine. Never better. Come along, there's work to be done. I have to calculate the best route to Betelgeuse by sea. Where's my sextant?"

Iris took my tentacle, looking worried. "You don't seem to be your usual self, Sir Dogalogue. Why don't you take a little rest and have something to eat. Come with me to the cabin."

Eikelbohm strode up. "What's with you, Dogalogue, jumping over the side like that? Have you lost your last remaining marble? This is an emergency. We all have to pull together you know."

"Sorry, sir. Yes, of course, I understand." I hesitated. "Er, one thing though. Could you remind me, what was the reason we couldn't recover my umbrella again?"

Eikelbohm looked about to manhandle me, but Iris stopped him, "Don't you see, Eikelbohm? There's something the matter with him."

"She's right. He's behaving abnormally," said the dragon. "Don't you see how pale he is? It must be the aftereffects of the attack by that wizard, or maybe the depth pressure affected his brain. Or both."

I did not appreciate being discussed as though I was some sort of mental patient. People should have the decency to conduct such conversations behind one's back. "Me?" I said. "My brain's perfectly fine, thank you. Now get out of my way so I can deal with this so-called sea monster. Oh. Where's it gone? It was here a moment ago, but now it's turned into a seagull. What's a seagull doing out here at sea? Must be on holiday. Did you know that seagulls have the greatest biomass of any animal on earth? Oh no, that's ants, sorry. But if the seagulls ate all the ants, then it would be the seagulls, wouldn't it?"

"Someone take this lunatic below," Eikelbohm growled. "Here you—rodent thing—badger. You're on Dogalogalunatic duty. Take him into the cabin and make sure he doesn't touch anything important or jump overboard chasing umbrellas. And above all, make sure he doesn't get in my way or I'll throw him overboard myself."

"Aye, aye, Captain," said Brains, proud of his new duty.

Mina scowled. "He threatened to throw Sir Dogalogue overboard," she whispered to Iris. "Who does he think he is?"

"Well, I suppose he thinks he's the commander of an interstellar mission to save a planet who just defeated a giant sea monster in battle," said Iris. "But I'm sure he was jesting about throwing Sir Dogalogue into the sea."

On the way to the cabin I stopped to speak to Iris and Mina. I glanced around to ensure we could not be overheard and whispered. "A word of advice. You two ought not to be out on deck without an umbrella. Don't you know it's wet down there?" I pointed to the ocean. "There's a perfectly good umbrella store not far from here. I have the address." I started searching in my pocket. "Oh no, silly me, I left it on Betelgeuse. There it is, up there," I pointed up at the blue sky where there was no sign of either impending rain or the great red star.

"Sir Dogalogue," please come with me," said Brains, taking my hand and leading me to the hatch. "Perhaps your umbrella is below deck."

"I'm worried about the captain," I said, keeping my voice low. "He is behaving very strangely. I think the deep water affected his brain. It's the pressure, you know. He can't handle the pressure." I had another concern. I was beginning to suspect that Eikelbohm might go back on his promise of fifty gold-plated umbrellas.

"Don't worry, we'll take care of the captain," Brains said. "Now you just come down and have a nice rest."'

I gazed at him in pity. "I understand that you are suffering from a delusion that an evil wizard has turned you into a badger. Don't worry, it will pass. It's the pressure, you know. I once knew someone who had a pet ant. But, sad story, it died. Ants do that. They don't live long. Nor do humans, when it comes to that. Or badgers. We Zondgrazians live pretty long. I know one or two I wish wouldn't. My crucifixion practice instructor for a start."

I could see that poor Brains didn't understand me, but what do you expect from someone who is convinced he is a badger? I'd had little hope of talking any sense into him from the outset. It seemed that I was the only one on the ship who realized that the captain had gone mad with power. He'd convinced them that I was the one who was mad, when in fact there was something very fishy about him. He seemed to have cracked under the pressure. I would have to arrest him and probably the badger as well. But where was I going to find a policeman in the middle of the ocean? I knew it seemed ungrateful, but I was afraid I would have to ask Joe to eat Eikelbohm.

Once we were in the cabin Brains brought me some lunch.

"Why thank you," I said. "I couldn't help noticing that you're a very short person. Did anyone ever tell you that you look remarkably like a certain small mammal, don't tell me... yes, I've got it, that's it. A badger!"

Up on deck Captain Eikelbohm was hurriedly checking the rigging before we set sail. The Sweep, claiming to be an expert, had reorganized the sails and rigging after the storm. Eikelbohm grabbed a rope and pulled it taut. "What's this?" he said, turning to The Sweep. "Did you do this? This boom is on the wrong side of the mast! If the wind blows from the stern, the sail will blow into the mast and tangle with the rigging. And what about this? This isn't right! ! This is a sheet, not a stay. You've attached it to the mast—it's supposed to be fastened to the boom. This is a disaster. If you attach a sheet to the mast and try to pull the sail in, nothing's going to happen, unless you pull really hard and the mast comes down, which is just possible since you've got it running through a block and tackle. And what's this you've tied to the end of the halyard? Have you ever been on a boat before? The halyard is supposed to pull the sail up. You've gone and tied a toy rabbit to the end of it. What were you thinking?"

The Sweep was bouncing and taking notes, ever eager to learn. "What was I thinking? Well, I thought some of the ropes didn't seem to be doing much, and they were sort of in the way, so I used them to lower some barrels into the bilges."

Eikelbohm was livid. "Go and fetch them at once. And send Iris here. She's the only one around here with any sense at all." He glanced nervously down at the water. "Here you, mole. I'm making you the official sea monster lookout. Climb up to the crow's nest and give a shout if you see anything that looks like a giant sea monster."

"Aye, aye, sir." Maurice felt his way carefully to the mast and climbed skyward, feeling mightily pleased to play such an important job in the adventure and determined to keep a sharp eye on everything less than two feet from his face. Why, he could even be the one to save them all.

If there was one thing we learned during that journey, however, it was that when you are being pursued across the Atlantic by a giant sea monster, it is better not to post a mole as your lookout, considering that moles are legally blind.

The Sweep fetched the ropes and gave them to Iris to deliver to Eikelbohm. He was in no hurry to go back to his work while Eikelbohm was in such a bad mood, so instead he went to the back of the ship, putting as much distance between the captain and himself as possible.

Iris found Eikelbohm sitting on his favorite barrel, resting his head on one hand, looking worried. "At this rate we'll sink the ship without any help from the monster," he said. "Your brother seems to imagine that he knows everything, but in fact he is a complete idiot. I can't believe how badly he's screwed up the rigging. It's going to take some time to set it straight and meanwhile we're like sitting ducks here if the creature decides to come after us again. Not only that, we're shorthanded. Dogalogue's gone completely loopy and everyone else is a useless landlubber except the dragon who has to sit still on the foredeck so that he doesn't tip the boat over. How am I supposed to manage a ship with this lot?"

"I know my brother is sometimes a little overoptimistic about his abilities, but he means well. Don't worry, I can fix the rigging. When we're under way, The Sweep can steer. He's good at that. You should get some rest, you're completely exhausted. Go and lie down. I'll send for you if there's anything urgent, OK?"

Eikelbohm sighed. "Thank you, Princess. I don't know how I'd manage without you." He rose and went below to his cabin.

As she watched him go Iris felt protective. Beneath that strong exterior he just wanted to be taken care of. She wondered if... no, it wasn't possible. They were too different. But he really was very handsome and he was so brave and responsible. And she certainly seemed to be making a good impression on him. And so she set to work sorting out her brother's mess. Not for the first time.

Meanwhile The Sweep was back in the aft castle talking to Maurice and Mina. "Eikelbohm seems very tense," said Maurice. "He ought to do yoga, like Sir Dogalogue."

"What about Dogalogue, though?" said The Sweep. "He's acting very peculiar. I hope it's only temporary."

"So do I," said Mina tearfully. "I really hope he recovers soon. He's my best friend, and I don't have many friends."

"You've got me," said Maurice, taking her paw in his. Mina sniffed gratefully.

"You need more friends?" said The Sweep. "I'm an expert at making friends. By the way, Maurice. What are you doing here? Aren't you supposed to be up in the crow's nest watching for the sea monster?"

"I was, but I got bored so I came down to see what was happening," said Maurice.

"Fair enough. Now as I was saying, I happen to be Europe's number one friend-making expert. Gather around." He gestured to a couple of passing sea gulls, plus a flying fish that had accidentally landed on the deck and was flapping about, feeling undignified. "Would you care to join my impromptu seminar on how to make one hundred new friends in four minutes?"

The sea gulls and the flying fish were curious so they waddled and flopped over to form a little semicircle of disciples. The Sweep frowned at the flying fish. "It is customary that persons attending my seminars possess at least one sound leg." The sea gulls began strutting around, showing off the soundness of their legs. The fish flapped sadly. "But in light of your pathetic expression I will make an exception." He spied Iris approaching with a determined look on her face. "Er, I think we might have to continue this lesson a little later," he said. "If any of you need to learn how to make friends or study the ancient martial art, Yubby Wuzza, or learn how to gesticulate with unmatched style, here is my card. Which only leaves one question to be answered, and that is, how come there is a giant tentacle coming out of the sea reaching for my sister?"

Four green tentacles had appeared over the starboard rail, groping blindly. Iris jumped back with a scream. "Gross! It's gotten slime on me."

The *Dodecahedron* lurched to the starboard. Everyone fell or stumbled toward that side of the ship, which would not have mattered much if that everyone did not include a forty-ton dragon. Joe slid across the deck trying to grip the surface with his claws but he only succeeded in tearing up strips of wood and making a terrible screeching sound. His shifting weight caused the ship to list still further so that it threatened to capsize.

Eikelbohm erupted on deck at a run and leapt for the bridge, cutlass in hand. With a great swashbuckling blow he sliced through a tough rubbery tentacle and landed in a crouch, spinning out of reach as another writhing limb lashed out at him.

"Iris," he cried," get below and play your harp! It's our only hope!"

As Iris raced for the cabin across the heaving deck, everyone else did their best to protect her from the flailing tentacles. Joe managed to claw his way to the port side of the ship, away from the mass of heavy tentacles pouring over the starboard side. This balanced the vessel so that we were in no imminent danger of sinking. But the monster now had the dragon trapped on the side furthest from its attack. Joe did not dare join the fight lest the ship capsize. Instead he leapt into the air with a roar and flew upward in a glow of red and orange scales, narrowly avoiding the rigging. With his weight removed the ship listed wildly to starboard again. Everyone grabbed something to hold on to. The Sweep grabbed the unanchored mole, missing by scant weeks the historical Vessel Safety Act passed by the British Parliament, stipulating that any mole traveling aboard a Royal Navy ship must be bolted to the deck.

I emerged from the cabin just in time to see Maurice and The Sweep tumble and roll down the steep slope of the deck right into the monster's arms. Looking back, it is clear that this must have been the moment when Ingrid, the lonely sea monster, first began to develop feelings for The Sweep. The prince, unaware of the amorous mood he had inspired in the salty breast of the leviathan, leapt free of the clutching tentacles, mole in hand.

"Back, creature of darkness," he cried, brandishing a rusty boathook. "Disturb not our righteous quest with thy nefarious disturbing-type activities. Miscreant monster, misshapen mammal, lascivious leviathan. Repent now before it is too late."

But the creature did not repent. A fresh tentacle took The Sweep unawares from behind and lifted him in its great sticky suckers clear off the deck and out over the water.

"Heeelp," cried The Sweep. "I'm in what can only be described as trouuuuuble!"

"Iris, now! Get to the harp!" cried Eikelbohm, desperately fencing with half a dozen tentacles.

With the monster's attention focused on The Sweep, Iris dashed across the wildly rocking deck for the hatchway. She bounded down the stairs into the cabin and quickly unwrapped her precious instrument. I had been attempting to catch some sleep, but there was not much hope of that with all this commotion.

"I say," I said, pulling up a chair. "That's an excellent idea, a bit of music. Would you mind playing something soothing, perhaps in the Aoelian mode? Everyone around here seems kind of edgy."

"You can play in Martian mode for all I care!" yelled Brains over the creaking of the ship and the shouting of our companions. "The monster has your brother, Iris! Start playing already!"

Iris hesitated. "I'm not sure whether to play a folk tune in D minor, or the more traditional Gregorian chant in F, adapted for harp. I don't know how sea monsters' tastes run."

Joe's great voice came from the sky as he swooped down, spitting fire at the monster. "Hello? Could we have a little music up here, please?"

The boat rocked dangerously and Iris almost fell off her stool. She clutched the harp and tried to ignore the tentacle probing blindly through the hatch. "Maybe I should transpose it," she mused. "The higher frequencies might lull the creature to sleep."

"Just play the damn thing!" screamed the badger as another cluster of writhing arms appeared in the hatchway and ripped away the stair railing. A boom smashed into the water with a great rending sound, tearing the sail in half. Ropes snapped like cotton under the terrible strength of the monster's arms and the ship listed wildly to starboard.

"How in the world can I play in this madness?" Iris cried in desperation

"Just relax," screamed the badger over the din of splitting wood and churning water.

"Relax!" Iris laughed and struck up a merry tune. Her fingers danced across the strings and the notes flew up through the hatch and out over the ship. Time seemed to slow so that all movement flowed like a dream and fear melted into mist. The tentacles massing around the ship relaxed and slid back into the water like overcooked spaghetti. The monster's body broke the surface and floated there flaccid, all pockmarked and pale like a pole-axed moon. I came on deck with the badger and we stared aghast at the hellish creature, now fully visible for the first time. An idiotic grin spread across its face and it began to dance a grotesque dance in time to the music, rotating slowly in the water, its deadly mane of limbs undulating on the swell.

"Helloooo, can someone please throw me a rope?" cried a voice from the water. We hauled The Sweep aboard. The monster continued to ignore us, absorbed in it's hideous dance.

Iris came on deck and continued to play, holding the monster under her spell. I was fascinated by the way her fingers plucked each string, sure that my tentacles could do it just as well. More than a little irritated by the denigrating remarks directed at my person by the Horizontalists, and by Eikelbohm, I felt it was high time I demonstrated that tentacles are at least the equal of fingers. And anyway, the harp was from Zondgraz, designed by my master. This earth simian had no right to monopolize it.

"That looks like fun. Mind if I have a go?" I asked.

"Please don't bother me now, Sir Dogalogue, I have to concentrate."

Iris's eyes were focused on the dreaming monster, willing it to sleep, but in my fey mood I was not about to be brushed aside or naysaid by a monkey, princess or not. "You simians are not the only ones around here with culture. I can play too, you know." I wrapped my tentacles around the harp and wrested it from her.

The moment the music stopped, the monster snapped out of her dream. Her cluster of baleful eyes turned on us once more and an army of thick green tentacles erupted from the water, pouncing on the ship like a team of leopards. A snaking arm wriggled across the deck and grabbed the harp. I clung to the golden frame and yelled, "He's back, folks! And I think he wants to play."

Iris, still on her knees, drew her dagger and lunged forward, stabbing at the serpent arm. Eikelbohm leapt over her, drawing his cutlass, and slashed the tentacle in half. I fell backward with the instrument on top of me. The water around the boat seethed and foamed and the ship shook. Everyone was shouting at once. Iris rose and fought her way across the swaying deck toward me crying, "You fool! Give me my harp!"

Really angry now, I confronted Eikelbohm. "You never intended to give me those gold-plated umbrellas, did you?"

"You moron," cried Eikelbohm in fury, trying to twist the harp out of my grip. "By Zond's teeth, let go before you get us all killed!"

At that, something in me snapped. Fool? Moron? How unjust. All I wanted was to play a little music. I relinquished my grip on the harp and seized Eikelbohm in a cephalopod stranglehold. "It's not fair," I said. "It's my turn."

With a violent lunge Eikelbohm tore free of my hold, my suckers popping like rice cakes as they released his flesh. He backed away, breathing hard, one hand wrapped so tight around the harp that his knuckles were white. The other held his sword, pointed not at the monster, but at me.

Iris lurched across the quaking deck but before she reached us the ship tilted violently again and she pitched forward, hands flung out to break her fall. Three giant tentacles descended on us, grabbed the instrument, Eikelbohm, and me, and lifted us high above the deck. Iris screamed from below, "Don't drop the harp!"

The Sweep rushed at the monster who, seeing her beloved's apparent show of affection, suddenly released us. We fell to the deck with a loud, twanging crash and lay stunned. But it was not to us that Iris ran. The harp lay broken like a wounded bird, its frame twisted, its strings snapped and curled. Iris knelt weeping with her beloved instrument in her arms, "My harp," she sobbed, "you fools, you've broken it!"

Then the monster reached out with one tentacle, thick as a python, pressed her down, took the harp from her arms, and was gone.

We stared about in the sudden silence, sprawled on the deck, not knowing where the creature would strike next, hoping against hope that it would be satisfied with the princess's golden treasure and leave us in peace. No such luck. Seconds later a fresh battalion of tentacles appeared along the gunwale near the stern.

"There is nothing to fear but fear itself!" declared Brains grandly.

Maurice turned on him. "Are you insane? That's the silliest philosophy I ever heard. There are at least eleven things to fear other than fear itself. Allow me to elucidate: snakes, witches, vampires, dogs, bad poetry, floods, public speaking, hunters, foxes, sharks, the monster dragging the ship down to the depths with us in it, and that boom swinging across and cracking you on the head. Watch out, duck!"

"A duck? Where?" Brains looked about and luckily saw the boom coming just in time to duck. "Ah, that kind of duck. You should have specified." He had turned a little pale. "OK, OK, enough, you've made your point. There are one or two things to fear other than fear itself."

"Not one or two. Eleven. Minimum."

The monster, not wanting to be left out of the conversation, butted in. "You forgot the fear of putting on too much weight during the winter so that you are too fat to appear in your bikini in summer. Even giant sea monsters have their fears."

Brains quailed as the creature loomed over them, but Maurice, too shortsighted to appreciate Ingrid's sheer monstrosity, kept his cool. "Ah, but you are very slim," he said. "Svelte, even. By the way, did you know that moles are one of the most fattening foods in the world?"

The monster leaned closer to peer at the mole. "No, I didn't know that. That's extremely interesting. What's a good low-fat food I could eat instead of a mole?"

Maurice cast about desperately. His gaze fell on Brains, but he thought better of it. "Er, vegetables, bats, dogs, leaves, plants, wood, oat bran, you know—high-roughage foodstuffs."

"Like this mast?" cried the monster gleefully. She pounced on the forward mast with a hundred tentacles, ripped it out of the deck, and began crunching on it with gusto, clawing away the clinging ropes. "Yum yum! Roughage! Tasty and healthy! Give me more!"

We skittered aside as shards of splintered mast showered the deck. The monster licked her lips and moved toward the main course—the central mast.

Eikelbohm cried out, "Don't let her get the main mast. It's anchored to the hull. It will sink the ship!"

He turned and snarled at the mole. "Thanks, treacle brain, for suggesting she eat wood! Next time I hope she sticks to her mole diet."

He rushed toward the mast, raising his hands in defiance as the monster towered over him. Great fragments of wood spattered her mouth as she eyed the main mast greedily. As she reached for it, The Sweep leapt forward to support Eikelbohm and stoutly hacked through a tentacle, but a dozen more took its place, thrusting forward in a single motion to overwhelm him and thrust him overboard as if he weighed no more than a balsa wood doll. Maddened with greed, the monster appeared to have forgotten her affection for the prince. More tentacles grabbed Eikelbohm before he had time to muster an energy blast and casually swept him aside. The monster seized the mast and cries of terror filled the air as the entire ship shook.

"I'm getting really sick of ending up in the water," grumbled The Sweep, catching a rope and clambering back on board.

Tentacles writhed into the air, higher than the mast. Our crew and the exhausted dragon were like fleas attacking a dog, pitting our pitiful strength against the leviathan. Eikelbohm threw himself at one of the dozen arms that, like a clutch of boa constrictors brought their might to bear on the main mast, bending it back until it ripped free of its base with an awful tearing sound, opening a gaping hole in the hull into which the sea rushed.

We'd lost the fight. The ship began to sink.

"Retreat to the aft castle," shouted Eikelbohm, leading the way through the wreckage toward the stern.

"Oh look," I cried. "A dolphin!"

"Ooh, ooh, where?" said Brains. "I've never seen a dolphin."

"I'd kind of like to see it, too," said The Sweep. "Which way is it?"

"Over there to the north," I said. They joined me at the rail to see if it came up again.

Eikelbohm stormed up, steaming with fury. "If you idiots don't get back on the aft deck I'll feed you to the goddamned dolphin! Wretched tourists! Unbelievable!"

"Captain Eikelbohm," said Brains as we followed him aftward, "I couldn't help noticing that you're very negative sometimes. It's not healthy, you know. You'll give yourself an ulcer."

The sea monster, mostly absorbed in chewing on the mast, swiped absently at us all with a long tentacle. Eikelbohm grappled with it and gasped. "Brains, throwing you overboard right now would be negative, and if you add that to my negative remark, that makes a positive. How does that sound?"

"By golly he's right," said Maurice. "A negative plus a negative is a positive. That's mathematics, that is. Yet somehow it still doesn't sound very positive."

"Don't worry," said The Sweep. "My latest invention, The Ambivalent Logic Pot, will resolve everything. If you put things in it, it gives you the answer. Here's a free sample: Two wrongs make a right, just as two lefts make a right, two insults make a fight, some dogs bark but do not bite, Greek philosophy is somewhat trite, and two darks make a light. It's all explained in my two-bowl theorem."

Meanwhile, our trusty bark, the *Dodecahedron*, was foundering fast.

"Quick everyone," cried Joe. "Get on my back. We'll have to fly for it!"

While everyone else ran for the aft deck, I went below to the cabin. I'd begun to worry that I'd forgotten to turn the gas off. When I saw the microvita seed casket it dawned on me! This was what Eikelbohm had been after, all along! I couldn't see the iPoss. Perhaps it was sleeping inside. I didn't want to disturb it, so rather than opening the casket I brought the whole thing along. The cabin was already filling with water. What a foolish idea. I had a good mind to complain to the captain. What if someone wanted to have a little lie down? They'd get all wet. This was no way to manage a ship. I really ought to fire him.

I was struggling up the stairs with the casket when Eikelbohm appeared at the top of the steps. "Ah, loony tunes, you did something right for a change. We went to too much trouble to let the microvita seed sink now. Let's go."

"Get away!" I cried breathlessly. "Not satisfied with one harp, one princess and all the glory, now you want the microvita seed as well. Keep your distance or I'll throw the whole caboodle overboard."

Eikelbohm raised his empty hands and took a step away. "Hey, take it easy. Whatever your nutty inner voice says, just so long as we get that casket onboard the dragon."

When I reached the deck I saw the princess sitting there, soaking wet, mourning the loss of her harp. "Come along, Sis," said The Sweep gently. "We have to flee to safety."

He took her arm and drew her away. Weeping, she ran with her brother for the dragon. But just as they approached the aft castle, the monster shook the ship again. The Sweep fell sprawling, losing his grip on Iris's arm. She stumbled, lost her balance, and with a scream tumbled over the side into the churning sea. Without hesitation Eikelbohm dived into the water after her. I thought it looked like a cheap PR stunt, but everyone else was impressed.

By then the rest of us were on Joe's back. With a rush of shining wings the dragon leapt into the air. As we swept upward I looked back to see the ship settling in the water, the monster happily munching on decking planks. Joe flew around in a curve, so close to the water that his dangling claws touched the waves. Eikelbohm and Iris were swimming away from the sinking ship as fast as they could and with a rush of wings and water and clutching hands Joe scooped them up from the surface and shot upward. Our little troop let out a cheer. The monster looked up and waved happily, as though we were applauding her.

"Oh Joe, thank you, thank you." Iris was weeping and hugging the dragon's neck. She cast a grateful look at Eikelbohm but seemed too shy to say anything. "Are you going to be all right, Joe?" she asked. "This is quite a load and we have a long flight."

"I'll let you know when we get there," said Joe. "At least I won't feel seasick any more."

Below us the faithful *Dodecahedron* lay low in the water. We looked down in awe as a host of tentacles rose and clutched her from all sides. Then the ship slowly upended, slid beneath the waves, and was gone. I think I was the only one who noticed a small bat spiral upward and settle on the end of the dragon's tail.

The Cephalopod Who Mistook his Friend for an Umbrella

The dragon's wings beat out a hypnotic rhythm while the sun warmed me, but the wind was chill, so I was cooked on one side and underdone on the other, which felt strange but not unpleasant. We'd been flying for more than an hour now, but I wondered if Joe could keep this up all the way to the coast. The unasked question was like an elephant in the room, and with all the extra weight on board the last thing we needed was an additional elephant.

Suddenly Brains laughed. "This is a bit like one of those stories where everyone is stranded on an island with no food, and they have to decide which of them they should eat."

"Excellent suggestion," I said. "Let's start with the cannibalism option. We should also consider flavors. I must warn you not to select me unless you are partial to seafood. And I'm told that my tentacles are awfully rubbery."

"Except that cannibalism wouldn't work in this situation," said The Sweep, "because even if, just to choose a random example, we were to eat Brains, that would not reduce the total amount of weight the dragon has to carry, because he'd still be with us, except that he'd be in our stomachs."

"Oh yeah," said Brains. "I didn't think of that. What a relief not to have to make that decision, eh?"

Iris, her nerves frayed, flared up. "Will you stop talking nonsense. Joe is getting tired. In a couple of hours it'll be too dark to see the coast even if we are getting near. This is a life or death situation."

This didn't exactly cheer everyone up.

The next hour was one of the longest of our lives, especially the dragon's. Time seemed to have forgotten the whole idea of marching along regularly, seconds ticking by in an orderly fashion. Instead it dawdled and paused, meandering and stopping to watch the clouds. With each passing moment we became more anxious as the dragon's strength was whittled away.

For my part, I was not worried. The solution was obvious. I was just waiting for the right moment to reveal it and get my due recognition as the hero of the day. I settled back against the dragon's warm neck and admired the view, which was really quite magnificent. We were flying low, surrounded by a circle of deep blue ocean overlaid with endless small waves that rippled in the light breeze. The surface shimmered like silver. The blue dome above with its painted, chalky clouds had never seemed so round, as though a translucent sphere had been cut in half and placed over the world to keep the dust off. What an elegant planet.

Soon I noticed a subtle change in Joe's breathing. It was a little more rapid and strained. Leaning on his neck, I could feel his strength gradually fading. The beating wings, the pumping heart, the rush of blood through his veins—all seemed a little less sure than when we had taken off. We'd flown a good distance since the sinking, but that elephant was becoming increasingly difficult to ignore. Finally Eikelbohm spoke up.

"We have to reduce our weight," he said. "I will discard my sword. Yours will have to go too, Dogalogue."

Excalibur rattled in his scabbard at The Sweep's hip. The Sweep started.

"I think Excalibur wants to say something," said Mina.

The Sweep moved to take the weapon out of its scabbard.

"I wouldn't do that if I were you," I warned.

"Why not?" said the Sweep. "The poor creature's fate is at stake. Surely it has a right to be heard."

This was of course exactly what Eikelbohm wanted. An argument over my sword. I'd end up looking bad because I didn't want to give it up, and he would look like the hero when he tossed away the worthless chunk of iron he'd gotten cheap at the local supermarket.

"Ignore it," I said. "It just wants to plead for its life and believe me, that sword is capable of continuing a discussion all the way to Iberia. Dying in the service of its betters is supposed to be a sword's dearest dream. It really ought not to make such a fuss."

At this the scabbard rattled violently.

"Don't worry. My sword is noble and selfless. It will be glad to make the sacrifice."

"I do think we ought to let it speak," said The Sweep.

"Very well," I said. My moment had come. I reached over, grasped Excalibur's hilt in my tentacles and drew the blade from its sheath.

"You are right, Sweep," I announced. "It hardly seems fair that a helpless sword should have to sacrifice itself, just because it has no brain."

"Thanks a lot," said Excalibur.

"Keep quiet, fool," I hissed. "I'm trying to save your life."

"The problem is simple," I said. "If we don't get rid of some weight, we're all doomed. Fortunately, we have something onboard more worthless than my sword, and much heavier. I'd say a traitor is the kind of object worth dumping. Providence has been kind enough to place one in our midst."

I turned to my enemy. "The game's up, Eikelbohm. Jump, 'ere I spit you on this vorpal poniard." I advanced on him, creeping forward on my tentacles, the sword outstretched.

"What are you doing, Sir Dogalogue!" cried Iris. "Have you gone *completely* insane?"

The Sweep hesitated, unsure which way to turn. He seemed torn between loyalties. As I intended.

"What's going on back there?" said Joe harshly. "No fighting on my back. It's against flight-safety regulations. You might stab me by mistake. Everyone calm down."

"I'm quite calm," I said. And I was. My purpose was clear. I felt cool as ice and twice as efficient.

Eikelbohm glowered red with fury. "I've had about enough of your mad antics, you crazy cuttlefish," he snarled. "Prepare to meet Zond!" Ignoring the dragon's plea, he swept out his own cutlass.

On level ground, even with Excalibur's help, I was no match for Eikelbohm. But here, for the second time in one day, I was in my element. My tentacles gave me a huge advantage. Some of them latched like limpets to the dragon's hide, and another contingent was assigned to wielding-Excalibur-and-stabbing-my-enemy duty. So long as my fifteen legs continued to cooperate and didn't get into some kind of argument amongst themselves, it shouldn't have been much of a stretch, but I'd reckoned without outside interference. I felt the prick of a blade in my back.

"Hold it right there, Sir Dogalogue, this has gone far enough."

Iris! I couldn't believe it! After all I'd done for that girl. Then I got to wondering if I had ever actually done anything for her, and I couldn't think of anything. Dammit, I thought. That evil power monger has won her heart. Thinking fast, I surrendered Excalibur to Iris, but just as Eikelbohm lowered his own blade I leapt and grabbed him around the waist, breaking his hold on the dragon's back. Iris screamed as my enemy and I, grappling one another furiously, plummeted toward the waiting water.

As we fell, I twisted and shifted so that when we hit the water he was beneath me. That winded him nicely. Pretty cunning move for a cuttlefish, I thought. The impact broke us apart and I had a few seconds to watch the dragon above us swerve and turn back. Judging by his dark red color, he wasn't too pleased. Never mind. When I had a chance to present the evidence, he would understand. Meanwhile, the sea felt cool, swishing around my body. Adrenaline coursed through my veins. I was enjoying this.

A few yards away, Eikelbohm was shaking with shock, cold, and rage. "You imbecile!" he spluttered. "I'm going to finish you once and for all." He started to swim toward me and there was murder in his eyes, but before he could reach me a shout came from above and with a rush of wings the dragon swooped toward us, claws outstretched.

"Catch hold!" The thought came clear but it was not needed. Trying not to feel like a field mouse facing an owl, I reached up and grabbed a reaching talon. Eikelbohm missed and one of my tentacles took it into its head to lash out and wrap itself around his wrist, bringing the conniving swine along with us. I cursed my soft-hearted tentacle. I'd have been happy to let him drown. With a surge the dragon dragged us through the water, carving a furrow of spray and then lifting us free into the air. Once again my independent-minded tentacle stretched like a rubber band as we dangled beneath the mighty beast. Decidedly uncomfortable, but it was fun watching the water flash by just a few feet beneath us. An astonished young tuna stared up and begged its mother for a dragon of its own on its birthday, then wept when she refused, saying, "And who's going to feed it?" I would have done it all again, but I was hesitant to suggest it to Joe.

What happened next was slightly less fun. Once we were back on board the dragon, my so-called friends clapped me in irons! Or at least the nearest equivalent. They lashed me to one of the dragon's dorsal spines. Can you imagine? I was a prisoner on my own planet-saving mission. I'd never been so humiliated! Joe, however, was awesome. He didn't chastise me—unless you count his sarcastic question, asking if I was planning on any more detours. He flew on like a hero, each wingbeat punctuated by a gasping breath. Lulled by the rhythm of the dragon's body, I dozed until the sound of low voices woke me.

"Do you think he'll get the death penalty?" said the badger. "We may all drown, but at least we won't be walking the plank like poor Dogalogue."

"No one is walking the plank. That's on pirate ships," said Maurice. "This is a Royal Navy ship. We never do barbaric stuff like making people walk the plank."

"So what do we do?" said Brains.

"We give criminals a fair trial and then cut their ears off and hang them."

"Ah," said the badger, nodding. "That's much more reasonable."

"Thanks a lot," I said. I did not much relish hearing my fate discussed by a couple of rodents. But they did not hear me. Or perhaps I did not actually speak. In fact, I'm pretty sure I imagined the whole conversation. By this time I was fully delirious.

Just as the sun touched the edge of the ocean behind us and the prospect of ever setting foot on solid ground was slipping away, we sighted land. A strip of dark shadow on the horizon, just a hint, like a mirage at first but quickly solidifying until the coast lay spread out before us in a line of hope.

I had ceased caring about the injustice of it all. I could tell that Joe was really struggling now. We'd most likely all drown and the microvita seed with us. It would probably end up in the stomach of some random fish and this sad world would be condemned to endless centuries of war and conflict. And once these crazy humans developed advanced technology, they'd blow the place to bits. I vaguely recall The Sweep making good on his claim that he could lighten the load, diving overboard to swim for it. We were still at least two miles from the shore. Iris wept, but she could not restrain him.

"No need to argue," said The Sweep. "I can easily swim a thousand miles, if need be."

"Don't be absurd, Sweep." Iris was furious in her grief. "This is not a joke. No one can swim a thousand miles."

"Fish can," said Maurice brightly.

"And turtles," said Brains.

But rather than argue, The Sweep dived into the water and struck out for shore with confident strokes.

"I can swim, too," declared Iris, unbuckling her boots.

"No, Iris," said Eikelbohm. "You must stay and take care of the small animals and the prisoner. I'm sure I can make it to the shore from here." He, too, dived in.

The skyline was ablaze with color. Our shadow no longer flitted across the water beneath us. We were flying closer to the ocean's surface now. Joe had no strength to spare for climbing. It is said that the best comes out in men and beasts when they face death or danger, and so it proved. Iris, a true princess to the end, comforted the small creatures. She kept Mina, who dreaded water almost as much as owls, close in her pocket. She held proud Maurice in her arms when he succumbed to fear at last and ceased cracking jokes, and she restrained brave but foolish Brains when he volunteered to dive in as well, though he could barely swim. Even the bat took off and flew for itself, sparing the dragon a full two grams.

As for Joe, never have I witnessed a greater act of sustained determination than the dragon's heroic flight. During those last moments, I could not understand how he kept going. It felt as though each wingbeat would be his last, that his strength would fail at any moment. But I could feel his great will driving his body past endurance, straining and then tearing powerful muscles worked far beyond their capacity, burning great clouds of oxygen to fuel his mighty frame. He could have tossed us all overboard and saved himself anytime. He risked his life for us, but he accepted it as his duty without question or complaint. In that hour I gained new respect for dragonkind.

SANCTUARY

I woke to find myself lying on a blanket on the grass under a clear morning sky. I propped myself up on one tentacle and saw that I lay on top of a hill overlooking the ocean.

"Where am I?" I asked.

"You're awake at last! About time, too." Iris hurried over to me. "We're on the coast of Navarre. How do you feel?"

"Rested. Confused. Is everyone OK? What happened to the ship? And the microvita seed?"

"Everyone's OK and the seed is safe. The *Dodecahedron*? Well, let's just say she's had better days."

I felt as though I had twelve iPosses stuffed inside my head. "The last thing I recall clearly is Insidious attacking me and sucking my life force, and Eikelbohm rescuing me. The rest is all mixed up. I dreamed a lot of strange dreams, and now I'm not sure what was a dream and what really happened."

"Well," said the princess wryly, "if you take all the craziest parts and put them in a row, that was probably what happened. Anything normal was a dream. But it was not your fault. We don't quite understand it, but it seems that the depth pressure and the poison Insidious injected when he attacked you caused a temporary madness. But I think that has passed."

I found this more alarming than illuminating. "So when we were back on the ship, I was behaving a little strangely?"

"Just a little."

"And did I mention something about my umbrella?"

"More than once."

"Oh dear," I said. "I was sort of hoping that was the dream part.

But surely I didn't break your harp and attack Eikelbohm or accuse him of being an enemy? That was the dream part, right?"

"No, you really did all that."

Damn. This was awkward. "Is anyone upset with me right now—like for example, Eikelbohm? Or maybe you?"

"Well, I must admit that when you broke my harp there was a moment there when I would not have minded if the sea monster ate you. But now that I understand you were not yourself, I am OK. I can't guarantee the same for Eikelbohm."

"Do you think he would feel better if I let him keep the umbrella?"

Iris looked at me in alarm but I laughed and she saw that I was joking. "I think you'd better let me talk to him first. Why don't you take some more rest?"

"Ok. Just tell him I'm really sorry, but it was the pressure. I just couldn't take the pressure." I lay down, feeling sleepy again. Yesterday had been a long day.

TIME TO PLOT, TIME TO PLAN

Nefarious watched the dragon as it flew the last few yards to the shore, its wingtips drooping so low they touched the crests of the waves, and with one last feeble flap collapsed on the beach. The wizard let out an evil chuckle and a small bat landed on his shoulder.

"Sinistru, there you are! So? Did they succeed? Did they recover the seed?"

Parinte Sinistru, exorcist, spy, part-time dentist, and full-time vampire, shed his disguise and transformed into his human body before answering. "Yes, Master, they found it. They have it in a casket that they just managed to bring ashore."

Nefarious let out another laugh, this one so evil and so full of hilarity that it has been imitated by evil geniuses ever since. Especially in the movies.

"Victory is within my grasp at last! Those fools have brought the treasure I've sought for millennia within my reach. Come, Sinistru. It is time to plot; it is time to plan!"

He laughed again and Sinistru snickered nervously in pale imitation.

"It is time," said Nefarious, rubbing his knobbed hands together in delight, "to call upon the services of my new disciple, Eikelbohm!"

Epilogue

"Time for bed, Miranda," said Dr. Dogalogue. He stood to escort the human child to her quarters.

She really was tired, and she had so much to think about that she did not even protest.

"Thank you, Dr. Dogalogue. That was a wonderful story! I'm so looking forward to seeing earth for myself. But you're not finished yet. You still have to take the seed and plant it in the Himalayas, and I'll bet those baddies didn't make it easy for you!"

"Indeed they did not. But remember, I had Dragon Joe on my team, and the fearless Sweep, and capable Iris, and my animal companions. And we had right on our side and the goodwill of our great master. Now sleep, my little earthling, and I'll tell you more tomorrow."

Miranda hugged him goodnight and lay in her bed, her eyes glowing. Sleep overcame her and she dreamed of her home, a world she'd never seen, and of colored dragons floating on the wind with wings of flame.

The End

No Aliens Were Harmed in the Writing of This Book

I imagine that the main question you have after reading *Real Dragons Don't Cry* is, "Is this story true?" I find it difficult to give a straightforward answer to this question, for while I do harbor doubts about the existence of dragons, many of the key characters in the story were inspired by real people. Saint Lucifer, for example, is the spitting image (minus the tentacles) of an Irish friend of mine, whom I cannot name since he has threatened to sue me if I publish. And the inspiration for The Amazing Sweep comes from a wonderful friend who deserves far better than to be made fun of in my book.

Perhaps I should tell you how I came to write this story so that you can judge its veracity, or otherwise, for yourself.

It all began as a game between me and a delightful little girl named **Taruna Mclean**. Our adventures together as Space Nurse Miranda and Doctor Dogalogue sowed a seed that remained in my heart for many years. In fact, so much time has gone by that Taruna is now all grown up with a child of her own. But the seed did not die. Years later it sprouted into a series of short stories and new characters were born: The Sweep, Dragon Joe, Saint Lucifer, and more. I knew even then that these stories took place in a common universe but their relationship to one another was a mystery.

Then in 2004, during a long illness, that hidden relationship revealed itself, as though the sea surrounding a group of islands had withdrawn, showing that they were the peaks of a single landmass. I had my plot: the quest for the microvita seed.

After that it was all uphill. I discovered at some point that writing a novel is really hard work. But I did not despair, for I was not alone on my journey. I know no better source of ideas for bizarre personalities than the characters populating my own life. As a result, my friends have been an enormous help in creating this story — though not always intentionally, I fear. I wish I could thank them all, for this, and for the many names, incidents, and odd details they contributed but I'm sure I cannot recall them all. My profound apologies if you are one of those who slipped my mind. Please remind me for future editions.

My deepest gratitude goes to my guru, **Shrii Shrii Anandamurti**, for being the greatest inspiration of my life and for contributing the concepts of microvita and sadvipra, which I took straight from his amazing philosophy.

Next I would like to thank my family for instilling in me a love of books and storytelling and many other good things. My parents emigrated from England to New Zealand in 1950, five years before I was born. My mother's wealthy father evidently imagined that there were no proper shops in the wild colonies, so every couple of months for years afterward she would receive a huge box from Harrod's of London, full of clothes and food and everything you might need to survive on a primitive island. My brothers and I anticipated these shipments from the motherland with great excitement. A favorite regular item was a delicious English breakfast cereal called Frugrains, an ancestor to granola. But **my mother** called them Dogalogues. So there you have it, the secret is out: our hero is named after a kind of toasted muesli.

My brother **Christian** was my chief mentor during my formative years. He convinced me that he was a wizard and tried to teach me philosophy when I was eight. It was the best education a young boy could wish for. Christian wrote three books when he was twelve. My favorite was a comic fantasy story, Mysteriasa Mediocre, starring the original Doctor Eikelbohm, who was actually a very nice man with back to front feet. Sorry for turning your hero into a baddy, bro.

The key characters were modeled on some of my favorite people in the world. I hesitate to mention their real names for legal reasons already noted. **Didi Ananda Gunamrta** however, did grant me permission to mention that she was the inspiration for the character Princess Iris.

Here are some more of the extraordinary people who've helped to breath life into the world of Doctor Dogalogue:

Alexandra McGee, who made me a little wool Doctor Dogalogue octopus that now watches me from his seat on my desk, for inspiring me to write about cephalopods.

Alok for fine-tuning the whole thing with his meticulous proofreading and for renaming Nefarious.

Amal Jacobson for beta reading and giving me incisive feedback that helped me improve the story dramatically by eliminating 37,000 unnecessary words.

Ben Stafford, my eldest brother, for naming his turtle Bert, thus inspiring me to give the glorious dragons down-to-earth names.

Dada Gunamuktananda for entering into mourning when his pet ant, Harvey, sadly died.

Dharmapriya for still being my friend even after I dared to say that Harry Potter was "a novel idea but hardly a seven novel idea."

Dhyanesh Fleury for pointing out that the microvita tree must be located in Atlantis. Of course!

Didi Ananda Devapriya who actually speaks Romanian and came up with the name for Padre Sinistru.

Didi Ananda Jayati for inventing the iPoss and saying that my story is "like a Christmas cake, full of nuts and raisins."

He whom we do not name for inspiring the character of Insidious.

Jyotirmaya Hull for pointing out the non-funny dad jokes.

Kesari Fleury for missing her dinner because she was so engrossed in my book, thus inspiring the patented Doctor Dogalogue weight-loss program, and for being such an insightful beta reader.

Krsnapriya for her enormous impatience and for volunteering to translate this book into Spanish.

Maribel Steel, Arati Gonzalez, Melissa Gabriel, and **Didi Ananda Nirmala**, for their encouragement and being official members of the Doctor Dogalogue Fan Club.

Matthew Pierse, **John Flange H. Lowe**, and **Paddy Neville** for helping me to develop the special kind of madness it takes to write a story like this, and for being the greatest of friends and helping me stay sane through those difficult adolescent years. And to Paddy for co-writing the Grend song.

Mina, a little girl from one of the Ananda Marga children's homes in Bali, for lending her name to a very special mouse.

Mina Donelly for beta reading and giving me the youth perspective. Sorry I didn't name the mouse after you, Mina. You were beaten to it by a much smaller girl.

Prashanti for offering to translate the book into Portuguese, even though she has not read it yet.

Svarna Prabha for providing the name of Princess Iris.

Tara Dolezal for beta reading and pointing out the places in the story where it didn't make sense (although I'm afraid she may have missed a few).

Vidya Feathers for believing in Doctor Dogalogue and putting up with me telling her the entire story on a long journey.

Last but far from least, I cannot overstate how much **Devashish**, my friend, writing mentor, ruthless poor-prose-eliminator, music producer and super-editor, has contributed to this project. I've enjoyed peaceful months at his farm in Puerto Rico, listening to the cutest frogs in the world, writing my story. And at his house in Brazil, entertaining the parrots and toucans and giant spiders, and waiting in vain for a sighting of the invisible monkeys, editing my story. Seven years ago we took a week together sorting two thousand pages of notes into a coherent plan for a series of five books. He taught me how to develop a structure, showed endless patience with my abuse of the English language, my horrible punctuation, and my confusing shifts in point of view. He even came up with a couple of very funny lines that have survived the editing scalpel and remained in the story. At which point I became concerned. Humor writing is one of the few things I can do that Devashish does not do better. I do not want him to become good at this as well. I only hope that his enormous generosity will be sufficient to offset the karmic debt he acquired when he told me to rewrite the entire story in the third person, and then blamed me for doing it and made me switch it all back to the first person again! For this, may Zond have mercy upon his soul.

The Microvita Tree

I hope you enjoyed *Real Dragons Don't Cry,* book one of the Microvita Tree series. This is the first book of five:

Book One: Real Dragons Don't Cry (2015)
Book Two: The Way of the Banana (2016). This is already in second draft, so it should actually come out on time.
Book Three: The Detox Clinic from Hell. Due some time after book two.
Book Four: The Egg from Earth. Due some time during my stay on your weird planet.
Book Five: The Battle of the Orange Dog. Hopefully this will be published pre-posthumously.

So that's the plan—unless I change my mind. Bear in mind, the original idea was to write one book.

Feel free to submit your questions, comments, or suggestions on Amazon reviews or The Microvita Tree Facebook page or my blog at www.TheMicrovitaTree.com. Maybe one of your ideas will appear in the next book, in which case you will be entitled to a complimentary signed copy and a free hug from my mouse.

Of course, being a fantasy writer, I fantasize about making this into a movie series. A couple of penniless directors are already interested, so that's a start, I guess. Just remind me to leave your planet before they release the Doctor Dogalogue action figures.

About the Author

Born in New Zealand, Dada Nabhaniilananda was ordained as an Ananda Marga Yoga monk in 1979. He is a meditation teacher, an author, a musician, and a corporate keynote speaker. He has spoken or performed in more than forty countries, including Brazil where he appeared on stage with the Dalai Lama at the 1992 Earth Summit. Dada currently lives in Northern California.

You can visit him at www.themonkdude.com